Key MOMENTS

Book One in the Key Series

ROSIE POLITZ

Published by

Cypress Moon Publishing

Author photo © Tate Tullier Photography

Cover and interior design by Damonza

ISBN: 978-0-9998877-0-7 (Paperback)

ISBN: 978-0-9998877-1-4 (eBook)

Library of Congress Control Number: 2018902769

Published by Cypress Moon Publishing

8165 Rustic Rose Court

Baton Rouge, LA 70818

First edition

For my Tommy. This book would not exist without you. You are my muse and I love you truly.

ACKNOWLEDGMENTS

IF YOU ARE reading this, thank you. If you bought my book in any shape or form, I thank you. If you borrowed my book, or lent out my book, you have my thanks. Basically, if you read my book, I'm forever thankful.

Huge thanks to my first guinea pigs – Padra, Erin, and Shawn – for reading the chapters as I wrote them from the beginning, and giving me your honest, sometimes painful, no-holds-barred feedback. I'll always be grateful for your input, suggestions, and excitement as new chapters were written. Thank you for telling me that what came out of my head was (mostly) better than I thought. Erin, I can't thank you and Chad enough for your insight and helping me understand certain aspects of the Army National Guard and deployment. Thanks for letting me know those scenes were realistic. Shawn, thank you for challenging me to think outside the box and for your enthusiasm after every chapter. Special thanks to you, Padra, for being my partner in crime, putting up with my constant Snaps about Clynn, and for dreaming with me. Keep your fingers crossed that this book may one day land in the hands of the Overwind Book Canon.

Leslie, Alicia, Sharon, and Leigh Ann – thanks so much for letting me throw you into the deep end of the beta pool and for letting me know that you couldn't put it down. Heartfelt appreciation goes out to you, Leslie, for the phone call. That conversation meant a lot to me. Big thanks to you, Leigh Ann, for making sure I got my New York accent as close to authentic as possible on paper. I'll never fuhgeddaboudit. Sharon, thanks for believing in me and for all of your encouraging words. Alicia, thanks a million for all of your excitement, but most of all, thank you for being my Annie.

To Billy and Chantelle, my extraordinary editors. Thank you both so much for your expertise and helping me improve my content. I appreciate it more than you know. This book is so much better because of y'all.

Shout out to Allen and Kellie Rasberry Evans. Thanks a bunch for letting me use your special phrase. Men really are such simple creatures. Everybody reading this should tune in to their podcast, *A Sandwich and Some Lovin'.*

Dr. Lawler, thank you so much for your knowledge and suggestions in getting my medical material straight with my timeline.

Jess and Josh, thanks for confirming that my police jargon was right.

To my parents, Harvey and Sandra. So much love and gratitude go out to both of you. Dad, thank you for drilling proper grammar and their rules into my second nature for as long as I can remember. Having that knowledge made my book easier to write. I can't imagine the corrections and edits Billy and Chantelle would have given me if it weren't for the grammar foundation you instilled in me, so thank you for tolerating all of my teenage eye rolls when you made me correct myself. It paid off. Mom, you have encouraged me in every aspect of my whole life, and never had a doubt in your mind that I could do this. Thanks for always letting me run wild with my imagination. You'll always be my favorite teacher. Thank you both for your nonstop faith in me and for being the best parents ever.

Endlessly, I want to thank Tommy, my one and only, for the constant reassurance, support, inspiration, and being my number one cheerleader throughout this whole process. You gave me the extra shove I needed when I had my first and last doubt. Thank you for putting up with my late nights in front of the computer screen, even when I said I was right behind you on your way to bed. You are my absolute. There are no words for how much I love you. May we one day take the road trip of Clay and Lynn.

Chapter 1

I NEVER UNDERSTOOD PEOPLE that retire and go back to work because they're bored. I mean, really? Find a hobby. Read a book. Do anything else besides find yourself in that daily grind again. When I retire...oh wait. Is that today? You bet your sweet ass it is.

Thirty years. Plus a few months. It's actually flown by rather quickly, though it hasn't all been fun, that's for sure. I started working for the government just one week after my eighteenth birthday. At forty-eight, by today's standards, I'm quite young to be retiring.

My first job was as a receptionist at the Department of Fish and Game. I loved it there, but it was only a temporary position, so I was forced to move on. After several years of transferring to different agencies, taking promotions along the way, while also going to school, I landed my dream job. My degree in Fine Arts helped me earn it. My minor in art history helped me perfect it.

I worked my way up to one of the head curators at a museum in downtown Baton Rouge. I love my job, and I'll miss the people I've worked with, but I won't miss waking up to this dreaded alarm.

My husband, Clay, is stirring around in the kitchen, which is odd, because I'm usually the first one up. Maybe he just wants to wish me well on my last day.

Clay retired three years ago as a lieutenant with the state police. He put in thirty years of service and had a great career, but after a close brush with death, he was ready to get out. I was ready for him to as well. We've been counting down to this day since his last shift. He was also an Army National Guard Firefighter and held the rank of First Sergeant when he retired. I'm so proud of him. He's my triple threat. He decided to let the Guard go when he retired from the state police. He did a tour overseas with Operation Desert Storm, and after the September eleventh attacks, he was deployed again with Operation Enduring Freedom.

I linger in bed for a few more minutes, thinking about what this final day as a working woman might bring. I plan on doing as little as possible. I finished all the paperwork I had on my desk yesterday, put the final touches on my latest exhibit, and signed a few more forms required for my departure. I'm sure as hell not starting any new projects. It's not like they'll fire me. FIGMO. That's a military term meaning, 'Fuck It, Got My Orders.' I smile at the thought. I'm sure there will be the usual cake, cards, well-wishers, and sad good-byes, but I won't cry. If I do, it will only be because I'm ecstatic. My life is mine now, well, mine and Clay's.

Since retiring, Clay has been spending his days building small furniture, restoring his old '67 Dodge Charger that he drove in high school, and going to the gym. See? Hobbies. My hobbies have been on the back-burner for a while. Ceramics, pottery, painting…mostly anything having to do with art. Anyway, my plan is to pick up all of my neglected paint brushes, acrylics, clay spatulas, tints, glazes, etcetera, and start fresh. I can't wait to fire up my kiln again. Clay and I might do some traveling too.

It's time to get out of bed. At least it's a bit easier this morning. I stroll to the bathroom counter to brush my teeth and put my wavy, auburn hair in a half-ass ponytail on top of my head with a scrunchie. Splashing cool water on my face helps me wake up, but despite my efforts to keep my hair from falling down, my lazy ponytail falls into the sink and the water wets the ends of my thick locks. Green eyes look back at me in the mirror. I need to fix this. My hair, I mean. Not my eyes. I like my eyes.

I undo the scrunchie and let the rest of my long hair fall. Spritzed with conditioning spray, the fly-away hairs are no more. After finishing my morning routine, I head towards the kitchen.

It's seven in the morning and I'm on time for once. I can swing by the drive-thru at Flo's Café with time to spare. Normally, I'm guilty of running ten minutes late leaving the house and still stop anyway. Flo's is just around the corner from our neighborhood. Clay and I love that place. It's rare that you can get good, hot, and fresh down-home cooking in a drive-thru. It never takes longer than five or six minutes from the time you give your order to getting a warm paper bag with your hot breakfast. Best. Biscuits. Ever. On days that I would run late, I'd get my boss, Kaye, one of Flo's famous biscuits. If there were ever any traces of irritation on Kaye's face due to my being tardy, they were gone the second she took a bite of that biscuit.

Clay hands my coffee to me in my favorite travel mug, the one with the manatees on it. He bought it for me on our honeymoon in Florida after we took a boat ride and saw some in the wild. Over twenty-five years ago. Can't believe I've kept up with this mug for that long.

"Have a great last day at work," he says. He kisses me good-bye with a peck on the lips. I start to leave and he holds me in place. His expression beckons. Clay kisses me again, but this time it's sensual. Then he slowly whispers into my ear, "I'll be eagerly awaiting your return."

I almost drop my coffee. "You're not going to make this an easy last day for me, are you? God, you smell good." His cologne has always driven me wild, with its notes of bergamot, sage, amber, and sandalwood. "Maybe I should call in sick."

"Do it."

"I can't. I've got a few loose ends to tie up."

"Well, I've got a loose end of my own that I want to tie up," he says as he grabs my butt.

"Shit, Clay. That's not fair. Hold that thought, though. I'll be back before you know it." I kiss him again and leisurely brush my hand against the front of his boxers.

"Now who's not being fair? You're killing me, woman."

I smile and wink at him. What a sexy-ass husband I have. I've always thought that he looks a lot like Kevin Bacon. How did I get so damn lucky?

When I first met him, I knew I wanted to get to know him better. It was the summer of 1990. July seventeenth to be exact. I was running an errand for work and had to drop one of the vehicles off for maintenance.

I walked into the shop, and there he stood, dressed in his BDUs. There are few things sexier than a man in battle dress uniform. It was like looking at Ren McCormack if *Footloose* had been about the military instead of dancing.

Clay was checking out at the counter, getting ready to leave. When he turned around, our eyes met, and he smiled at me. He didn't even leave right away.

"Hey, you," he said, as if we already knew each other.

Instant sparks.

"Hey, yourself, soldier." I don't know where that came from. I'd never been that brazen before. My face became warm, like it had turned ten shades of red. Butterflies started pirouetting in my stomach. I couldn't believe he was actually talking to me. But I thank God that he did.

"Oh. Uh, I'm sorry, I just…I thought you were somebody else." He smiled nervously.

"Oh. That's okay." I grinned at him. *Dammit*, I thought. *It felt like he was flirting with me. Figures.* "I guess I have one of those faces," I said to him. *God, I'm such an idiot. Of course he's not flirting with me. The one day I forget to put on lipstick.*

"Yes. You do. And it's a beautiful one. Well, you have a good day, now."

"Uh, you too." I gave him an awkward smile and he winked at me as he walked out the door. *Hold on…maybe, just maybe, he was flirting with me. Wait, did he say 'beautiful'? He thinks I'm beautiful? Even without lipstick? How could I just let him walk away?* I mentally kicked myself for not running out after him. I almost did, but the clerk behind the counter had already greeted me. Oh well, at least I had a cool story to tell when I got back to work.

I finished my business with the car dealership, which took forever because of a mix-up with an account number, and I finally got the key to the loaner car they gave me. I walked outside, and there he was, standing by his truck. I stopped dead in my tracks. My cheeks began to flush again and the ballerinas in my belly came out for an encore. *Has he been waiting for me?* He waved and motioned me over to him. I looked behind myself to be sure. Nobody else was in the parking lot. He laughed a little.

"Yeah, you," he said. I couldn't hear him, but I could read his lips.

Oh my God. He was waiting for me. He had been standing out there nearly thirty minutes. For me. Yes, that's right…for me. Hot damn. *Who needs lipstick?*

"I have to apologize," he said as I walked towards him, when his voice fell within earshot. "I was kind of rude back there."

"Are you kidding? You called me 'beautiful.' That's hardly rude. I should apologize to you for not thanking you for the compliment. You just caught me off guard. That's not something I hear every day, especially from guys I don't know." My heart was doing cartwheels.

"My name is Clay," he said, his hand outstretched. "Sinclair." He pointed to his last name on his uniform.

"Lynn Boudreaux," I told him as I shook his hand. More than just sparks ignited that time. Fireworks. No, bigger still…my chest was a battlefield of *rat-a-tat-tats* and missiles being launched from one side to the other. I thought it was going to explode. He felt it too. The second we touched, his eyes dilated. "It's nice to meet you, Private Sinclair."

"That would be Sergeant."

"Sorry. Sergeant." I saluted him and he smiled.

"The pleasure's all mine, Miss Boudreaux. It is 'Miss,' right?"

"It is."

"Good. So…now we know each other."

Well, maybe not yet. But we will. Oh yes…we will.

Chapter 2

I OPEN THE DOOR to go outside and I'm pleasantly surprised. Sunny, not too warm, low humidity. Usually, springtime in Louisiana seems like a sticky summer to people from other parts of the country. But even if it were a hundred degrees right now, I wouldn't let it get me down.

We live in a small town called Pride, a bit over twenty miles from Baton Rouge. There's not a whole lot around, but I love it here. I mean, we have all the small town necessities…a few convenience stores, a few more churches (it *is* Louisiana), a post office, schools, a grocery store, park, an auto repair shop, a Dollar General, several great eateries (again, Louisiana)…that's all you really need, right? And here's a fun fact about Pride: Donna Douglas, who played Elly May Clampett on *The Beverly Hillbillies*, was born here. Our claim to fame.

Our small town is still close enough to Baton Rouge in case you need something that you can't find here in Pride. And now there's Amazon. Is there really anything you can't get online these days?

Sometimes, if Clay and I just want to live it up for the night, we'll go into the city for dinner at a nice restaurant and then get a hotel room. We love going to the sushi place, Tsunami, in downtown Baton Rouge. It's on the top floor of The Shaw Center for the Arts. The restaurant is decorated with silver beaded curtains and huge bamboo shoots. But while the ambiance inside is warm, it doesn't compare with the atmosphere outside at sunset, where the view of the Mississippi River is incredible, and can literally take your breath away. Okay, not literally. But it's a sight to behold, with the orange glow of the sun hovering over the horizon and reflecting off the water, casting sparkles on the surface all the way down the meandering river.

Anyway, I get in my car and head to Flo's. Almost as soon as I pull out of the driveway, my phone rings through the car speakers. It's Clay. I press the button on my steering wheel. "Hey, babe. Did I forget something?"

"Yeah, you forgot to stay home."

"I wish. You certainly got me all riled up to walk out the door, Mr. Sinclair."

"Hey, you can't blame me for trying."

"After today, I'm yours. All day, every day."

"Yes you are. Maybe I should get some of those little blue pills."

"You don't need that."

"Couldn't hurt." He laughs. "I'll see you when you get home, then. Be careful. I love you."

"Love you too. Bye." I pull into the drive-thru at Flo's. I order my usual, one sausage biscuit and one plain biscuit, with extra napkins, because Flo doesn't skimp on the butter. I get Kaye a biscuit too, even though I won't be late. Oh man, I love the aroma that emits from that greasy-bottomed paper bag. My car is filled with the smell of fresh hot biscuits. They should make a candle out of this scent. I'd buy it.

I drive into the parking lot at work and finish up my extremely buttery biscuit. I get out and take my last walk into the building where I have worked for eleven years. I head up the elevator to the second floor, where the administrative section is. You could play football in here, were it not for cubicles as far as the eye can see. It reminds me of one of my favorite movies, *Office Space*, but thank goodness, my time here has not been as crazy, and there's way less monotony. Kaye has *never* asked me to work weekends, even though the museum is open on Saturdays. That's probably because of the biscuits.

I step into the break room to refill my coffee mug. Dammit, who left the creamer canister empty again? Good thing I have the key to the supply closet. Shit. No I don't. I turned it in yesterday. Ugh. I let out an exasperated sigh and roll my eyes. Some people in this building have no respect for the unwritten rule: if you empty it, refill it. I shake my head and heave my heavy purse onto the counter. I rummage through it, finally finding a few packets of creamer from the last time Clay and I stayed at one of the hotels a few blocks from here.

Fresh cup of coffee in hand, I wave to a few of my co-workers on the way to my office and they congratulate me knowing this will be my last day. I open the door and flip on the light. Well, there's my workspace. Nearly empty. I stare at the blank walls, devoid of my accolades, and my bottom lip starts to quiver. I wasn't supposed to get emotional. This is a glorious day, one Clay and I have been looking forward to for so long, but here I am, starting to tear up. It's the end of an era.

I set my purse down in its usual place in my desk, inside the drawer to the left with the loose handle. I sit down. I don't know what to do. Everything is done, except for a few emails I need to follow-up on regarding some artifacts I inquired about several weeks ago. I turn my computer on and gaze at the flashing screen while it powers up; the whir of the fan inside the CPU crescendos.

I walk down the hall to Kaye's office and she's not there, so I leave her biscuit on her desk. I'm hoping she will let me go home early. Is that possible? I bet so. She's been known to do that a time or two. Plus, she loves me. It's the biscuits, I tell ya. It'd be nice to get home a little early so Clay and I can pick up where we left off this morning. Time will tell. Only eight hours to go. Tick tock.

Well, no such luck. It's going on 4:30 now and still no word. I can't believe Kaye hasn't come in my office and told me to leave. I haven't even seen her in the last couple of hours. She did make sure I had a nice going-away luncheon though, so there's that. It was in the big break room, with a spread of finger foods, punch, and cake. And I got a lovely gift. Kaye and a few other of my work friends and employees got me a leather picnic backpack. Complete with real plates, goblets, flatware, and even a bread knife, cheese board, and corkscrew. So, you know they also got my favorite bottle of

Cabernet Sauvignon to go with it. It's all so charming, I can't wait to have a romantic picnic with Clay under the trees at Cypress Park. That's our favorite park, and it's not too far from our house. The park is small, but there's a certain secluded spot under a huge oak tree where we can chill out and take in nature.

I finally make my way home, so ready for my celebratory dinner date with my main squeeze and the rest of my family. My parents, my sister Cecilia, my great-aunt Mitzi, and Clay's dad are joining us. I didn't want to make a big fuss over my retiring, but they seem determined to. We have reservations for 7:00 at Antonio's Steak House. There's a glass of wine and a big, juicy steak calling my name. But right this second, I can't get my mind off my husband and resuming our frisky behavior from this morning. I'm getting a little tingly just thinking about it.

I pull into the driveway of our modest two-story home. It's a Craftsman bungalow style with several triangular pitched rooftops. The house is painted light beige and trimmed in white, with a small covered front porch. Not too small for a swing though. Every southern girl must have a front porch swing, and I love mine.

Clay has recently planted some hot pink azalea bushes in the front flower beds, lined the walk with monkey grass, and put caladiums around the oak trees in the middle of the yard. It looks like the cover of *Southern Living* magazine. Spring is the best time of year for yard work down here. The only time, really. Our summers are so hot, nobody can stand to be in the yard for too long.

I enter the house and it's too quiet. I don't hear or see Clay anywhere. "Clay? Babe?" No answer. "Where are you?" He must be waiting in bed for me. The corners of my lips nearly touch my ears and I make a beeline down the hall to our room. But he's not here. My shoulders slump and my smile abandons my face. A note on the bed takes the place of him. *L, I'm out back. Come get me when you get home. – C.* Why isn't he eagerly awaiting my return, like he said he would be? I head to the back door and open it.

"Surprise!" shouts a crowd of about fifty people, and it works. I am literally surprised. I jump back and put my hand to my chest. I'm speechless. I almost start crying. I really had no idea Clay was putting this together.

"Oh my gosh," I say. I look around and take it all in for a second. There are friends and former colleagues of mine that I haven't seen in so long. I see Dr. Norwood, one of my favorite art history professors; Edie, my supervisor before Kaye, who taught me the ropes when I started at the museum; Stu, who showed me the delicate way to properly handle antiquities; cousins, too many to name; some old high school friends; and Kaye. I'm bursting with joy. "No way. I can't believe this." Clay is beaming. I know he's proud of himself for pulling this off without me getting wind of it. I gambol over to him and give him a giant hug and kiss. "Thank you, you sweet thing. How did you manage to keep this from me?" I look around and notice tables of food. There's even a wine station and a huge galvanized bucket with assorted bottles of beer. "What about Antonio's?"

"I cancelled the reservation and had them cater instead." Clay hands me a glass of wine. "You would have been here earlier, but I couldn't let that happen. I called Kaye this morning and made her promise not to let you leave early. Couldn't take the chance of you walking in during the set up." He raises his beer in her direction. I smile and shake my head at her. She laughs and shrugs her shoulders.

"Well, now it all makes sense. Sneaky McSneakerton. Thank you, babe. I love this." I raise my voice and address the crowd. "Thank you all so much for being here to celebrate with me. With us. This man never misses a chance to surprise me. I'm genuinely shocked."

"To Lynn!" Clay toasts with a raise of his Corona. The crowd follows and I hear various sentiments of "Cheers!" and "Congrats!" from my party guests. Clay clinks his beer bottle on my wine glass and leans down for another peck on the lips.

Everybody resumes mingling. I list into Clay's direction and lower my voice to where only he can hear me. "I'm not complaining, because this is super special, but, on my way home, I had visions of something else dancing in my head."

"Oh yeah? What's that?"

I give him another hug and whisper in his ear, "You and me. In bed. Picking up where we left off this morning."

His eyes widen. He kisses me on the cheek and whispers back into my ear. "This will not be a long party. I promise," he says. He looks me up and down and I wink at him.

I find my mom and dad, Eliza and Lee, talking to Clay's dad, Lane. I hug them all and tell his dad, "That boy of yours is something else. I can't believe he did this."

"Well, you know how it is. We Sinclairs love to dote."

"That you do," I tell him.

"You and Dianne sure raised him right," my mom says to Mr. Lane.

"Yeah," Dad says. "Thanks for that."

"Where's Aunt Mitzi?" I ask Mom.

"I called to see if she wanted us to come pick her up, but she wasn't feeling well. She sends her love, though. She's so sorry she couldn't be here for your big night. I'll go by her house in the morning and check on her."

"Good idea. And please, take her some food. It looks like there's gonna be a lot left."

I make my way over to my friend Annie. We've been best friends since the first grade. I give her a big hug, as I haven't seen her in a couple of months, though we talk or text almost every day. "Thanks so much for coming just for me," I tell Annie.

"I wouldn't miss this for the world, you know that."

"We need a girls' night soon."

"Yes, we do." She raises her empty glass. "I'm going to get another glass of wine. You want?"

"Definitely, that sounds great, thanks."

I socialize, eat, and drink, as a couple of hours pass. I open a few presents that my friends and family were so kind to give me. I insist that they were not necessary, but that they are sincerely appreciated. Annie actually got Clay and me both something: a set of lounge chairs with cup holders for the backyard. Yes, we'll be doing a lot more lounging from now on. I'm even thinking about telling Clay I want to put a pool out here.

I look over and see Annie talking to Clay's older brother, Stone. He's making her laugh. Interesting. Annie was married to her college sweetheart, Martin, for nearly two decades, but they got divorced about two years ago, so this is good to see.

I walk over to Annie and Stone to see if anything might be budding. "Hey, you two. Y'all having a good time?"

"Yeah," Stone says. "Congratulations, sis-in-law."

"Thanks, bro-in-law."

Annie tells me, "Stone and I were just catching up. It's been what… ten years since I've seen you?" she asks him.

"Something like that. Hey, I'm gonna get another beer. Either of you ladies like another drink?"

"No, thanks," I tell him.

"Sure," Annie says, handing Stone her glass. "I'll have some more wine. White. Thanks." She smiles as he walks away.

"Soo…what's all that about? Spill it."

"We were just catching up."

"That's not a 'just catching up' smile on your face, girl."

"I don't know. Am I crazy?"

"No. Y'all have known each other forever."

"I know, I've just never looked at him that way before."

"Well, before, you were both married. Now, you're both not. I think it's worth exploring. And if he's anything like Clay in a particular department, well, let's just say, you'll be happy in the dark. And the daylight." I nudge her with a wink.

The tips of her ears turn red. "Oh my God, Lynn. Stop it. He hasn't even asked for my number," she says with a laugh.

"He will. Watch."

Stone comes back with Annie's wine and I decide to make myself scarce and let things happen.

It's almost 9:00 and things are winding down. My parents and Mr. Lane start picking up the food. Stone and Clay gather up the leftover alcohol and fold the tables and chairs up. My party guests are starting to hug my neck on their way out, and they each have a comment about all of my newfound free time.

"You won't know what to do with yourself now," says Stu.

"Oh, I've got a few plans. Gonna get back to painting and stuff."

"Every day is Saturday," Dr. Norwood says.

"Thank goodness," I tell him. "You would know."

My cousin Ralph ribs me with, "Hey, now you can do nothing all day long and not worry about getting caught."

"Get outta here. I was a stellar employee. Got the plaques to prove it."

"Horse shit," he says in a good-natured tone. You can always count on Ralph to make you smile.

"I'm so jealous," Kaye says. "Everybody at the museum is going to miss you so much, especially me. And I'm definitely going to miss those biscuits."

"Maybe I'll surprise you one day and bring you a few," I tell her.

"I'd love that. Sorry I left work without saying good-bye, but I had to leave so I could get here before you."

"I wondered what happened to you, schemer. Thanks for everything. I'll miss y'all too."

"Let's do lunch one day. Bring Clay."

"Sounds great," I tell her.

As I hug Annie good-bye, she whispers in my ear, "You were right. He did ask for my number."

"I knew it. Are you okay to drive?"

"Yeah. He's going to follow me though, to make sure I get there safely. What a gentleman, right?"

"It's those Sinclair genes. I'm telling you. Nothin' but nice all the way around." I give her another hug. "Be careful. Love you."

"Love you too, girl. Goodnight."

Clay and I head back inside after watching my parents and his dad drive away.

It's been an exciting day and a wonderful evening. I'm now ready to take a relaxing bubble bath and cuddle up with my man. After I soak for what seems like hours, I slink into bed.

"Now, you sly fox...where were we?" I ask Clay, and we are finally able to let nature take its course.

Chapter 3

I AWAKEN TO THE smell of bacon. Is Clay up early again? I stir a little, not really wanting to get up yet. I open my eyes and sure enough, my husband is missing from my side. So now, I'm trying to figure out what else is about to hit my belly. Coffee. Surely there's coffee. There's always coffee. What is that sweet smell? Is that pancakes? Oh, please let it be pancakes. I hear Clay utter a few expletives. Eggs. We're having fried eggs, too, and he just popped the yellow. He's going all out for breakfast this morning. His phone rings and I can hear him answer it.

"Hello? … Hey, good morning. … Thanks. It was a good party. She deserved it. And thanks for all your help. … No, she's still sleeping. … What happened? … Oh my God, I'm so sorry. … I'll let Lynn know as soon as she gets up. Let us know the arrangements as soon as you hear. … Okay, thanks. Love you, too."

Oh no. Somebody died. I jump up and rush to the kitchen. "Who was that? Who died?"

"That was your mom. Aunt Mitzi died. I'm so sorry, Lynn."

I put my hand to my mouth as a hard lump forms in my throat. My legs tremble and I sit down. I shake my head from side to side. Tears sting my eyes. Clay sits down next to me and takes my hands in his.

I know Mom said Aunt Mitzi wasn't feeling well last night, and she was old, but she seemed to be in relatively good health for her ninety-three years. I'm going to miss spending time with her.

She was my grandmother's sister, the youngest of nine. My Grams died when I was very little, so Aunt Mitzi sort of played that role for Cecilia and me. Maybe because she and Uncle Sid never had kids of their own.

Clay and I never had kids either. As an adult, I felt a little closer to Aunt Mitzi because we shared that. I don't know why she and Uncle Sid never had any children. We didn't talk about it. She never volunteered the reason and I never asked. It's a touchy subject. I hated it when people would ask me if Clay and I were ever going to have kids. The questions finally stopped when I hit forty.

I often wondered who would take care of Aunt Mitzi when she got up in age. Turns out, she took pretty good care of herself till the day she died. Clay and I would check on her every week, but she didn't really need a lot of tending to. She still had all her wits and most of her faculties. A rare breed.

Ritzy Mitzi, I used to call her. She lived in this great, big house and always dressed in something sparkly. She wore fancy jewelry and never went a day without her hair done. But she wasn't one of those highfalutin ladies. Uncle Sid's family had money, but Aunt Mitzi never let it go to her head. My great-grandparents had a tremendous work ethic and were able to keep their grocery store during The Great Depression when other businesses were failing left and right. Their work ethic rubbed off of them and onto Aunt Mitzi. She stayed grounded and never took anything for granted. She didn't boast about things she had, and she loved to give. She and Uncle Sid even gave us a thousand dollars as a wedding gift.

Spunky, she had a sense of humor that could make the surliest man throw his head back in laughter. Aunt Mitzi was also an artist. Her framed gouaches of mountains with sunsets, forests with wildlife, coastal lighthouses with crashing waves, and flower gardens with butterflies are scattered throughout her house. That's where my love of art comes from. Spending summers at her house while my parents worked, she taught me a lot about the use of color, textures, and the easiest way to paint trees. A rare breed indeed. Her beautiful soul will be missed by many, especially me. My face contorts and the tears fall, my chest heaving as I try to catch my breath between sobs.

Clay hugs me. My head buries into his shoulder. After a minute, I wipe my puffy eyes. He crooks his index finger under my chin and lifts my head up to meet his cerulean eyes. "I'm going to miss her, too," he says, and gives me a tender kiss on my forehead. "Do you feel like eating?"

"No."

"Well, how about some coffee?" he asks, as he pours me a cup anyway, knowing my answer. "But I know Aunt Mitzi wouldn't want you to let this fine breakfast go to waste. You know how she loved bacon."

Boy, did she love bacon. She had a full stock of bacon in her refrigerator and freezer. Not just regular bacon. She had all kinds of bacon: maple, thick sliced with black pepper, hickory smoked…you name it, she more than likely had it.

"You're right." A smile crosses my face. "Okay, then. For Aunt Mitzi." Lifting our coffee mugs, we clink them together and drink a toast to her.

Chapter 4

TWO DAYS LATER, on our way home from the funeral, we stop at Aunt Mitzi's favorite florist, Bloomies, and I buy her favorite flowers to brighten our home. Pink hyacinths and Candy Swirl roses. You know, the ones that resemble peppermints.

We pull into the driveway. "Go ahead, babe. Just give me a minute. I'll be in shortly." My voice wavers. Another tear breaks free.

"Okay, love. Take all the time you need," he replies.

Eyes closed, I smell the flowers. I'm instantly taken back to Aunt Mitzi's house. Years of memories flood my mind. Running up the stairs and sliding down the bannister. Helping her paint. Bacon frying. Playing dress-up in her old clothes from the closet under the stairs. Easter egg hunts and water balloon fights with my cousins. Climbing fig trees. Playing Chinese Checkers. The salt of my soul escapes from the corners of my eyes, leaving streak after streak down my face.

I collect myself, go inside, and put the flowers on the kitchen table. Clay has a pot of coffee on. I swear, sometimes I believe he can literally read my mind. The brewed dark roast hits my nose with a strong whisper, its comforting smell floats across the kitchen and tangles with the perfumed fragrance of the flowers I've just set down. It kind of reminds me of Sunday mornings at Aunt Mitzi's. The only thing missing is bacon, of course. I head down the hall to change clothes and Clay follows.

"Are you okay, Lynn?" he asks as he slips into a t-shirt and shorts.

My navy peplum dress falls to the floor. Not in the mood, I'll pick it up later. I rummage through the closet for something more comfortable to wear. "Yeah, I will be. Just really sad, you know? But I'll be okay. She was the last one left." A disappointing thought hits me. "Oh no." Sitting on the bed, my head hangs.

"What's wrong?"

"No more holidays at her place."

"Aww, babe. I'm sorry. Maybe we can start having them here."

"Okay. I'd like that. So what happens now? Does hers go up for sale?"

"I don't know how that all works. Surely she had her affairs in order. She was too smart not to. Since she had no heirs, maybe she left everything to the church. Some people do that. That sounds like something she would do."

"Yeah, sure does. She loved going to mass at St. Gerard, and it's such a beautiful old church. Father Angelo is going to miss her. You could tell he was genuinely upset today giving the eulogy. I swear he was a little sweet on her. If he weren't a priest...hmm...who knows? I've been to other funerals there for little old ladies, and he never spoke of any of them the way he spoke about Aunt Mitzi."

I hang up my dress. Can't stand to see it on the floor, no matter how melancholy my spirit is right now. It's the minor bit of OCD in me.

We head back to the kitchen for some fresh coffee and a piece of pie from Flo's that Flo herself insisted we take home from the funeral. Flo and Aunt Mitzi were great friends (though Flo is only in her early seventies) and she donated all the food for the 'after party,' as Aunt Mitzi would always call family gatherings following funeral services. So. Much. Food. I take the first sip of coffee and a bite of the sweet buttermilk chess pie as the doorbell rings.

"Probably Flo," I say with a mouth full, "bringing us more leftover food on her way home."

Clay answers the door and a strange man's voice greets him. Curious, I walk over to the front door. Clay doesn't have a chance to answer the young man before he turns his attention to me.

"Hello, Mrs. Sinclair?"

"Yes, can I help you?"

"This is for you. Can you sign here please?" He hands me a large brown envelope and a clipboard to sign for the package. "Thank you. Have a good day."

"What is it?" Clay asks.

"I don't know. It's from the Law Offices of Chase and Hunter. Chase and Hunter? For a law firm? That's too spot-on," I say with a chuckle. We walk back to the kitchen and sit down. I open the flap and dump the contents onto the table. There are two envelopes. 'Number One' and 'Number Two.' Four unfamiliar keys, together on a keychain with an 'S' on it, also wait to be explained. I open the first envelope. Oh my God. Is that what I think it is? My eyes grow huge and my mouth is agape. I look at Clay, then back inside the envelope, then back at Clay. "Holy shit."

"Come on, Lynn. What is it?"

"It's a check for a quarter-million dollars." I can barely get the words out.

"What the hell? From who?"

"I don't know. It has the law firm's name on it, signed by Jefferson Chase." I immediately open envelope number two, assuming there's an explanation inside. Papers unfurl. "Oh my God. It's a copy of a will." I skim it and find an address. "From Aunt Mitzi's estate? I can't believe she did this." I read the papers aloud to Clay. "It says, 'From the Law Offices of Chase and Hunter...' That name still cracks me up. 'I, Bernice Lorraine...' Bernice Lorraine? I swear I never knew her real name. I always thought it was like, Minerva or Matilda, or any other name that started with an 'M.' Where in the world did 'Mitzi' come from? Okay, anyway..." I continue to read.

"'I, Bernice Lorraine Chauvin Santini, of 1120 Lancaster Park Place, Baywood, Louisiana, declare this as my last will and testament. I hereby revoke, annul, and cancel all wills and codicils previously made by me, either jointly or severally. I declare that I am of

```
legal age to declare this will, and that I
am of sound mind. This last will expresses
my wishes without undue influence or duress.
I bequeath my house at the address listed
above and all of its contents to my great-
niece, Cheralynn Jade Boudreaux Sinclair…' "
```

I look up at Clay, taken aback. So far aback. Clay's eyes are wide and his face crinkles. He's as stunned as I am.

"What? Her house too? Are you serious?" he asks.

I reread it, then glance at the rest. "Yeah. It goes on, a bunch of legal mumbo jumbo, but holy shit, Clay. I mean, how did she even do this? I thought it was supposed to take months for a will to be distributed, not days. And isn't there supposed to be an executor or we're supposed to be called into court or something?"

"This is definitely a first. Are you sure that's all there is?" Clay asks.

"Looks like it." I'm still flabbergasted. The thoughts in my head are bouncing from one end to the other. "But what about the rest of the family? She has umpteen nieces and nephews. Why us? What should we do? I need to call Mom and see if she knows anything about this." As I start to get up, another folded piece of paper falls independently from the legal ones. I open it up. "Oh, sweet Jesus. It's a handwritten letter from Aunt Mitzi herself." I read it to Clay.

> *"My darling Lynn,*
>
> *'Don't look so surprised. You and Clay were always there for me anytime I needed anything. I guess living the shortest distance from me over the rest of the family helped, but nevertheless, I would call with the silliest of requests and y'all came to my rescue with bells on. Sometimes without me even asking. The fact that you would both come all the way out to "The Boonies," as you kids say, just to check on me and bring me something to eat so I wouldn't have to cook was always such a blessing. Fifteen miles up this dark and lonely stretch of road is not that close, but yet, there y'all were. At least once a week.*

'Now, don't get me wrong...of course some of my other sweet nieces and nephews would make an occasional visit here and there, and were always eager to help me with anything I asked of them while they were here, but I have always felt a special bond with you. There's something there that I don't have with anybody else.

'Sid and I talked about it before he died and we both agreed to leave the house and everything in it to you. I know my decorating style is not yours and Clay's, as you are always so quick to poke fun at my "ugly duckling" barnyard kitchen backsplash, and my green "shag carpet" in the den and the stairs. But, no worries, my lovely. That's what the money is for. Please, make my house your home.

'I know this seems a little sudden after my death, but don't you fret. Nobody is going to take the house away from you. I had it all worked out down to the dime for everything to be expedited before I left this earth. We had such a great life, Uncle Sid and I, and you and Clay were a very big part of it long before he died and even more so for me after. Don't worry about the rest of the family. They have all received letters of their own, with decent checks, so don't you go feeling guilty that you have the house.

'You remind me so much of myself at your age, you always have. I have loved watching you grow up to be the beautiful woman you are today. And you couldn't have picked a better husband to cherish you. Tell Clay that I thank him, so very much, for taking such great care of my favorite girl (don't tell your cousins I said that!) and for being the best great-nephew I could ask for.

'The house is ready for you, my sweet girl. The locks have been changed and these are the new keys. Everything now belongs to you and Clay. Enjoy your new adventure, my darlings. Until we meet again.

All my love, always, Aunt Mitzi.'"

"Whoa." Clay brushes his hand through his hair.

"Right? Wow. Just wow. I can't believe it. My emotions are all over the place right now," I say in a voice that borders on crying again. "I'm so sad that she's gone, you know? But, she gave us her house. That's unreal.

I've always loved that house and now it's ours. That makes me happy. But, I'm also anxious about what everybody else in the family will think about us and the house, regardless of what Aunt Mitzi said about giving them money too. Dang, she and Uncle Sid must have been loaded, way more than I ever imagined. And then, of course, I'm just still in shock that she did any of this to begin with. And the money? For remodeling? How fun will that be? I'm overwhelmed and overcome with all kinds of crazy feelings."

"So am I," Clay replies, as he takes a deep breath and exhales, puffing his cheeks out like a blowfish. "So, what do you want to do? I mean, I guess we're moving to Baywood. I'm assuming you're okay with that."

"Of course. Aren't you?"

"Yes. I'll miss this place, but, sure. Moving to Baywood is okay with me."

"I know, I'll miss this house too. It's the first place we bought together, lots of great memories here. But, I never dreamed I would get to live in Aunt Mitzi's house, so I'm excited about that."

"Me too. It'll be a new chapter in our lives. Should we start packing? Put our house on the market? Where do we start?"

"Well, right now, I'm more interested in finishing. Finishing this pie. My coffee is cold. Will you please pour me another cup? Then, sit down with me so we can figure things out?"

"Sure thing, love." Clay gets up and pours my old coffee out and refills my cup, adds my creamer, and comes back to the table. He, too, is partaking in this wondrous pie we have before us.

Chapter 5

"WELL, I THINK that's the last of the boxes," Clay says as he shuts the trunk of my car. "The movers are coming tomorrow. The rest of the stuff, what little we're taking, should be at Aunt Mitzi's house by tomorrow afternoon. I mean our house. That seems so weird to say."

"I know. And I can't believe our house sold so quickly. Two weeks? That must be a record for Pride. I'm glad we donated everything else we didn't need to the Wildcat Ransack." The mascot for the local high school is the Wildcats. The football team is having a fundraiser to get new bleachers installed at their stadium. "What are you waiting for?" I slap Clay's butt and get in my car. "Let's go, we're wasting daylight." He steps into his truck and we're off to Aunt Mitzi's house. Our house. Our new home.

I've always loved this drive up to Baywood. It's so peaceful. There's never any traffic. Huge oak trees dripping with Spanish moss line both sides of the road, making a canopy of shade all the way down. Rustic farmhouses are scattered every few miles or so, and all of the mailboxes are colorful and mounted on old farm equipment.

This time of year is my favorite. I open my sunroof to let in the intoxicating perfumes of the wisteria, sweet olive, and banana magnolia, giving me the full effect of the day outside. I look in my rearview mirror and stick my arm through the opening above my head and wave at Clay. He blinks his lights back at me.

I pull up to the gate of the wrought-iron fence that surrounds the property and enter the code for it to open. As I make my way up the driveway, which is more like a small street, I'm seeing the house with new eyes. It's a fancy house for Baywood, a two-story Tudor style home boasting three sharply pitched gable roofs with scalloped bargeboards, several dormers, and the unmistakable half-timbering. Two prominent brick chimneys rise high above the rooftop with ornate chimney pots, adorned with rich lattice patterns. It's always been such a beautiful place.

Aunt Mitzi and Uncle Sid moved into the house in 1943 when they first got married. It was a wedding present from Uncle Sid's parents, Giovanni and Mariella. Salvatore Santini, Uncle Sid's grandfather, opened the first bank in Baywood in 1893. He built this house for his wife, Francesca, in 1896.

It was tradition in their family to pass the house down to the eldest son upon his nuptials. Seeing as how their family had money, it wasn't that big of a deal. Since Uncle Sid and Aunt Mitzi never had children, they remained in the house.

I get out of my car and stand between the door and the seat, looking up at the house in awe. Slack-jawed, my eyes wander across the façade of the house, which is the length of a football field. This is surreal.

A brisk wind carries the aromatic hot-pink puffs from the mimosa tree throughout the front lawn. The sun, though still shining, is going down now, and shadows of the pecan trees dance along the front of the house. Clay drives up after me and gets out. He shuts his truck door and comes up behind me, wraps his arms around my waist, and pulls me close. I lean back into his chest.

"Let's get these boxes unloaded tomorrow," he says. Then he whispers in my ear, "I'm starving." He walks us backwards, with me still latched to him, and shuts my car door.

We make our way to the entrance. I mosey through the elaborate arched porte cochère, up to the porch (with a swing, of course), and stop just before the solid wood door. I run my finger over the beautiful beveled glass in the center. My eyes wander to the sidelights and I notice something for the first time. The design etched into the elegant glass is an inconspicuous repeating 'S' pattern. For 'Santini,' I presume. Now it will stand for 'Sinclair' as well.

Clay unlocks the door and opens it as if he's trying to sneak in. We stand at the entrance to the house and nothing has changed. Except it's ours. Sunbeams stream in through dozens of casement windows with diamond patterned lead glass, illuminating the walls and the floor. My steps are soft and apprehensive, like I'm being judged by the heavens. I'm taking it all in.

The foyer emanates an unfamiliar air. The beautiful antique furniture strikes me as being in vogue. The tick of the grandfather clock is more pronounced. The arches separating the rooms convey fancier carvings. The art on the walls comes to life. Her art. Watching Aunt Mitzi create a new masterpiece was hypnotic, and I was here when she painted most of these.

There is one large abstract framed photograph hanging to the left in the foyer that's out of place compared to the rest of the art. It's a close-up, black-and-white print. I believe it's the entrance to a building. The structure isn't remotely familiar, but I've always liked the photo. The lower half resembles tall vertical windows in an Art Deco style. They are either very tinted, or the photographer waited until the sun was almost down, because what I believe to be the tall windows are black. Above that, rows of more windows, climbing up to what I envision as a skyscraper. Something Ansel Adams would have photographed, if his subject matter had been primarily architecture instead of landscape. Clay says the picture has always reminded him of a guitar, as if somebody set a camera near the bridge of the instrument, zoomed in, and took a picture of just the strings, climbing up the neck to the tuners and head.

We walk into the den, my eyes still surveying everything. Crossword puzzle books sit next to Aunt Mitzi's favorite recliner, waiting to be solved. A bookshelf full of mystery novels, most of them written by Agatha Christie, anticipate their next reader. A Victrola, one of many Aunt Mitzi and Uncle Sid owned through the years, stands tall in the corner. Next to the couch is her curio cabinet, which contains a plethora of collectible tea pots. I run my hand over the arm of the couch and it's softer than I remember. Clay is at my side and rubs my back.

"You okay, love?" he asks.

"Yeah. It's all so familiar, just different. Does that make sense? I mean, the last time we were here, she was alive and this was all hers. Now she's gone, and it's all ours. It even smells different in here. Sweeter. Like cake. It used to smell more savory."

"Like bacon," he says.

"Yeah. Like bacon." I laugh.

"Come on," Clay says.

He grabs my hand and we head for the kitchen. He did say he was hungry and now I am too. My eyes hit the backsplash. It repeats all around the room, just above the countertop. Barnyard animals. Ducks, cows, chickens, and the like. A passé trend. That will have to go. Aunt Mitzi loved it, but she's right, it's not for me.

We open the fridge and find it empty except for a box of baking soda. "Mmmmm…baking soda…" Clay says in his best Homer Simpson. We look at each other and laugh.

"Well, I guess that's better than having a smelly kitchen to come home to first thing," I say. "I bet Aunt Mitzi made sure the house was cleaned out of all things perishable in her last wishes as well."

"Probably so," Clay replies. "There really is nothing money can't buy. What about the pantry?"

"Nah. Aunt Mitzi hadn't cooked much in a while. Stuff's probably old."

I open the freezer. Bacon. I should have known. I smile and silently thank Aunt Mitzi for all the bacon. I take out a couple of packs and put them in the refrigerator to thaw out for tomorrow's breakfast. Come to think of it, BLTs sound good for lunch tomorrow too. I make a mental note to go to the store in the morning for some lettuce and tomatoes, plus bread, mayonnaise, and—jeez, I've got a whole kitchen to stock.

I call Flo's.

"Flo's. How can I help you?"

"Hey, Flo. It's Lynn."

"Lynn! Great to hear from you, darlin'. What can I do for you?"

"Is there any possible way you could have somebody deliver out here to us tonight? We'll pay extra." It's at this moment that I realize I'm going to miss having that place around the corner.

"I'll have my best delivery guy on it. And there's no extra charge for family." I love her.

"Aww, thanks, that's so sweet."

"So, the usual?"

"Yes, thanks so much. Make sure it's somebody you trust with the code."

"You got it. I'll send Austin. It'll be about forty minutes, will that be okay? I know you're used to getting your food in fifteen."

"Perfect. Thanks so much, Flo."

"You're more than welcome, Lynn. Hope to see you both soon."

"Yes, ma'am."

I hang up the phone and tell Clay the food will be here before six.

"Did you say sex?"

"No, silly. Six." I smile at him.

"I heard 'sex.' Whaddaya say we christen every room in the house? Starting with the dining room. This table looks pretty sturdy." He tries to shake it and it doesn't budge.

"I thought you were hungry."

"I am. I'm all kinds of hungry."

He raises his eyebrows up and down at me and starts walking in my direction. He scoops me up, carries me over to the table, and sets me down, my legs dangling off the edge. I pull my maxi skirt up a little and lean back on the palms of my hands. I wrap my legs around his waist and pull him towards me. He takes off his shirt, then leans down and kisses my neck while unbuttoning my top. I tilt my head back and let him have at it. He reaches around, unhooks my bra, and slides it off my shoulders, trailing his fingers down my arms, triggering a clashing uproar of chills on the surface and heat within. He's gentle as he circles my breast with his thumb, but then takes the tip in his mouth like it's essential to his existence. His other hand reaches under my skirt. He grabs my pink lace panties and I lift up, hovering my end over the table, making it easier for him to take them off. He jerks my skirt down with them, throwing both on the floor. We kiss with fervor. I arrest his belt with urgency and unbuckle it. The zipper on his jeans slides down at my determination and I try to take hold of him. He brushes my hand away and lets out a mischievous laugh in the middle of our kissing. I want to touch him and he knows it. He kisses me down my neck, hot breaths in between. I run both of my hands through his short hair and scrunch my fingers, grabbing small fistfuls at his scalp. He lets out a startled groan. I release him and he looks me in the eyes. He takes his jeans off, smiles, and changes course. He signals me to move further back on the table and I obey. He idles, tracing a languid finger up my inner thigh and then down the other one, skipping my middle. My eyes narrow and I shake my head at him with a bitter smile. My reaction tells him, "That's not fair and you know it." He smiles even wider. He's toying with me, his eyes still on mine. My mouth is getting dry with each longing breath I take. I lick my lips. I need him. Dammit, he's sexy as hell. He goes up and down my inner thighs again, and this time he pauses at the area just above my center. With soft contact, Clay taps his fingertips on the triangular region of naked skin, teasing me further. Then he moves down a bit, cupping my entire middle with his whole hand, rubbing it up and down, still taunting me. I moan as he finally gives in and touches me right where I want him to. Need him to. He feels how much I crave him. That's all it takes. He's done playing. Before I know it, he's inside of me and we damn near act like we're trying to break that table. Our momentum intensifies, and at one point, the table actually moves. We burst out laughing but keep going. Kissing, rocking, grunting. Ceaseless, breathless, shameless. We devour each other, until our session comes to an end. We collapse on the table, totally sated.

"That…was just…sensational…" I express between my panting.

"Damn straight," Clay huffs out. He takes my hand and softly kisses each one of my fingers. "I love you, you know that?"

"Yeah, I know." I trace his lips with my finger and he playfully bites it.

"Okay, now I've really worked up an appetite," he says.

As if on cue, the doorbell rings.

"Oh shit, do you think he heard us? Or saw us?" I'm a little embarrassed. I mean, the end of the dining room table is visible through the front door, beyond the den, even though the beveled glass obscures the inside somewhat. We'll have to get used to the new lay of the land.

Clay jumps up and puts his jeans on in a flash, foregoing his shirt. "Maybe. I'll be sure to tip him well. Or maybe the free show was a good enough tip."

"Clay!" I shout, blushing. I gather my clothes and retreat to the kitchen to get redressed.

Clay grins and bounds to the front door, yanking it open. "Hey there, Austin. Sorry to keep you waiting."

"Uh, no problem, Mr. Sinclair. I, uh, hope you, um, enjoyed it, I mean, *enjoy* it. Enjoy it. Enjoy your dinner. I'm sorry. I, uh—"

Oh, no. Poor Austin. Flo's great-grandson. He must be mortified. I cringe for his sixteen-year-old, socially awkward self.

"Austin. It's okay. Relax. Thanks for coming all the way out here. I know we're not in the regular delivery area."

"Sure. It's nothing. I don't mind. Just got my license a few months ago, so Granny says we can expand some."

"Good to know. Thanks. Here's a little extra for your trouble."

"Oh, it's no trouble. Thank you, Mr. Sinclair. Have a good wife. Um, oh crap. Night. A good night. I'm going to shut up and leave."

"Don't worry about it, really. Be careful driving back. Good night, Austin."

Clay comes back in the dining room and sets the food on the table.

"Poor kid," I say. "I'm so embarrassed. I sure hope he makes it back okay. His cheeks are probably as red as mine."

"Yeah, that's why I didn't give him shit about it. The look on his face was torture enough for him. Hell, I was sixteen once. I remember. And you have nothing to be embarrassed about, love. Now, what do we have here? The norm?" He opens the bag and takes a deep sniff of the burgers and fries I ordered. "Mmm…greasy and delicious."

We finish eating and I ask Clay to please get our suitcases out of the car so we have some clothes to change into tonight and tomorrow morning. He gets them as I clean up the mess from dinner.

We go upstairs and start unpacking, hanging some of our clothes up and putting the others away in drawers. Then, we start looking around the house. We realize most of the décor isn't our style, as Aunt Mitzi must have known. I love the furniture. We'll keep that for sure, but some of the other things will have to be redone. Flooring, curtains, some of the light fixtures, the aforementioned backsplash…you know, cosmetic stuff.

"Wonder why they never made any updates to the house to keep up with the times," I say. "I mean, look at that wallpaper. Dragons and peacocks? I'm sorry, but no thank you. I love peacocks, but not with dragons and not on wallpaper. I'm sure it was in style when the house was built, but I've always thought it was so hideous. I know it's an old house and they probably wanted to keep it authentic, but c'mon. There's shag carpet. So they had to have made updates in the seventies. Why stop then of all times? It boggles my mind."

"Good question. I don't know. It is a strange combo for wallpaper." Clay shrugs it off.

Maybe it was that Aunt Mitzi was very practical. She was no miser, but she didn't spend money if she didn't have to. The only renovation she and Uncle Sid ever made to the house was adding a master bath to their bedroom.

Clay and I start talking and pointing around and determine what we want to change and where to start. I'd definitely like to start with the shag carpet, my least favorite thing about the house. So we make a decision that after we unload the boxes from the vehicles tomorrow, we'll start pulling up the carpet. Clay used to work for a flooring and carpeting company in high school, where he did a lot of ripping up and installing carpets, so he knows what he's doing.

"What about the stairs?" Clay asks.

"Yeah, I want to take the carpet off of them, too."

"No, I mean, are you ready to christen them?"

I smile. "How about we do the master bedroom next instead, huh, horndog?"

"Fine by me," he says as he nods and locks eyes with me.

"You'll have to catch me first though," I say as I make a run for it.

He chases me up the stairs and down the halls. When he catches up to me in what is now our bedroom, I let out a playful scream. He stops and turns me around. Our faces centimeters apart. Clay touches his forehead to mine. We begin to breathe as one. He takes my hands, interlocks our fingers, and my lips surrender to his. We undress each other, in no rush. With his eyes, he commands me to lay back on the bed. I love it when he takes charge. I comply, ready for round two.

"Relax. Just let me love you."

Chapter 6

I OPEN MY EYES, not really ready to wake up, but I have no choice. The sun is piercing its way into this room like a sword. Note to self: add room-darkening shades to my list of things to buy for the house. The clock on the bedside table tells me it's almost 8:00 in the morning. I should get up. Might as well wake Clay so we can get started downstairs. I oughta repay him for last night. Yes, there's a surefire way to get him up this morning. I turn over in his direction, but he's not there. I put my robe on and head downstairs. He has unloaded all the boxes, moved the furniture, and is almost finished pulling up the carpet in the den. He's already sweaty from working and the day has barely begun.

"Good morning, beautiful. Coffee's ready and I've got biscuits in the oven," he says from the floor. Clay is on his knees with his butt resting on the heels of his shoes. He looks up at me and wipes his forehead with his shirt sleeve.

"What are you doing? I would have helped you, you know? Let me go get dressed. Then you can take a break while I drink my coffee and we'll finish the rest together."

"Deal. I'll fix your coffee for you. Biscuits should be just about done too." He gets up from the floor and heads to the kitchen while I go upstairs to change.

Wait, did he just say biscuits are in the oven? He went to the store too?

My hero. I rifle through the closet for the most comfortable clothes that I don't mind getting messed up. I head back down for some much needed coffee. Clay has fixed me a plate of two buttered biscuits, slathered with blackberry preserves. We sit down to eat. "You have certainly been a busy bee this morning, Mr. Sinclair. When did you go to the store? What time did you get up? And why didn't you wake me?"

"I woke up at about six, I guess. I couldn't go back to sleep and I knew we'd have a full day, so I got up and got started. I went to the Stop 'N Go down the road and got a few things for the fridge. I'm sorry I didn't take time to fry the bacon. I wanted to get as much done as I could before you got up. I almost woke you, but you looked so sweet and peaceful. I figured you were still pretty tired from last night." He gives me a sly grin.

I smile back at him. "Well, you did do an ab fab job of depleting me of all my energy. So, since you're almost finished with the carpet in the den, why don't you give me one of those hooky knife thingies so I can rip the carpet off the stairs?" I ask.

"You mean the carpet knife?" He laughs at my childish term for the tool.

"Whatever it's called." I stick my tongue out at him.

"Okay, sure. You'll just have to be careful that you don't cut yourself. The blade is pretty sharp. And you'll need some locking pliers and a nail puller to pull up all the staples. That's going to be the real pain in the ass."

We finish eating breakfast and Clay gets back to the den while I start on the stairs. The carpet detaches easier than I expected. As I'm ripping it up, it stops short. It's been cut in the middle. That's weird. Maybe they ran out of it and picked up where they left off. I walk up the stairs and pull the rest up. I feel pretty proud of myself. I'm not very handy. Clay is the skillful one. And he's right about the dang staples. How tedious.

I'm in the middle of working on the staples when the movers get here to unload the rest of our things and a few pieces of furniture that we want to keep. Clay and I show them where we want our belongings, at least until we get done with our renovations, and they go on their way.

Clay is finished with the den and we work together on the rest of the staples, stair by stair. We are about to take a break when we get to a loose board in one of the steps halfway down, right about where the carpet was cut. The board on the step wiggles, but it's jammed. Clay finally gets it to shimmy off. We look inside and notice a box. It's black, hard plastic, about a foot square, and maybe six or eight inches deep.

"Oh my God. I wonder how long this has been here." I try to get it out, but it's awkward.

"Here, let me try." Clay reaches in the step with both hands and takes it out. It's a fireproof safe, and it looks heavy. He brushes the dust off of the top and shakes it. It makes a lot of noise.

"Dang, what the heck is in it?" I ask. "It sounds like a box of rocks."

He tries to open it. "Dammit, it's locked. Of course it's locked."

"Can you smash it?" I ask him.

"No, I don't think so. We'll have to find the key. There's definitely something curious inside though." He shakes the box again. We hear jingling. "Coins?"

"Oh wow, I bet it is a bunch of old coins. I think Uncle Sid had a rare coin collection at one point. I always heard about it but never got to see it. Maybe because they were all locked in the dang stairs."

"Why would he lock his coin collection in the stairs?"

"Safe keeping? Maybe it's worth a lot. It does seem a little out of character for them, though. Maybe it's something else."

Clay brings the box to the dining room and sets it on the table. We start rummaging through drawers in the house, looking for any kind of key that might fit this box. It's got a tubular lock on it, so at least we know that's what kind of key we're looking for. We separate and dig into every nook and cranny we see.

"Find anything?" Clay yells to me from upstairs.

"No, nothing yet." I shout back. I go from the dining room to the kitchen. Jeez, the backsplash will definitely be replaced next. Wait...I think back to the letter she left with her will...the backsplash...she mentioned the carpet on the stairs and that's where we found the box. I run upstairs and find the letter.

Clay sees the excited look on my face. "You found it?"

"No, but let's look at the letter again." I get it out of the dresser and skim it. "Yeah. See? Look. She has 'shag carpet' and 'ugly duckling' in quotes. I didn't think anything of it before, but she had to be giving us a clue to find the box and we didn't even know it. Let's go find that key."

We run downstairs back into the kitchen. "Okay, three of the six different tiles have ducks," I say. "Jiggle all the duck ones and see if any are loose."

Clay is on one end and I'm on the other. We're laughing like we're on a crazy scavenger hunt. I guess we kind of are.

"I bet I'll find it before you do." he says.

"Oh yeah? What do you want to bet?"

"If you find it first, I'll give you a repeat of last night. If I find it first… well, I guess it'll be my turn to—"

"Found it." A tile with two white ducks pops right off and the key is tucked into a hollowed out hole in the wall. I can't believe it was that easy.

"You're shittin' me. Dammit," Clay says. His brows crinkle and he lets out a sigh.

"Suckerrr." I don't think Clay cares that I found it first. He just likes to win. He doesn't know I already decided to flip the script before he even made the wager. Clay will get his turn.

"Way to go, babe."

"Come on. Let's see what's in this thing."

We rush to the dining room table and I insert the key in the box. Please open. I turn it and it unlocks. I take a breath and lift the lid. What in the world?

Chapter 7

"MORE KEYS?" CLAY asks. "There must be a hundred more keys in here."

Our hands dive into the box and start examining the different keys. I see several antique keys. Some look like regular house keys. A few are very odd. One looks like a wind-up toy key, another is long with a double bit at the end, and one so small it looks like it might be for a suitcase. Each key is on a keychain and the keychains are all numbered. Some of them have more than one key. We take them all out and lay them on the table in number order. There are fifty-one keychains.

"I'm guessing each keychain is from a different place," I say. I go through them and start thinking out loud. "Some of the keychains are of locations and some are random. Number one's keychain is a picture of Houmas House Plantation near New Orleans, with an old-fashioned key attached to it. The second keyring is from a First National Bank with what looks like a safety deposit box key. That would make sense. But it doesn't say where. Shit, how are we supposed to know? Let's see, the number three keychain is in the shape of Alabama. Number four is a picture of an old car." I look up to the sky and say with laughter in my voice, "Aunt Mitzi, could you be any vaguer? Throw us a bone, huh?"

Then I notice an envelope taped to the top of the inside of the box. It's like she really heard me. I open it and it's a computer printout, but instead of text, it's just a bunch little pictures.

"What is that?" Clay asks. "It looks like that crazy symbol font. Wang-dongs or something," he says, talking about the cryptic typeface.

"Oh, I bet you're right. That's exactly what it looks like. Wingdings. Get the computer, let's decode it. This is going to be fun."

The cipher is incredibly long, but all we had to do was search the internet for a translation chart. This will be easier than I had originally thought, though still no easy task.

"Let's see." I scan for the first character in the chart. "Okay, it looks like the first symbol is for a capital H. Then lowercase e, followed by l, another l, an o…oh, it's 'Hello.'" I laugh at myself.

We get through the whole thing after about three hours. Yes, it took that long. The beginning says:

> *Hello, my angels. If you're reading this, then that means I'm gone, and you have moved in to my beloved home. It also means you have found the box of keys. As I'm sure you probably noticed, each keychain is numbered. They are numbered for a reason. That's your first clue. It's your job to use the numbered hints below to either figure out where to go, or use the clues as directions once you get there.*
>
> *Many of the keychains are clues in their own right. Some are obvious, others are not. Some have two keys. On those, one key could open a door or something else; the rest is up to you to find what is locked away somewhere inside. Take what you find in each place with you, though some places may not have anything tangible for you to take. Use your own judgment.*
>
> *You will have questions. But don't worry, you'll get answers as you go on.*
>
> *The following is the list of clues to help you with each destination. The numbered clues correspond to the numbered keychains:*
>
> 1. *In the room of the one that played Baby Jane, there's an ornamental closet with a secret pane.*

2. *Near the Crossroads where a man sold his soul, go inside and ask for Miss Cole.*

3. *In the town where "The Heaviest Corner on Earth" has surely seen its share of hijinks, file into the Empire Building and look for hidden pinks.*

4. *In Florida's capital, there's one of these on display. Look in the back, and find what you may.*

It goes on down to number fifty-one, with riddle after clue after hint. We realize after our sixth one that the keys will open something somewhere in every state and Washington, D.C. That was easy enough to figure out, but we have our work cut out for us.

"I love how at the end, she signed it, 'Happy road tripping, my sweeties.' She was something else. I guess it's a good thing I'm retired now. We actually have time and money to go on this wild goose chase. I wouldn't really call it that though. And no wonder she said, 'Enjoy your new adventure' in the letter she wrote from her will. I thought she meant us living here. Now, I see she meant a real adventure."

"Yeah, I guess she did," Clay says as he puts his arm around me and pulls me in for a hug.

Chapter 8

CLAY AND I get ready for bed. I put on my favorite tank top and boy shorts and situate myself under the covers. I watch Clay in the mirror as he finishes brushing his teeth. He's shirtless and sexy as all get-out. He looks up and catches me staring at him.

"What?" he asks, mid-brush with a mouth full of toothpaste, catching my eyes in the mirror.

"Nothing. I'm just watching you."

"Why?" He spits in the sink and rinses his mouth out.

"Why not?" I smile at his reflection as he reaches for the hand towel and dries his face. "I like watching you. You're easy on the eyes."

"You little voyeur, you." He returns my grin. He heads into the closet and I can hear him opening drawers looking for something.

"So, what do you want to do?" I ask, my voice a little elevated to compensate for our distance. "I mean, how do you want to go about this? There are things we need to get straight before we just pack up and hit the highways. Obviously we need to sit down and figure out a route. At least for the first few states, then I guess we can just play it by ear and plan day by day. Or do you think we should figure all the clues out first? Do you think we should buy an RV? What about the renovations? Oh my God, Clay, what if we hadn't decided to pull the carpet up? We would never have found the box! Should we put a hold on our mail? We don't really know anybody around here to ask and there aren't really any neighbors for miles anyway. Or I can see if Cecilia can come house-sit for us." Cecilia is divorced and all three of her kids are grown and out of the house. "Or maybe we can just have our mail forwarded to her place while we're gone. No, nevermind, I really don't want that either. We need somebody to come and check on the house at least a couple of times a week and I don't want our mail piling up in our box so—"

"Babe." He pokes his head around from the closet, still rummaging.

"Yeah?"

"Relax. We'll figure it out. Asking Cecilia to house-sit is a good idea though. She will have to pass by her place to get to work, so she can still keep hers in check. If she's okay with that," he says.

"I'm sorry, I know I'm rambling. I'm just excited and anxious about it all. What are you looking for?"

"My favorite t-shirt. I don't remember unpacking it."

"It's in the laundry room. So, I'll call Cecilia tomorrow. And I'll tell her she can bring Fred, if you're okay with it. I don't think he'll mess up anything. Plus, they're kind of a package deal anyway."

Fred is Cecilia's Polish Lowland Sheepdog. I got him for her as a puppy right after she split from Frank four years ago. We were trying to come up with names for him and she said he was the shaggiest puppy she'd ever seen. She picked him up, looked him in the eyes, and then got nose to nose with him before she spoke.

"I would name you Shaggy," she said, "but that's not original enough for you. What about Scooby? He was Shaggy's best friend in the cartoons."

"That's not exactly original either," I said.

"Fred," we said in unison. We laughed and the name stuck. Fred licked her nose to seal the deal, as if he totally agreed with his name. He's such a sweet dog and has been wonderful company for my sis.

Clay turns off the bathroom light and stops to spray himself with cologne. I know what that means. His sexy scent makes its way to me before he does.

"Of course. Fred is more than welcome here," he says as he climbs into bed. "I love that dog. I think we should figure out all the clues first, so we know exactly where we're going. The renovations can wait. If we wouldn't have decided to pull the carpet up, I bet there would have been a clue hidden in the house somewhere that we would have found instead, leading us to the box. And no, I don't think we need to buy an RV." He leans in for a kiss. "If...we...do...that..." he says softly, kissing my lips between words, "we'll miss...half of the fun...and adventure...that is a real road trip." His hand finds its way under my shirt.

"I...see..." I play his game. "Well that...is fine...with me then." I move my arm below the covers and touch him. Yowza. He's already hard. I reach in and stroke him and he makes a deep sound with his breath. His hand moves from under my top to inside my bottoms and he touches me. He doesn't play around this time. He goes straight to the right spot and slowly circles his thumb around as he inserts a finger inside of me. I moan at the simultaneous magic he is working between my legs. I keep stroking him and our breaths get a little louder. I'm so ready for him. I don't want him to stop, but I want to feel all of him. We undress in seconds. I straddle him and lower myself slowly. I rock back and forth as he reaches up for my breasts. I arch my back, taking him in deeper, all the way. I move faster, then slower, then speed up again. I lean down while still moving and I slow to almost a stop. I try something different by kissing my husband passionately while I'm still slightly in motion on top of him. It's one of the most sensual feelings I have ever experienced. I sit back up and we go until we are satisfied. I collapse on top of Clay and lie there until I catch my breath.

"Well, that was new," Clay says, his breathing back to an even keel. "Me likey. We must do this again sometime," he says through a smile and kisses my forehead. I laugh and kiss him back. I roll off of him. Neither of us bother with getting redressed, and we drift off to sleep.

Chapter 9

THE NEXT MORNING, Clay nudges me awake before the sun invades our bedroom. "Wake up, sleepyhead. We've got some decisions to make."

I stretch, but keep my eyes closed. "What time is it?" I ask, in my raspy morning voice.

"Ten after six."

"Six? It's still early. Do we have to start now? You know I'm not a morning person. I need coffee." He kisses my eyelids and gets out of bed, turning on the bedside lamp. I sneak a peek at him walking naked to the bathroom. He catches me.

"Stalker." He smiles. "Come on," he says from the bathroom. "After we get dressed we'll go to Flo's and get some breakfast. We'll work out our game plan. And you need to call Cecilia." He comes back dressed in jeans and his faded Led Zeppelin t-shirt. "I'll go down and put the coffee on."

I sit up and catch him at the doorway. "Hey. I know we're gonna have to put our renovations on hold for now, but when we're done with this road trip, we should put one of those morning bars in here with a coffee pot, a small sink, and our own little fridge."

"That's a great idea. Done. Now c'mon, woman, get dressed."

I get out of bed, begrudgingly, and head to the closet. I take my time looking for something to wear. I find my favorite jean shorts and a soft, pastel, tie-dyed t-shirt with a pocket on the front. I don't bother with makeup. I put my hair in a scrunchie, throw a pair of sandals on, and head downstairs.

Clay has fixed our coffee in go-cups and we head out the door to Flo's for breakfast. The sun is barely up.

"Let me drive." I just throw that out there, knowing Clay's answer.

"I don't think so." He's very particular about his truck.

"Why?" He hates the way I drive.

"You're not even awake yet." That's true.

"Fine." It was worth a shot. "But if I were awake, you'd let me?"

"Not bloody likely," he says in a British accent. Then he smiles at me and shakes his head.

I get in the passenger side and look in the mirror. "You're right. I'm far from being awake." I rub my eyes as he starts to back out of the driveway.

"Here, this will help." He blares the radio and I jump, spilling coffee on my hand.

"Ow! Dammit, Clay! Okay! I'm awake now, fool!" I look in the glovebox for a napkin and wipe my hand off where my coffee splashed out.

"Oh, shit, babe, I'm sorry." He turns the radio off. "Are you okay? Did it burn you?"

"A little. I'm okay. Lucky for you the lid was on tight enough not to pop all the way off." I give him my mean eyes. "That's it. You're buying my breakfast."

"Oh, like that's different than if you were buying mine," he chuckles. He puts the truck in park and takes my hand. "Let me see. I'm so sorry. It is a little red. We'll get you some ice at Flo's." He kisses the top of my hand where the small burn is. "I'm really sorry, babe. You know I didn't mean to do that."

"I know. It's okay. Really, I'm fine. But you scared the crap out of me. I'm fully awake, so mission accomplished."

"Yeah, but it came at the expense of you getting hurt. Not worth it. I'll make it up to you. Whatever you want." He kisses my hand again and puts the truck back in gear.

"Hmm…whatever I want? I'm going to have to think about this."

"God, what have I done?"

That's a haunting question coming from Clay. Old feelings stir, but I ignore them.

"I know. I'm in control of the radio for the first week of our trip," I declare.

Our music tastes vary slightly. We both like pretty much everything, but he's more classic rock, heavy metal, punk, and alternative, while I'm more Top 40, pop, and disco, with a little country thrown in here and there. And I love old school rap. But so does Clay.

"Oh lord, okay, that's fair. But please, no diva ballads."

"Deal. That's not exactly good road trip music anyway."

Clay pulls into Flo's and my mouth starts watering for those biscuits. As we walk inside, the first thing I notice is Austin, who turns beet red and escapes to the kitchen when he sees me. At first I'm confused. Then I remember the dining room christening and I feel my own cheeks flush. But I smile at the fun Clay and I had on that table.

We sit at our usual booth in the corner and I already know what I want, but I look at the menu anyway. The list of options is printed on the placemats, which is rather convenient and a smart marketing move. It was Aunt Mitzi's idea.

"Good morning, y'all." Flo says as she brings us a carafe full of coffee. She knows us well.

"Good morning, Flo. Can I get a cup of cool water please? No ice. This knucklehead made me spill my coffee in the truck and I burned my hand."

"Oh, goodness gracious. Shame on you, Clay." She yells to the café counter, "Shelby, can I get a cup of water over here? Ixnay the ice. Stat!"

"Mornin', Flo," Clay replies in a low tone. His head hangs down, having been scolded by Flo. "It was an accident." He looks up at her. "You know I wouldn't hurt my girl on purpose."

"That I know for sure," she says.

"How's Austin doing?" he asks.

"Fine, besides the fact that he hates the morning shift. Why do you ask?"

"No reason," Clay smiles and winks at me from across the table and I smile back at him.

"What happened? Did he forget something the other night?" Flo asks.

"No," I step in. "Everything was great. He just may have been witness to something he didn't expect to see."

"Or hear," Clay adds.

"Oh, for heaven's sake. You two crazy kids. What am I going to do with y'all? Hell, who am I kidding? I wish I had the kind of fire that the both of you do. Still on your honeymoon after all these years. Don't worry about Austin, he'll get over it. Now, what can I get you this morning, Lynn?"

"I think I'll have the biscuits and gravy with a side of smoked sausage," I tell her.

"Good choice. Clay?"

"I want the country man breakfast special. But I don't want any frou-frou whipped cream on my pancakes. And do you have an extra tablet and a couple of pens we can borrow?"

"Country man. No whip. Paper. Pens. Got it. Sure. Be right back." Flo flits off to put in our order.

"No whipped cream on your pancakes? Are you crazy? You don't know what you're missing, babe."

"Country men do not eat whipped cream on their pancakes. Only on their women."

I can't help but laugh. "Touché, Mr. Sinclair. Touché."

"Hey, you want me to put some butter on your burn? There's some right here in a bowl."

"No, that's a myth. It will actually seal in the burn. Thanks, though."

Shelby brings the cup of water over for me. "Here you go, Mrs. Lynn. Is there anything else I can get you for now?"

"No, thank you, Shelby. That's it. Tell your mom 'hello' for me."

"Okay, will do. And you're welcome."

Clay immediately starts to doctor me up. He really does feel bad. "Which one of your friends is her mom? I forget."

"Loren. We went to high school together."

"Oh yeah. Dark hair, drives a Viper?"

"That's the one. Why? You got a thing for her?"

"I've got a thing for cars. You should get one of those, by the way, before they stop making them."

"A Viper? No thanks. Too small for me. You're lucky you got me into a Challenger. How you ever got me to switch from being a loyal Toyota customer, I'll never know. I miss my Camry."

"I put a spell on you."

"Yes you did."

Flo comes back with the tablet and pens. "What's this about? You makin' your Christmas list already?" she asks.

"No, we're going on a cross-country road trip and need to try and map out our route," I tell her.

"A road trip, you say? Hmm…this wouldn't have anything to do with some keys, would it?"

"You *know*? Of course you know. Well, yes, we found the box of keys yesterday afternoon. I can't believe Aunt Mitzi did all of this. For us."

"Honey, you and Clay were like her own. I know she's got a bazillion nieces and nephews, but you were her favorite," she says as her eyes start to water. "Oh, I miss her so. I'm truly going to miss talking to her, and our card nights, and that laugh. Sweet Jesus, she had an infectious laugh."

"That she did. I miss her like crazy too. But, I'm thinking this little adventure she's putting us on will keep her close to us. First stop, Houmas House." That's always been my most favorite plantation in the state. At least of all the ones I've ever been to. It is such a grand house and has the most beautiful gardens I've ever seen.

"Well, y'all let me know when y'all leave. Swing by here and I'll fix y'all up with some snacks for the road," she says with a smile.

"Thanks, Flo," Clay says. "We'll take you up on that, for sure."

"Yes, thanks so much, Flo. You're too good to us."

"Well, you're family and I gotta take care of my family. Speaking of family, here comes Austin with your breakfast. I'll let y'all eat in peace."

Austin puts our food on the table and gives us an uncomfortable smile. I can tell he's still embarrassed, but I won't say anything to try and ease his humiliation. I'll just pretend like nothing happened.

"Thanks, buddy," Clay says.

"Yeah, looks great, Austin. Thanks," I say. That sounded okay, right?

"Welcome," he says, and it doesn't seem like he can get away fast enough.

"Short and sweet," Clay says. "I'm guessing he didn't want to say too much for fear of fumbling with his words again and expelling another Freudian slip."

"Man, I hope we haven't polluted his untarnished mind."

"Babe. He's sixteen. No matter how much of a social misfit he is, he has impure thoughts. Probably about you. You're hot. Our table sex was hot. You don't unsee or unhear that."

"Oh, lord have mercy…okay, next subject…" I focus on the breakfast in front of my 'country man' of a husband. There are four plates and a bowl. Three eggs, bacon, sausage, grits, fried hash browns, a pork chop, and we can't forget about the pancakes with no whipped cream. "Hungry?" I ask as I steal a piece of bacon off of his plate.

"I'm a country man," he says as if that explains it.

"A country man that doesn't listen to country music."

"What can I say? I'm an oxymoron."

"You got the moron part right." I wink at him.

"Touché, Mrs. Sinclair. Touché," he says with a laugh.

Chapter 10

SORTING OUT OUR route while trying to eat was a bad idea. It's hard to write while eating, especially with so many plates on the table. We decide to put it off until we get home. Clay and I finish up our breakfast and pay on our way out.

"See ya later, Flo!" Clay yells to her through the window of the loud kitchen.

"Bye, kids! Now, don't forget to come back before y'all leave. But call first so I can have it ready for ya!"

"Will do! Thanks, Flo!" I shout. We wave good-bye and head home.

"Holy shit. I'm so full," Clay says.

"Well, I guess so, country boy."

"That's country *man*, ma'am."

"Oh, excuse me. Right. Country *man*."

We pull into the large, three-car garage and get out. Clay puts his arm around me as we walk up to the side door that leads into the kitchen. "I'm gonna miss this place while we're gone. I was just getting used to actually saying it was ours," he says.

"I know. We've barely had time to enjoy it. How long do you think we'll be gone?"

"I don't know. Depends on what we find when we get to each stop, I guess," Clay says, as he opens the door. "But there's no need for us to rush if we don't feel like it. We can just go at our own pace."

"Yeah, you're right. We could be gone for a while. I guess it might be easier to get the computer and figure out our route. Can you hook up the printer before we get started, please? I'm gonna go ahead and call Cecilia."

"Already ahead of you. Did it last night," he says proudly.

"Sweet. Okay then. Thank goodness Aunt Mitzi caught up with the times enough to have WiFi. She loved playing *Words with Friends* and *Pearl's Peril*, said it kept her mind sharp. She also said looking at *Facebook* was like getting a Christmas card every day. It was her way of keeping up with family. She was so giddy when I set her page up for her and showed her how to use it. I never thought she'd catch on, but that was one smart lady. She didn't let computers intimidate her." I get my phone out of my purse and call my sister.

"Hey, Lynn. What's up?"

"Hey, sis. I was wondering if you might be free the next few months."

"What? What do you mean?"

I tell her the whole story and she sounds excited about it. I'm glad, because I was almost afraid she might be a little upset. I still haven't really talked to a lot of family about the house situation. But she said she's totally fine with everything and that Aunt Mitzi left her enough to get a new car, so she couldn't be happier. She is more than willing to house-sit for us. Especially since I let her know Fred can come too. I ask her to give us a few days to work out a few things and I'd call her when I had a decent timeline on when we'd be leaving.

"I'm sure I'll chat with you before then, though," I say. "Thanks for doing this for us. I'll talk to you soon. Love you."

"No problem. Love you too, sis."

I hang up and look into the den. The carpet is cut, but still there. Clay rolled it up after he finished, but we got sidetracked with finding the box of keys, so there it sits. "We need to get all this carpet out of here before we leave," I say to Clay. He doesn't answer me. I turn back around and he's in a daze. "Hey. You with me?" I snap my fingers in his direction and he looks at me. "Did you hear me?"

"Sorry. What?"

"The carpet."

"Yeah, I know. I'll get it. May need your help to carry it out though," he says.

"Okay, sure." I focus my attention on the laptop. I get the list of clues we translated and we start with number one. "Alright, we know where Houmas House is and that it will be our first stop. Now we have to figure out where or what 'the Crossroads' is and obviously we're going to a bank. Hey, you know what might actually be more fun?" I ask.

"What's that, love?"

"What if...I know you said we should figure out everything first, but instead of trying to solve everything right here, right now, what if we do them one at a time? Like, wait until after we find whatever it is at Houmas House, and then work on clue number two. I think that will make it more fun and exciting. And suspenseful. Plus, whatever is at Houmas House might help lead us to the second place, so there's no use in wracking our brains over it now."

"That does sound pretty cool. Okay then, we'll do it your way. Let's start packing. We've got all day. We might even be able to leave tomorrow," he says.

"Awesome. Alright then, I'm going to put the clothes in the wash. Would you mind going to the store and get some groceries for the house to replenish the fridge and pantry? Actually, the pantry isn't that empty, but we should check some of the expiration dates, since I'm sure Aunt Mitzi hadn't cooked in a while. Plus, you know how she would keep some stuff past the date anyway. One time, my cousin Nikki and I were spending the night with her and Nikki made us some hot chocolate. We thought we were crunching on stale marshmallows. Turns out it was dead weevils."

"Oh my God, that's disgusting," he says with a laugh. "I'm never kissing you again. How did you not see they weren't marshmallows?"

"It was dark and we were watching a movie. At one point, I finally realized what I thought were the marshmallows weren't sweet. They were gritty. And not like old sugar gritty. I spit the one I had in my mouth out into my hand and it was a dark color. So I went into the kitchen, looked in my cup and that's when I noticed. Nikki and I were a little grossed out, but we survived. We were also only about twelve and didn't think to check for stuff like that beforehand. Let's just chunk everything and stock it from top to bottom. And I dare you not to ever kiss me again," I say.

"Oh yeah? Okay, Mrs. Sinclair. We'll see who caves first. My bet's on you." He throws the proverbial gauntlet down.

"Challenge accepted. Now, go to the store."

"Yes, ma'am." He stands at attention and salutes me in jest.

I sort through our clothes and put them in the washer. Coats and jackets are thrown onto the couch to be hung in the closet later. Then I move to the pantry. I go through each item, and sure enough, almost everything is expired. I throw it all out except for some of the cans that are still in date. Aunt Mitzi is probably rolling over in her grave. If she were still here, she'd shake her finger at me. "Those cans are still good, young lady. You're wasting too much food," she'd say.

I head upstairs and pack. While I'm waiting for the rest of the clothes to dry, I go down and look at all the furniture everywhere. I move the rolled up carpet over so I have a path to walk around. So now we have no carpet. But the beauty of it is, the original hardwood floors are presenting themselves in such a dull magnificence. I had noticed the floors when we were ripping up the carpet to begin with, but I didn't realize how pretty they are. Being covered for over forty years hasn't done them any favors, though. I search the cabinets for some Murphy's Oil Soap. I know Aunt Mitzi had some. Found it. I get the mop and shine those floors right up. I do the stairs next. I rearrange the furniture the best I can by myself and bring a few small tables and lamps from our old house up to our room and a couple of the spare bedrooms.

The last of the laundry is finished and packed in our suitcases. Everything is clean except for the clothes on our backs. Now I need to store our coats and jackets. I put them all on hangers and bring them to the closet under the stairs. I turn on the light and notice the underside of one of the steps has a little door on it with a latch. That's new. I put our winter wear on the nearby chair as I wonder what's in there. As I open the door, it dawns on me. This is the step where we found the box of keys on the flip side. Clay was right: we would have found it anyway. Pure genius, Aunt Mitzi. Pure genius.

About two hours have passed, and I wonder where Clay is. He must be buying the store out. I text him to see what's going on. **You ok babe?**

He replies. **Checking out now. Be home soon. Love you.**

I answer. **Ok. Be careful. Love you back.** Followed by a kiss emoji.

Thirty minutes later, I hear the side door creak open downstairs.

"Lynn? I'm home. Can you come help me put up the groceries? I don't know where you want everything," I hear Clay yell from the kitchen. I bop down and start putting things away while he gets the rest out of the truck. Cereal, macaroni and cheese, eggs, beef jerky, steak, fresh fruit...basically Clay's six food groups...and pretty much everything else a house needs for its first supply of food. Except bacon. We've got that stockpiled already. And he even got Fred some doggie biscuits. How sweet.

"I don't think CeCe likes beef jerky," I comment.

"That's for me. For the road. I got you some chocolate covered sun-flower seeds and dried pineapple chunks. You know, the ones coated in sugar that you love? And some other stuff for us, too. Fig bars, trail mix, and that kind of stuff. And oatmeal cream pies."

"Aww, thanks, babe. Those kinds of things weren't even on my radar, but you're right, we'll need a few snacks for the trip. I know Flo isn't going to supply us for the whole time we're gone. I wonder what she has in mind as 'snacks for the road' from a café. She'll surprise us with something great, I just know it."

"Whoa, you've been busy," he says as he looks into the den. "The floors look great. I can't believe they've been covered up all this time. What a shame, right? I'm glad we don't have to get new carpet. I was going to suggest hardwood anyway. I was pleasantly surprised to see the original floors as I was taking the carpet up yesterday morning."

"Yeah, me, too. Oh! I almost forgot. Come see this." I take Clay's hand and bring him to the stair closet.

"The closet?"

"Yeah."

"What about it?"

"Open the door."

It creaks like a century-old door should. "Hmm. Okay. Great place for our jackets. That's what you wanted to show me?"

"Move them over."

The hangers scrape against the metal rod as he shoves them all to one side. "A little door? What's in there? Did you look?"

"Yeah. It's nothing."

"Noth—oh! See? I told you we would have discovered it some kind of way or another. Aunt Mitzi was one smart cookie."

"That she was. I'm so relieved though, aren't you?"

"Yeah."

"You were right."

Clay puts the coats back in order and shuts the door. "Hey, I'm gonna go pull my truck up to the front door. We can put the carpet in the back and I'll take it to the road," Clay says.

"Okay."

He comes back in and I walk over to help him with the carpet. He picks up the brunt of it and I pick it up at the end and we haul it to his truck.

"Dang, this is a little heavier than I thought it would be. Are you sure I'm even helping? I barely have a hold on it." He's so strong. He's not a beefcake, but definitely fit. As a state trooper and an Army National Guard Firefighter, he had to be. I bet he could totally have done this by himself, but I don't mind helping.

"You are. Even if it's the slightest bit, it's alleviating some of the weight." He shoves it in the bed and drives it to the street.

I get an idea and throw it at Clay when he comes back inside. "I just thought of something I want to run by you."

"Shoot."

"Well, you know, since Houmas House isn't that far from here, we don't need to leave especially early. Maybe CeCe can come over for lunch, I'll cook, and we can leave after. Maybe spend the night at Houmas House and do dinner there. I've heard their restaurants are really good."

"Sounds like a plan. So you want to cook? Or do you want me to grill the steaks?"

"Steak sounds great actually, so yeah, that's all you then. I can do a salad and make some mac and cheese. I'll call CeCe and tell her our plans have changed slightly and she needs to start packing and be here for lunch tomorrow."

"Okay, it's settled. Let's load up what we can in the truck tonight and we'll call Flo and let her know we're leaving tomorrow, do breakfast there and pick up what she has for us, and then we'll be back here for lunch. Then after that, it's just you, me, and the road, babe."

"I can hardly wait," I say.

Chapter 11

I'M AWAKENED BY Clay wrapping himself around me from behind. I keep my eyes closed, but I can tell it's still dark outside since my eyelids aren't being stung by sunshine. I still haven't gotten the shades. I peek into the blackness and the clock shows 3:16 in the morning. I love when he wakes me up in the middle of the night. I don't reveal that I'm awake. I let him continue trying to rouse me. He's closer to me than usual, and by that I mean there's only one layer of fabric between us. Mine.

His soft lips visit my neck, then he reaches under my shirt and traces around my belly button with his index finger. He licks the edge of my ear, then follows up with light breeze from his lips. Butterflies excite my insides, but I don't acknowledge him. This is more fun. He's growing harder with every imaginary tick of the clock. Clay lifts the back of my shirt and runs the tip of his tongue all the way up my spine. Chills come over me and I almost can't stand it.

He gets back up to my ear, his words dragging in a whisper, "I know you're awake, goofball. You can't fool me. I know your body. I know you feel how much I want you right now." Then he presses himself into my backside for emphasis.

Okay, he wins. I turn into him, he kisses me, and I release a quiet giggle into his mouth. I whisper, "It's more fun to torture you sometimes. I like to make you work for it. And you just lost the bet."

"Shit," he says out loud, and we laugh.

He takes my shirt off, followed by my bottoms. He's rock solid. A sudden flush of warmth spreads from the center of my being outwards to my extremities. My hands ache with need to explore him. I press my body to his, sliding my hands up and down his back, going over the defined curves of his muscles. I run my fingernails up and down his body as far as I can reach. He shudders. He grabs me by hips and pulls me on top of him. He presses his lips to mine, deepening the kiss with a push of his tongue and a hold on the back of my head. I open myself to him and the ultimate contact occurs. We make love. And I use that term loosely.

Chapter 12

THE SUN SHINES as brightly as ever through the windows again and wakes me up for the second time since we've lived here. Have we really only been here three days? The big, red, digital numbers on the clock scream 9:15. Nine fifteen? I bolt upright. Clay is missing from my side again. Have we switched roles?

We leave today and lunch is in three hours. How could he let me go on sleeping? I start to head downstairs and I can see Clay in the dining room bobbing his head to Guns N' Roses' "Sweet Child o' Mine" while setting the table for breakfast. It's funny to hear that song playing so low. That's one of our favorite songs to blare. He doesn't see me yet so I stand there, halfway down the stairs, watching him dance around the table. He bursts into playing the air guitar and I snicker to myself. He must have heard me because he looks up, right at me, and then darts to where I'm standing on the stairs. He picks me up and carries me down, through the den, and into the dining room, all the while singing the chorus to me. I laugh and sing along. He sets me down and gets my plate for me.

"I wanted to let you sleep, so I've been keeping your plate warm in the oven for you. I went to Flo's already, got us breakfast, and our snacks from her. You're gonna love what she put together for us."

"Just when I think I know you, you find another way of surprising me, Clay Sinclair. I really didn't feel like leaving the house today until after lunch. We have so much to do before we go. Thanks, babe, these are my favorite biscuits on the planet. I'm going to miss them."

"Well," he says, "it's like I told you last night…" His voice turns to a whisper, the same whisper that he hissed in my ear, just six hours earlier, "I know your body." He winks at me and clears his throat. "And I knew you'd be tired this morning, so I let you rest. I'm going to need you as my navigator. I need your mind sharp, ma'am."

"That's what GPS is for. But you're right, it's no fun being on a road trip if the other person is conked out next to you. Thank you for letting me sleep." I give him an air kiss and take a bite of what is to be one of my last biscuits from Flo's Café for a while.

As I'm putting an end to my breakfast, well, brunch really, Clay is getting the grill ready for the steaks. He marinated them all night so I know they'll be awesome. I make the macaroni and cheese and put the salad together.

Cecilia gets to the house at about 11:30 and Clay helps her with her bags. Fred dashes in like he owns the place. He jumps on me like we are long lost pals. I give him some love and one of the doggie treats that Clay bought.

Lunch is wonderful, as usual, when Clay is in charge of the barbeque pit. He is a master griller. He always gets my steak perfect, medium rare. I can't grill a steak to save my life. We visit for a little while longer and then CeCe helps me with the dishes. She thanks Aunt Mitzi for getting a dishwasher a few years ago.

"I hate doing dishes," Cecilia says. "I'm so glad she put this thing here." She points to the fairly new stainless steel appliance with her foot.

"Yeah, I think it was getting a little harder for her the last few years to do things. Last summer, she asked us come over and help her move into the downstairs bedroom. She just couldn't do the stairs anymore. She even had to get a housekeeper, you know? Not that her house was ever that dirty, but she just couldn't keep up with it all anymore," I say.

"I can understand that. You and Clay are the perfect people for this house. I love it, but it's just too much for me. We've had some good times here, though. Lots of memories. Thanks for thinking of me to sit for y'all. I know I'll enjoy being here again."

"Well, we really appreciate you doing this for us. And I know we've got the best guard dog ready to tackle anything that gets in his way, right, Fred?" He barks in agreement and I pet him on his head.

We load up the last few things and Clay fixes us some drinks for the road. I hope he remembered to pack our Community Coffee. You can't get that everywhere, mainly just here in Louisiana. I think a couple of other southern states carry it now though. And of course you can always get it online, but that can take longer than you're willing to wait for coffee. It's our favorite.

"Hey, babe?" I yell from the front door as he's putting our drinks in the truck. "Did you remember to pack enough coffee for the road? And our thermos?"

"No, I thought we'd rely on generic hotel coffee the whole time," he says. I can't tell if he's joking or serious. He's good at that. But he better be joking.

"Um, 'hotel coffee'? Do you kiss your mother with that mouth?"

"Babe, please. Of course I packed the coffee," he replies.

Clay comes back in and we hug Cecilia good-bye and give Fred some belly rubs and tell him to be a good boy.

"We'll be in touch," I tell her. "Thanks again." I'm about to close the door behind me when I notice my picnic backpack sitting in the kitchen. "Oh, we can't forget this. I'm sure it will come in handy." I pick it up and sling it over my shoulder. I give CeCe one last hug, Fred one more 'good boy,' and I'm out the door. I put the backpack in the seat behind mine and climb in the front. "Let's rock and roll, babe."

"Yes ma'am." Clay puts the truck in gear and we're off.

Chapter 13

I CONNECT MY PHONE to the truck radio and hit my *Funky Disco* playlist. Clay is already giving me grief.

"Aww crap, I forgot you're in control of the radio for a while."

"Don't worry. I'll mix it up. But right now, get ready to boogie." I hit the shuffle button. The first song to come on is "Love Rollercoaster" by Ohio Players. "Well, you got lucky on that one." But Clay rolls his eyes. "Don't act like you don't love this song. I know you dig the Chili Peppers' version of it." He smiles and we both start singing and grooving to the beat.

"According to the GPS, we should be at Houmas House in a little over an hour," he says. "What do you think the clue means exactly? Something about a baby named Jane?"

"No, it's Baby Jane, you know, from the old movie *What Ever Happened to Baby Jane?* with Bette Davis and Joan Crawford? Bette Davis was the Baby Jane character."

"Yeah, not exactly my genre of movies," Clay replies.

"I watched it with Aunt Mitzi. She loved Bette Davis. It was quite the horror movie for its time. Well, creepy and sadistic anyway."

I pull the sheet out with all of our interpreted clues and reread it out loud. "Okay, it says 'In the room of the one that played Baby Jane, there's an ornamental closet with a secret pane.' Hmm...let's see...well, as I said,

Baby Jane was played by Bette Davis, and she also starred in the movie *Hush…Hush, Sweet Charlotte*, which was filmed at Houmas House back in the sixties. If I remember correctly, there's a room in the house that they call the 'Bette Davis Room' because that's where she slept during filming." I pull up the internet browser on my phone and start a search for 'Houmas House Bette Davis Room Closet' and nothing comes up except for the Bette Davis room itself with its impressive canopy bed, covered in a pink floral bedspread with matching tester drape and curtains. I show Clay. "Well, I guess we'll just have to find the closet when we get there. What do you think she means by 'ornamental' closet? Like maybe there's a design around the door frame with a secret hiding place? Or what if it's not even really a closet at all? What if it's like a trap door?"

"I don't know. Try not to overthink it before we get there," he says, and he's right. I'm not going to let this stress me out. Aunt Mitzi wouldn't want that and I know that was not her intention, by any means.

"Okay, you're right. So, subject changer. Tell me then, what did Flo fix up for us?" I ask.

He smiles and points at the thermal tote between us. "See for yourself."

I open the tote and it's still relatively warm. I take one of the bags out and open it. I gasp, look at Clay with wide eyes, and close the bag without thinking about it, as if to make sure that what I'm looking at doesn't escape. "Oh my God, is that what I think it is?" Clay nods his head with a smile. "Little buttery biscuit bites?" I pop one in and I'm not even hungry. It melts in my mouth. I make a deep moan at how good they are. "Oh my goodness…oh my goodness." One turns into two and then Clay opens his mouth. I start to give him one and instead of eating it, he bats it away and catches my hand. He draws my index finger into his mouth and slowly swirls his tongue around it. He knows that's one way to get me in the mood. "What the hell are you doing, Sinclair? Don't start something you can't finish." I remove my finger from his mouth.

"I can pull over," he says with one of his sexy, sly smiles.

"Uh, that's a negative, Ghost Rider." He laughs. "I can't believe you wasted one of my biscuit bites. Jerk." I turn my attention back to the tote and there must be four bags full of my all-time favorite biscuits, but in spherical, bite-sized form. "Flo rocks. These are the best. I hope she knows she's created a monster. I'm gonna want all my biscuits in little orbs from now on."

"Biscuit balls," Clay laughs.

"Jeez." I roll my eyes at him. He's such a guy. Any chance to use the word 'balls' and he's all over it.

"She even made some up with cinnamon and sugar so they are kind of like a dessert. And if you like them, she'll add them to the menu. Regular size though. And she said she would name them 'Lynn's Cinns.' C-I-N-N-S. Isn't that funny? I mean since what happened with Austin and all? I thought it was pretty freaking hilarious when she told me that. I told her I thought it was a great idea." He can't stop laughing.

"Oh my God. You are shameless, Clay Sinclair." I thought about throwing a little round biscuit at him, but I didn't want to waste another one. "I don't know whether to cry, laugh, or just be happy she wants to name something after me. But, she's gonna have to change the name. Cinns and sins? Too close for comfort. That's not happening. Makes me sound like I have a biscuit fetish."

"That's why it's so funny. And anyway, don't you? Did you hear the sound you made when you ate the first one just now?" he asks.

He mocks the noise I made. And dammit if it doesn't sound like somebody in the middle of foreplay. His face is slightly red from his amusement.

"Touché, Mr. Sinclair. Touché."

Chapter 14

I KNOW WE'RE GETTING closer to our destination because we're on the Great River Road. This stretch of highway is lined with plantations. Some are right next door to each other. The long clusters of Spanish moss dangling from old oak trees are the curly beards of invisible old men lying watch in the branches.

We finally pull into the parking lot of Houmas House. I haven't been here in forever—at least fifteen years. The grounds are as beautiful as I remember, lush and green, with flowers blooming everywhere. The plantation house is a Greek Revival mansion, a charming shade of deep yellow with green shutters and white trim. Brilliant, white, stately columns surround three sides of the residence. Yes, residence. It's not just a tourist attraction. The owner actually lives here. As you face the front of the house, there's a set of three dormer windows on top of the hipped roof. A belvedere, enclosed by a widow's walk, crowns the massive home.

One of my favorite things about Houmas House is their garçonnières. These are small tower-like houses that were used as bachelor pads for the young men of the family once they got up into their teens. There are two on Houmas House property. One of them has been turned into a small tavern named The Turtle Bar.

I can't wait to tour the gardens again. But not before we figure out what's hidden in the Bette Davis room closet.

"You got the key, right?" Clay asks.

"Yep, right here." I dangle it by the keychain. "It's an old skeleton key, but seems shorter than what most closet skeleton keys look like." It's only about two and a half inches long, so I'm a little perplexed by it.

"That's actually called a lever tumbler lock key. Could be called a mortise key. Or simply, a bitted key. Skeleton keys are master keys, where the serrated edge has been filed down so that it can open more than one lock."

"Huh. I always called these old-timey keys skeleton keys, the way they're shaped, with the teeth that stick out at the end and the big loopy top part. Learn something new every day."

"It's a common mistake. Probably because a lot of those old keys were in fact skeleton keys and were used for hundreds of years."

"I'll probably keep calling them skeleton keys out of habit. And how is it that you know so much about keys? You a locksmith in your past life?"

"No," he laughs, "but my great-uncle was. I'd help him in his shop during the summers while my parents worked. Taught me a thing or two."

"I love learning stuff about you. I can't believe I never knew that. Even after being married this long."

"I bet I'll learn more about you on this trip too. Surely I don't know everything there is to know about Lynn Sinclair."

"That's where you're wrong. You know Lynn Sinclair. It's Lynn Boudreaux you don't know everything about." I smile at him.

"Touché."

There are a few things about Lynn Sinclair that he doesn't know, but I'm not ready to tell him.

"Hey," he says, "we're gonna have to be sneaky, you know? Even though Aunt Mitzi left something for us, it might look like stealing."

"Yeah, I thought about that. The owner and employees probably have no idea what's in the closet. We'll figure it out," I say.

We buy our tickets and browse the gift shop before the tour starts. This has to be one of the biggest gift shops I've ever seen. There are candles, works of art, cookbooks, handmade collectibles, Christmas ornaments, and so much more. I can't help but pick up a coffee mug with a picture of Houmas House on it stating, 'The Crown Jewel of Louisiana's River Road.' That it is. I look at the ornaments as well. I get an idea.

"I think I'm going to try and find an ornament in every place we go on this trip and keep a tree up year round with all the ornaments we collect along the way, as a permanent scrapbook on display," I tell Clay.

"That is such a 'you' thing to do. I love it. But you're gonna be responsible for watering it. Get ready to start sweeping up needles year round. At least until they all fall off and it becomes a Charlie Brown tree."

"Psh." I roll my eyes at his lame attempt at a joke. Surely he knows I mean an artificial tree.

"Just promise me you won't buy a coffee mug everywhere we go. We don't have room for fifty coffee mugs in the truck."

"Deal. But I'm getting this one." I hold up the Houmas House mug and tap it with my nail three times, making a *tic tic tic* sound on the ceramic.

There are two ornaments that I like. They each depict the garçonnière. I can't decide, so I get both.

"Oh, it looks like our tour is ready. Let's go, babe." I check out and we get in line with the rest of the group.

We enter the house through the front door and on the foyer walls is a detailed mural depicting a field of sugar cane. There are ornate polished brass chandeliers hanging from decorative medallions under a ceiling painted as a cloud-filled sky. Our group moves on, room by room. Clay and I take it all in. We are trying to absorb all the history and the details of the furniture from our lively and entertaining tour guide, who is in full-on character in a period costume as an antebellum lady of the nineteenth century, complete with hoop skirt and southern drawl, albeit quite an exaggerated one, even for Louisiana. But there's really only one thing I can think about. I'm itching to ask when we're going to get to the Bette Davis room, but I don't want to appear uninterested, or more importantly, bring any attention to myself or Clay.

We move on to a new room. This one is royal-blue and has a lovely bed and interesting display cases, as well as an old rocking horse and bassinette. The tour guide is going on and on and I'm tuning her out. Not on purpose, my mind is just preoccupied. Clay nudges me and brings me out of my daydream. "What?" I whisper. He points with his eyes to the room next door, connected to this one. The room we recognize from the internet. The room with the pink canopy bed. The Bette Davis room. My insides are giddy and I start bouncing on my tippy toes like a kid. I want to bypass the current room and move right past the tour guide.

We finally begin to shuffle in to the Bette Davis room and the guide starts telling us about the room and the time the actress spent here during the making of the film as well as her feud with Joan Crawford. We are at the back of the group, in the doorway of where the two rooms join, so we can't get a good look of the entire Bette Davis room. Clay and I are scanning the room the best we can for anything that resembles an 'ornamental closet.' I spot what appears to be a small closet in the corner of the room to the left of the bed, but there's nothing remotely ornamental about it. I lean over to him and continue whispering, "That can't be it. It's not fancy enough." People start moving further into the room looking at the mementos from the movie, so we're able to get in all the way. We are standing inside the doorway now. I still don't see what I'm looking for. Then, Clay nudges me again. I look at him and he cocks his head to his right. There's an armoire. An exquisite armoire. An absolutely extravagant armoire. There…is our ornamental closet. It's mahogany, or maybe cherry wood, and is carved with intricate filigree designs on the doors. Similar carvings are above them, with rounded pediments that come to a point. They look like jumbo two-dimensional Hershey's Kisses.

My palms start to sweat. How are we going to open it and find the secret panel with all these people around?

I text Clay. You follow group. I'll stay and try to open. Hope next group isn't close. Distract if need be.

He responds. Ok. Good luck. We got this.

He pulls me close, sticks his hand in the back pocket of my jeans, and squeezes my cheek.

The group moves on and Clay lags behind, looking back at me as they head to the next room. I rush to the armoire and fumble in my pocket for the key. I put it up to the keyhole. My hands are shaking. Naturally, I drop the key and it clinks on the floor. I hear somebody ask what that noise was. Crap. I duck between the Bette Davis bed and the armoire, lift the bed skirt, and shuffle myself under the bed. It's a little dusty under here. Please don't sneeze. Footsteps enter the room. It's the tour guide. I can see her feet under her historic garb. I'm starting to sweat. My face is hot. She stands there for a minute. I'm guessing she's looking around, I can't tell. She makes a comment about 'the ghost again' and goes on her way. Whew. That was close. I need to hurry though. Wait...ghost? Forget it, I don't have time to worry about ghosts right now.

I scoot out from under the bed and get down to business. I put the key in and holy cannoli, it unlocks. I take my time disengaging the door, praying that it doesn't creak. It opens in my favor and I start feeling around on the inside panel of it. I notice a slight dip in the seam near the edge. This must be it. I can see where I would be able to pry it loose, but I need something like a butter knife to pop it off. Well, this is frustrating. We must plan ahead better next time.

I hear the group move again and I start freaking out. I'm not worried for too long though, when I hear Clay pipe up in the hallway. "Can you please tell me a little more about this old map on the wall?" My man. Saving the day.

I'm at a loss as to how to, number one: get the panel off the door; number two: do it without breaking it, anybody hearing or seeing me; and number three: put it back on with the same instructions I just gave myself for number two. Don't panic. Think, Lynn, think. My heart is racing. I'm about to cry. I should have let Clay handle this. I put my hands on my hips and slide them into my back pockets and feel something. That sneaky dog slipped me one of his multi-tools. It's a flat one, about the size of a credit card. Well, hallelujah.

I use the tool's screwdriver edge and go straight into stealth mode, prying the panel off. It comes free easier than I thought it would. I pull it back and I see what I believe is meant just for us.

Chapter 15

I T'S AN OLD postcard. I don't recognize the picture on it, but I grab it and stick it in my back pocket. I hurry up and snap the panel back in place and close the armoire just as the next tour group comes in.

"Are you lawwst, sweet-haw-art?" a different lively tour guide asks me in the same embellished southern accent. Hers has even more drawl than our tour guide had. She's probably not from here at all, doubly playing up the accent. I know it's all part of the gig, and I get it, really, but this isn't how we Louisianans speak. At least not in the Deep South. But, maybe they did way back then. I don't know. I wasn't there.

"Um, yes, actually. I went to the bathroom and lost my group. Mine was the one right before this one. I think."

"Try down-stay-uhs," she says, with a look on her face like she doesn't believe me. She has good instincts.

"Thank you," I say as I rush out.

"You're way-uhl-com." Her reply chases me down the hall with reverberation.

I text Clay again as I head downstairs. **Mission accomplished. What's your 20?**

He replies quickly. **Awesome. I knew you could do it. Outside kitchen.**

The outside kitchen. I think I remember where that is. I want to stop and look at the postcard, but I want to wait for Clay so we can check it out together.

Couldn't have done it without the skillful slip of your tool. Outside where exactly?

I've got another tool I'll slip you later. Out back. Follow the people.

Ok, gutter brain.

I'm out now and I'm looking around. I hear the theatrical drawl and track it through a breezeway where the kitchen appears to be off to the side. I see Clay standing near the entrance looking around and he spots me. I make a motion for him to come here, and he slithers out the door.

We walk down the brick-paved path, away from the crowd in the outdoor kitchen. Now that the deed is done and we are far enough away from everybody, my senses are on overdrive. I'm jumpy, almost to the point of hyperventilating. I could be found out at any second. I start fanning myself with my hands.

"What's wrong with you?" Clay asks.

"I feel like I'm about to faint. I didn't notice any security cameras, but that doesn't mean they weren't there. What if we get caught?" I look around. I'm paranoid, as if I'm carrying Elvis Presley's stolen high school ring.

"Come on, let's walk over here and sit on this bench by the tree."

"Okay." We stroll about twenty feet and sit down. "I don't know what just happened. I was fine up there, for the most part. I think I'm okay now."

"You sure? You need some water?"

"No. The less attention, the better."

"Babe, I think everything's going to be fine. Just breathe. If you were going to get caught, you would have by now. We're in the clear. Now... what did you find?"

I take a few deep breaths and pull the postcard from my back pocket. It's one of those old postcards where the picture looks more like a drawing made with colored pencils, and it's printed on that fancy linen paper, not the cardstock of postcards you get these days. I show it to Clay. As we're looking at it together now, I see at the top that it's identified as the Field Building in Chicago. I've never been to Chicago, so maybe that's why I couldn't determine it at first glance. But, what does it have to do with

Aunt Mitzi? I don't remember her ever mentioning it before. I thought I knew all of her stories.

"The Field Building," Clay says. "Hmm...not familiar with it. Are you?"

"No, I don't recognize it either. She never spoke of this 'Field Building' before, at least not that I can recall."

"Do you think the number two keychain leads us to Chicago? Should we go there next?"

"I don't think so. Remember in the letter, she said that the keychains were numbered for a reason, which is our first clue. So, I believe she's leading us on a sensible course that we should follow by the order of the keychains. Since we know number three is Alabama, I doubt she'd make number two Illinois."

"Yeah, that wouldn't make much sense logistically. What does the message say on the back?"

"I don't know. I've been anxiously waiting to find you before I looked at it. I wanted to share this together." He smiles and kisses me on the forehead, knowing that had to be hard for me. I flip the postcard over and read it out loud.

>*"Dear Rita,*
>
>*I'm fine. I promise. Please tell Mama and Papa not to worry.*
>*It's not what they think.*
>*Love, B."*

"Wow," Clay remarks.

"Right? I don't know what to say. This is intriguing. I'm assuming 'B' is Aunt Mitzi since we just learned her real name was Bernice."

"Rita was your grandmother, right?" Clay asks.

"Yes. Aunt Mitzi always told me that of all her brothers and sisters, she was closest to my grandmother. Let's see. It's postmarked June twentieth. Nineteen-forty-one." I do the math in my head. "Aunt Mitzi was only seventeen when she sent this. Just finished high school. What was she doing in Chicago at seventeen? My great-grandparents couldn't have afforded to send her there and she sure didn't have enough money to get herself there. Was she alone? This was before she married Uncle Sid. They got married when she was nineteen and he was twenty-two."

I look at the picture of the building again and decide to do an online search for it. The image results come up. Holy crap. I do recognize this building. "Shit. Clay."

"What is it?"

I show him. "Take a look at the picture on my screen and then look at the postcard again."

"I don't get it."

On my phone screen, I use my fingers to zoom in to the entrance of the Field Building.

"Oh…damn. It's the building in the picture from the foyer. The entire thing. Total high-rise."

"Yes. I would recognize those long, vertical windows anywhere. The postcard shows a different perspective and angle than we are used to seeing, that's for sure. But this is it." I read the description of the building on the back of the postcard aloud. "Okay, it says here, 'Located at LaSalle, Clark, and Adams streets. This structure, five hundred and thirty-five feet high, is one of the most imposing office buildings in Chicago. Owned by the Estate of Marshall Field.' An office building? This is getting more fascinating by the minute."

I read more online about the Field Building. "It's a bank building. That makes a little more sense. That is, if she went there with Uncle Sid. Before he was Uncle Sid of course. She was just a kid. Why was she there?"

"A better question is, how did Bette Davis get a hold of this postcard and plant it in the armoire?" he asks, like he's seriously contemplating how Aunt Mitzi and Bette Davis could have known each other.

I sneer at him. "Get serious, Clay. Come on, this is a little unsettling for me."

"Sorry, babe. Okay, so how the hell did that postcard end up in an armoire here at Houmas House?" he asks.

"No idea. What in the world does all this mean? It sounds like she was in trouble. Or at least my great-grandparents thought she was in trouble. I never knew of this incident before."

"Do you think she was pregnant and went away to have the baby? They did that back then."

"No. No way. I know it in my heart, she would have never given a baby up. Born out of wedlock or not. Nobody in the family ever spoke about this particular jaunt of hers though. I just can't wrap my head around it. I need a drink."

"Come on," Clay says as he stands up and holds his hand out for me. I grab it and he helps me up. "You good?" I nod. He puts his arm around me and brings me in for a hug. "Let's go. I hear the Turtle calling us."

"That sounds great. But I'm hungry, too. I don't think they serve food at The Turtle Bar."

"Then let's go eat at their restaurant."

"Okay, which one though? There are like, four to choose from. We should maybe go ahead and book one of the cottages for the night, too," I reply.

"Whichever one you want, babe. I'll book the room as soon as we sit down."

"Alright, let's try The Carriage House." We walk over to the restaurant, and since it's a little early for supper time, the elegant restaurant is relatively empty. We are seated at a table for two near the baby grand piano and I look over the menu. Clay books a room for us at The Inn at Houmas House online.

Our waitress comes over and I order a glass of wine and Clay opts for a martini. We go ahead and request our entrées as well.

I look around. Pure elegance. The chandeliers hanging over the table are incredibly striking. I'm all about some fancy chandeliers, and these are exquisite. Hundreds of pieces of vertical crystals are raining down from all three tiers of the light fixture.

I switch gears in my head and wonder about the postcard again. "Okay. I'm at a loss as to what any of this means," I say. "I'm so confused."

"Babe. This is only our first stop. Remember, Aunt Mitzi said something about it making more sense as we go on. This is just the first piece of the puzzle. And there are fifty-one pieces. At best, we could only hope to see less than two percent of the picture."

I breathe a little sigh of relief. "You're right. Again." I smile at him.

"You always know just what to say to make me feel better. I don't know what I'd do without you. My life would be off course."

He takes my hands in his and holds them across the table, stroking the backs of them with his thumbs. "We are a good match. Partners in crime. Lovers in righteousness."

"Ha...definitely. I was so freaking nervous when I was trying to get the panel off of the armoire."

"Well, you were vandalizing a house on the National Register of Historical Places."

My face gets hot. "Shut up!" I yell in a whisper, looking around to see if anybody heard what he said. That's all we need. "As if I wasn't terrified enough already. I don't know how I even got through that. How did you know I would need something to pry it off? Why didn't you tell me you put that tool thingie in my pocket? You could have saved me a little grief, you know. I almost got caught."

"I knew it wouldn't be that simple and I knew you'd find it. And you didn't get caught. If you had, I know you would have come up with a perfectly good explanation. You're quick on your feet with stuff like that. Plus, now you have a better story to tell." He smiles at me and takes a sip of his drink.

"That's a risky little game," I say. "Thank goodness it worked out."

Dinner is enjoyable. Perfectly seasoned. Clay and I take a bite of each other's meals and agree on how scrumptious it all is.

"So, does our room have a fridge and a microwave? We're going to have to make sure of that for the first week or so, you know. I can't let my biscuit bites go to waste. They need to be refrigerated."

"Hmm...I don't know. I'm sure they'll be fine either way. They may not be as good as the days go on, but even three-day-old biscuits from Flo's are better than none."

"You got that right," I tell him.

"Our room includes breakfast though, so you may not want your little biscuit bites after that."

"You hush your mouth, Sinclair. There's always room for biscuit bites."

We finish up dinner and order the Bananas Foster to share for dessert. One of my most favorite ways to end a meal.

As we're walking to our cottage for the night, Clay puts his right arm around my shoulders and I lean into him. I put my left arm around his waist and I reach straight up with my other one to grab his hand and I lock our fingers together.

"This has been a great day. Thank you," I say.

"Beautiful drive, great food, being an accomplice on a heist at an antebellum home; I guess it was a pretty good day for me too."

"Stop it." I nudge him playfully.

He stops under one of the gigantic looming oak trees. The ambiance of this place is magical. He turns and stands in front of me and takes my face in his hands. He leans down for a quick kiss. "You don't need to thank me. We are in this together. This is our adventure." He kisses me again, a little longer this time. Then he whispers, "Now. Let's hurry to our room. I want a second dessert."

Chapter 16

I WAKE UP AND Clay is actually still sleeping. I look around the quaint bedroom of our cottage. Clay booked us one of the deluxe suites on the property. It's so nice. Well, nice is an understatement. The cottages are relatively new, but are decorated with the old-world charm of the main house. And they have porches with rocking chairs.

I have to use the bathroom, but I don't feel like getting up yet. This bed is so comfortable. And gorgeous. It's a dark wood with a solid canopy and the roof of the bed is lined with tightly pleated material, satin maybe, gathered in the center with an embroidered medallion. I snuggle up close to Clay and drape my arm over his side. He moves and stretches his long, fit body. He grabs my hand that's resting near his stomach and kisses it. I return a kiss on his shoulder.

"Good morning, love," he says, his voice raspy.

"Morning, babe. Sleep well?"

"Slept great. You?"

"Yeah. I'm loving this mattress. Comfy." I stretch. "We've got another big day ahead. I'm gonna go get started on a shower." I sit up and kiss him on the cheek. "You stay in bed and rest some more."

"Don't have to tell me twice."

"Sleepyhead. I'll wake you when I'm finished." I rub my hands through his hair and proceed to the bathroom.

This shower is luxurious. And huge. Hell, Clay could have come in here with me. I bet that would have woken him up if I would have offered him the chance. I finish up and put on my robe. As I'm brushing my teeth, Clay walks in and slaps me on the butt. He strips and gets in the shower. I put on my clothes and as I start blow-drying my hair, he gets out. He's always been so dang fast getting ready. I guess from being in the military, and old habits are hard to break. He's dressed before I know it. I finish my hair and put on my makeup.

We move into the living area of our cottage. Clay makes our coffee for us and I fetch the cipher out of my purse with all of the translated clues so we can go over them again. I dig in the box of keys for the one labeled with the number 2—the one we presume is a safety deposit box key.

My husband brings me my cup of coffee. Apparently we missed break-fast, so I eat a couple of my day-old biscuit bites. Still good. He sits down next to me on the couch and opens his jaws. I toss one into his direction and he catches it in his mouth. I give him a thumbs up and mumble, "Good catch," as I finish chewing my biscuit. "Okay, now for the second clue. It reads, 'Near the Crossroads where a man sold his soul, go inside and ask for Miss Cole.' I'm just gonna go out on a limb here and guess that we are headed to Mississippi. Like I said yesterday, with keychain number three being Alabama, it just wouldn't stand to reason that we'd be going to Arkansas or Texas next. Or Illinois for that matter. This keychain is from First National Bank. So, I'll look for that bank in Mississippi and see what comes up. Not sure about these Crossroads. And somewhere a man sold his soul? Like, to the Devil? You have any idea?"

"Nope, sure don't. You'd think with all the traveling I did with the Guard I would know a few of these things. Let me see the list again." I hand the paper to Clay and he notices something. "Hmm…the 'C' in Crossroads is capitalized. Maybe that means something. But, otherwise, I'm sorry. No idea," Clay replies.

"Oh, wow, I didn't catch that. Maybe it's an actual street name." I get my phone out and search for 'First National Bank Mississippi Cross-roads.' The results come up. "Well it seems there is a First National Bank in Clarksdale, Mississippi. So that's something to go on I guess."

"How far is that from here?" Clay asks. "Try just searching for 'Crossroads Mississippi' and see what happens," he suggests.

"Good idea. Okay. I don't know how far that is from here, I'll have to check in a minute." After performing the new search, I gasp at what I find. "Holy shit. The first thing that pops up says 'Clarksdale, Mississippi – Devil's Crossroads – Roadside America.' I think we just found it." I click on the images heading. "Oh. It's the intersection of highways forty-nine and sixty-one. There's a sign with guitars." I show Clay the picture. "Okay, there is definitely a story here. What did Aunt Mitzi get herself into?"

As it turns out, nothing. At least nothing having to do with selling her soul to the Devil, thank goodness. Legend has it that at these Crossroads in Clarksdale, Mississippi, Blues musician Robert Johnson sold his soul to the Devil for success. I give Clay all this information. "I find it strange that I've never heard of him. Doesn't seem very legendary to me, but then again, you know, Blues isn't really my favorite kind of music. And he died almost a hundred years ago, so there's that," I say. "I'm sure his music is big in the Blues world. We should look up some of his stuff and play it to get in the spirit."

"Go for it," says Clay. "And, my guess is that Aunt Mitzi just needed us to know what town to go to, in order to find the right bank. Or, maybe she wants us to sell our souls for the answer to her fifty-one part riddle."

"Very funny," I say sarcastically. "Why wouldn't she just say, 'Go to the First National Bank in Clarksdale, Mississippi'?" I ask.

"Well now, what fun would that be? And look, we learned a little urban legend along the way. So now we know these infamous Crossroads are in Clarksdale, Mississippi and there's a First National Bank there as well. That's where we need to head next. So how far is it?"

"According to the route online, five hours and twenty-two minutes. But, that's taking the interstate." I drag the highlighted course to the more scenic route. "If we take highway sixty-one all the way up, which will be a prettier drive, and it's not like we don't have the time, it will take us five hours and forty-four minutes. Not that much out of our way."

"Alright. Let's pack up and get ready to go," he says.

"Wait, I want to see the gardens first before we leave. This place has given us such a wonderful start to this quest of ours. Let's finish it right."

"Sure, love. That sounds nice. I'll start loading up."

We browse the gardens and there are so many different beautiful flowers in bloom: lilies, azaleas of just about every color you can imagine, pansies, daffodils, and more. There's even a cactus garden. On one part of the grounds, there's a sweet little turquoise bridge going over a koi pond with plentiful lily pads, surrounded by a lush green setting of ferns, palmettos, palm trees, and other flourishing greenery. A pagoda-like gazebo with a rock waterfall in the front of it is the backdrop for this charming area.

"I'm so in love with this place," I tell Clay. "We should come back here every year for our anniversary."

"Why does it only have to be for our anniversary? I'll take you here anytime you want as long as you promise not to dismantle any more furniture." He winks at me.

"Deal," I say with a smile.

"It is rather peaceful out here. It's like we're in another world."

"Yeah, it is. So enchanting. And you're too good to me."

"I want to be," he says. He kisses me under a group of oak trees that must be three hundred years old.

We finish up our leisurely stroll through the grounds at Houmas House, eat an early lunch at Café Burnside on the property, and then get on the road for Clarksdale, Mississippi.

First thing I do is search for Robert Johnson's music. "Hey, look. There's one called 'Cross Road Blues.' We gotta play that one."

"Hit it."

Chapter 17

I TAKE A SIP of my coffee. "Alright, it's just after noon," I say, looking at the clock on the dashboard of Clay's truck. "It doesn't look like we'll get there in time for the bank to still be open. They close at four. So, we'll have to stay there for the night and check out the bank first thing in the morning. But we can swing by the mysterious Crossroads and see what's there. I wonder if there are any Christmas ornaments depicting the Crossroads. I need one. But if I can't find anything, I'll just take a picture of the intersection and make my own ornament."

"I'm sure whatever you come across will be fine either way."

"Yeah. Okay, I've got enough of the Blues. The legendary Robert Johnson is bringing me down. But, I gotta admit, he's good at it." I switch my playlist and "Saturday Night" by Bay City Rollers comes on. "Oh, I love this song." I start clapping my hands and spelling out 'Saturday' along with the song, antagonizing Clay.

"You're such a goofball." He laughs and shakes his head at me.

"So, what do you think could be in the safety deposit box?" I ask. "Do you think it has anything to do with the Field Building in Chicago? I mean, since that's a bank too? I just don't understand. What the—"

"Babe. Stop freaking out. No stressing. Remember? Whatever happened in the past is in the past. Your family thought the world of Aunt Mitzi. As far as I could tell, there was never any bad blood or animosity when it came to her. Not from one person in your entire family," Clay says, trying to reassure me.

"Yeah, but, unless...what if this is a fact-finding mission and secrets and truth will come out. Maybe something we never knew about. I mean, my grandmother died when I was four, so I don't even really remember her and Aunt Mitzi being together in the same room. I was too young. And my great-grandparents were wonderful people. I've never heard anybody say anything bad about them. From what I understand, GiGi was kind and generous to a fault. When Granpop would get a shipment of rice in at the grocery store during the Depression, he would give her a twenty pound sack to take home for the month. Any time anybody would go over to visit GiGi, she would give them a cup. Before you knew it, those twenty pounds were gone, much to the dismay of my Granpop. But, what if my family has a deep dark secret? I don't know if I want to know."

"Deep dark secret, huh? Maybe it's just a bag of rice in the safety deposit box."

"Jesus, Clay. Can you be serious for one freaking second? I'm worried."

"Sorry. But come on, babe. You're doing it again. Just stop stressing your pretty little head about it. It's probably nothing, you know? This is supposed to be fun. Aunt Mitzi would not have done this if it was going to hurt you."

"Ugh. There you go again, talking sense into me. Okay, alright, okay. I'm done speculating." Out loud anyway. I'm quiet for a while, contemplating as I stare out the window. The faint sound of the Bee Gees' "How Deep Is Your Love" plays in the background.

"Right?" I barely hear Clay ask. "Hellooo...Earth to Lynn," he says, snapping me out of my daze.

"I'm sorry, babe. What's right?"

"Aunt Mitzi. Didn't she work at the bank Uncle Sid's dad owned? Or am I dreaming that?"

"Oh, crap. You're right. She did. She worked for him after she graduated high school. God, how did I not put that together earlier? Well, that answers one question. Maybe. We can just assume right now that she was in Chicago with Uncle Sid. It must have been some sort of business trip. But now, that raises the question...why would Uncle Sid's dad send two kids to Chicago for business? Granted, I guess being in your early twenties in the nineteen forties was like being middle-aged though. But sending a seventeen-year-old girl, fresh out of high school?"

"Hey, if twenty back then was like forty is today, then seventeen was like thirty-five. She was a woman by those standards. I'm guessing there was a little banging going on in between the banking."

"God, Clay. Could you be any crasser?" I ask, shaking my head.

"No, I'm being serious. I mean, most girls were married by then. Some even had to drop out of high school to help take care of the family, right? With Aunt Mitzi being the youngest, I would imagine enough of her siblings dropped out of school to help around the house and the store. So, Aunt Mitzi was allowed to finish school. Make sense?" he rationalizes.

We cross the state line and I tell Clay, "Hey, pull over. I want to get a picture of the 'Welcome to Mississippi' sign. I'm going to do that for every state. So prepare yourself." He pulls over and I lean out the window and snap my picture. "I guess the last one I get will be 'Welcome to Louisiana.' Fitting, right?"

"Okay, yeah. Now, back to our conversation. It makes sense, what I said. Agree?"

I'm out of coffee so I refill my mug from our thermos and check to see if Clay needs some. Nope, he's good. "It does make sense, actually. But I know most of my great-aunts and uncles finished school. A couple of them died when they were very young though because of childhood diseases that had no cure at the time. One died at birth. They just couldn't ever get him to start breathing on his own. Really sad. I believe it was just the oldest two or three that didn't finish high school."

"Okay, so…Aunt Mitzi was no dummy, right? She always beat me at Trivial Pursuit. Maybe Uncle Sid's dad hired her because he knew she was smart."

"How would he know that?"

"Wasn't she valedictorian of her class? That's big news in a small town. Makes the paper every year, right? A whole page devoted to the smartest graduate."

"True. I remember seeing the article in one of her scrapbooks."

"He saw her potential. And if there was any big business going on in Chicago, he needed his two best employees on the job," Clay says.

"Could be. I would just think that if it were that important, Mr. Santini would have gone to Chicago himself," I offer.

"Maybe he couldn't. Or maybe it wasn't that important. Maybe he wanted Uncle Sid to see the world a little bit. I'm assuming Aunt Mitzi hadn't set foot outside the state of Louisiana at that age. He probably wanted to let her have a little taste of something bigger, too. Broaden her horizons. Maybe that's why your grandparents were upset. Because he took their baby and shoved her off to Chicago without any real street smarts. And with a middle-aged man she barely knew, no less. I can understand why they were worried."

"Wow, Clay. You think you have this all figured out, don't you? You don't really have any idea what happened. Neither do I. So, just stop trying to put a scarlet letter on Aunt Mizti, *okay*?" I say, miffed.

"Whoa, Lynn. That's not what...I'm not...I know she...fuck...just forget it." He cuts the radio off.

"Fine!" I turn to the window again and fold my arms across my chest. How can he say that about her? She wasn't a floozy. If she were here and heard him say that, she'd...well, I don't know what she would do. Slap him across the face? Pinch him by the ears until he fell to his knees? Dare I wonder...would she laugh because he's right?

It begins to rain. It's like Aunt Mitzi is sad because we're fighting. And fighting about her. She would hate that. We sit in silence for miles. I don't want to believe any of his theories. That's all they are. We don't know.

It's storming now and the visibility is getting worse. We pass a road sign that says we are a few miles from Vicksburg. Great...we still have three hours to go.

Clay slows down and exits the highway. I don't say anything. He pulls into the parking lot of a hotel. I don't move. "What are you doing?" I ask without turning away from the window. I'm so annoyed with Clay that I don't want to look at him. "We're only three hours away." He puts the truck in park and shuts the engine off.

"Babe. Lynn. Look at me. Please." I turn my head and squint my eyes at him. "I'm sorry. I didn't mean to imply anything inappropriate about Aunt Mitzi. I was just thinking out loud, trying to figure things out. Trying to think of an explanation. You're right." My expression softens.

"We don't know what happened. But we will. She said we will." He takes my face in his hands. "And if there's one thing I can promise you right now, again, it's that she did not want this for us. This fight. This silence. This wedge." He unbuckles his seatbelt. "I love you."

"I love you too. I'm sorry I blew up at you. What are we doing here?"

"The rain is really getting wild and I'm tired. This weather makes me sleepy. I thought it would be a good idea to just call it a day here. We can still make the bank tomorrow with plenty of time to go by the Crossroads. You stay in the truck and I'll go get us a room. I'll be right back." He starts to get out of the truck, but turns around. "You never read *The Scarlet Letter* did you?"

"No. Why?"

"It was about a woman who went to prison for committing adultery with a minister and conceived a child with him. It's deeper, darker, and much more complicated than that though. Nowhere close to resembling Aunt Mitzi and Uncle Sid." He smiles.

"Well, same ballpark. I was supposed to read it in high school. I didn't even read the *CliffsNotes*. I thought it was just about a woman who had sex before she was married. In the olden days, that was criminal. So yeah, you can guess that I failed that literature test. Now, go get us a room. And make sure it has a microwave."

Chapter 18

CLAY GETS UP early and says he wants to hit the hotel gym for about an hour, to stay in his routine of working out. "It's leg day," he tells me. I groan. I hate working out, but I decide to join him. I can't stand exercising in a gym. It bores me. I'd rather get physical in other ways, besides in the bedroom. I'm a runner. I guess I can hit the treadmill while Clay does some weight training. I do love watching him work out. That's the only reason I'm going.

This gym is one of the biggest ones I've ever seen for a hotel. Clay is about thirty feet in front of me doing squats while lifting weights. I'm running on the treadmill, but I slow down and then stop so I can stare at him. He's so serious, grunting through clenched teeth with every rise. It's his lowering to the floor that I'm fond of though. That tight ass. His callipygian physique makes me swoon. There's a really pretty girl on the treadmill beside me, probably in her late twenties. I see her checking him out too. I smile inside. That's my sexy guy.

She looks at me and takes her earbuds out. "Hey," she says in a breathy whisper, "could you be any more obvious? I mean, I know he's hot, but it's rude to stare." She chuckles.

"You think he's hot?"

"He looks a little old for me, but yeah. I'd do him."

"So would I. In a heartbeat."

Clay drops his weights to take a break and looks over at us. It must be obvious that we're talking about him. "What are you looking at?" he asks.

"Uh…nothing," I say, pretending like we're strangers. I restart the treadmill and begin jogging again.

"Impressive control you've got there," the girl says. "We were just admiring you."

He smiles. "Thanks," he says, clearly flattered by the sweet young thing's compliment. He replaces the weights back on the rack and takes a long swig of water. He gives a side-eye look over here while he drinks. Strictly for the chick next to me, he tilts his head back and pours the last couple of sips from his water bottle over his forehead, which streams down his face and chest, then he rubs his hands through his now wet hair. I'm laughing inside. But holy shit. That was hot.

"Oh my God," the girl whispers.

"I know, right?" I whisper back.

Clay struts over to us and he stands next to my treadmill. "Hey," he says.

"Hey," I reply.

"Why don't you shut that thing off and follow me up to my room."

"Um…okay." I slow the machine down to a stop.

The hot chick shrugs her shoulders. "Go for it, girl," she says out loud with a smile.

Clay kisses me right there and then walks off, but not before he slaps my butt.

"That's my husband," I say with a snicker.

"Are you serious? Oh shit. I'm sorry. I should learn to keep my big mouth shut." Her face is as red as her Ole Miss sports bra. "You're a lucky woman though." She winks at me.

"I know." I smile back at her, the color of my face undoubtedly close to hers.

"Really," she says, still running, "I'm sorry. I had no idea. I didn't think you knew him. You're good." She smiles and shakes her head.

"Don't worry about it. Seriously, it's cool." I surprised myself by having remained calm on the inside. I have a bit of a jealous streak.

"I can only dream about having that kind of relationship one day."

"You'll find your guy. He's out there."

"Thanks, I hope so."

"You coming, Lynn?" Clay asks from the door.

"Yep." I step off the machine and turn back to the girl. "Have a great rest of your workout," I tell her.

"You too," she winks at me and I laugh as I walk out the door.

Clay is waiting for me in the hall.

"Spectacular performance," I tell him. "The waterfall was a nice touch. You got that poor girl all worked up."

"What? That was just for you, babe." He laughs and swats my bottom again.

"Good job, picking up on my pretend-I-don't-know-you vibe. That was fun."

"Yeah, that was sexy. We should do that again sometime, Mrs. Sinclair."

"Agreed, Mr. Sinclair."

We get back to the room and shower. I warm some of my biscuit bites for breakfast. I ate some for dinner last night too, because I know they won't be good for much longer. They are almost all gone anyway, I just don't want them to go bad. I need to call and thank Flo. And I've gotta beg her not to name the cinnamon and sugar ones 'Lynn's Cinns.' No way, no how. Maybe I'll send her a postcard. She'd love that.

We load up, hit the road and plot our route to the Crossroads. I decide this morning to give Clay a little break and surprise him by playing something that's a little more his speed. I hit the play button on my *Badass Songs* list. Billy Idol's "Rebel Yell" blares from the speakers.

"Yes indeed," Clay says. "Now that's some road trip music right there." He accelerates his truck like he owns the highway.

I laugh. "Well, I owe it to you for giving you such a hard time yesterday. I hate when we fight, I shouldn't have given you the silent treatment for so long."

"Hey, I know when to give you your space. And it wasn't all you. Our makeup sex was intense though," he says as he looks me up and down like he could go again at any minute. Who am I kidding...he could. I shake my head at him. Men...

"Slow down, Meatloaf. You're driving like a 'bat out of hell.' The last thing we need is a string of speeding tickets on this trip."

He smiles. "I see what you did there. Nice one." He eases just a little and sets the cruise control to seventy miles per hour.

I flip through one of the magazines I brought with me to pass time on the road. "Ain't Talkin' 'Bout Love" by Van Halen comes on and Clay starts singing.

We're in Clarksdale before I know it. I see the big, blue guitars at the intersection of the highways. The Crossroads. It's not much to see, but I have to get out and take a picture. Especially if I can't find a Christmas ornament with those huge, blue guitars on it.

We head down the road to the bank. My knees are bouncing up and down on their own. I close my eyes and take a few deep breaths. I roll my neck around and try to relax myself.

"What are you doing? Are you nervous?"

"Yes. We're supposed to go in and ask for Miss Cole. But what if she's off today? What if she switched banks? What if she died?"

"Babe. Love. Stop. You've got to quit doing this to yourself. Deep breath. Let's just go in and ask for Miss Cole and see what happens." He parks the truck. "Shall we?"

I get the key out of the box. "We shall."

Clay opens the door to the bank, and everybody in the building looks up. Um, were they waiting for us? "Hi," I say. "Is Miss Cole here?"

"Who?" a young lady asks.

"Miss Cole?" I repeat.

"There's no Miss Cole that works here," the girl says.

My shoulders slump and there's a heavy pulse in my throat.

Clay speaks up, "Are you sure? We were told to ask for Miss Cole. We have a key."

An older gentleman about seventy comes around the corner upon hearing Clay's much louder, more confident voice. "I'm sorry, did you say 'Miss Cole'?" he asks.

"Yes, sir," Clay replies.

"Follow me," the man says.

We do. My spirits rise.

"I assume your presence means Mitzi has passed. You must be Clay and Lynn. I'm Mississippi Coltrane. I'm your 'Miss Cole.' That was Mitzi's idea. Everybody calls me Colt. Mitzi was such a dear friend, I'm sorry to hear she's gone. But let me tell you, that woman lived. Let me go get the key for the box. I'll just be a minute."

"Oh my God," I whisper and hit Clay on his arm. "How long has she been planning this? Watch, we're gonna find out she was like a smart lady version of Forrest Gump, with a hand in every notable thing on the planet."

"Shh…" Clay puts his finger over his lips and laughs.

Mississippi Coltrane aka Miss Cole aka Colt comes back with the bank's key for the safety deposit box. Number 237. He puts his key in and I put mine. He takes the box out of the wall and leaves us in privacy. He smiles on his way out and says to let him know when we're finished or if we need anything else.

"Thank you," Clay and I say in unison.

I take yet another deep breath and open the box.

Chapter 19

THERE ARE FOUR envelopes. "I'm seeing a bit of a trend here," I say to Clay as I open the one that has the date of 1945 and the number one circled on it. It's thick. I unfold the papers. My eyebrows furrow. I don't understand.

"Adoption records?" Clay asks.

My mood plummets. The temperature in my face soars. My hands start shaking. I can barely hold the documents. "That's what it looks like. Apparently Aunt Mitzi and Uncle Sid adopted a baby in 1945. A boy. What happened to him? I've never heard about this. Not once in my whole life. It says here that it was like a done deal, but there are a couple of signatures missing. What happened to the baby? You know, I always wondered why they never had kids, but I never asked. It was none of my business. Besides, I hated when people asked us so I know how it feels." I look in the envelope again. "Oh, look, here's a picture." It's a very young Aunt Mitzi and Uncle Sid, holding a little baby. They look so happy. "I don't get it. Did the baby die?"

"Open the one with number two circled," Clay says.

I unseal the envelope and unfold the papers. "Oh no." My words are barely audible. "Disruption of Adoption? What does that mean? That can't be good."

"It looks like the birth mother took the baby back," Clay says.

"What? How heartbreaking. I can't believe this. The pain they must have felt." I look at the picture again. "This photo is taken in the den of the house. They had the baby home, Clay. How could he just be taken away after that?" My vision blurs with the onset of tears.

"I guess maybe the laws weren't as strict back then for the birth mother to change her mind. Hell, they can change their minds even today. The window is small, but it happens," Clay says in a somber tone.

I open the third envelope, marked 1947 with another number one circled. It's the same thing. Adoption papers. A girl this time. And another picture of them with this baby. "Oh my God. Another one? Don't tell me. I don't want to look at the fourth set of papers."

Clay opens it instead. "Yeah, I'm afraid so. Looks like another disruption of an adoption. Jeez. What are the odds of this happening twice to the same couple? Two of the most loving people."

"It's not fair." My voice cracks, teetering on the edge between sorrow and anger. Thoughts race through thick clouds in my head as I try to understand. I sniffle. "I guess they didn't want to try again. I wouldn't either. Can you imagine the fear they felt with the second baby? And then to have their worst nightmares come true? The anguish and torment. Dammit. Unreal. Those babies would have had the best life." Clay hugs me and I weep into his shoulder, my chest heaving up in down in rapid successions. "This is so sad," I say, my tear-filled words muffled by his shirt. He rubs my back to try and calm me down.

"I know," he says. "I'm sorry this happened to your family. This is awful. Come on. Look at me, babe." I raise my head up and look into his eyes. They've never seemed bluer. "I'm willing to bet Aunt Mitzi knew this would upset you, but she obviously had her reasons for letting you in on this. And who knows, maybe those babies still wound up having great lives. Let's wrap up here and find somewhere to go and figure out clue number three. Maybe there will be more information at the next place."

"Yeah. Okay. Go get Mr. Cole, or whatever his name is, and I'll put the papers back together. Can you see if they have any tissues please?"

"Sure thing, love," he says.

I wipe my cheeks with the backs of my hands and put the papers back in their respective envelopes. Clay comes back with Mississippi Coltrane, a handful of tissues, and a bottle of water. I blot my face, open the water bottle and take a huge swig.

"Thanks for the water, babe. I didn't realize I needed any, but I was thirsty." My voice is less shaky now. "Mr. Cole, how did you know Aunt Mitzi?"

"Colt, please. We met in the early sixties. I was a young buck, just finished college with a degree in accounting. Through certain channels, I went to work for Mr. Santini, Sid's father. I'm not from Louisiana, I was new to the place. Mitzi and Sid kinda took me under their wing."

"I see. Did you know what was in this box?"

"No, not exactly. But Mitzi had alluded to it a time or two. I made my own inferences, drew my own conclusions. I'm guessing it's nothing good." He hands me a big, brown envelope and I tuck the papers inside it.

"No. Apparently they tried to adopt two children, both fell through," I tell him.

"Tragic," Colt says. "I figured it was something like that. You kids finished here? I've got a meeting I need to get to."

"Uh, yeah," Clay says.

"Alright, I'll walk you out. It's been great meeting you, finally. I wondered if I'd be around to see this day. Lynn, I see some of Mitzi's features in you," he tells me as we're walking out the door.

"Oh, thank you, that's so nice of you to say, warms my heart. And thanks for your help today. I'm so glad you were here."

"My pleasure. Say…is Flo still around?" he asks.

"Flo? You know Flo?" I ask him.

"Oh yeah. We go way back. Way, way, waaay back. The four of us used to paint the town red every chance we got." He stops for a second, like he's remembering something, and smiles. "Tell her I asked about her, will ya? Tell her, 'The mustang has missed his Sally.' She'll know." He gets into his car and rolls the window down.

"Uh, okay, sure, I'll pass along the message," I tell Colt.

He backs out as we both stand by the passenger door of the truck. As an afterthought, I shout to Colt as he's driving off, "Hey, Colt, where are you from?"

"Chicago!" he yells back, and takes off with a wave of his hand.

Chapter 20

WE LOOK AT each other with our mouths to the ground, our eyes as wide as we can open them, while Colt drives away. Clay unlocks the truck and we get in.

"Well, how interesting," I muse. "Okay, that makes me feel better. I have a feeling we'll find out more about Mr. Mississippi Coltrane along this trip."

"Maybe," Clay says.

"Hey, babe, I'm getting hungry. Let's find something to eat. And somewhere that might have an ornament with the Crossroads on it for our tree."

"Okay, that sounds like a good idea. What are you in the mood for?"

"Um, I don't know. I kind of feel like pizza."

"Oh, man, pizza sounds great. I could go for some myself," Clay says.

I search for the nearest pizza joint on my phone. "Hey, there's a place called Stone Pony Pizza just around the corner. Let's go there."

"Stone Pony. What a slick name for a pizza place. Let's check it out."

We drive down the street and come to Stone Pony Pizza in a strip of old buildings. It's sandwiched between an empty, archaic bank building that looks like one Bonnie and Clyde could have robbed, and an old general store with naturally distressed bricks.

"I love these old small-town buildings. When mom and pop stores were the only place to shop. Times were simple," I say.

"Yeah, but life was harder," Clay replies.

We get out of the truck and Clay notices something cool on the back of the building that we passed to get here. "Whoa, check out that awesome mural of Clint Eastwood. That's from *The Outlaw Josey Wales*, one of my favorite movies."

"Man. That is badass. Very cool," I say, and I snap a picture of it.

We head inside Stone Pony Pizza. It's a rather nifty place. There are some really groovy, black-padded, semi-circular booths. A museum's worth of memorabilia dons the walls: sports jerseys, movie posters from *Animal House* and several Spaghetti Westerns, a boxing poster commemorating the big fight between Mike Tyson and Lennox Lewis from 2002, vintage ads for Pearl Beer and Lucky Strike Cigarettes…just to name a few. There's also a bar.

"Let's sit in one of the booths. They look cozy," I tell Clay.

The waitress introduces herself as Learline and gives us the menu. We both order a beer and she lets us have a minute to look over the choices while she gets our drinks.

Learline comes back with our beers and Clay tells her we want the Buck Wild pizza. I take the list of clues out of my purse and look at number three.

"Alright, listen up, Sinclair."

"All ears."

"This one says, 'In the town where The Heaviest Corner on Earth has surely seen its share of hijinks, file into the Empire Building and look for hidden pinks.' This one is going to be a doozy. All we know is it's in Alabama, going by the keychain. Is there anything here that you know anything about? Do any words stick out as clues within the clue? Aunt Mitzi seems good at that."

"Well, nothing stands out, but it doesn't make much sense right now. I wonder what she means by 'hidden pinks.' A collection of Pink Floyd albums? *Pinky and the Brain* action figures? The famous hot dogs from Los Angeles?" He laughs and I shake my head at him. "Okay, I'm being serious now. So, what does the internet say about this so-called heavy corner?"

I look it up. "Oh it's in Birmingham. So, we have a place. Okay, let's see…according to the internet, it's at the corner of Twentieth Street and First Avenue North in Birmingham. Good, we have an exact location. Says here, it was given that name because, at the time, the height and mass of the four buildings were so great, that it was dubbed The Heaviest Corner on Earth. Back in the day I guess it was rare to have that many skyscrapers in one place. These buildings were finished long before construction of the Empire State Building and the Chrysler Building in New York even started. How crazy is that?"

"Wow. So, what are the other buildings? How tall are they?" Clay asks.

I scroll through the information. "There's the ten-story Woodward Building, sixteen-story Brown Marx Building, sixteen-story Empire Building, and the twenty-one-story American Trust and Savings Bank Building. Check it out, here's a picture of it from 1916." I show Clay the picture.

"Yeah, that's a lot of concrete for back then. Next question…how long will it take us to get there? If my geography is right, Birmingham is almost smack-dab in the middle of Alabama. We are in east Mississippi, near the Arkansas border, so having to travel all across this state and half into the next, I'm gonna guess about four hours."

"Wow, very good, Clay. Three hours and fifty-four minutes. You get an A plus."

He takes a sip of his beer and holds it up like he wants me to hold mine up, too. I raise it up and he clinks our beer necks together.

The pizza comes and it's really good. Some of the best pizza I've ever had. I ask Learline if there's anywhere I might be able to find a Christmas ornament with the Crossroads on it and she doesn't know of any, but says I might be able to find one online. So after a little bit of searching, I find one, but it's not exactly like I wanted. It's basically a scalloped edge sign imprinted with '61/49 Crossroads, Clarksdale, MS' with a picture of a guitar and the shape of the crested highway sign. At the bottom it says, 'Come hear that Clarksdale moan.' I wanted one that looks like the actual guitars at the intersection. This guitar isn't even blue. I can't believe they don't have anything like that around here. They are missing an opportunity. It's possible that I'm just overlooking the obvious, but I mean, don't Blues fans (and, supposedly, people wanting to sell their souls) come here from all over the world? Either way, I will definitely make my own ornament with the picture I took, but I go ahead and order the one I find online anyway. I'll text CeCe and tell her to be on the lookout for it.

Learline comes back to clear our empty pizza pan and Clay asks her about the mural. "What can you tell us about Clint Eastwood?"

Her head tilts to one side and she purses her lips together as her eyebrows crinkle. Then she realizes what he's talking about. "Oh," she laughs, "that's one of our most popular murals. Clarksdale has several all around town. If you have time, you should drive around. We're a very artsy town. And if you like the Blues, you won't be disappointed in any bar you step into," Learline explains with a smile. You can tell she's proud of her quaint little town.

"I wish we had time. I know we'll be back at some point in the future," I say. "Thanks for all the information. And we thoroughly enjoyed this pizza. It was wonderful." We pay the check, leaving Learline a nice tip, and get back in the truck, our bellies full of yummy pizza.

"Yes," Clay says, as he starts the truck. "We'll definitely be back. I bet we're going to be saying this sort of thing plenty along this trip. I can only imagine what Aunt Mitzi has in store for us. The things we'll learn. About her, the country, and ourselves."

"You're so right." I turn on my *Anything Goes* playlist and "Babe" by Styx comes on. "Aww, it's our song," I look at Clay and smile. He gives me a wink. This song always makes me want to cry, as much as I adore it. It gives me mixed emotions of gloom and love.

Clay and I hadn't long been dating, just a couple of months, when he got deployed for Operation Desert Shield. He was going to be gone for about a year, give or take, he wasn't really sure, not that he could tell me anyway. He couldn't even tell me exactly where he was going, besides somewhere in the Middle East. We were spending as much time as we could together. The night before he was going to leave, this song came on the radio and he sang it to me. It was fate. The words were perfect, like it was written just for us at that moment. It was the first time Clay told me he loved me. I cried. Happy tears and sad tears. That night was our first time in bed together, believe it or not. And we've been calling each other 'babe' ever since.

Chapter 21

W E'VE BEEN DRIVING for a while and I've been occupy-
ing myself with texting Annie, Flo, and CeCe. Flo got a
kick out of the message from Colt. Said she hadn't heard his
name in years. I ask her for the details.

She replies. That story is best told over a bottle of wine. Tell you
when you get back.

Can't wait to hear it. I'll bring the bottle.

Deal. Bring two.

"Disarm" by The Smashing Pumpkins is playing. Clay has been
extremely quiet. I look over at him and he's not here. He's on another
planet. His face is irritated and cross.

"Clay." Nothing. I speak up. "*Clay.*" I snap my fingers and jar him.

"What? What?"

"Where's your head, babe? You okay?"

"Yeah. Sorry."

"What's going on in there?"

"Nothing. Just…thinking."

"About what?"

"Nothing, babe. Don't worry about it."

"Are you sure you're okay?"

"Yeah. Fine."

"Okay. If you're sure." Sometimes he just doesn't want to talk, but he reaches over and grabs my hand. I shuffle through my playlist and look for something that will take his mind off of whatever it is he's reflecting on. I decide on "Rock You Like a Hurricane" by the Scorpions. I watch him for a minute. His face has relaxed and he's mouthing the words to the song. He looks over and winks at me. My husband is back.

We finally make it to Birmingham. I booked us the Presidential Suite at a hotel on the way here, so we head there first to unload and rest. We both wind up crashing and take a nap for a couple of hours. I wake up and it's almost dark outside. I gasp.

"Clay, wake up. It's getting late. Crap. I can't believe we slept so long. Get up." I'm on the side of the bed tugging at his arms. He's not budging.

"Babe, calm down," he says in a tired voice. "The building isn't going anywhere. It's too heavy, remember? Let's just relax. We can check out the Empire Building tomorrow." He stretches and pulls me back down. I lose my footing and fall onto him. "Ugh," he grunts, and I giggle.

"You did that to yourself." He returns my laugh and opens his legs. I lie between them, resting my chin on top of my folded arms on his chest. He gazes at me and tucks my hair behind my ears. "What?" I ask. "Why are you staring at me?"

"You're just beautiful."

"Now who's the stalker?"

"Touché, Mrs. Sinclair."

I scoot up to kiss him and he rolls me off to trade places with me. He continues kissing me, rubbing my center through my shorts. Then he gets up. "I'm going to take a shower. Order us some room service."

"What? You're gonna work me up and then leave me here? That's dirty, Clay."

"Precisely. I love making you squirm. And don't even think about joining me in the shower, or you'll pay."

I sit on the bed, dumbfounded. I'm hungry for my husband, not room service. Clay has never done that before. I guess this adventure we're on has made him more adventurous in other ways too. But I have to admit, that was kind of hot. A jerk move, but a hot one. I want to know what he'll do to make me 'pay' if I try to get in the shower with him. Maybe that's exactly what he wants. Okay. So I don't. I order room service instead.

I hear the water shut off in the shower at the same time there's a knock on the door. Our food is here. Perfect timing. The guy wheels the cart in, I sign for it, and tip him. I bring it to the dining table and set it up for us.

As I'm waiting for Clay to come out of the bedroom, I strip down to my sheer, lacy bra and panties and sit at the table. I hear the bathroom door open. The zipper makes its way around our suitcase. He's looking for something to wear.

"Babe," I practically have to yell, this room is huge. "When you get dressed, I'm in the dining room with dinner," I say, as unassuming as possible.

"Okay, I'll be right there," he says. "You were a good girl while I was in the shower."

"Just obeying your orders, Mr. Sinclair."

He rounds the corner dressed in a t-shirt and boxers. As he nears the table and realizes I'm half naked, he immediately stops walking, his face stunned. "What are you doing? Where are your clothes?"

"Sit down."

"What the—"

"No talking."

He sits down and looks at me, waiting for further instructions. I don't say anything. I pick up my fork and signal for him to do the same. He does. His demeanor has shifted from domineering to subordinate in a matter of minutes. We eat in silence, staring at each other. He gives me a nervous smile. The muscles in his arms twitch. He's vulnerable. Serves him right. I'm loving it. I hold my smile back so he doesn't know how much I'm enjoying this role reversal. But I'm also getting more turned on. And so is he. I can see it in his eyes and his actions. His eyes dart up and down from my face to my boobs. He's fidgeting with his food. He licks his lips. Clay is uncomfortable below the table. I almost can't stand it anymore myself. Warmth spirals at my core. The tips of my breasts strain to break through the diaphanous fabric of my bra. But I wait. And I make him wait.

We finish eating and I get up. My steps towards him are lax. When I finally make it around the table to him, he tries to touch me. I hold up my index finger and wiggle it from side to side, telling him that's a no-no. His eyes get wide and he swallows hard.

"Babe, please," he whispers.

"Shh. I said no talking," I whisper back.

I take my bra off and he starts to reach out again. I tilt my head and raise my eyebrows. He retreats. I drop my panties and stand there for a bit, watching him resist while he's eyeing me up and down. He wets his lips again and swallows hard once more. His eyes are fully dilated, begging. I know he must be aching. A bit of guilt sneaks in to my psyche. But this is fun. Different. Stimulating.

After another minute or so, I finally take his hand. The contact after the tension sends sparks through my body. Clay stands at attention, in more ways than one. I lead him to the bed. "Stay put. But take off your shirt. And don't touch me." I sit on the bed and target his boxers. I pull them down, taking only a few seconds, but they probably seem like minutes to Clay. After I release what's been trapped beneath his boxers, I stop and take the tip of him in my mouth, circling my tongue a few times. He shudders and lets out a deep moan.

"Lynn," he whispers.

"Shh. Don't move." I get up and pull all the covers off the bed, stretching my body in the process. I flip my hair to one side, exposing my neck. I get in, and take my time to spread eagle. His jaw drops. He's ready to pounce. I wait another thirty seconds or so before I give him permission.

"Now," I demand.

"Holy fucking shit, that was extreme," Clay says, more breathless than I've ever seen him before, during, or after sex. "Babe, seriously. What came over you?"

"You did," I pant, laughing hysterically.

He loses it, laughing so hard he can barely get the word out. "Touché!"

Chapter 22

THE NEXT MORNING, we get up and eat breakfast. I look up the route to the Empire Building location and we head that direction.

"It's only about a mile from here," I tell Clay.

"So what kind of building is it exactly? An office building? Another bank?" he asks.

"I'm not sure. I figured we'd just see when we get there. We still haven't even figured out the clue. We don't know what we're even looking for."

"What's the key look like?"

I take out the key and examine it. It's a small key, but modern. I show it to Clay. "What do you think? Key to a desk?"

"Hmm, maybe. Read me the clue again."

"Okay. 'In the town where The Heaviest Corner on Earth has surely seen its share of hijinks, file into the Empire Building and look for hidden pinks.' Clear as mud."

"Maybe it will become clearer when we get inside," he reasons.

The streets are lined with cars and we see that we won't be able to park near the building, so we find a parking spot about two blocks down and Clay starts to get out.

"Wait," I tell him. He shuts the door.

"What is it?"

"I really think we should figure out the clue first, so we know what we're looking for. In case we have to scope things out or something."

"Okay, good idea. Alright, let's think. Let me see the paper." I give it to him. He reads it a couple of times and then gets his thinking face on. He closes his eyes and opens his mind. He's repeating the clue to himself, his lips barely moving. If he told me that he astral projected himself inside, I'd be inclined to believe him. He opens his eyes with a start. "I think I have something," he says.

"What? Do tell."

"Okay, if we take out the nothing words and focus on what's left, we have 'file', 'hidden', and 'pinks.' But, why would she say to 'file into the building'? She makes it sound like we'll be with a group, like walking into the building in a single file line. It's just us. She knew it would be just us."

"Okay, so what does that mean? What about the hidden pinks?"

"Well, I think we're looking for filing cabinet with some important papers," he smiles at me, proud of himself. He's always been better at puzzles than I have.

"Alrighty then. That makes sense. So, you're thinking the hidden pinks are like pink carbon copies of forms hidden away in a filing cabinet."

"Exactly."

"Oh, Aunt Mitzi, you are really testing us, aren't you?"

"Let's do this," he says.

We walk hand in hand up the street to the building. As we get closer, I notice that it's not an office building. Or a bank. It's a brand spanking newly renovated hotel. I start to panic.

"Oh no, Clay. This hotel just opened. There's no way our filing cabinet is there. What do we do?" I start to hyperventilate. "It's probably been thrown out. Junked. What the hell do we do?"

"Come on, love. Calm down. Breathe. Who's to say that filing cabinet isn't still there, huh? We haven't even walked inside. C'mon, let's go."

"We don't even know who or what to ask for. Sure, let's just waltz in there like we own the place. 'Um, yeah, I need to see all your filing cabinets please.' Right, that's going to go over well."

"And exactly what did you expect to do before we knew it was a renovated hotel?" he asks.

"I don't know. But at least if it was a hundred-year-old office building, instead of a brand new hotel, chances are our filing cabinet would still be here. I should have seen this coming."

"Babe, listen. This isn't going to be our only bump in the road, I guarantee it. We may run into this problem down the line too. Let's just go inside, take stock of our surroundings, and hang out in the lobby for a minute. You need to collect yourself."

"Don't tell me what I need! This is important, don't you see? This is Aunt Mitzi's legacy. She left it to us to find and it could all be ruined. How could they do this? I already don't like this place. This hotel is tainted."

He puts his hands on my shoulders and rubs up and down my arms. "Okay, I'm sorry. Let's just go see. And hey, better an open hotel than a locked up abandoned building, right? At least there's a possibility it's here." He brings me into his side with his arm around me and we walk up to the doors.

I stop before going in, just to take in the beauty of the building. The words 'Empire Building' are still above the entrance, though it's now the Elyton Hotel. But it will always be the Empire Building. Probably because it's on the National Register of Historic Places and maybe they can't ever remove its original name. I don't know if that's true or not, but it seems logical. At least I hope so…its initial name should remain with it forever.

This enormous structure is stunning. If there's one thing I learned minoring in art history, it was style. And this skyscraper is of the Classical Revival persuasion. Well, it was definitely a skyscraper for its time. The entry is flanked by a massive set of Doric columns made of pink granite. Breathtaking. There are carvings in between the windows and on the sides going all the way up to the cornice. I can't make them out, but I'm sure they mean something. I inhale and exhale deeply, and Clay opens the doors.

The inside is gorgeous. The lobby is decorated in soothing colors. The walls are painted in an ombre of blues from almost royal at the top to baby-blue at the bottom. The furniture is cream colored and there are black, white, and blue accents all around. Marble is abundant throughout: at the check-in counter, the walls, the floors, the railings…it's exquisite. And I bet it's all original to the building. Even the chandeliers look original. They don't erect structures like this anymore.

We sit down on one of the couches in the lobby, and I'm trying to get a glimpse behind the counter, looking for any sort of filing cabinet. Of course I won't be able to see one back there. That would just be too tacky to put behind such a lovely front desk. I don't want to like this place, but my God, it's downright dazzling. I wonder what the rooms look like.

My nerves are on edge. My hands are shaking and my mouth is dry. I don't know what to say to the clerk behind the counter. I defer to Clay. "Babe, please, can you go and ask them whatever it is you think we can lead with? I'm at a loss as to where to go from here."

"Of course I will. It's going to be okay."

"How do you know that? What if we can't find it and we miss a huge piece of the puzzle?"

"Then my bet is, Aunt Mitzi will have prepared us for it. Give me the key." I hand it to Clay. "Sit tight, love." And he takes charge.

I watch him walk up to the front desk. I don't know what he's saying. He looks back at me and the desk clerk follows Clay's pointed finger in my direction. The hotel employee leaves the counter and comes back with who I believe must be the manager. A fifty-something, slender, blonde-haired lady wearing black slacks with a blue silk blouse and a black blazer, instead of the uniformed blue blazer of the clerks behind the check-in desk. I'm guessing Clay is having to repeat himself as he does the whole thing again with pointing at me. Then I see the hotel manager smile and she lets out what can only be described as a joyful shriek. Clay waves me over with enthusiasm. Seriously? Have we hit pay dirt?

She introduces herself. "Kitty O'Brien," she says, with her hand outstretched.

"Hi. Lynn Sinclair," I reply, as I shake her hand.

"Come. Come. Follow me," she says, and we follow her through a series of rooms to a back office. I look at Clay with huge question marks in my eyes. He seems as clueless as I am. "Sit, please. Can I get either of you anything? Water? Soda? Mimosa?"

"Mimosa? Really?" I ask.

"Yes, really. We've been waiting for you. For years. So, mimosa?"

"Years? How many? I don't understand what's going on. And yes, I'm going to need that mimosa. Maybe two, if I should be so bold."

She looks at Clay. He asks for some water. She presses a button on her phone, "Eileen? Two mimosas and a water please."

"Coming right up," Eileen replies.

"Okay, Mrs. O'Brien, can you please tell us what's going on?" I press.

"First things first. Call me Kitty, please. Now...you're here for the filing cabinet, right? We've been dying to know what's inside."

"How is it you've been waiting years for us?" Clay asks. "Didn't this hotel just open?"

"Yes, but when the hotel group bought the building in 2015, it was of course abandoned, since 2009, and the place was a mess. The only thing, and I mean, the *only* thing that was intact and upright, besides the walls themselves, was your filing cabinet. Locked away in a storeroom all the way at the top of the building. There were specific instructions not to take it out of the building. Not to open it, trash it, sell it, nothing. It's in my office. Upstairs." She points up.

"Are you serious? How?" I look at Clay. "How in the world did Aunt Mitzi pull this one off?"

He shrugs his shoulders. "I don't know, Lynn. She was an amazing woman. Maybe she was magic too."

Eileen comes back with my mimosas and a tall glass of water for Clay.

"Thank you," I tell Eileen, and I gulp that first mimosa down. Kitty lifts a single eyebrow and gives me a nervous laugh, like she's afraid I might get tanked. "I'm sorry," I tell her, "I'm just really thirsty and very confused." I sip the next one.

"Wow, I think this is the best water I've ever had," Clay says.

"It's infused with blackberries, blueberries, watermelon, and cucumber," Kitty says. He holds his glass up and toasts in her direction.

"Okay, so wait. Let me understand, now. The filing cabinet was here when the hotel started to renovate?" I ask.

"That's correct," she says.

"So it was here before then." Clay replies.

"Right."

"Alright, so what was this building before it was the hotel?" I ask.

"Oh, it's been many things, housed many occupants over the last century, but the last tenant, when the building was forced to close its doors in 2009, was Colonial Bank."

Clay and I burst out laughing. "Of course it was. Oh, this just keeps getting better," I laugh to the point that my eyes water from the corners.

"I'm sorry, now I don't understand," Kitty says.

We explain everything to her, start to finish, and in the end, she's laughing with us. She calls Eileen to bring another round of mimosas and she takes us up the elevator to her office.

We go up a few floors and follow her out of the elevator and down the hall. Her office is smaller than I would imagine for a hotel manager, with a less than favorable view, but I imagine you have to save the good views for the guests. At least she has a window. She opens a closet in her office and gives us our space.

"I hope this isn't more sad news," Clay says as I unlock the cabinet.

I pull the top drawer out and find nothing. Second drawer, nothing. Third and fourth drawers, nothing and nothing. I want to cry. "How can there be nothing here? We were on a roll," I tell Clay. Once again, I'm crushed.

"Hey, it's not over. Just because there's nothing in the drawers doesn't mean there's nothing in the cabinet. If it was something heavy, or even made a sound, you can bet somebody would have broken that lock. But if somebody thinks all they're storing is an empty filing cabinet, then no harm, no foul. Right, babe?" he says to me. "No offense, Kitty," he tells her.

"Oh, none taken. You're absolutely right. I can't say that I would have broken the lock, but I wasn't sure there was anything in there to begin with. Sorry, sugar."

"Let me see," Clay says. "Kitty, can you get me a flashlight from your maintenance department?"

"Sure, let me call."

"Babe, I hope you're right. I'm getting my hopes up again. I hope it's not for nothing."

"And if there's nothing, truly nothing, we'll just move on. And it'll be okay."

A maintenance man comes in with a huge Maglite and hands it to Kitty, who in turn hands it to Clay.

"Now, let's see. Cross your fingers, babe." He pulls the drawers out and looks all down the sides of the cabinet. Nothing. He sticks his head in the best that he can and shines the light up to the top of the inside of the cabinet. He comes out smiling. Now I'm giddy again. He reaches in and I can hear something tearing off the top. And...it's another envelope.

"Oh please don't let this be anything depressing," I say as I cross my fingers.

Clay hands me the envelope. "No, you open it," I tell him.

He opens it up, pulls out a couple sheets of paper, looks them over, and meets my eyes. His reaction is completely indifferent.

Chapter 23

THEN HE GIVES me one of the biggest smiles I've ever seen on his face. "Babe. I'm glad you let me open this, because you wouldn't have any idea about what I'm looking at right now."

"What? What is it? By the look on your face, it's gotta be good."

"Oh, it's not good. It's incredible. For me anyway."

"What the freak is it, Clay?"

"It's the title to a 1957 Cadillac Eldorado Brougham. With my name on it. All I have to do is sign it and register it. And find it."

"So it's just an old car?" I ask.

"No, it's not just an old car. It's the motherlode of old cars. As far as I'm concerned anyway. There were only four hundred made. Ever. This baby was so far ahead of its time. The options and engineering on this bad mamma jamma were unheard of for a vehicle back then. She sported a roof made totally of brushed stainless steel. Quad headlamps. It was the first car to have air springs."

"I don't know what that means."

"Basically, you were riding on butter. And there were over forty some-odd choices of interior color and trim combos you could order. With mouton carpet."

"Mouton carpet?"

"Yeah, the softest, velvetiest, carpet. Specially processed from lambs.

They also used it in Rolls Royce and Bentley. And most limos. In fact, the Brougham actually cost considerably more than a Rolls at the time. Over thirteen thousand dollars. In the *fifties*. And I believe it was one of the first cars to have rear heat and air. It might have even been *the* first. Plus, it had power steering, brakes, seats, and windows."

"Wow. I've never heard of this car. And only four hundred exist?"

"No, only four hundred were manufactured. So you can guess how many still exist sixty years later. I could go on and on about this car. I never would have dreamed in a million years that I would get to own one. I'm floored. Pun intended."

"Har, har, har."

"Oh, and check this out...the kicker...it was loaded with a bunch of vanity items in the glovebox. Like a cigarette holder, notepad, Kleenex dispenser, some other odds and ends, I think it even came with some French perfume, and get this...magnetic shot glasses. I shit you not. You could line shots up on the fold-out tray of the glovebox. Totally badass."

"Get outta here. Shot glasses?"

"Hand to God."

"And, what, so this was Uncle Sid's car? They always drove Caddies when I was little, but I don't remember one with a stainless steel roof. But, this car was probably long gone by the time I was old enough to be able to remember it."

"Aunt Mitzi left a note with the title here. *'Dear Clay and Lynn, but mostly Clay—*"

"It does not say that."

"It does too. Look." He shows me the letter. He had read exactly what was written.

"Well, alright then. Proceed."

"As I was saying..."

> *'Dear Clay and Lynn, but mostly Clay,*
> *As the car enthusiast that I know you are, Uncle Sid wanted*
> *you to have this beauty of a car of ours. I have tracked it down and*
> *bought it back for you. It's not in great condition, per the previous*

owner, so it's yours to restore how you see fit. Please enjoy it. Once you find it. More later.
    Love, Aunt Mitzi.'"

"Okay, so all we have to do is find it and it's ours? Well, yours. That's so cool. I'm so glad this was a happy find. Oh, God, Clay, can you imagine if we hadn't found the filing cabinet?" I turn to Kitty who has been so patient during our excavation and discovery. "Kitty, thank you so much for keeping this safe for us."

"It was no problem. It's not like I had a choice, not that I minded anyway. My job could have been on the line if anything had happened to it. Especially before the renovations were done."

"Wha—what do you mean?" I ask her.

"Well, the architectural firm that designed our hotel is from New Orleans, and when we had our first meeting, the owner came to both my supervisor and me, about this filing cabinet. He was very adamant that it was to stay here, no exceptions. He even checked that it was still here the day we opened."

"You're kidding. Was it Santini Architect Firm by chance? Enzo Santini?" Clay asks.

"Yes. You're familiar with them?"

"You could say that," I say. "That's my Uncle Sid's brother's son."

"So that's how she did it," Clay says.

"And you said you're from Louisiana. Now it makes sense. Full circle," she says. "I'm so glad I was here to witness this, thank you for letting me be a part of it. Would you like to see the rest of the hotel? Have a drink at our rooftop bar or dinner in the restaurant? If you need a place to stay tonight, we'd love to have you. On the house."

"Oh, wow," I tell her, "That sounds marvelous, thanks so much for the offer, but we really have to get back on the road. Next stop is Tallahassee. The hotel is truly beautiful though, I wish we didn't have to leave."

"Yes, Kitty, thank you," Clay says.

"Well, next time then. Anytime really. Here's my card. I'll give you my personal cell." She writes a number on the back of the card and hands it to me. "Whenever you're in town, or just want another little getaway, please, call me and I'll have our best room ready for you. The two of you have been a pleasure. It's been a real treat meeting you and being involved, however small a part I may have played." I put her card in my purse.

"Small part? Please, Kitty. Without you, we may never have found it. So, thanks again, so much." I give her a hug. "You are now free to destroy the filing cabinet. Clay, put the drawers back in for her please."

"It'd be easier to destroy without the drawers."

"Clay!"

"Of course. Sorry," he says.

"Destroy? Are you kidding? I'm keeping this forever. This cabinet will go wherever I do. What a story I have to tell," she says, genuinely thrilled. She walks us back down to the lobby and she asks if we'd like anything from the restaurant to take with us.

"No, thanks, but I'd love some more of that water if it's not too much trouble," Clay says. "Babe? You?"

"Yes. That sounds great actually. Thanks, Kitty."

"No sweat. The next time we meet, we can say we go way back. I'd really love for y'all to spend some time here when you're back in the area."

"You got it," Clay tells her.

"Yes, Kitty, it's a deal. Thanks again, for everything."

Kitty gets us a carafe with the hotel's logo engraved on it. It's full of that delicious water, and she says we can keep the carafe as a memento of this stop on our quest. We walk back to the truck and Clay is beaming. I love seeing him so happy. He's on cloud nine.

"Well, babe," I say to him, putting my arm around his waist, "you have another project to work on when we finish this trip. Wherever and whenever we find this car, how are we going to get it back home? It doesn't sound like it's drivable. And I wouldn't want to be separated from you anyway, on the road. That's no fun."

"Oh, no, that won't happen even if it is drivable. I can call Stone and see if he can get it. It'll probably have to be towed, so he can bring his trailer."

"That sounds like a good idea. Are you sure he won't mind?"

"Not when I tell him what it is. And that I'll need his help restoring it. It'll probably be hard to keep him away from it."

"Good point. So, now we need to figure out the next clue." My stomach starts to growl. "I'm getting hungry, though. Maybe we should've taken Kitty up on her offer to eat at the hotel. Let's just get some drive-thru right now. We'll make better time if we eat on the road. Does that sound okay?"

"Sure, love. Whatever you want. I know you hated to throw out the last of your biscuit bites. They were pretty hard though, I don't know what Flo was thinking giving us so many to take with us. But they were good while they lasted. So, you want burgers?"

"Yeah, that's fine. Nearest one we come to is a-okay with me." We climb into the truck and head south on I-65 towards Tallahassee, Florida.

Chapter 24

"SERIOUSLY, CLAY, WHAT if we hadn't found the filing cabinet? Or if the papers had been stolen? What would we have done? We'd never know about the Caddie."

"Well, the papers in the cabinet are actually copies, so in Aunt Mitzi's letter, when she says, 'more later,' I'm figuring at some point along the way, we'll come across the originals."

"Oh, thank God. That was some good thinking on her part."

"Yes, it was."

"I know we could have stayed the night again in Birmingham and taken Kitty up on her offer, but I'm kind of anxious to find out what's waiting for us in Tallahassee."

"Yeah, I almost stopped you from declining, but I figured you had your mind on Florida."

"Aren't you curious?"

"Sure I am."

"We can always go back to Birmingham. And we will."

"Um, Lynn? I just thought about something. Kitty said the filing cabinet has been there since at least 2009. That means Aunt Mitzi has been planning this for us for at least eight years. Probably longer. Even Uncle Sid had to be involved with bringing the papers here, since he didn't die till just a few years ago."

"Holy shit, you're right. Oh my God. I can't believe that."

"Right? Crazy." Clay shrugs. "I guess it's good to have a hobby. Planting these items and making up these clues was probably a fun job for them."

"I'm sure it was. I can see them sitting at the dining room table trying to come up with the clues, what to hide where, who to get in contact with to help them keep the things for us…all of that."

"Yeah, me too. But I see them on the couch, where it's more comfortable."

"True. That's probably more like it."

I get my phone out and start surfing through my playlists to find a good one.

"You mean it's not my turn to be in control of the music yet?" Clay asks.

"Sorry, babe, this is only day four. We still have three days before my week of full control is up. I'll take any requests into consideration though. Try me."

"Anything by Ozzy, Tesla, The Ramones, AC/DC…something along those lines."

"Hmm, let me see what I have up my sleeves." I scroll through all my lists until I get to the one titled *Animal Instincts*. Oh yes. I have just the perfect song after last night. I hit the play button on "Closer" by Nine Inch Nails.

"Perfect," he says, as he looks at me with a sexy smile. I return one. "Babe, I gotta tell you…we've always been good together, but damn, last night…what you did to me…it was unbelievable. Epic. I've never felt so powerless and ignited. Defenseless and aroused. At the same time. Without even being touched, mind you. And I've never seen you so aggressive and domineering. You had me so weak in the knees, Lynn, literally. I thought I was going to lose it when you bent over to strip the bed down. Your silky-smooth ass, staring up at me like that…you don't know how bad I wanted to take you right then. The anticipation was brutal."

"Aww, I'm sorry, babe. You started it," I smirk. "I just thought it would be fun to reverse it. Guess I was right."

"Oh, God, please, no, don't be sorry. That was the hottest thing ever.

Scorching. Fierce. Primal. I don't know if we can top that. We're gonna have to put that in our playbook."

"Okay, sure," I say. But I'm not sure.

One of the most sensual songs ever written, "I Wanna Make You Close Your Eyes" by Dierks Bentley, starts playing. I start staring out the window. I must be giving off a pensive vibe because the next thing I know, Clay asks, "What's the matter?"

"Nothing."

"Wrong answer. I know when something's bothering you, Lynn. Your actions and the expression on your face betray you. Tell me what's on your mind, babe."

"I just feel like...maybe...if you think last night was so epic and can't be topped, you'll be disappointed from now on. Like you're always going to expect it to be that hot. And it won't be good enough for you now. I won't be good enough."

"What? Are you serious? Where is this coming from? Why are you feeling insecure all of a sudden?" He looks at me, forehead furrowed and mouth open in shock. But these feelings aren't new. I have my reasons. "Babe, come on. If anything, I think it made us better all the way around. Being with you...it's so right. There's nothing I love more. And no, I don't expect that every time. Last night was just so raw and unrestrained," he says. "You know, sometimes I like to take it slow and savor every inch of your body, head to toe. Like our first night in the house. Remember that?" he asks. Oh, I remember. Boy, do I remember. I look at him and nod. He reaches over the center console that's separating us, grabs my hand, and kisses it with his soft lips. "You and I make the best love, that's all I meant." He slows down and pulls off the interstate at exit 246 near Pelham.

"Where are we going?" I ask him.

"Lunch."

"Oh yeah." But my appetite is gone.

He pulls into a parking spot of the burger joint and kills the truck. Why are we stopping?

"Don't get out." He exits, walks around to my side, and opens my door. "Come here." I unbuckle my seatbelt and slide down. He wraps me in his arms and hugs me in a way that's reminiscent of the time he came home after his second deployment. "Look at me." I lift my head up. "Don't you ever doubt my love for you or my want and need to be with you. You are my world, babe, and nothing will ever change that. People say there are no absolutes, but I promise you, they do exist, and that's one of them. Got it?"

"Yeah." He kisses me, long and hard, right there in the middle of the parking lot, in front of God and everybody, not caring in the least bit.

I'm startled by somebody honking their horn. "Get a room for crying out loud!" yells a woman with a car full of children.

We laugh like we've just been caught making out in the schoolyard. "Sorry," Clay tells her. "Not really," he says to me, and kisses me once more. "Now, let's get back in the truck and hit the drive-thru."

And just like that, I feel hungry again.

Chapter 25

I GET THE CLUES out of my purse and we try to figure out the next one. All we know for sure is that we're going to Tallahassee, Florida.

"Okay, check out this keychain," I tell Clay. It's kind of small, about one inch square with a red classic car on it. The key itself is a regular car key, from before remote keyless entry became the norm, of course. "I know it's an old car but I'm not a hundred percent on what make and model it is. Maybe a fifty-seven Chevy?" I give it to him to look at.

He barely gives it a glance. That's a man who knows his classic cars. "That's exactly right, babe. Good job. You can tell by the chrome head-lights and the wide grille, not to mention those distinctive tailfins."

"Well, it looks just like one Uncle Sid used to have. Not that long ago, actually. They drove more than just Cadillacs over the years."

"Oh yeah, I remember that car. What ever happened to it?"

"I don't know. Sold it I guess," I answer.

"That's a shame. I woulda bought it. Oh, wait. Do you think we might be going to get that car now, too? Maybe that's what we're going to find. What does the clue say again?"

"It says 'In Florida's capital, there's one of these on display. Look in the back, and find what you may.' I don't know. Doesn't really sound like we're going to be leaving with another vehicle. It sounds like something else. You think she's talking about 'one of these' meaning the car? Like on a showroom floor or something?"

"Yeah, I bet you're right. We're probably looking for a car museum and we'll need to find the fifty-seven Chevy on display. And 'look in the back' probably means the trunk. I doubt there would be anything in the back seat, you know? Then everybody would see it. Unless maybe if it's hidden under the seat or something, but my first guess would be the trunk. So we're off to another caper. I'll slip you my tool again and let you do the dirty work."

I playfully punch him in the arm and search for car museums in Tallahassee as "Let's Get It On" by Marvin Gaye starts playing. "Tallahassee Automobile and Collectibles Museum. Should we head there? I don't see any other car museums listed in Tallahassee."

"Alright, yeah. Sounds like we have our destination then," Clay says.

"They close at five, so once again, we'll have to check it out in the morning," I tell him.

"You know, that's actually better, I think. Because we'll be awake and can start fresh. If we try to do too much in one day, we'd probably be exhausted," he replies.

"True. Okay, I'll find us a room."

We drive a few more miles and a hitchhiker comes into view on the side of the highway. I ignore the guy. But not Clay. "Hey, you think we should pick him up and see where he's going? He can ride in the back." Again, I can't tell if he's serious or joking.

"Uh, no sir. That's how horror movies start."

"And pornos," he says laughing.

"I wouldn't know," I say, laughing with him. Frankly, it's the most exciting thing we've seen in a while. We pass him up and his sign says, 'Tallahassee.' "Well. That's interesting. Are we in the Twilight Zone? What are the odds?" I ask rhetorically.

"Yeah, really. Weird." Clay literally shakes it off as a strange coincidence. "Okay, remind me not to acknowledge the next hitchhiker we come across."

"Um, yeah. What, you have some sixth sense or something? That was just too creepy."

"Well, hey, now we have another cool anecdote to add to our stories we can tell. You are keeping track of everything, right?"

"You mean like a travel log? I hadn't really thought about it. That would be cool. I mean, I did bring a notebook just to have if we need it and I've jotted notes on our clue sheet as to what we've found, but that's it. So far I can pretty much remember everything. Plus I have all the pictures I've taken."

"That's true. You should start a blog. Shit, can you imagine if cell phones hadn't been invented yet? We'd have to rely on stopping at gas stations for directions, pray for hotel vacancy signs, and wait to get all our pictures developed. Now, thanks to the tech nerds, we don't have to worry about that."

"Advancement in technology has its pros and cons. But in this instance, I think it's great. I'm not staying in any seedy roadside motels. And did you just say you would stop and ask for directions? As if. Who are you trying to fool, Sinclair?"

"I meant society in general," Clay says with a smile.

"No, you meant you would make me get out and ask for directions. That is, if you would even admit you were lost."

"I don't get lost."

"Sure, okay. That's why it took us six hours to get to Nikki's college graduation when it should have only taken four. Thank God we went a day early or we would have missed it."

"One wrong turn. You're never going to let me live that down, are you? Shit, you'd think the statute of limitations would be up by now." He rolls his eyes and huffs.

"I'm just giving you a hard time, babe."

"Well it pisses me off! You have no idea." He turns the radio off.

"Jesus, Clay. Calm down. God. What is wrong with you?"

"Nothing. Forget it. I'm over it. Just. Nothing."

"Whatever."

I let Clay cool down. I guess I really hit a nerve. I turn my attention to my phone and decide to text Cecilia to check on things at the house. **Hey sis. How are things going?**

She replies. **Fred and I are holding down the fort. He loves exploring the backyard. Y'all having fun?**

Awesome. Give him some belly rubs from Aunt Lynn. Yes, we're having a great time. Hey I ordered a Christmas ornament. Should be there this week. BOLO.

You got it. Y'all be safe. Love you.

Always. Love you too.

Then I text Annie to get the latest scoop on her and Stone. Hey girl. How are things with Stone?

I get an answer about a minute later. So far so good. We're having dinner tonight. How's the road?

I love hearing that. I think the stars have aligned for y'all. The trip's been great. We're on our way to Tallahassee.

Ha. Maybe. What's in Tallahassee?

Auto museum.

Sounds fun!

We'll see. No idea what we'll find.

Good luck! xoxo

Thanks! xoxo

We've been driving for about three and a half hours now, in silence for the last hour though. We're nearly halfway to Tallahassee and are entering the college town of Troy.

"Home of the Trojans," Clay says. "The other Trojans."

Okay, good. I guess he really is over it. I never know with him sometimes.

"You're such a goofball. You sound like a teenage boy."

"I'm far from being a teenage boy."

"That you are. In more ways than one," I say in a seductive voice, and wink at him. He smiles a pleased-with-himself smile and I swear he almost looks like he's turning red. "Are you blushing, Mr. Sinclair?"

"Are you trying to make me, Mrs. Sinclair?"

"Hmm…maybe…"

"Maybe? Maybe? Okay. Alright. Keep going. We've got nothin' but time."

"Remember last night?"

"Uh, yeah, we've already had this conversation. I'll never forget last night."

"Maybe there's more."

"More? More what?"

"That's all I'm saying," I tell him.

"Are you insane? I'm driving. And we still have two hours to go. You're not making me blush, you're giving me blue balls."

"Oh, God, I'm sorry," I say laughing.

"It's not funny, Lynn."

"Okay, I'm sorry, try to forget it." Still laughing.

"Forgetting what you looked like last night all sprawled out on the bed is not happening."

"Okay. Think of something totally unsexy, like…constipation. Paperwork. Earwax. Worms. Cleaning a barbeque pit that a dinosaur sat on."

"What? Where did that come from?" he laughs.

"I don't know, just trying to think of something to relieve you."

"Well, that helped. I literally pictured a dinosaur sitting on a nasty-ass barbeque pit. Nicely done, babe. Hold up…barbequed dinosaur… MMMmmm…" He shakes his head at me and laughs. "Whaddaya think that would taste like?"

"Chicken. Of course."

I turn the radio back up, and not wanting to make Clay's balls any bluer, I look for any other playlist besides my sexy-time one. He sees me scanning my lists.

"Play something to keep my mind off of wanting to ravish you."

"That's what I'm looking for, goofball. How 'bout disco?"

"Perfect."

"Okay." I press play and "Get Down Tonight" by KC and the Sunshine Band starts.

"Lynn, what the fuck?"

"What? It's disco!"

"Change it."

"What's wrong with this one?"

"The lyrics. Change it or we're pulling over."

"Shit, I'm sorry," I say as I think about the lyrics and start laughing. "Alright. Scrolling down. Got it." Surely this one will be okay. "Don't Worry Be Happy" by Bobby McFerrin plays. Clay actually loves this song. I do too. It's such a fun little jam.

"Yes. Much better." He starts whistling along with the song. I love watching Clay dance behind the wheel. He's so animated.

We drive another hour and I realize I need to go to the bathroom. "I have to pee. Good as it was, all that fruit-infused water is finally catching up with me. Plus, I really need to stretch my legs," I tell Clay.

"Ooooh...there's an image." He closes his eyes like he's picturing me and smiles.

"Clay! Keep your eyes on the road! Jeez..." I guess his blue balls are long gone.

"Sorry," he says with a laugh. "Okay. We're almost to Dothan, we'll stop there. I need to go too, now that you mention it."

"Hey, there's a Barnes and Noble ahead. That's good, go there. Their restrooms are clean. And we can get a little snacky-snack from their Starbucks."

He eases off the highway and drives into the Barnes and Noble parking lot. We both head to the restroom. "Whoever finishes first," I tell him, "go get in line and get us something to munch on for the road. If it's you, get me a banana nut muffin. If it's me, what do you want?" I ask him.

"Get me one of those big-ass chocolate-chip cookies. Let's just meet up there by the coffee area," he tells me.

"Ohh, that actually sounds really good. Get me one of those too. See you shortly." I go in the bathroom, knowing Clay will finish first. He always does. He's a guy. But when I get to the Starbucks, I don't see him anywhere, so I go ahead and get in line. Good thing, too, because the line is long. I wait about ten minutes before I order and still no sign of Clay. I hope he's feeling alright. I ask for two of the gargantuan chocolate-chip cookies and two banana nut muffins. The barista rings me up and hands me our items. I turn around and Clay is finally there. "You okay? I was about to start getting worried."

"Yeah, fine. Sorry, I took longer than I expected to."

We get back in the truck and there's a present on my seat. "What's this?"

"I got you a surprise," he says to me.

"Aww...is that what took you so long?"

He smiles. "I wasn't in the bathroom the whole time."

I open the package and it's a travel journal. "Oh, Clay, I love it. Thank you." I lean over and give him a big kiss. "It's perfect," I tell him. And it is. It has a brown hardcover and it's got one of those elastic bookmarks that you can stretch over the pages to save your place. It's embossed with all the best travel words and phrases on the cover: adventure beckons, wanderlust, discover, experience, enjoy the ride, and more. But my favorite one is: cherish every moment. Because I do. Even our little spats. "You're so sneaky," I tell him. "I can't believe you even had time to wrap it."

"I was trying to hurry. I didn't want you to catch me. I saw you in line when I was checking out and came and wrapped it in the parking lot. You didn't even see me come back in. I'm skillful and covert like that. He makes a static noise with his mouth and then speaks into his shoulder, "Operation Surprise Lynn was a success. You may now fall back," followed by another static sound. I giggle.

"I'm sorry about earlier, Clay. I didn't realize the whole 'getting lost' thing was such a sore spot."

"Forget about it. It's just me." He starts the truck and we continue to Tallahassee.

Chapter 26

THE NEXT MORNING, we wake up, hit the hotel gym, shower, eat breakfast, and are on our way to the Tallahassee Automobile and Collectibles Museum. "Do you think this is where Uncle Sid's Caddie is?" I ask Clay.

"No, I doubt it, because Aunt Mitzi said she bought it back and it needed restoring."

"Oh, that's right. Yeah, I doubt it's in a car museum then."

It doesn't us take long to get there and we are some of the first people in the door. We pay the admission fee and start looking around. There are classic cars everywhere. Clay is in heaven. It's more than just cars and trucks though. There are also motorcycles, bicycles, and boats. Then there are sections with collections of pianos, knives, guns, vintage toys, cash registers, dolls, and more. They even have Abraham Lincoln's hearse. There's so much to see.

We scope out the place looking for the '57 Chevy. Clay is lagging behind, admiring everything. Naturally, and rightfully so, all of the cars are behind ropes with DO NOT TOUCH signs posted. How are we going to do this without getting caught?

"Baaaabe," he says to me, like a whiny little kid. Uh oh, I know that tone.

"What, Clay?" I ask in a whisper. "Catch up. What do you want? We have to get in and out of here as slick as possible without anybody seeing or hearing us open and close the trunk."

He's now at my side, whispering back. "That's what I want to talk to you about. Look at this place. It's incredible. You know I could spend all day here. I don't want to be in and out. Let's find the manager and just ask him if we can open the trunk. Then we can check everything out till our hearts are content."

"You mean your heart," I say out loud to him, putting my index finger to his chest. But he's right. This place is pretty spectacular. I wouldn't mind looking at everything myself. We should have just asked for the manager in the first place. Duh. "Alright." I smile at him. "Let's go see if we can find the person in charge."

"I love you."

"I know."

We ask for the manager and an older gentleman comes back and introduces himself as the owner, Mr. Moe Castinella. "What can I do for you?"

I look at Clay. I figure he can sweet-talk our way through this, with all of his expertise and admiration for the vast collection Mr. Moe has here.

"Mr. Castinella, my name is Clay Sinclair. This is my wife, Lynn. I just want to say that you have yourself an impeccable assemblage of vehicles here, sir. I'm looking extremely forward to checking everything out. I'm an enthusiast as well. Restoring my old sixty-seven Charger back home, and I'm on my way to retrieving a fifty-seven Brougham. But, we're rather interested in the fifty-seven Chevy you have."

"Ah, well, thank you, Clay. This place is my pride and joy. Love when my customers can appreciate what I've got. And just what do you mean by 'interested'? It's not for sale. And which one exactly? I've got more than one," Moe says.

"Of course you do. Um, the red one? See, thing is, we have a key for it that was passed down to us. There's something in the trunk that was meant for us. We don't want the car, we just want to be able to open the trunk and see what's in it."

"You kids related to Sid and Mitzi Santini?"

"Yes," I say. "Mitzi was my great-aunt."

"I see. Okay, follow me," he says. We accompany him as he leads us through the one hundred thousand square foot time capsule.

"So, how did you know my Aunt Mitzi and Uncle Sid?" I ask Moe.

"I didn't. One day, about five years ago, the red fifty-seven Chevy just showed up as a donation from Sid and Mitzi Santini. Said I could have it under one condition."

"Let me guess," Clay said. "Don't open the trunk."

"Bingo. So, I never did. I'm a man of my word. I was awfully worried they were hiding a bag of bones or something in there. Almost said, 'No,' but a fifty-seven Chevy? My all-time favorite car. Had to have another one. Please, by all means, let me allow you to pop the trunk. I've been dying to know what's in there," he says, right as we arrive to its spot on the showroom floor. He lets us go under the yellow rope between the stanchions.

"Babe? You have the honors," Clay says to me.

I put the key in and unlock the trunk. As I lift it, I pray there are no more envelopes, at least for now. Well, that's weird. It's Aunt Mitzi's Bible.

Chapter 27

"WHAT? HOW? WHY? I don't understand. Mr. Castinella, you say this car arrived about five years ago?" I ask him.

"That's correct. Haven't opened the trunk. Scout's honor." He holds up the three fingers in the Boy Scout salute.

"I could have sworn I saw her Bible, this Bible, within the last five years at the house," I say to Clay. I pick it up and thumb through it. It's definitely hers. There are notes in her handwriting and highlights on her favorite passages. Verses she used to read to me all the time as a child, to teach me life lessons. Verses that she would read to me when I was having fights with my friends, when I felt all alone. Verses she read to me when my boyfriend broke up with me in high school, and I thought the world was ending. Verses for when I thought my parents had lost their minds, to show me that they only wanted what was best for me. Verses for when I had my first big fight with Clay, and I thought our marriage was over. These highlighted passages were my therapy sessions. My healing stages. The phases where I grew as a girl, a woman, a wife. I'm flabbergasted. Something that I'm getting used to these last few days.

"Maybe the one she had recently was a new one."

"Maybe you're right," I tell Clay. "Mr. Castinella, may we sit in the car?"

His thumb and forefinger skate along his jawline in a point towards his chin. He stammers a bit, but not wanting to refuse the great-niece of his benefactors, he obliges. "Sure, be my guest," he says.

We get in and I take a whiff. Waxed vinyl, fresh paint, polished chrome...it still smells the same. I know this car was in mint condition when it was donated to this museum. Clay and I take a picture of ourselves to remember this stop. I haven't come across any other ornaments of our locations, so I'm probably going to have to make most of them myself with pictures. I get a little nostalgic for Aunt Mitzi and Uncle Sid and days gone by. I just want to sit here a minute. I take a few more snapshots of the dash, the back seat, the steering wheel, and a couple more of us together. Then we get out and I take a couple of the car itself, from all sides.

Clay extends his hand to Moe. "Thank you so much, Mr. Castinella. We really appreciate it."

"Not a problem. So, just a Bible eh? No buried treasure?"

"This is not just a Bible. This is a lifetime of memories and counseling and prayers being answered. And unanswered," I tell him. "Thanks for letting us have this time with the car. I know we'll enjoy looking at the rest of your collection, Mr. Castinella."

"Nothin' to it. A Bible's certainly a better find than a body. Glad I could be part of your story." I smile at his joke.

"Clay, I'm gonna go put this in the truck." I point to the Bible. "I'll be right back."

"Okay. I won't be far from here."

I go outside and put the Bible in the truck. As I'm walking back up to the museum, I notice a scraggly man heading straight in my direction, glaring right at me. Oh, shit. It's the hitchhiker.

Chapter 28

OH GOD, HE looks mad. I avert my eyes and alter my path. He mirrors my course. He is getting closer and I'm really starting to freak out. The blood has rushed out of my face. My breathing increases. Do I run? Do I scream? There's nobody else in the parking lot. I know Clay won't hear me; he's completely preoccupied inside. I take my phone out and call him. I grasp the keys in my hand and spread them between my fingers, sticking out in case I need to punch the homeless-looking man. Clay's phone rings and rings, then goes to his voice mail, which is full, so I can't even leave a message. Great. I hit redial, put my phone on speaker, and slip it back into my purse. Again, no answer.

The man is about five feet from me now with squinted eyes and pursed lips. Breathing through his nose in short huffs, he sounds like a bull getting ready to charge.

"Get back!" I yell at him.

"No. I have to ask you something. Why were you laughing at me?"

"What?"

"I saw you laughing! I saw you pass me up. I'd recognize this truck anywhere." He points to Clay's truck. I don't know what's so identifiable about it. It's just a black four-door Dodge Ram pickup. The tires aren't especially huge or anything. How did this guy know this was our truck? And what are the chances that he'd end up here? How did he see us laughing? We were going about seventy miles per hour when we passed him. Twilight Zone revisited.

He takes some steps forward and I take them backward. "Stay back!" I continue to yell. I have my grip on my keys at the ready. He keeps his distance, but he's still a little too close for comfort. "We weren't laughing at you. We were laughing at ourselves. How did you see us? And how did you know this was our vehicle? How did you follow us?" He continues to move towards me and I keep stepping back. I'm almost at the truck again.

"CLYNN," he says.

The license plate. Okay, well that explains it. We officially need to change that as soon as possible. Done with the cute name-combo vanity plates. No more CLYNN 2 for me, either.

"What do you want?" I ask him. He seems harmless enough, just dirty. But I'm not letting my guard down. "I don't have any money."

"Bullshit. Anybody drives a truck like this has money. I need some money." He grabs me and pushes me into the side door of the truck and tries to snatch my purse, but luckily I have it slung diagonally over my torso, cross-body style.

My phone buzzes in my purse. The hitchhiker hears it too, and as I reach to answer it, he brings my arms up and slams them above my head, pinning them against the truck. He holds my wrists together with one hand and the frame of the window digs into the back of my hands, hurting them. I yell out in pain. He towers above me and snatches the keys out of my grasp. He drops them and they land on the pavement with a jangle.

He demands money, as he continues trying to take my purse with his free hand. I try to kick him but he's too close for me to get my leg or my knee up. He reeks of body odor and liquor.

"Leave me alone!" I yell at him.

"Hey! Get away from her, motherfucker!" It's Clay. Thank God. He's running towards me and the guy starts fleeing, but not before Clay catches him and proceeds to beat the crap out of him. I have to make him stop after he gives the derelict a bloody nose and a few punches to the gut. The guy is rolling around on the ground moaning and clutching his stomach. Clay runs up to me, out of breath. "Are you okay, babe? Oh my God, I'm so sorry. I'm so sorry." He hugs me close. "When I realized you weren't back yet and then saw I had two missed calls, I knew something was wrong." He looks me over to make sure I'm alright. "Did that fucker hurt you?"

"My hands, but that's it really. I'm okay." Clay takes my hands and examines them. They're a little red, but no broken bones. "He was asking for money, then he tried to grab my purse. Clay. It's the hitchhiker."

"The hitch—...from the highway yesterday? How the...what the...?"

"He recognized our truck. The plate."

By this time, people had witnessed what happened. Moe comes running out, a lady at his side, to see what's going on.

"She's okay!" Clay shouts to Moe.

"Dammit, Dillon! What the hell are you doing here? I fired your ass months ago, for good. If you don't leave right now, I'm calling the cops. And if I catch you on our property one more time, I'll follow through with that restraining order. Get the hell outta here." Moe tells the man on the ground.

"I wasn't trying to hurt her," the hitchhiker says from the concrete. "I promise. I just need some money."

"Shut up, you lazy bum." Moe says. He turns his attention to us. "You kids alright?"

"Physically, yes. She's a little shaken up, but otherwise alright."

"You want to press charges?" Moe asks me. Do I? I can't think straight yet.

Clay intervenes. "You know that guy?" he asks Moe.

"He's our son," the lady says.

Whoa. Their *son*?

"Yeah, some son he turned out to be," Moe says.

"Moe, did you have to so harsh?" the lady asks.

"He's a good-for-nothing, piece of shit, Eden." He turns to Clay and me. "We weren't even sure if he was still alive. Look at him. Forty-five years old. Wasted his damn life on drugs and booze and gamblin'. Threw away his family. Stole from us." He pauses and points his thumb back at the lady standing next to him. "I'm sorry, this is my wife, Eden." We nod at each other.

Eden is an attractive lady, about Moe's age, with blonde hair pulled into a bun and jewelry from head to toe. "We tried to help him a hundred times over," she says. "It never worked. There's only so much you can do. He has to want to be helped, you know? So...sadly, we washed our hands of him. Thank God our daughter-in-law and grand-kids don't hold us responsible. We still get to see them."

"I'm very sorry he attacked you, hon," Moe says to me. "I can't apologize enough. So do you wanna press charges, darlin'?" He asks me again. "He could use a few good nights in jail. Might finally straighten his ass up."

"Oh, my goodness. Uh, no. I'm okay," I tell Moe. I take a few deep breaths and calm down. I think I'm good.

"Well, alright," he says. "I'm gonna go keep an eye on him. Make sure he can walk his ass out of here. You've got a great right hook there, Clay. Nice job laying him out like that. He needed a good ass-whippin'." He and Eden walk over to where their son is still lying on the ground. I can hear Moe yelling at him and Eden yelling at Moe. I guess no matter what kind of trouble your kids get into, they're still your kids, and you still want to protect them.

Clay looks in the direction of the hitcher on the concrete and shakes his head in disbelief, then turns his attention back to me. He takes my hands and kisses the back of them where they are red. "Come on, love, let's get in the truck and go."

"No, I know you haven't seen everything inside that you wanted. I feel like we just got here. I'm fine, really. We can finish the museum."

"No, not now. I can't. I just wanna get out of here. I should have never let you out of my sight. God, if anything had happened to you, I would never have forgiven myself." He hugs me again. "I'm sorry." His voice starts to crack. "I'm sorry, babe." He sniffles into my hair.

"Hey," I look up at him and his eyes are red and glassy. "Clay. I'm alright. You saved me."

"Yeah, but...what if..."

"Stop. No 'what ifs.' Let's just go ahead and get in the truck. Are you okay to drive?"

"Yeah." He sniffles again and in one nonchalant move, he flicks the water from the corners of his eyes with his thumb and middle finger. "Where do we go from here?" he asks.

"North I assume. Georgia probably. That's my best guess, since it's the only border near our location that we haven't been to, besides the Atlantic Ocean. C'mon. We'll figure it out together."

He hugs me again and kisses me. It's delicate, gentle, and tender, like he's afraid of breaking me. "I'm not much in the mood for driving for hours. Can we just stop somewhere over the state line and pick this up tomorrow? Are you sure you're okay, babe?"

"Yes and yes. Okay, let's go," I tell him.

Clay waves his arms to get Moe's attention and he walks back over to us while Eden stays with their son.

"We're heading out," Clay tells Moe. "Sorry we can't stay, but you understand."

"Yes. And again, I apologize for Dillon's behavior. Please let me refund your money. It's the least I can do," he says to us.

"No, that's okay, it's not necessary. Thank you, though," Clay says. "We'll be back. I promise you that. But it'll be a while."

"Well, next time's on me. I mean that." He shakes Clay's hand then turns towards his wife's direction and shouts, "Eden, honey, they're leaving." She starts walking over and their son starts to follow. "Dillon, you stay put!" he yells.

Eden, visibly shaken, says to me, "I'm so sorry, hon. Dillon was brought up better than that. He's never raised a hand to anyone. That I know of, anyway. Please, accept our apologies. Is there anything we can do?"

"No, thank you. I'm really okay. He didn't hit me. Maybe this is rock bottom for him. Maybe now, he'll want to be helped."

"I hope you're right, dear," Eden says to me. "You seem like such sweet people. Please, if it's not too much to ask, would you mind saying a prayer for him?"

"Of course," I tell her. I can't say the same for Clay though.

"Thank you." She hugs me. Her hair smells like peaches and honeysuckle. It reminds me of Aunt Mitzi. I close my eyes and let Eden's hug last a bit longer than necessary.

"Lynn. We need to go," Clay says. His tone is curt. He means now.

"Yeah. Okay."

We say good-bye to Moe and Eden. They wish us well and good luck in our travels. They again apologize for their son's actions.

As I'm getting in the truck, the hitchhiker, who is now standing up, cries out, "I'm sorry! I'm sorry!" Then he looks up to the sky and I can barely hear him say, "God, forgive me. I'm sorry." He buckles back to the ground on his knees, and weeps. Eden rushes over to him and consoles her son. Maybe this really is rock bottom for Dillon. I do hope he gets some help.

I shut the door and pull the list of clues out. "Okay, listen, we'll just figure out where we need to go first and we can solve the rest later, alright?" I start reading the clue. "So…'In a town the same name as where the Parthenon lies—"

"Athens." Clay cuts me off. "Athens, Georgia. Alright. Find the closest town with good hotels on the way there." He starts the truck and heads towards Highway 90.

"You want me to finish the clue at least?"

"I can't think about that right now. Let's just put it on hold for a minute, please. I just want to get somewhere and rest with you. How can you be so fucking calm, Lynn? That asshole could have really hurt you. I could've lost you. I can't believe I was so selfish. God. I just…I don't know what I would have done. I would have killed that son of a bitch. That's what. If I hadn't gotten there when I did…I can't believe I didn't hear my phone ring. Shit!" He slams his hands down on the steering wheel.

"Clay, please don't do this. It wasn't your fault. You couldn't have known. Don't beat yourself up. I'm okay. Stop blaming yourself, babe." I reach up and touch his face. "I'm right here. I'm safe." He grabs my hand and kisses it. Doesn't let it go. I resume looking up hotels, with one hand, in the nearest city over the Florida-Georgia line. "Can you do about forty minutes? There's a town called Thomasville. Doesn't look like they have any luxurious hotels with presidential suites, but there's a Best Western. Those are nice. And they have studio suites."

"Yeah. Sure. I can do forty minutes. Be there in twenty-five." He floors it.

Chapter 29

WE ARRIVE AT the hotel in twenty-seven minutes. We check in and head up to our room. It's a little after lunchtime and we are both starving. We decide to order pizza.

After we eat, Clay takes his shoes off and lies down on the bed. "Come here," he tells me. "I need you. I want to just hold you close to me." I take off my sandals and lie down next to him. I scoot into him with my back to his chest. He envelops me with his arms and legs, pulls me even closer, and buries his head in the crook of my shoulder and neck. He inhales. "God, you smell so good," he whispers. "Babe, I'm sorry I—"

"Shh." I cut him off. "I know. We don't need to go there again. Stop doing this."

We stay there, unmoved, for a while. Just when I think he's about to drift off to sleep, he unties the string at the top of my shirt and loosens the laces. He kisses my neck, near where his head has been this whole time. He breathes into my ear, "I love you, Lynn. God, I love you. I'm never letting go of you." He peppers my ear with little bitty kisses, up and down the outer edge, his favorite place to get me revved up. He playfully bites my earlobe and moves his hand between my legs. He pulls me closer still, as he rubs me there, and I feel him, hard at my backside. He unbuttons and unzips my shorts and reaches inside. Oh. Yes. I turn on my back and he sits up to wriggle me out of my bottoms. He lifts up my shirt and I take it off along with my bra. I'm completely naked and he's totally dressed. Touching. Kissing. Squeezing. I reach for him to undo his shorts. "Don't. Not yet," he whispers. "I just want to concentrate on you. I want to relish in your every curve. Cherish each of your corners." He rubs his hands along my sides as he kisses me up and down my stomach. His hands are roving, mapping their way over the topography of my entire terrain. He moves to my middle, parts my legs, and caresses me with his mouth. He does what he does best. I quiver as I'm overwhelmed with tingling. My body relaxes, my arms and legs transforming into warm rubber bands as the tension from earlier dissipates. I let go. Responding involuntarily. Answering my husband the way he wants me to. Needs me to. My back arches and I grab the sheet beneath me with my fists as a wave of euphoria washes over me, and I breathe his name.

Chapter 30

T HE NEXT MORNING, we get up and head to Athens. It's
roughly a four and a half hour drive.

"Okay, love, I'm listening. What does it say?" Clay asks about
the clue before I even mention it this morning.

"Well, let me see." I dig the keychain out of the box first and examine
it and its key. The keychain is a running dog. It's heavy, possibly made of
solid silver. I show it to Clay. "Greyhound?" I ask him.

"Looks that way," he says.

The key itself is small and stubby with a cylindrical, red plastic head.
"The key looks like it might be for an old locker. There are three numbers
on it: one, five, and three." I get the list out of my purse. "It says, 'In a
town the same name as where the Parthenon lies, you'll find a bus station
locker to which this key applies.' Ha, I was right. I guess we're looking for
locker number one-fifty-three. Okay, now...searching for a Greyhound
Bus Station in Athens, Georgia. Well, looks like there's one on Atlanta
Highway. When we get closer to Athens, we can stop somewhere and put
the address in the GPS," I tell Clay.

"Sounds good, babe. Now, hit me with some music."

"Alright." I scroll through and find my *Chow and Beverage* list and
press random. "Cake by the Ocean" by DNCE starts playing.

"Not bad," Clay says. "I like this song."

"We're on day six now. Another day and a half and you can have some power over the radio," I tell him.

"Some?"

"Well, don't you think it's fair that we switch up? We'll alternate days. So, day after tomorrow you can have it, next day it's me, then you, and so on."

"Alright. That's reasonable," he says.

"Hey, you have to admit, I've been doing very well at deejaying, right?" I ask.

"I suppose so. Nothing has made me cringe. So far, anyway."

"Psh. Whatever. It's not like I'm a huge fan of all your stuff. I can tolerate most of it, but some, not so much."

"Okay, I get it. You don't like heavy metal and hard rock."

"Only some. I can't stand guitar solos. That grates my nerves so freaking bad, I don't know how you stand it."

"Can we just move on?"

"Uh, okay. Touchy-touchy. Jeez. So what do you want to talk about? Obviously not music."

"Obviously. Let's take stock of everything we've picked up and learned so far," Clay says. "A postcard with the Field Building in Chicago saying that whatever Aunt Mitzi was doing there, she wasn't in trouble. And she was seventeen. Then we learned that she and Uncle Sid tried to adopt two babies, which were both disrupted. Third, I got myself a fifty-seven Brougham to restore. I think that's just a bonus. How am I doing so far?"

"So far that sounds right. And then last, we got Aunt Mitzi's Bible. Now, we're heading to a bus station locker. What do you think is in there?" I ask.

"Let's hope it's a waterfront beach house," he says.

"Ooh, I would love that. But, I kinda doubt it. It wouldn't fit in the truck." He smiles. "And as far as I know, Aunt Mitzi and Uncle Sid weren't beachgoers. They liked the mountains."

"Hmm…maybe a mountain cabin then. That wouldn't be bad either. Besides, we're learning a lot about them, so who knows?"

"You're right. A beach house, or a mountain cabin, could be in our future." I laugh.

"Yeah, we can drive there in my restored Brougham. Hey, any one of those could still be in our future, even if we don't get it from Aunt Mitzi and Uncle Sid's treasure hunt. What do you think?"

"I love the sound of that," I tell Clay.

"Alright, when we're done with this quest, we'll look into it," he says.

"Man, it's gonna be hard to decide which one…beach or mountains."

"If we can find a good deal, we'll just get both. Maybe not at the same time, but eventually."

"Sounds like a plan," I tell him. "Strawberry Wine" by Deana Carter plays from my song list and it reminds me of Gatlinburg, Tennessee. "Hey, speaking of mountains, whenever we get to Tennessee, let's try and go through Gatlinburg, if it's not too far out of the way from wherever it is Aunt Mitzi leads us. Remember that winery there? They have the best strawberry wine. I'd like to pick up a few bottles. Maybe even a case."

"Sure thing, love. We can swing by that jelly place, too, and get some of that banana-pineapple jelly."

"Oh, yeah. That's good stuff."

I open my journal and start jotting down notes about what Clay and I just talked about. At some point, when we come across a drug store or some other place where I can instantly print pictures from my phone, I'm going to do that and put them in the journal with my comments and explanations of our findings.

My stomach rumbles. I look at the clock and realize it's closer to lunch time than I thought, though my belly-thunder was my first clue. "Hey, babe. You hungry yet?"

"Yeah, I could eat. We're almost to Macon. Let's grab something there."

We get off I-75 and head down Forsyth Street. We much prefer exploring rather than relying on the internet for places to eat. Sometimes, the best places are just stumbled upon. "I see a Subway. I love Subway, but I'm not really in the mood for a sandwich. Dunkin' Donuts, Which Wich, which I'm assuming is another sandwich place. Nope and nope. I want to sit down somewhere," I say.

"Yeah, me too. Need to stretch my legs a while."

"Oh, slow down a little. Looks like there's a restaurant up ahead." We get closer. "H and H Restaurant. Looks like a little hole-in-the-wall. Those are usually the best places," I tell Clay.

"Oh, I've heard of this place. The Allman Brothers made this restaurant famous. I forgot this was here. H and H is iconic to AB fans. To the whole world, really. It's soul food. And you're right, I bet it's some of the best we'll ever have." He pulls into the parking lot on the side of the building.

"How did The Allman Brothers make it famous?" I ask as we walk to the entrance.

"Well, from what I understand, they were just starting out and pooled their money together for two meals to share between all of them. The owner felt sorry for them and gave them each their own plate and told them to pay it back when they had the money. You can guess they probably paid her back a hundred times over," Clay explains.

"Aww, what a sweet story."

We go in and sit down. The waitress brings our menus. She's around our age, has a beautiful dark complexion and long blonde hair with a natural flow.

"Good afternoon. I'm Jean," she says cheerfully. "You'll find today's specials under 'Wednesday.' You have your choice of a meat, bread, and up to three sides."

"Sounds great," Clay tells her.

"Thanks," I say.

"I'll give you a minute. Wave me over when you're ready, sugar," she says as she walks away.

"Thanks," we say in unison. We laugh.

"I think she was talking to me," I say.

"Uh, negative. She was talking to me. Because I'm so sweet. Plus she gave me a wink and a smile."

"Okay, fine. I'll give you that one. So, what are you in the mood for?"

"I'm always in the mood for—"

"Food, goofball."

"You asked."

"H and H does not stand for 'Hungry and Horny.'"

"Does for me."

Food and sex. Is that all they think about? Men are such simple creatures. All they really want is a sandwich and some lovin'.

"So," I say with a smile, "what are you going to order?"

"I think I'm gonna go for the fried catfish, green beans, and macaroni and cheese," Clay says. "And a roll."

"I knew you'd get the mac and cheese. I bet you have macaroni and cheese running through your veins."

"That would feel weird. What are you getting?"

"I guess I'll go with the meatloaf, collard greens, and deviled eggs. With cornbread. And a sweet tea," I say.

"Sweet tea goes without saying."

I read about the history of the H & H on the menu. It's been opened since 1959. Inez Hill, along with her goddaughter and cousin, Louise Hudson, were the H & H. They are better known as Mama Hill and Mama Louise. Mama Hill died in 2007, but as of today, May 3, 2017, Mama Louise is still with us. I write that on a napkin so I can enter it into my journal later.

Jean comes back and we put in our order. I look around and the place is decked out with lots of The Allman Brothers Band memorabilia, as well as moments from the lives of the owners, and pictures of other celebrities that have visited and eaten here over the years.

"So, what's your favorite Allman Brothers song?" I ask Clay.

"Well, I mean, it's gotta be 'Midnight Rider,' right? Classic."

"Oh, yeah. Good one. I should add that to our playlist."

"You should. That's a good road trippin' song."

"Okay, deal."

Our lunch is served. "Can I get you anything else?" Jean asks.

"No, ma'am," Clay says. "Thanks."

"I'm good," I tell her. "This looks great, thank you."

"Just call me if you need me, darlin'. Anything at all."

"Will do." Clay winks at her this time and she smiles.

We dig in. I take a bite of my main dish and Clay starts with his macaroni and cheese, of course.

"Mmm. Man, this meatloaf is so good. How's your mac and cheese?"

"Fucking delicious."

"Clay, watch your mouth. We're in public."

"Sorry. You wanted to know," he laughs. "Here, try a bite." He gives me a forkful.

"Oh my goodness. Yep." Soft and creamy with just enough cheese. So. Good. I mouth the words 'fucking delicious' and then giggle.

"Told you."

We finish up eating some of the finest fucking delicious southern soul food on the planet, and Jean comes over to check on us.

"Ooh, you both made happy plates. Dessert?" she asks.

"Oh gosh," I say, "I'd have to put it in my pocket. Everything was so good. I'm stuffed."

"How 'bout you, sugar?" she asks Clay.

"Same. I think I'm gonna have to pass."

"You can take it to go. We have the best banana puddin' in the south."

"Okay, you sold me," Clay tells her. "We'll take two to go."

"Comin' right up."

Clay stops her before she leaves the table. "Have you ever met the Allman Brothers?"

"No. Sure haven't. But, you're in luck. My great-aunt Mama Louise is here today. She loves talking about them. Would you like to meet her?"

"Are you kidding?" Clay asks. "Yes, I'd love to."

"Me too," I say. "Aren't great-aunts the best?"

"They sure are, sugar. I'll go get her."

Mama Louise comes over to our table and sits down. We introduce ourselves and tell her we'd love to hear a couple of stories about the Allman Brothers. Her face lights up as she talks about the band, going on tour with them in 1972, and her overall fondness for them.

By the time we leave, we're all laughing. We hug Jean and Mama Louise good-bye and take pictures with them. Clay pays the check and leaves Jean a sweet tip. We each buy an H & H t-shirt on the way out and waddle back out to the truck.

"Oh my God," Clay says. "That was awesome. One of our best experiences yet. And I'm still stuffed. Why did you let me do that to myself? I need a nap."

Clay starts the truck and we keep heading north to Athens.

"You are so right. Definitely one for the journal. And I didn't force any of that food down your throat, Mr. Sinclair. That was all you. I'm full, too. It was really good though. I'm so glad we happened upon it."

"Me too. I've always wanted to go there. It's been in the back of my mind. It all came back to me when you spotted it. Good eye, babe."

"I know. I spotted you, right?"

"That you did. And I'm so glad you were looking up, so I could catch your beautiful green eyes when we first met."

"Oh, whatever. It was a case of mistaken identity. You thought I was somebody from your past. And as I recall, you were disappointed that I wasn't."

"Um, that's not how I remember it."

"What? What are you talking about? You said you thought I was somebody else. And then you left."

"But then I didn't. Believe me, I knew what I was doing. When I turned around and saw you, my heart dropped. I had to make you think that I recognized you, so I could see if you would remotely give me the time of day. You passed my test."

"Oh, really? *I* passed? How do you know I didn't just feel obligated to talk to you after you waited for me out there?"

"Because. You still look at me the same way. When our hands first touched, your eyes went from flirty and lit to downright seductive and scorched. I saw it. I felt it. I know you felt it. You had to. Those eyes. Your eyes. They had me. You had me."

"All according to my plan," I tease him.

"Touché, Mrs. Sinclair. Touché."

Chapter 31

WE ARRIVE AT the Greyhound bus station in Athens, Georgia at about 4:00, only to learn that they closed at 1:00.

"Crap. I can't believe I didn't see that on their website," I say to Clay.

"Well, good news is," Clay says, "they open back up again at eight tonight."

"Yeah, but I don't think we need to get back on the road again tonight, so we might as well make the best of this afternoon and find a place to stay. Then, we'll come back in the morning when they open," I tell Clay. I look online and find a Hotel Indigo. We have one of those in Baton Rouge, so I know they're nice. I book us the Presidential Baby Grand Suite.

"So, it seems we've found ourselves with some free time. What do you want to do?" Clay asks.

"I'm not sure. Let me investigate a minute." I search online for things to do. "Let's see…botanical gardens?"

"Nah."

"Museums or galleries?"

"No, and please, God, no."

"You don't want to go see who let the 'dawgs' out?"

"What?"

"There's a 'We Let the Dawgs Out' art exhibit featuring creative painted bulldog statues."

"In honor of Uga, I presume."

"Precisely." Uga is the name of the live mascot of the University of Georgia Bulldogs. Clay starts singing "Who Let the Dogs Out" by the Baha Men, 'woofs' included. I laugh.

"No thanks. What else you got?"

"Craft breweries?"

"Now we're talkin'." He rubs his hands together like he can't get a beer down his gullet fast enough.

"Okay. There are five."

"Which one is the closest to the hotel?"

I check. "Well, there are three downtown, near the hotel. Each are literally a two-minute drive from the Indigo, just in different directions. So, how about the one called Creature Comforts? I like the name."

"Then that's where we shall take up residence for the next few hours. Let's roll."

"Okay. Should we check into the hotel first?" I ask.

"Yeah, that's actually a good idea, then we can just go up to our room after instead of waiting in line later tonight," he says.

We make the drive to the hotel and check in. Our room is ultra swanky. There's a baby-blue baby grand piano in the room, with furniture to match. I wish one of us knew how to play. I can play a little by ear and I can even read music, thanks to taking choir in junior high for two years. I know where to put my fingers on the keys, but I can't play fluidly at all. Some people just have the gift. But not me.

We put our stuff down and use the bathroom. I need to freshen up my hair.

"You ready, babe?" Clay asks.

"Just about. I need to fluff my hair a little and touch up my makeup." I revive my look and we are out the door.

We head into Creature Comforts Brewing Company, and it's got a really laid-back college-town vibe. First off, it's in an old 1940s Chevy dealership, which was later converted into a tire plant, so Clay loves that, right off the bat. Even though he's a Dodge man, it still has the undertone of classic cars, and that's all him. He's right in his element. The owners even left the garage bay door in and have it opened, letting the breeze through. It's like a little block party. And it's pet friendly. A couple of dogs and cats on leashes are laying around, just chillin' with their owners. I love that. Maybe that's part of their shtick, with having 'creature' in their name.

The bar itself looks like it's made from reclaimed wood planks. Pallets maybe. The boards are actually a little wide for pallet slats, but that's what it reminds me of, in color and in rusticness. Is that a word? Rusticity. That sounds more like it. The tanks are not far from the bar, which I think is rather smart. A great conversation starter.

We walk up to the bar and I opt for their Tropicália, which is brewed with ripe passion fruit and a citrus hop. It's not my usual go-to type of beer, but I've always been a little more adventurous with my palate when I'm on vacation. When in Rome, right? Clay orders their Reclaimed Rye, an amber ale of French oak and rye malt. There's live music playing and we just people-watch, listen to the band, and have ourselves some beer.

I thought the Tropicália would be really good. At least it sounded good, going by the description, but it's not my favorite. It's not the worst beer, but I've had better. I'm going to keep drinking it though, maybe I'll acquire a taste for it. Fingers crossed.

Clay drinks a few more beers than I do, having had the sense to order normal drafts and not some weird hipster shit. I know I'm going to have to wind up driving back to the hotel. But we're having a good time, so I don't mind. After the other day, I know he needs to unwind a little.

"Babe," Clay half slurs, "what if…think about it…what if…Uncle… Sid's…sifty-shevven Fevvy…" I snicker at his spoonerism. "…was made… right…here."

"Whoa. That's some mind-blowing shit, Clay. Like, seriously. You never know. Maybe it was."

"The car's ghost. It's heeeeere," he says, reminiscent of the girl from *Poltergeist*.

"How could it be a ghost when the car is still 'alive' in Tallahassee?"

He looks at me wide-eyed with an open mouth, like I've just discovered the whereabouts of Jimmy Hoffa's final resting place. "Touché, woman."

We finally get ready to leave the brewery at about 10:00. It was great to let loose for a little while. We haven't really done that this whole trip.

We walk out to the parking lot and Clay is swaying a bit as we head to the truck. He puts his arm around me, probably to steady himself more than anything, and starts singing "Family Tradition" by Hank Williams, Jr. Country? He's definitely a bit inebriated. I start laughing and walk him over to the passenger side.

"Um, babe...whatchadoin? Thisisyourside." His words run together.

"Not tonight it's not. You can't drive, Clay. Surely you know that."

"I'm fine. I can so trive my duck."

"Nope. Right now it's my truck. You're way too tipsy. You're getting all your words mixed up."

"Fine," he huffs. "If you shay sho."

"I say so. Get in the truck, Sinclair."

"Okay, boss. Don't wreck 'er."

Clay and I make it back to the hotel and get ready for bed. He goes to the bathroom and splashes water on his face. I lie down and my eyes are heavy and a little dizzy, like I've been given anesthesia. I close them and drift away. Sleep is my friend. I'm barely aware of Clay turning off the lamp and getting into bed. He nudges me. When I don't respond, he starts whispering in my ear. I have no idea what he's saying.

"Stop, Clay," I mumble. "I'm trying to go to sleep." I keep my eyes closed.

"No, Lynn. Wake up."

"Why?"

"I can't sleep. I'm hyper."

"I'm tired."

"Come on, babe."

"Shh. Lay down and close your eyes. Go to sleep."

"I can't. I'm a little drunk. And a lot horny."

"I'm neither of those things."

He takes my hand and makes me feel him. "Are you turning this down?"

"I am."

"Seriously?"

"Seriously."

"*Seriously?*"

"Yes. Go to sleep, Clay."

"Please? Pretty please? With you on top?"

I turn over in slow motion. I'm such a sucker for his groveling. He rarely begs.

"With you on top. I'm too tired for all that."

"Deal."

I wake up and Clay's not in bed. I look at my phone. It's 4:42 in the morning. I hear the shower running. What is he doing up so early? I get out of bed and open the door to the bathroom. It's foggy with steam. Clay is standing under the hot water with his eyes closed. Not moving. Tense. Fists clenched. I undress as fast as I can and quietly get in the shower with him.

"Clay." No reaction. "Babe." I touch his chest using just my fingertips. He jerks and opens his eyes. "I'm sorry. Are you okay?"

He wraps his arms around me and hugs me close. I hug him back the best I can, but I know it's not tight enough.

Chapter 32

THE ALARM ON Clay's phone wakes me up out of a deep sleep. I open my eyes and Clay is still knocked out, oblivious to the noise coming out of his cell. I try to shake him awake.

"Clay. Wake up, babe. Turn off your alarm," I tell him. Nothing. "Clay." I nudge his leg with my foot.

He stirs. "What time is it?" His blind fingers fumble around the night-stand for his phone and he hands it to me to silence.

"It's almost ten. The bus station closes at one, remember? We need to get ready to go." I rub his back to coax him. I know he had a rough night, so I try to go easy on him. "Come on, Clay. Get up please."

"Okay. I'm up. I'm up." He stretches and turns over in my direction. "Sorry about last night. The shower."

"Don't be." I snuggle into him and kiss him on his neck. "It's okay. Do you want to talk about it?"

"No."

"Clay, you know you can talk to me."

"I said no, Lynn. I'm sorry."

"Okay. It's okay."

Whatever it is, he'll come around. Eventually. I think. I hope.

We get to the bus station about 11:00. We walk around and look for the lockers, but don't see any. That crushing feeling of dread washes over me again. Hot flashes. Sweaty palms. Lump in the throat.

"Clay, I don't see any lockers anywhere. Do you? What if they're gone? What if they tore them out? I mean people don't really use that kind of stuff anymore, do they?"

"I don't know, Lynn. Let's ask around. I don't see any though."

We look around and find a young desk clerk.

"Excuse me, ma'am. Can you tell me if there are any lockers here?" I ask her.

"Lockers? Uh, no. We don't have any lockers," she replies.

"None? Did you ever? Where were they located? I have a key to a locker and I need to get something out that belongs to me. It was left for me." I can hear the anguish in my voice as it shakes and I ball my hands into fists, digging my nails into my palms.

"I'm sorry," she says, "I don't know of any lockers that have ever been here."

Clay sees how upset I'm getting and intercedes. "Can you ask somebody? Is your manager here? It's really important," he says.

"Um, okay, sure. I'll be back in a minute," the girl says.

"Babe, you need to calm down. They could still be here. Breathe."

A few minutes later, she comes back with an older man that has to be at least eighty. He's wearing a brown plaid newsboy cap on top of a presumably bald head. A prominent nose, white mustache, and horn-rimmed glasses take up most of his face. "Good morning, my friends. How may I help you?"

"Hello, sir," Clay says to him. "We're looking for a set of lockers. Specifically, number one-fifty-three." Clay shows him the key.

"I'm sorry, son. We don't have lockers. How long have you had that key?" the old man asks.

"Um, I'm not sure exactly how long. It was left to us," Clay tells him.

"Well, it looks rather old. You know, we used to have another bus station that had lockers. It was built in the nineteen-forties. Closed a few years back. I think it's been converted into retail space, but that'll be your best shot for finding your locker."

"Oh, really?" I ask, a little hopeful.

"Yes, but I wouldn't be surprised if they ripped them out."

"Can you tell us the name and where it is please?" I ask.

"It's at the corner of West Broad and North Hull. I worked there for years when it was still a bus station. Not sure of the name now, but it's some kind of junk shop or something. At least I know 'junk' is in the name," he says.

"Thank you." Given his age, I have to ask… "Sir, did you know Sid and Mitzi Santini?"

"Sid and Mitzi…Santini…hmm…naw, can't say I do. Name's not familiar." I feel a little let down.

"Okay, thanks so much for your time and the information," Clay tells him.

"You're welcome. Hope I was helpful. Good luck to the both of you."

"Yes, you were, thank you," I tell the man.

Sitting in the truck now, I let out a heavy sigh and look down towards the floor. I start pulling at the string hanging out of the hem of my shorts. "Clay, you know if that old bus station is a retail business now, those lockers are long gone."

"You don't know that. C'mon, what have we learned all this time? Aunt Mitzi wouldn't have let that happen. And even if the lockers aren't there anymore, maybe whatever was inside still is."

"True."

Clay keys 'West Broad' into the GPS while I do an internet search for junk shops in town. "Okay, nothing is really coming up under my search except for a shop called 'Junk in the Trunk' on Olympic Drive, so that can't be it. Unless they moved. Let's just go to the intersection the man told us about and see what we find."

We get there in about ten minutes and it definitely looks like an old bus station built in the forties. It's a Streamline Moderne style cinderblock building, with rounded edges above the door and on the sides. This is the style of architecture that came after Art Deco. They've painted it green and white though. It's not the typical blue of Greyhound. Above the door are huge, colorful, spray-painted letters that spell out 'Junkman's.'

"Junkman's?" I ask.

"Looks more like 'Junkman's Daughter's Brother.' See, over there off to the side are the words 'Daughter's Brother.' But most probably just goes by Junkman's for the most part. Not as much of a mouthful," Clay says. "I'm guessing there's a Junkman's Daughter shop somewhere that came first."

"Oh yeah, I see now. Well, this is it," I say. "Let's cross our fingers that the lockers are still here. Or at least, like you said, whatever was in number one-five-three is still here."

It's kind of busy, and the parking lot looks full, so we park in the front of the building where the street parking is.

The first thing I see upon walking in is a rack of Halloween costumes and a stand with lovely scarves and purses. Cardboard cutouts of movie characters hang high on the walls in the back of the store. We walk a little further inside and Clay nudges me and points to his right. Holy crap. The lockers. I didn't see them at first because they are flush in the wall, right by the door.

"Oh my God. I can't believe it," I say. "They're still here. Intact. Should we ask for the manager? Or just hurry and open it?" I ask Clay.

"Well, let's just open it. If we get caught, then we'll explain ourselves."

"Alright. Good enough for me." There are sixteen lockers, stacked four by four. They are about one foot square. I get the key out of my pocket and look for number 153. It's all the way in the top left corner. "Babe, you're gonna have to do it. I'm a little too short." I give him the key. "Be quiet about it."

He gives me a side-eye sneer like I've insulted him. "I know what I'm doing."

He scans around and nobody is really paying attention to us, so he goes for it. He puts the key in and opens it. Inside is, you guessed it, an envelope. It looks like there's a note on the front. Clay snatches it out and closes the locker back, but not before we're busted.

"What in the Sam Hill do you think you're doing? How did you open that locker?" asks a man. His arms are folded across his chest, legs shoulder width apart, and he's glaring at us with a crumpled brow. "Give me that folder. That belongs to me." He's dressed in a tie-dyed t-shirt, faded jeans with holes, and sports a long gray ponytail. He's probably in his late sixties. A definite hippie.

"Sir, with all due respect," Clay says, as calmly as possible, "this is—"

"I said hand it over!" the man yells. His tone of voice turns heads and now all eyes are on us.

Clay hands over the envelope and I shoot daggers at him with my eyes. What the hell is he doing? We don't even know what it is yet.

"Babe, it's okay," he says, as the dude snatches it from him. "Possession is nine-tenths of the law."

Patrons of Junkman's Daughter's Brother have moseyed their way to our side of the store, pretending to check things out on the nearby racks so they can see and hear what's going on with us.

The man reads the note written on the envelope aloud with a sardonic attitude. "'*If you find this, please lock it back in the locker or file it away somewhere in this building for safe keeping. Clay and/or Lynn Sinclair will come looking for it. I promise you that. Any questions, please call Mitzi Santini at two-two-five...*' blah, blah, blah."

He rolls his eyes and opens the large brown envelope. Out comes some old, yellowed newspaper articles. But I can't see the headlines, as the guy is facing us. I can tell they are laminated though. Once again, Aunt Mitzi thought ahead. Thank goodness for that. The longer they sat in there, the worse they would have deteriorated without being protected. Who knows how long they've even been in there.

"What is this?" the guy asks.

"We don't actually know yet," Clay says to him. "Sir, please, let us explain."

"You got sixty seconds."

Clay and I tell him everything, as short as we can make it. He's engrossed in our story, nodding and raising his eyebrows, tilting his head to the side with curious eyes. Then he laughs. Belly laughs. Like Santa Claus himself has just been mistaken for the Easter Bunny. His guffaw echoes throughout the whole store and the crowd around us grows.

"So...you're tellin' me," the man says, "that what I hold here is part of your cockamamie scavenger hunt key game? Okay, Fred and Daphne. Where'd you park your Mystery Machine? Scooby waitin' outside for ya?" He's making fun of us and I want to cry. Or punch him in the face.

"Mister, please," I beg him. "We have the key to that locker. You've obviously never been able to open it, right? Or you would have known what was in there. That envelope with those articles was left here for us. They mean something."

"Did it ever occur to you that this aunt of yours is sending you both on a wild goose chase?"

"What? No. She isn't." Or is she? No. I won't believe it. I won't give it another thought. "We've already found some personal items and information along the way." He's not listening.

"That would be the best practical joke of all-time. My wheels are turning...I might do that to my kids." He laughs and shakes his head, like we're idiots.

"That would not be very funny." My tone is meek. Clay bows up, muscles tight, just waiting to take this guy out. But I give him another sharp look and he relaxes. He knows if he does something to let the contents of that envelope get destroyed, I'll go off on him in a way he's never seen.

"You don't know me," the man says. "It would totally be something I would do. Especially after I'm gone. And anyway, I'm just messin' with y'all. Really. Have you looked around this place? I'm a jokester. A regular clown. Here ya go." He hands the envelope to me and I breathe a huge sigh of relief. "Ya coulda just asked me though. I'm an easy-goin' guy. And I figured we really didn't need that locker. Got fifteen more just like it. I'm the owner, by the way. Zeke Jacobs."

"Lynn and Clay Sinclair," Clay introduces us and the two of them shake hands.

"Figured as much."

"Thank you," I tell him. "You had me going there for a minute. I thought you were making a mockery of everything. It's nice to meet you."

"Usually I'm the one being made a mockery of. Feel free to look around after you take a gander at them articles. Don't understand what the big deal is though. Everybody already knows Al Capone was a cheating mob boss. Catch ya later." He walks away.

"What?" Clay is at my side as I pull the articles out of the envelope. There are clippings from the late twenties and early thirties. All Chicago papers. The headlines read *U.S. Jury Convicts Capone, Al Capone Guilty of Tax Evasion – Owed Over $215,000 in Back Taxes – Sentenced to 11 Years* in Prison, Capone and 68 Named in Beer Plot, Killing Exposes Capone Death Plot, Massacre 7 of Moran Gang, and State Starts Gang Cleanup. I'm at a loss for words. My mouth is hanging open. I look at Clay.

"What the hell," Clay states. "Was Aunt Mitzi involved with the mob?"

"No effing way," I say with declaration. "And even if she was, she wasn't old enough to be involved with Al Capone. No. Just…no. There's no explanation here though. No letter, no clues, no codes to figure out. I don't get it. Again. No answers, just more questions."

"Which I'm sure will be answered in due time," Clay replies, as he hugs me and rubs my back for comfort.

"I know. I just want all the answers now," I say into his shoulder.

"I don't," he says. I look up at him with a blank stare. My eyebrows crease and I start to ask him why, but he answers me before I get the chance. "Because as soon as we have all the answers, this road trip is over. And I'm having too good of a time with you to be done with it already," he says. "I want this to go on. Don't worry, we'll get our answers. Be patient, love."

"I love you." I give him a peck on the lips as Zeke comes back around and sees us.

"Hey, none of that. Plenty of hotels around here," he says. "Or I got a room in the back I rent by the hour, if y'all would prefer?" He winks at us.

"Very funny," Clay says.

"Mr. Jacobs, can I ask you a question?" I inquire.

"Mr. Jacobs was my father. I'm Zeke. Shoot."

"Zeke—"

"Mr. Zeke."

"Uh, okay, Mr. Zeke—"

"It's really just Zeke. Told ya. I like to kid around. If you could see the look on your face. Sorry. Go ahead. What's your question?"

I hesitate to address him now. "Okay then, *Zeke*, how is it that you didn't destroy the lockers here?" I ask.

"Well, I know this building is pretty historical in its own right. I wanted to preserve as much history as possible. The lockers were a given. Plus, I thought they'd be great for my employees to keep their personal stuff in and all that. Of course, I didn't have all the keys." He winks.

"We also uncovered the original flooring." Zeke points down to the floor, which definitely suggests 'old bus station.'

"Oh that's wonderful," I express, "and lucky for us."

"Yeah," Clay says, "thanks for keeping them intact. I think we're gonna look around. You have a pretty groovy-looking place here."

"Be my guest," Zeke says with a wave of his arm like a model on *The Price is Right*.

We peruse the aisles of nifty items. There are Mardi Gras masks, wigs, a gay pride section, soaps and bath bombs with funny descriptions, a jewelry case, racks of stuff for marijuana lovers, rows of sunglasses (from which Clay picks out a couple of pair). There are a lot of other neat items too. Among the bongs and rainbow t-shirts, I see the perfect thing that makes me burst out laughing. It's an oven mitt with a '50s style rendering of a young girl sitting at the table with her dog, enjoying a plate of spaghetti. And it's captioned, 'this is fucking delicious.' Given our lunch from yesterday in Macon and the conversation we had about Clay's mac and cheese, I have to get it.

"What's so funny?" Clay asks. I'm laughing so hard I can barely breathe, so I show him. He cracks up right along with me. "Get two of them," he says.

We head to the check-out counter and grab some snacks and canned drinks for the road while we're there. Impulse buys. We need to restock our ice chest anyway. Clay and I gather up our purchases and tell Zeke good-bye and thanks again.

Back in the truck, I open up a bag of Peanut Butter M&Ms and a Cherry Coke Zero while Clay opens a Kit Kat and a Mello Yello.

"Where to now, babe?" he asks.

"Not sure. Hold on, let me get the key first." I search the box of keys for number six. "Ooh, this is one with two keys. Our first one like this." The keychain itself is round, about two inches in diameter, and has a pattern that resembles a circular maze on it. I show it to Clay. "Any idea what this is?"

"Nope. Looks like a Chinese symbol though."

I look in my purse for the list of clues. "Okay. 'In South Carolina, in a town called Prosperity, a house on McLeary, could barely be kept for posterity. You'll know it when you see it, it's in quite disrepair, look inside for a chest, and see what's in there.' Wow, that's our longest clue yet."

"At least she gives us the place straight up. Hey, I bet that's the symbol for prosperity," Clay says.

I look it up, and dang if he's not right. "Well, aren't you smart?"

"No. If I was really smart, I would have known that from the get-go." He gets on the road and we head east to our new destination. "Now, what's on tap for tunes?"

I hit the shuffle button on my playlist called *Elements*. I love this playlist of songs about air, water, fire, and earth. And just for fun, there are a few songs by the band Earth, Wind, and Fire. I mean, you can't have a playlist about that subject without them on it, right? "Into the Mystic" by Van Morrison starts playing.

"Oh, nice one, babe. Love this song."

"Me too. See, I have good music in my lists. Tomorrow, it's all yours."

"Sweet."

Chapter 33

AFTER ABOUT AN hour of driving, we cross the border into South Carolina. I love how Clay has remembered to pull off to the side of the road every time so I can get a picture of each state's welcome sign. Even when he was upset about the hitchhiker fiasco and flooring it from Florida into Georgia, he pulled over without a word. And swears the ten seconds it took to do that is what made us get to Thomasville two minutes later than he expected to.

I switch my playlist over to the one titled *Dos and Don'ts*. "Don't Let It End" by Styx comes on. This song brings me such anguish, I don't even know why I put it on here. It reminds me of when Clay and I almost separated.

It was right after we got married. We had our first big fight and I just knew he was going to leave me for good. I was so young, so naive.

It was May of 1991. I went to meet him at the airport the Friday night that he came home from his deployment. It was the first time I met his parents. I guessed who they were by the signs they had made that said 'Welcome Home Clay.' I was a very nervous twenty-two-year-old. I knew they would be there, but I didn't expect to be so ill at ease. I introduced myself to them and his dad was very receptive. His mom, not so much. We're fine now, amicable anyway, but that night, she was very cold and standoffish. She barely acknowledged me. I got the feeling she was one of those you'll-never-be-good-enough-for-my-baby type of moms. We were waiting for the troops on the tarmac and I was so excited and anxious to see Clay, plus tense and edgy on top of that because of his mom. I saw him get off the plane and I started tearing up. He made his way over to us and winked at me as I stepped aside to give him a moment with his parents. Then he turned his attention to me and gave me a huge hug. He asked me to marry him right there. I didn't hear him at first because I was crying just from seeing his face and being in his arms again. Then he kissed me for a solid minute. At least it felt like that. It could have only been ten seconds. Time stood still. I didn't even care that his disapproving mom was standing right there, watching. I hadn't seen him in eight months. *In your face, Clay's mom.* I gave him another tight hug. I didn't want to let him go.

"Did you hear me, babe?" he asked. My arms were still around him.

"What? No, I'm sorry. What is it?" I asked, wiping tears from my face.

"Will you marry me? Will you be my wife?"

I gasped. "Yes. Oh my God. Yes!" More tears. The apprehension in my veins vanished and turned to pure contentment.

We hugged some more and kissed again and people were cheering and clapping. I looked around, and apparently, Clay wasn't the only one who proposed to his girl right off the plane. I'm guessing almost a year in combat will put things into perspective for a man. And what a fine man I had myself. I was over the moon with happiness—much to the dismay of his mom. She wasn't thrilled in the least. I swear I saw her roll her eyes. We made eye contact and had a silent conversation that we both understood.

You better get used to me, woman.

You better get used to me, girl.

But his dad was genuinely pleased. "Congratulations, you two," Mr. Lane said to us. "Welcome to the family, Lynn. Pleasure to have you." He even gave me a big bear hug.

"Yes," his mom added, "what a nice addition you'll be." *Was that sarcasm?* She faked a smile and gave me one of those insincere side hugs.

My parents weren't a hundred percent on board either, but they wanted me to be happy, and Clay made me happy. They loved Clay, but knew we hadn't spent that much time together. They never tried to talk me out of marrying him or told me I was making the wrong decision. They supported us. I think they would have just rathered we waited a little while.

We had a short engagement. That's an understatement. We literally got married as soon as we could. We applied for the marriage license the Monday after he got home and were married right after the waiting period of three days, on Thursday May 16, 1991. He didn't want to wait any longer. Like I said…perspective. I was fine with that. I never wanted to make a big fuss over a huge wedding. Even as a little girl, I always desired something small, with just my immediate family. So that's how it was.

Cecilia got everything together for us, what little we needed. Aunt Mitzi and Uncle Sid offered their house as our venue, so we took them up on that. And of course Flo did the food.

After we got married, I moved into Clay's house. It was a different house from our Craftsman. A much smaller house. Something only a bachelor needed.

I stayed there the whole time during Clay's deployment. I took care of his dog, Shadow, a brown-spotted Catahoula Cur that he had just gotten about nine months prior to his leaving. I kept his house up for him and drove his truck every so often so it wouldn't sit dormant and deteriorate. Since we didn't know how long he would be gone, he gave me permission to do so. And that was something. He didn't let anybody drive his truck, not even his dad or his brother. I felt honored. I felt loved. I felt grown up. I was playing house. My guy was in the Army National Guard taking care of our country. And I was taking care of him from afar. I missed him so much while he was gone.

The first week I was there, every single night at about 8:00, I noticed the same car pass by very slowly in front of his house. By the time I got up to the door, I couldn't see who it was. Every time. I was too slow. All I could see by the streetlight was that it was a dark gray Honda Civic.

One night, I decided to turn off all the lights and see what would happen. Like clockwork, said Honda Civic drove by. I was waiting. I got up. But then it stopped. It backed up, and pulled into Clay's driveway. I got a little scared, not having come up with a plan of action if something like that actually happened. I got on the ground and crawled back to the couch.

Clay's truck was in the driveway, so it looked like he was home. My Corolla was parked behind his truck. If Clay had been home, my car should have been a clue that he had company.

I heard the Civic's car door shut. I heard somebody walking up the front steps and onto the porch. I heard keys jingle and then a zipper. The unmistakable zipper of a purse. A girl? A fucking girl? Who the fuck was this bitch? She tried to peer through the blinds on the door. Then she moved over to the window and tried to look through the small hole where Shadow had chewed the blinds up as a brand new puppy. I was as still as I could be and stayed in the obscurities of the living room. There's no way she could have seen me. Then she knocked on the door.

"Clay?" she asked. "Are you home? Are you there? I changed my mind. I can't do this. I still love you. I'm sorry I broke your heart again. I miss you. There's something I need to tell you. Please. Open the door. Take me back."

My heart sank.

Shadow started barking.

"Shadow! Where's Daddy?"

Oh, hell no. Game on, bitch.

I shot up off the couch and stormed over to the door. As I proceeded to fumble with the barrage of locks my security conscious boyfriend had, I could hear her saying, "Oh, Clay, I knew it. I knew you still loved me."

I stopped. Just as I was about to open the door. My insides were boiling. I took a deep breath to calm myself.

"Clay? Open the door, baby."

I opened the door. I wish I had a picture of that bitch's face.

"Where's Clay? Who the fuck are you?" Shadow was growling at her.

"No ma'am. You don't get to ask me that. Who the fuck are *you*?"

"I'm Alexa, Clay's girlfriend. Now tell me who you are. What are you doing in his house? Where is he?"

"No, you're not. No, I won't. None of your business. And *really* none of your business."

"Tell me where he is, bitch."

I took another deep breath and smiled. "If you were Clay's girlfriend, you would know where he is. And since you don't know where he is, then you're obviously not important to him. If I catch you here again, even so much as driving your skanky ass down this street, one more time...you'll be sorry. You're not welcome here."

"Are you threatening me?" she shrieked.

I didn't answer her. I slammed the door in her face and locked all the locks back. I let her think what she wanted. I immediately ran to Clay's bed and cried into his pillow. I could hear her banging on the door, demanding I open it and let her in so she could kick my ass. Right. Like that was going to happen.

Clay's scent was all over his pillow, which made me cry harder and miss him more. And I was dying inside. Unravelling. Breaking. Crumbling. Shadow jumped up on the bed and started licking my hands.

"Who was that, Shadow? You didn't like her, did you?" I pet him on the head and he rolled over for me to rub his belly. I scratched his tummy and his back legs started moving like he was running. His tongue hung out the side. He looked like a crazy hyena.

Clay and I hadn't had the conversation about our exes. I had no idea of his past. He had no idea about mine. We'd only been dating about two months when he left. I had never heard that girl's name from him. There were no signs of her in his house. None. No pictures anywhere. No girly things in his bathroom. Not even an old shirt that she may have left there. I checked. After that incident, you bet your ass I checked. I went through all of his drawers and closets. Nothing. Either she literally meant nothing to him, or she broke his heart so bad that he erased her from his life. Whatever the case, I was glad she didn't exist in his house.

A few days later, I saw her drive by again. I let it go. She must have assumed I was kidding when she thought I threatened her though, because she passed by again several days after that. I bought one of those cheap NO TRESPASSING – VIOLATORS WILL BE PROSECUTED signs and put it on the window sill. Then, I called my brother-in-law, Frank. He was a cop. I asked him to please sit outside a couple of houses down, and when he saw a dark gray Honda Civic with a girl driving slowly down the street, find any reason at all to pull her over. He had nothing but time, so there he sat, night after night, as a favor to me. It took six days, but she did it again. Except that night, she decided to make another appearance on the porch. I was ready for her.

She banged on the door, yelling. "I know who you are! And I know where Clay is!"

Not only did she pound on the door, she also proceeded to throw eggs at Clay's house. I was livid.

I waited for Frank to pull up. And did he ever…flashing lights and everything. I opened the door as Frank was getting out of his police cruiser. Broken eggshells were all over the porch. Yolks dripped down the door and windows. As much as I wanted to punch her lights out for what she had done, I ignored her. That was not easy.

"Ma'am is everything okay here?" he asked me.

"No, this girl is trespassing and vandalizing this house. I told her before that she was not welcome here. I told her not to come back. There's even a sign here, warning people." I pointed to my trusty notice, inconspicuous as it may have been. Frank nodded at me.

"Ma'am, I'm placing you under arrest for trespassing and vandalism. Please turn around and place your hands behind your back. You have the right to remain silent—"

"What? You can't do this," she protested.

"Oh yes he can," I said with a smile.

"You fucking bitch. This isn't over."

"Please, keep talking," I told her.

"…If you cannot afford an attorney, one will be provided for you…" Frank continued Mirandizing her, but she wasn't paying any attention. She just kept spewing obscenities in my direction.

After Frank hauled her off, I cleaned up all the splattered eggs and broken shells off the front of the house. There were even a couple on my car that I hadn't noticed at first. *What a twisted piece of crap this girl is. How could Clay ever be with somebody like that?*

The next day, I called Frank to find out what happened. Her parents bailed her out. She only spent about three hours in jail. Which was fine with me. Enough to scare her. I told Frank that I would drop the charges if he could get me a confident answer from her that she would stay the hell away. Done and done. I never saw her again. And I never mentioned it to Clay in any of our communications while he was deployed. He needed to be focused. He did not need drama thousands of miles away. I would not do that to him.

Chapter 34

THE SATURDAY FOLLOWING our wedding, after we moved all of my things in and I got settled, Clay and I were in the kitchen hanging up a painting we'd gotten as a wedding gift from Aunt Mitzi and Uncle Sid. I asked Clay the question I'd been dreading for eight months. "Who is Alexa?"

All of the color drained out of his face. He had to sit down. His voice cracked when he answered me. "Um, she's my ex. Why do you ask?"

"She came by here while you were gone. Claiming she was your girlfriend and she was sorry and wanted you back. She said she knew you still loved her and she had something to tell you."

"What? That's insane. She's insane. We broke up months before I even met you."

"How long were you together?"

"Two years."

"*Two years*? Why did you break up?" I sat down at the table with him.

"She said she couldn't handle being with somebody in the police force. And being a firefighter…in the military. The fear. Her best friend lost her boyfriend in the Panama Invasion in late eighty-nine. And her uncle died in the line of duty trying to break up a street fight. She said it was hard watching her aunt and best friend go through that and she couldn't bear the thought of losing me either way. She said she couldn't understand why I was putting myself in triple danger. We got back together a couple of times, but the last time she left, she called me 'selfish.' That was it. I told her she was a bitch for thinking I was selfish when I was only trying to help people. Plus, I couldn't have my feelings played with like that. So I ended it for good. Told her to forget about me, because I was going to forget about her. Then I burned everything I could find that was hers."

"Do you still have feelings for her?"

"No, babe. I don't. So what happened?"

"Well, she was very rude and demanded to know who I was and where you were. She was adamant and irrational. She stalked your house for weeks before I trapped her."

"What do you mean you trapped her?" He sounded a little upset.

"She drove by very slowly every night. I didn't know if it was you she was stalking or some other house. So one night, I turned off all the lights. She actually pulled into the driveway and came up to your door." I told him exactly what happened.

"So, you threatened her?"

"No. I didn't."

"Well, that sure as hell sounded like a threat. What did you do? Did you hurt her?" He stood up with objection. The chair scraped on the wood floor and flew back a few feet, hitting the cabinets.

"Jesus, Clay! Whose side are you on? I didn't hurt her." Then I stood up, matching his scowl. "I had her arrested."

"You had her *arrested*?"

"Yes! And why do you care? If you don't have feelings for her."

"You *fucking* had her arrested? For knocking on my door? Jesus Christ, Lynn! What the fuck! What is wrong with you?" I'd never seen him that angry. And then he said, "God, what have I done?" That haunting question. I just knew he was second-guessing himself for marrying me in such haste.

I started crying. Bawling. "For your information," I said through tears, "I dropped the charges the next day. And she didn't just knock on your door." Then I started yelling. "She egged your house! I didn't know that girl! I never heard her name cross your lips! I scared her enough to stay away. She never came back. And if you're so sorry you married me,

I'll make this real easy for you!" I grabbed my purse and stormed out the door.

I got in my car and didn't look back. My Styx cassette was in the tape deck. When I started my car, "Don't Let It End" just happened to be on, which was sadly appropriate for the situation. I drove straight to Aunt Mitzi's. I cried all the way there, listening to that song, thinking about what had just transpired. *How fitting is it that our love song and now our break-up song are both by Styx? I'll never be able to listen to this band again.*

When I got to Aunt Mitzi's, I ran straight inside, sobbing about how I ruined everything and that Clay was sorry he married me. I was afraid he wanted a divorce.

"Come here," she said, hugging me. "Sid, get her some water will you? Come now. Let's go sit down in the den and talk this out."

I told her everything that happened. She listened. She didn't ridicule me or Clay one time.

"Do you love Clay?" she asked.

"Of course I do. I wouldn't have married him if I didn't."

"Do you want your marriage to be over?"

"No. But I don't know what he wants."

"You need to go home and ask him. Talk it out. But not before you listen to this."

Then she did what she did best when it came to helping me get through tough times. She took her Bible off the shelf. Bookmarks and prayer cards were stuck between pages, and thin tasseled cords dangled from it, marking many of the passages she often referred to.

I was in dire need of another one of our counseling sessions. I sat on the couch. I pulled my knees up to my chin, wrapped my arms around my legs, and closed my eyes as she read to me.

"Are you listening, dear?" I nodded, my eyes still closed. "Alright then. From the First Letter to the Corinthians, Chapter thirteen, verses four through eight. Well, through the first sentence of eight. 'Love is patient, love is kind. It is not jealous, [love] is not pompous, it is not inflated, it is not rude, it does not seek its own interests, it is not quick-tempered, it does not brood over injury, it does not rejoice over wrongdoing but rejoices with the truth. It bears all things, believes all things, hopes all things, endures all things. Love never fails.' You hear that, Lynn? Love never fails. As long as your love is true, it will not fail you, dear. It will not end. I love that passage. It's my favorite.

"Now, pay attention. This is taken from the Letter to the Colossians, Chapter three, verses twelve through fifteen. 'Put on then, as God's chosen ones, holy and beloved, heartfelt compassion, kindness, humility, gentleness, and patience, bearing with one another and forgiving one another, if one has a grievance against another; as the Lord has forgiven you, so must you also do. And over all these put on love, that is, the bond of perfection. And let the peace of Christ control your hearts, the peace into which you were also called in one body. And be thankful.' That's some heavy stuff, dear. Think about that for a minute. Let it sink in. Put your love for each other above all of those other attributes. Love is the bond of perfection. The love between you and Clay. That love is the bond, the glue that holds you together. Perfectly.

"Here's another one of my favorites. The First Letter of Peter, Chapter four, verse eight. 'Above all, let your love for one another be intense, because love covers a multitude of sins.' You think Uncle Sid and I would still be together without that one? That one got us through some hard-hitting moments in our years. I know the love you and Clay share is intense. You don't get married as soon as possible after a proposal if your love is not intense. There's no separating you two. But that same intensity that you love with, that fire, can transfer itself into heated arguments. You love each other intensely, so you must forgive each other in the same way. Love trumps sin. There's no rock, paper, scissors here. It's just rock and scissors. And love is the rock.

"Now, I'm going to skip around a little on this next one, but I want you to hear me. From The Letter to the Ephesians, Chapter four. 'Be angry but do not sin; do not let the sun set on your anger, and do not leave room for the devil. No foul language should come out of your mouths, but only such as is good for needed edification, that it may impart grace to those who hear. All bitterness, fury, anger, shouting and reviling must be removed from you, along with all malice. [And] be kind to one another, compassionate, forgiving one another as God has forgiven you in Christ.' Sound familiar? You know, that's another one of our secrets. We never go to sleep angry with each other. We always talk it out, even if it's with heads on pillows. So should you. Solve this today, Lynn.

"Okay, I've got one more for you, and this is about you...yourself, as a woman and a wife. And if Clay doesn't see what he has in you, then you don't need him."

I opened my eyes wide and picked my head up. I blinked at her. I was shocked. How could she say that? I did need him.

"Are you paying attention, Lynn? This one is most important." I nodded and put my head back down. "Proverbs, Chapter thirty-one, verses ten through twelve. 'When one finds a worthy wife, her value is far beyond pearls. Her husband, entrusting his heart to her, has an unfailing prize. She brings him good, and not evil, all the days of her life.' Verse ten there is most profound. You are worthy. You are invaluable. You are precious and treasured. And if he doesn't realize that, he's a damn fool. Do you understand? Now, I love Clay. Not that I've had much interaction with him, but that boy loves you. I see the way he looks at you. His eyes sparkle at the mere sight of your beautiful face. When you walk in the room, his face lights up. I believe this is worth saving."

I got up off the couch and hugged Aunt Mitzi. This was our best and most meaningful 'therapy session' yet. "Thank you. I needed that. All of it. I heard every word. I knew you would know just where to go in your Bible and what to say to me personally. I love you. So much."

"I love you, too. Now, dear, you go on, drive safely, and fix this. I know you can."

"Yes, ma'am. Thanks again, Aunt Mitzi. I'll call you tomorrow." I picked up my purse and got ready to go. "Bye, Uncle Sid. Love you."

"Love you too, darlin'," he said.

I opened the door and Clay was standing right there, about to knock.

Chapter 35

"HEY," I SAID.

"Hey. Can we talk?"

"Yeah. You wanna come in? We can go upstairs."

"Sure." Clay came in and gave Aunt Mitzi a hug and shook Uncle Sid's hand, then we headed upstairs to one of the spare rooms and shut the door.

"What are you doing here?" I asked him.

"I left right after you, tried to catch you but you didn't even look back. I went back inside and I was going to chase you down, but I couldn't find my keys. So, after I found them, I went to your mom's. She hadn't heard from you. Told me you'd probably be here."

"This is where I always go when I'm upset."

"I didn't even know how to get here from your parents' house. Your mom had to give me directions. Look, I should have never blown up at you like that. It wasn't fair."

"Are you still in love with her?"

"No. I told you that."

"You don't just turn your feelings off like that after two years, Clay. There has to be something."

"There's not. I mean it. I shut myself off from Alexa. No, it wasn't easy. I did love her, but she jerked me around so bad, I couldn't take it anymore.

I didn't want that in my life. I never looked back after I cut her out. Five months later, I met you. You turned my world around. Showed me how good it can be. You stuck by me the whole time I was gone. To war, no less. And you never gave me any inclination that you would ever leave me because of it. Not once. I never doubted your love and faithfulness."

"Do you regret marrying me?"

"Why would you think that? You took off so fast earlier that I couldn't even ask you why you thought I was sorry we got married."

"Then what did you mean when you said, 'God, what have I done?'? Didn't you mean marrying me so fast after you got back? You had a change of heart? Maybe we should separate for a while. See if this is what you really want. Or if you want a…divorce."

"Is that what you want?"

"I don't know." That was a lie. I did know. I did not want to be away from him for a single day for the rest of my life. Yet I had to make sure he wanted the same thing. I could tell those words, 'we should separate' and 'divorce,' surprised him. But I couldn't tell if he was sad or relieved.

"Fine." He got up to leave. I caught him just as he was about to open the door.

"You didn't answer my question."

"What," he said tersely.

"What did you mean? When you said that."

"I was thinking out loud. I messed up. Not divulging my past was a mistake. What I had done, by not telling you about Alexa. It was wrong of me."

"Then why did you get so defensive about her? That broke my heart. Clay, you know me. I wouldn't hurt anybody. I'm not vindictive."

"Says the one who had her arrested."

"Whatever. I didn't even get a chance to tell you that she's the one who threatened *me*. The first night she came over, she kept banging on the door after I told her to leave. Said she was going to kick my ass."

"She did *what*?"

"Exactly. I was afraid to go to sleep that night. How was I supposed to know she wasn't a psycho, huh? She egged your house, Clay. Broken eggs all over the front porch. She could have come back wielding a gun at me for all I knew."

"Jesus, Lynn. God, I swear! She's not a monster!" he yelled.

"How in the hell would I *know* that?"

He sighed. He looked down and put his thumb and forefinger at the top of his nose between his eyes and squeezed, like he had a headache. Then he walked back over and sat down next to me on the bed again. I started picking at a thread on the bedspread to avoid eye contact.

"You wouldn't. You're right. And I'm sorry. I should've told you about Alexa. Lynn. Look at me. I don't want this." I looked at him in horror. "No," he smiled, "I mean, I don't want a separation. And I sure as hell don't want a divorce."

"You don't? Are you sure?"

"Yes. I've never questioned my decision to marry you. It's the best thing I've done. You're my world, babe. Just the thought of you kept me going while I was away. You were the light in my darkness. I couldn't wait to come back to you and make you my wife."

"I don't want to be separated from you either. Not for a minute."

"Then, why did you ask for it?"

"I just needed to know that being married to me is what you really wanted. I'm sorry."

"Hey, this is not your fault. I'm sorry I overreacted. I wish you'd told me that Alexa is the one who actually did the threatening. If she had gotten through the door, I bet you could have taken her. Alexa is the one who would've gotten an ass kicking." I smiled. "You had every right to feel scared and respond the way you did about Alexa."

"Please stop saying her name."

"Sorry. Her. I never want to hurt you again. Will you please forgive me?"

"Yes. Will you forgive me?"

"You didn't do anything that needs forgiving. I see that now. Here, I got you something." He reached behind his back under his shirt and pulled out a greeting card. I opened it and read it to myself. I started crying on the spot. I couldn't believe it. It said, 'You are far more precious than jewels. Proverbs 31:10.' I didn't even open it to read the rest. I just threw my arms around him and kissed him like there was no tomorrow.

"Lynn. Babe," he was trying to speak with my tongue in his mouth. I didn't let up. He had to pull away. "Seriously. If you don't stop, I'm going to have to take you right here, right now in Aunt Mitzi and Uncle Sid's house. I don't think that would be very respectful. Let's go home."

"Yeah. Okay. Let's hurry. I'm riding with you."

I got up, grabbed my card, and we were out the bedroom, down the stairs, and out the door. As we were running down and out, I shouted to Aunt Mitzi that everything was fine. We would be back the next day for my car.

Chapter 36

THINKING ABOUT ALL that makes me really sad. To know I almost threw it away over a misunderstanding. I never wanted anything less in my whole life. I think that's one of the reasons why we are still so sexual with each other, even at this stage in our marriage. Because we both know it could have ended differently and we don't take that for granted for a second.

God, I love this man. As I look at him sitting next to me in this truck and on this road trip right now, I know how lucky I am. I reach up and rub my hand through his hair and stroke the back of his neck with my thumb.

"What's that for?" he smiles.

"Just for being you. I love you, Clay Weston Sinclair."

"Wow. Middle name and all. Babe, are you okay?"

"Yeah," I sniffle.

"What is it? What's the matter?"

"Nothing. Really this time. I was just looking at you and I love you so much. I was thinking about when we first got married and how awful my life would be right now if we had gone through with separating. We might have actually ended up divorced. I'm so glad you were honest with me at Aunt Mitzi's that day instead of leaving."

"Aww, love...I haven't thought about that in years. Where is this coming from?"

"I don't know. I just look at you sometimes and wonder what I did to deserve you. Plus, that song takes me back there, knowing I could have ruined everything. And I'm so thankful that we got passed it."

"Babe. Come on, now. That was so long ago. So much water under the bridge. And hey, don't you go thinking I don't know how lucky I am. I love you too, Cheralynn Jade Boudreaux Sinclair. Lynn. Babe. Love. Shorty."

I laugh out loud. That sounds so funny coming from Clay, especially since, in slang, it's pronounced *shawty*. He's never called me anything but 'babe' or 'love.' Or by my name of course.

It's almost 5:00 and I know we should be getting to our destination soon. I've been daydreaming so long, I don't even know where we are. "Are we almost there?" I ask.

Clay hits a button on the GPS. "Yeah, look," he says. "We're on Sanctuary Street now. McLeary is just up ahead, perpendicular."

"Oh, cool." I start digging through the box of keys again looking for the prosperity keychain. Each of the keys are really old. "They're both skeleton keys," I say.

"Not skeleton keys, babe."

"I mean, level-tumble-tortoise-bit keys, or whatever you said."

He laughs. "Lever tumbler. Mortise. Bitted."

"Like I said. 'Whatever.'" One key is long, the other short. "Jeez, if one of these keys opens the front door, this house must be ancient."

We get to the end of Sanctuary Street and Clay notices a big, old house on the corner to the left of us, partially overgrown with bushes and trees. "Dang, look at this house. Spooky."

"Yikes," I say.

"Shit. Lynn. That's it."

"What? What do you mean? No, it can't be, this is Sanctuary Street."

He turns left on McLeary, and there's the front of the house.

"See?" he says.

"Shit. No mother effing way. Uh-uh. I'm not going in there this close to dark. Keep moving."

He pulls into the driveway instead. "Wait here," he says.

"Are you out of your ever-loving mind? 'Wait here' my ass. You're not going in there alone and I don't want to go in there at all right now. Can we please do this tomorrow?"

"Lynn, it's still broad daylight. It doesn't get dark for another two hours. Where's your sense of adventure?"

"Where's your beginning-of-a-horror-movie gauge? Clay, this house is huge. We don't know what we're looking for. The sun goes down fast. We're staying here tonight anyway, right? Let's just find a place and come back tomorrow."

"We're looking for a chest."

"We don't know what size. It could be a tiny chest in one of fifty closets."

"I'm going in. Give me the keys."

"No."

"Alright."

He opens the center console and takes out a flashlight, then gets out of the truck and starts to walk up to the front steps.

"Shit. Dammit," I mutter to myself. I get a flashlight out of the glovebox and follow him. This house is at least a hundred years old. Probably more. It's a Queen Anne style, and I know it was a beautiful house in its day. I mean, really, it's beautiful now. Freaking creepy as hell, but beautiful. The exterior is actually in pretty good condition, considering how old this place looks overall. White siding covers the house, though some slats have broken off, revealing the original wood frame. Gingerbread trim drips from the ends of the roof. The woodwork on the railings and posts are intricately carved. The double front doors are flanked by sidelites with a transom over the entry. Upstairs, directly above the main access, there's a matching set of doors with a small porch balcony. There's a huge bay window to the left of the entrance. So far, everything looks original: the wood, the doors, the windows, even the doorknobs. Which is why I now know, the reason we have a 'skeleton' key that will unlock it.

"Clay! Will you wait?" He's looking in the windows and trying to open the doors. "Shit. Stop. I'm coming." I give him the keys when I reach the door.

"Here goes nothin'," he says with a raise of his eyebrows.

It unlocks. He opens the door and it creaks all the way open. The noise is so amplified, making an echo throughout this huge empty house, that it reminds me of a horror movie sound effect. If there are any squatters here, there's no sneaking up on them now. It smells bad too. Not gross, but stuffy. Musty. Old and closed up, with stagnant air. You know that smell.

As we walk in, the flooring is a light-blue linoleum with filigree designs. It spreads throughout the foyer into what I guess would be the living room, where the big bay window in the front is. They are grimy and worn in the most traveled paths, so I bet all the flooring inside is original too.

I glance around, my eyes capturing some hair-raising details of this century-old home of affluence. Single light bulbs dangle from the ceiling by thin electrical cords. Rusted candlesticks left behind on one of the many mantles. A broken plate of china, with a floral pattern and gold rim, sits on the floor. Cobwebs in every corner. The only thing missing that would really up the ante on this house being any freakier is a wheelchair.

"Hello?" Clay shouts. "Anybody here?" Nothing.

"Thank God. Okay, let's start looking around. There's no furniture that I can see, so let's make a quick run through. In and out. Do not leave me alone," I tell him.

"Babe." A half smile, half smirk flashes across his face, like I just foiled his plans.

"Don't 'babe' me. I know you, Clay Sinclair. You'd love to scare the crap out of me in a place like this. Now come on. It's starting to get dark in here. I don't see any cabinets. Where's the kitchen?"

We look all around downstairs and it doesn't look like there was ever a kitchen or a bathroom built. Not even added on at some point. It's like this house just time warped. I guess the kitchen was outside, since back then they built them there for fire prevention. And there was probably an outhouse. I can't believe this house has not been vandalized. No graffiti, no signs of homeless people taking shelter, no traces of drug paraphernalia, nothing. It's shocking. Maybe this place is haunted and nobody *wants* to hunker down here. It does have that spooky vibe. Maybe it is occupied by ghosts.

"Clay, I'm getting an uneasy feeling." I turn around and he's not there.

"Clay? Where are you? Dammit, Clay, this isn't funny." I move to the middle of the room and survey my surroundings. There are no doors in here so he's not hiding in a closet. "Clay! If you don't answer me right now, I'm calling nine-one-one." Then I see him. There's a huge mirror sitting on the floor in the room adjacent to this one and he doesn't know I can see him. His back is against other side of the wall that's in front of me. He's amused. He puts his hand over his mouth to keep silent snickers from becoming audible. I sneak up on his ass and poke my head around the corner. "Boo, motherfucker!"

"Shit, Lynn!" He jumps about a foot back, sliding himself down the wall and falls down.

I crack up laughing. "Serves you right. I told you not to leave me alone. You know I was already freaked out before we walked in here. Get up."

"Got dammit, babe. You literally almost scared the actual shit out of me." He grabs my fingers and makes me feel the pulse in his neck. It's throbbing.

"Don't try to make me feel sorry for you. You were just waiting to do that to me."

"How did you find me?" he asks with a smile. I point to the mirror. "Shit. Lucky break."

"No, you're lucky that you didn't scare me, because I probably would have died."

I take a closer look at the mirror and it is gorgeous. It must be at least six feet tall and equally as wide, but it's not square. The middle is one big mirror and the side panels are split into four smaller mirrors. It's edged with a stunning opulent gold and the top and sides are curved all around, with the crown almost in the shape of a shamrock. It looks very regal, like it belongs in a castle. Not in this old dump. Total fish out of water. I wish we could take it with us, but I know there's no way it would fit in the bed of Clay's truck. Plus, it probably weighs five hundred pounds. Then I notice the staircase. Creep factor ten. It has the same woodwork up the rail as the ones outside on the porch. The white paint is dreadfully peeling from the railing and the wall.

"Whoa," Clay says. "Take a look at the staircase."

"I am. More like a scare-case. Freaky deaky. If Frankenstein, Dracula, and The Mummy would have ever lived together, this would be their house."

"Frankenstein's monster."

"What?"

"Frankenstein wasn't the name of the monster. He didn't have a given name. Frankenstein was the creator of the monster."

"Okay, Mr. Technical. Did you or did you not know who I was talking about?"

"Touché, Mrs. Sinclair. I'll give you that one. And you're right, this would have been a killer frat house for movie monsters. Throw in The Wolf Man and The Creature from the Black Lagoon for good measure."

"Thank you. Now, let's check out the second floor."

"Yes, ma'am. I'll go ahead of you to make sure the steps are safe, though the stairway looks pretty solid."

"Okay, but hold my hand. I'm not letting you get away from me this time."

We go upstairs and search the rooms. The flooring is all original hardwood. Probably heart pine. The walls are the same, constructed with planks of heart pine in every room. We explore the entire upper floor, room by room. I make Clay check the closets. Nothing. No chest anywhere. There's one more bedroom to investigate. As we walk in, I spot a chest. A big, dilapidated chest. It's almost the size of a coffin. The top is covered in a burgundy velour, its flocking partially detached and frayed due to age. "Alright. You open it," I tell him.

"Why me? You scared it might be Dracula?" he laughs.

"Very funny. I just don't know what to expect, that's all. This whole place gives me the heebie-jeebies. How did Aunt Mitzi come across this house? I don't know of any family here. This is crazy. What are you waiting for? Unlock it."

He does. Clay then lifts the cover of the chest. It squeaks and creaks like the front door did. He looks in, looks back at me, and smiles.

"Please tell me it's not another envelope."

"Nope. Much better. Come see."

Chapter 37

I WALK OVER AND peer inside the shadowy human-sized box. It's really getting dark in here now, so I turn on the flashlight and shine it inside. It's a quilt. It's zipped up in one of those big plastic bags that a comforter set comes in. The bag has a layer of dust on it, but the quilt is folded just so, where you can tell that it's a tree trunk. Clay picks it up out of the chest and dusts it off. It's cumbersome and hefty. At the bottom of the tree, 'Chauvin Family est. 1910' is embroidered with silky royal-blue threads. It's beautiful. I almost start to cry. A warm feeling of love washes over me and I swear I can feel Aunt Mitzi's presence.

Clay slings the bagged quilt on his shoulder so he can carry it downstairs. I shine the light in front of him to lead the way. The heavy blanket is teetering in his grip, not balanced as well as it should be. "Watch your step. Don't fall."

"I got it. My equilibrium is in check."

"Careful, babe. Steady going down, it looks hard. Oh, I can't wait to see the whole thing. I hope it's big enough."

"That's what she said."

My boisterous laugh bounces off the walls and ricochets around every corner of the house.

As we walk out the front door and lock it back up, it's twilight. I swear I see bats circling the tops of the trees. Clay puts the quilt into the protected bed of the truck. We climb back in the front to get ready to leave and I reach over, put my hand on the front of Clay's shorts, and lightly squeeze. "Yep. Big enough. But not hard."

"Jeez, babe, what are you doing to me today? First you try to give me a heart attack and now you're trying to give me a boner?" He starts the truck and begins to back out of the driveway as he shakes his head at me.

"I like giving you boners. Speaking of bones, look at the house now, at dusk. Spine-chilling," I say. "I wonder if kids have always been scared of this house, like you see in the movies."

"Yeah. I can't wait till we find out more about this place. Now, would you kindly remove your hand before I bring you back inside and have my way with you? Don't start something you can't finish."

"Oh, sorry," I chuckle and move my hand away from his shorts.

"Alright. Where to now, pray tell."

"Don't know. Let's get out of here though. Just drive. Find a place nearby to figure out the next clue."

He backs out of the driveway and heads north down McLeary, crosses some railroad tracks, and pulls off into the parking lot of a business that has obviously closed for the day.

I get the clue list out of my purse and dig for the keychain. It's pink and round, about one inch in diameter. The number 1268 is printed in white on a green frame. "Okay, let's see here. 'Go north to Glade Valley and find the office of post, the box for this key holds a letter from a ghost.'" I gasp. "Oh. Do you think it's from her?"

"Could be. So I wonder how far this Glade Valley is from here. I'm assuming it's in North Carolina." He punches the city into the GPS.

"Crap, it's like four hours away. Babe, I know you're tired, that's too far to drive tonight. We wouldn't get there till almost midnight. And all the towns near here look too small for a decent hotel chain, without backtracking or going too far out of the way. It looks like Charlotte is only about two hours north though. Can you do that? Or you want me to drive?"

"Oh, you got jokes, huh? Good one. No, I don't need you to drive. You're funny. And yeah, I can do two hours. See what you can find in Charlotte for us to stay in tonight," Clay says.

I look up the hotels in Charlotte and book a king suite at a nice hotel. "Okay, we're all set. Thank goodness you're okay to make this two hour drive, because literally, there is no other big city past that on our route up to Glade Valley. Hooray for Charlotte."

"God bless Charlotte."

I scroll through my playlists, for the last time as music manager, and look for something that will help keep Clay awake and focused. I decide on my *Good Mood Ditties* list. "Send Me on My Way" by Rusted Root starts playing.

"I gotta hand it to you, Lynn, your music hasn't been that bad. But, tomorrow…get ready for some guitar solos."

"Can't wait." Sarcasm: one of my many talents. But I know he's chomping at the bit for some Metallica. He's been a good sport this week. I close my eyes. At some point I drift off, despite the upbeat tempo of the music playing.

"Babe." I can barely hear Clay, he sounds miles away. "Lynn. Come on, love, wake up. We're here." I open my eyes.

"Wow, that was fast," I say as I stretch.

"Yeah, for you," he says, as he leans over and kisses my cheek. "C'mon."

I unbuckle my seatbelt and hop out of the truck. Clay gets our suitcase out and I grab our toiletries bag and my purse. We check in and head up to our suite for the night.

"We should shower," I tell Clay. "We need to get that old-house funk off of us. I'm not going to bed all grimy with one-hundred-year-old dust all over me."

"Yeah, that was my plan, too," he says. "You can go ahead. If you don't go first, you'll fall back asleep and I'll never get you awake to shower. And I'm not sleeping next to a dirty woman."

"I thought you liked it when I was dirty." I wink at him.

"Touché. Now, get your dirty ass in the shower."

I get in and take a long, hot shower. The steam encircles me. I close my eyes, take a deep breath, and relax. I let the warm vapor shroud me and do its thing to detoxify my body, open my pores, and relieve the tension in my muscles. This is so calming, but I need to get out soon before Clay falls asleep.

I get out and yell at Clay that I'm finished and he can take his turn. He doesn't answer. I get dressed and find him asleep on the couch. I knew it. I walk over and kiss him on his neck. "Clay," I whisper. "Wake up and go shower." He stirs. "Come on, you. I'm not sleeping next to a dirty man."

He smiles, his eyes still closed. "I'll show you dirty," he says as he tries to grab my boobs.

I move out of his reach. "Save it for later. Go. Now. Go." He doesn't budge. So I stand in front of him and take off my nightshirt. "Clay. Open your eyes." He does. He's up now. He reaches for me again and I run to the other side of the room by the bed and put my shirt back on. "Get in the shower. I'll be right here when you get out. Waiting for you." I crawl into bed. However unintended, I drift off to sleep again.

I'm slightly awakened by Clay turning off the lamp. He gets into bed and I don't think he even bothered with getting dressed. He slides next to me, my eyes still closed. He kisses my eyelids and traces my lips with his tongue. I kiss him in return. He reaches below the covers and strokes my center through my panties. I remove my shirt. He throws the covers back and exposes me. Clay kneels down on the bed with my body between his legs. He leans down and draws my breast to his mouth. I rub my hands through his hair, then my nails up his back. He shudders and presses himself against my bikinis and rocks in slow motion. He kisses his way down my stomach and grabs my underwear, taking his time sliding them down my legs. My thighs are marked with gentle kisses that follow the trail of my panties. Hot chills race from my head to my toes on a zipline. Clay repeats the exchange of kisses back up my legs and pauses at my core. He teases me with his tongue, just for a few seconds. So not fair. He stipples my belly with his lips as he finally gets back to mine. Lying next to me, he touches all the right places. He knows just the ones. He always has. As we kiss, I feel for him and take hold of his hardness. I move my hand up and down as he is moving fingers in and out. Just when I think he's about to reach his peak, I stop. He bolts upright and the moonlight reveals his face, mouth agape, eyes blinking like a neon sign in need of repair. Then I sit up, too, and push him back down. Clay's face relaxes and he lets out a chuckle that exemplifies sweet relief. I straddle him and we unite. We lock hands and our movements are in sync. We erupt together, which almost never happens. Must have been all that steam from the shower, clearing my mind and improving my circulation. I drop onto Clay's chest, the two of us panting.

Chapter 38

I WAKE UP TO Clay brushing my hair behind my ear and kissing me on the cheek.

"Rise and shine, valentine," he says. "Time to get up."

"What time is it?" I ask.

"Eightish."

"Okay. Fine." I turn over on my side and look at him. He's got his head resting in the palm of his hand, propped up by his elbow on the pillow. I trace the nail of my index finger down his chest. "Last night was great. We never finish at the same time."

"Yeah, I love it when that happens. We're good together, babe."

"Really good. I want to put a steam shower in our bathroom when we get back."

"Okay. Random. But okay, it's yours." He kisses me and then slaps me on my naked bottom. "Come on, woman, up and at 'em. Let's hit the road."

We get in the truck and the first thing Clay does is shake his phone at me. He can't wait to start cranking his music for a change. "Let's rock," he says, as he dons a pair of his new sunglasses that he picked up from Junkman's yesterday. He gets the truck running, turns up the volume, and hits the play button. "Man in the Box" by Alice In Chains starts and jostles me fully awake. I'm having flashbacks of coffee spilling on my hand. I shake my head and laugh at him.

"Oh no, Clay," I say. "I just realized I didn't get my North Carolina welcome sign."

"I got you covered, love. I pulled over for you while you were knocked out. I did the best I could, but it was dark. It's a little blurry."

"Do you know how much I love you right now?" He gives me his phone to find the picture. It's not bad. "Clay, that's good, it's not that blurry. Thank you, babe. That was so sweet. I can't believe I didn't wake up when you stopped."

"Well, luckily the interstate wasn't that busy, otherwise I wouldn't have been able to pull over. We may have had to get it at another time."

"You're my hero. Okay, no more crossing state lines at night anymore. Deal?" I ask.

"Deal."

We travel the short distance of only about an hour and a half until we get to the Glade Valley, North Carolina post office. It's a small building. It doesn't look like a post office at all, more like a little house, with cobble stones for bricks and a chimney on the roof. A post office with a fireplace? How cozy is that? We go in and greet the postal clerk and look for box 1268.

"There it is," Clay says.

I get the key out and unlock the box. The only thing in there is one large brown envelope. I reach in and take it. And then the tears start.

"Clay, it is from Aunt Mitzi. At least I think so. It's her handwriting, but there's no return address. It's addressed to us, here. Postmarked four years ago."

"Oh my God. This has just been sitting there that long?" He goes back over to the postal clerk and asks, "Ma'am, can you tell me how long this box has been rented for? Number 1268?"

"Oh? 1268? The Santini box?"

"Yes," he says.

"About five years. I've only seen them the one time they came to open it. They never get any mail, nobody ever comes to check it for them. Only junk mail comes, so I started throwing it all out after it wouldn't fit in there anymore. There's just one piece of mail in the box that looks legitimate. Are you relatives?"

"Yes," I tell her. "Clay and Lynn Sinclair, her niece and nephew."

"You're the addressees. Oh, I've been wondering how this would turn out. So glad to know you're finally getting your package."

I wipe my eyes and tell Clay we need to go somewhere else. I can't read this here. The envelope has more than just a few pages in it. I can tell by the weight. I know I will be shedding some more tears. I doubt there are any hotels around here, but I cross my fingers as I look online and find a bed and breakfast. I give my phone to Clay. He thanks the clerk again for her help on our way out. We get back in the truck and he drives to the B&B.

Chapter 39

THE GLADE VALLEY Bed and Breakfast is only about seven minutes away. It's a beautiful log cabin style home with a wraparound porch, set on top of a hill, with the gorgeous Blue Ridge Mountains for a backdrop. The view looks like a postcard.

Clay goes inside to see if there are any vacancies, though I can't imagine this place would be full, given the remote area of North Carolina we are in. Then again, a lot of people search these places out, just for that reason. And it is the weekend, so we have that going against us too. Please let there be a room available. I see him coming back to the truck and I start to get out, but he shakes his head 'no.' Great. Just fricking great. He gets in and starts the truck.

"They're all booked?" I ask.

"Yes."

"Shit." I start to cry again. I know I need to be somewhere relaxed to read this letter from Aunt Mitzi. I know we can't be on the road for this. I know I'll need Clay for his hugs and comfort. Dammit. Of all the times for a place to be booked up.

"Babe. It's okay." But it's not. "Come here." He reaches over the center console of the truck and wipes my tears away. "Hey, I've got something better. Our own secluded cabin. The B and B has one and rents it out too.

And it's vacant. I'm just going to drive to it, down the way there. It's going to be okay."

"Seriously? Oh, thank God. I wouldn't be able to wait much longer to read this and I really didn't want to do it on the road. Okay. Good. I'm okay."

He turns around and drives down a limestone path that leads to the cabin, which is about seventy-five yards away. Our own private little getaway. I'm so grateful that I breathe a huge sigh of relief followed by a couple of quiet tears. We get our bags out of the truck and walk towards the cabin, down the quaint passage of steps. On the way there, I notice just how peaceful it is. Trees blow in the wind, birds chirp, and water streams in the distance. I could live here.

We make our way inside. Wow. This place is just what I needed. Poetic. Organic. Bucolic. The cabin is decked out in hardwood floors, a planked cathedral ceiling, and walls lumbered with such a light wood that I can't tell if it's natural or painted. Pastoral scents of cedar, smoky ash, and honeysuckle fill my nose. My tension melts. There's a full kitchen, bathroom, and living room downstairs. A massive floor-to-ceiling stone fireplace separates the living area from the kitchen. Upstairs, I see a loft bedroom. "Can you please make us some coffee, babe? I have a feeling I'm going to need some. I'm a bit drowsy."

"Sure thing, love."

"Thank you. I need to get comfortable, so I'm gonna head up to make my nest in the bed."

"I'll put the pot on and be up shortly." Clay gives me a quick kiss and I grab our toiletries bag to bring with me.

I take off my shoes and realize there's a half bath up here too. I splash my face with water. Holy shit! It's frigid and it freaking stings. The water stabs my face like tiny stilettos made of icicles and I let out a breathy gasp. I'm taken back to my teenage years, when Nikki and I used to dare each other to jump into her swimming pool after sitting in the hot tub for an hour. That kind of gasp. I don't think I need coffee anymore. I'm wide awake. I catch my breath and pat my face dry.

I walk over to the bed. Its headboard is against the backside of the stone cladding of the fireplace. The handmade quilt on the bed has pastel shades of pink and green in what's known as the pineapple pattern in the quilting world. I only know that because Aunt Mitzi made one in the same pattern with a bunch of my favorite colors and gave it to me for my high school graduation. I even helped her quilt it, unbeknownst to me. I miss those times. Sometimes I would spend a weekend with her when she would have her quilting room all set up. We'd sit and quilt for hours…talking, laughing, crying…and snacking on what she always called her 'quilting cookies.' Those shortbread cookies with sugar sprinkled on them that come in those blue tin cans. I bet you know the ones I'm talking about. Those cookie tins would inevitably spend the rest of their lives holding nothing but sewing supplies. Aunt Mitzi would tell me stories about my grandmother and how close they were, tales about my great-grandparents and growing up during The Great Depression, and snippets of her young life with Uncle Sid that taught me lessons in life, happiness, and love.

Clay comes up with a mug of coffee for each of us and hands me mine. I take a sip and set it on the bedside table. I sit further back at the head of the bed against the pillows and stretch my legs out straight. Clay puts his coffee on the chest of drawers, near the foot of the bed. He sits at the end of the bed and gets in the same position as I'm in, but leans back on his hands and wraps both of his legs around one of mine. I smile at him.

"Are you ready for this, Lynn?" he asks.

"Yes." I open the envelope and there's a manila folder inside. I open the folder and find yellowed laminated newspaper articles with the same headlines that we got from the old bus station in Athens, along with a lengthy letter from Aunt Mitzi. "Whoa. I guess we're going to get some answers about these headlines."

"See? I told you Aunt Mitzi would have made sure we saw these," Clay says. "I suppose she thought there was a chance that we wouldn't have found them at the bus station."

"She was almost right. Man, she really thought ahead, huh? Didn't want to take any chances." I begin to read out loud to Clay. "Here we go.

"'My darling Lynn and sweet Clay,

'First off, these articles are the same ones you were meant to

find in the bus station in Athens, Georgia. I do hope you were able to find them, but if not, read the headlines before you finish this letter.

'I know you have so many questions, and I promise, I'm going to do my best to try and guess what they are, and answer them for you. I'll start at the beginning – the postcard of the Field Building in Chicago addressed to your grandmother. The message, as best as I can recall, said something about telling Mama and Papa that I was okay and it wasn't what they thought. Well, they thought one of three things: either that I had run off and married Sid without their blessing, that I was pregnant and went away to have the baby in secret and give it up (which I would have never done, regardless of my age and marital status at the time...you know that now), or that I was involved in something dangerous and/or illegal.

'Here's a little background: Sid and I had not even started dating yet. I barely knew him, except from seeing him around town from my going to the bank for Mama and Papa, and his coming into the grocery store a few times. The more I went to the bank, our pleasantries went from 'how's the weather' to 'how are you' and then one day he said he had a job opening and asked if I was interested. I could tell he was wondering if I was interested in more than just a job. And I was. I took the job without even giving Mama and Papa notice. I thought they would be happy and proud of me, because I would be earning money, and be able to bring more to the family. But they weren't. Papa did not get along well with Mr. Santini of the bank, and didn't approve of my working for him. Sid became guilty by association, even though Mama and Papa didn't know him at all. So, we had our differences, but eventually, they came to accept my working for the Santini family. After all, it was a good salary, and we really needed the money. We were still trying to recover from the Depression. Minimum wage was thirty cents an hour, and Mr. Santini offered to pay me forty-five. I couldn't say no.

'I had been working there a couple of weeks when an opportunity came up for Sid and me to go to Chicago for a

two-week long business trip. Or at least, what I thought was a business trip. I told Mama and Papa about it, I was so excited. It would be the first time I ever left the state of Louisiana. But they would not let me go. They didn't think it was proper for me to go on an unchaperoned trip with a man I barely knew. They still thought of me as a kid. Combined with their distaste and distrust for the Santini family, their answer was a hard NO. "It's not safe!" Papa yelled. I tried to tell them that it was my job and they were being irrational and stubborn, that they just didn't want their baby girl to spread her wings and fly. "You're not being fair! I'm almost eighteen!" I yelled back. But they wouldn't hear any of it.

'Even though they forbade me, I didn't listen. I was intrigued and curious about Chicago. The more I thought about it, the more I wanted to go. So I snuck off and went anyway. But I had very mixed emotions about what I was doing. I wanted to see the world, I wanted to impress my boss, I wanted to get to know Sid better, but I hated lying to Mama and Papa. I'd never disobeyed them before. But it was my choice. And I believe I made the right one.

'When we got to Chicago, we checked into our rooms and I rang home right away to let Mama and Papa know I was there. (It was a very fancy hotel, each room had their own phones). I was afraid to talk to them, but I had to let them know I was okay. Thank God Rita answered the phone. What a relief that was for me! That's when she told me Mama and Papa thought I ran off and got married or I was pregnant or in danger. Then someone knocked on my door. I had to hang up because I didn't want to leave your grandmother on hold since collect calls were very expensive. I didn't get to tell her that none of those were the reason I left, hence the postcard.

'We had very explicit instructions for us to go to the Field Building, meet with some people, and have some papers signed. I thought it had to do with the bank business, since we worked for the bank, and we were going to a bank. Sid told me to let him do all the talking, I was just there as sort of a buffer, to look

pretty, so that the people we were meeting would be nicer. I didn't understand. I was young and naive.

'There were several meetings over the course of the two weeks. All of the men spoke Italian, I had no idea what they were saying. Voices were raised, tempers flared. That needs no interpretation. At one of the meetings, I glanced at one of the papers and everything was typed in Italian, but I noticed the name Alphonse Capone. I couldn't believe it. You know, back then, the mob was very prevalent, especially in Chicago. Were we in fact there because of the mob? Was Papa right? Was my safety in jeopardy? I was so confused. I felt lied to and used and manipulated. And I was. But not how I thought.

'That night, at our hotel, I told Sid what I saw and I demanded to know what was going on and if my life was at risk. He assured me it wasn't. I made him explain or I was going to quit the bank and take the next bus back home. He didn't want that to happen, so he told me the truth.

'Mr. Santini had been a confidential informant for the FBI. He was one of the whistleblowers on part of Al Capone's gang. This ties in to the articles you have. You won't find Mr. Santini's name in the papers though. He had been sworn to secrecy, and put under a form of protection, which is what the papers we brought with us were about. Mr. Santini had signed his portion of all the documents: affidavits, testimonies, evidence reports, recounts, statements, non-disclosure agreements, etc. He was scared for his life in Chicago, therefore, he couldn't make the trip himself. I was shocked to say the least.

'It took nearly ten years of bureaucratic red tape to get it all done. Al Capone wasn't even the mob boss anymore when we went to Chicago. His time as mob boss ended the minute he went to prison (but he remained very powerful behind bars in other ways). The Chicago Outfit that Capone built was still prevalent, run by several men that were under Capone at the time of his imprisonment, but it was done a lot quieter. Big Al had finished his time in prison by the time we went to Chicago, but he had

been hospitalized and was in no shape to get back into the mob. (Many years later, we found out that he was very sickly, and died a slow and debilitating death from complications of syphilis, at his home in Miami, Florida).

'*I was surprised that Sid had trusted me enough to tell me all of this information. He didn't have to. This was big. He risked his own life by telling me the truth, at least the truth as he knew it. I was sworn to secrecy myself, by him, and this is the first time I'm telling anyone about that trip in its entirety. Sid said that he would have never suggested I go on the trip if he had any inkling my life would be in danger. He said I meant too much to him. I was so enamored with Sid at that moment, you can guess what happened after that. We had our first kiss. Sid and I fell in love on that trip. He was my first and only love.*

'*Before we left Chicago, we decided to secretly being courting each other. When I got back, Mama and Papa were not happy with me, but they were glad I was home, safe and sound. I told them that we went up there for meetings and to have some papers signed, which was true. I told them I also went to some classes for training and that's why we were there so long, which was not true. But Mr. Santini paid me an extra one hundred dollars for my time. I immediately gave the bonus to Mama and Papa, which seemed to soften the blow.*

'*Sid started coming to the store more often on weekends when I was off from the bank, and Mama and Papa would be polite, but never friendly. This went on for about six months. Even though I was eighteen by then, I was still not ready to tell them about us. It was hard to keep it a secret. It was really difficult for me to see them be so impersonal towards Sid. I loved him so much and I knew what a good person he was. Do you know how hard it was to try to spend time together? It was tricky. Sometimes we'd get lucky and be in the bank vault together with nobody else around. We would sneak a couple of kisses in. Sid was always a perfect gentleman, never tried anything further.*

'*One day, after I finally couldn't take Mama and Papa's*

indifference towards Sid any longer, I told them we were in love. They were furious. But, there was nothing they could do. They still believed that Mr. Santini was involved with the mob. And he was, to a certain extent. Only because, being in the bank business, he knew where money was going and who it was coming from. He had connections in Chicago. His connections had connections, and they all talked him into helping them blow the cover off Capone and his cohorts. But he could never say a word.

'He knew what some of the people in Baywood and the surrounding areas, like Pride, thought of him, Mama and Papa included. He was never discourteous to anyone, regardless of how other people treated him. Because he knew the truth, and knew how it looked to the outside. Mama and Papa figured all his money had to have come from being in the mafia, even though Sid's grandfather, a self-made man, is the one who opened the first bank in the town, long before anybody knew anything about the mob.

'Finally, after nearly a year of begging and pleading for my parents' blessing of marriage, they granted it and Sid and I got married. I did not want to marry him without their blessing. You just didn't do that back then. The longer time went on, and Mama and Papa began to really get to know Sid, they came to love him. I was so thankful for that.

'I didn't think things could get better for us, until we adopted our first baby. Which brings me to your visit to Clarksdale, and I will give you more information on that later. I hope this has cleared up a few questions for you. I love you, my sweet darlings and I'm watching over you. You're making me very proud.

Love always, Aunt Mitzi

'P.S. Please go back to the post office in Glade Valley and cancel my mailbox, as it no longer holds use for me.'

"Oh, Clay." I can barely get the words out before he untangles our legs and I am in his arms. We lie together at the head of the bed. I'm kind of surprised at myself though, I'm not crying. "I never would have guessed that Aunt Mitzi and Uncle Sid had to go through so much to be together. That makes me so sad for them, knowing what the truth was and they couldn't tell a soul. Keeping their relationship a secret…that must have been rough."

"I'm sure it wasn't easy. Nothing was easy back then. But luckily, it all turned out for the best. So, do you feel better, love? Did you get your questions answered?" he asks.

"Most of them. Except, we still don't know how that postcard ended up in a piece of furniture at Houmas House."

"Oh, wow, that's true. Maybe we'll find that out later too."

"Maybe. And, you were right. Sort of."

"About what?"

"There was a little bit of lovin' goin' on in Chicago between them. I can't believe they had to sneak around for so long. Getting their affection in any chance they could."

"I know the feeling," he says. He kisses me and pulls me close.

"Well, I guess it's a good thing we're still in Glade Valley and didn't leave town," I say.

"What do you mean?"

"We've gotta go back and close her post office box."

We both laugh and then proceed with an afternoon delight.

Chapter 40

AFTER OUR MID-DAY mattress dance and short nap, we go downstairs. Clay puts another pot of coffee on while I get the cipher with the clues so we can figure out our next destination. My sexy, shirtless husband suggests that we go out on the porch to enjoy our fresh coffee in the outdoor tranquility. I agree and bring him our coffee mugs. I ask him to look in the box of keys for number eight while he waits for the coffee to finish brewing.

I amble out the door to the charming porch. It overlooks a creek, and the babble of the water is so soothing, lightly rushing around large rocks and driftwood that have gotten stuck in its wake. I sit down in one of the two rocking chairs and wait for Clay. He soon joins me outside, hands me my mug, and looks down at the stream while sipping his coffee.

"This is the life," he says. "I could get used to this."

"Me too."

Clay takes the seat next to me. I feel like the world is ours right now. As if we are the only people on the planet at this moment. All we can hear are birds chirping back and forth, leaves rustling from a light breeze, and the murmur of the brook below us. We are completely blissful and content, surrounded by the calm and solitude of the mountains, the flora, and the fauna. Nature at its best.

"I never want to leave," I say to Clay. "This place is spectacular. I don't mean this cabin in particular, though I do love it. But, I mean, North Carolina and the Blue Ridge Mountains as a whole. Let's buy our mountain cabin here. I always thought I wanted to be in the Smokies, but that was before I saw these peaks and valleys. And right by the Blue Ridge Parkway? I don't think it gets much better than that. I've always wanted to drive down the BRP in the fall. Can you imagine the beauty, with all the leaves changing colors? Let's do it, babe. Please?"

"Sure thing, love. Whatever you want. I agree though, North Carolina is really nice. I could live here. At least for a few weeks a year as a getaway for us," he replies.

"Yeah, I mean, I don't want to move here permanently. I love having Aunt Mitzi's house. That's home."

"Yep. It is. But home for me is anywhere you are," he says.

"Aww, babe. I love you."

"I know. Okay, I got the key," he says as he dangles it in front of me. It's one of those old hotel keychains, in a diamond shape with rounded edges.

"You ready to go through the clue?" I ask.

"Lay it on me."

"Alright, the clue says, 'In the city formerly known as Big Lick—'"

"Big Lick?" Clay asks with a laugh.

"That's what it says," I snicker.

"I'll show you a 'big lick,'" he says.

"You already did." I give him an air kiss.

"I did, didn't I? And how was it?"

"You mean you couldn't tell?"

"I wanna hear you say it." He meets my eyes.

"Spellbinding."

He smiles and nods, proud of his sexual prowess. "Okay, sorry, babe, proceed."

I shake my head at him, clear my throat, and start over. "Listen up now, goofball. 'In the city formerly known as Big Lick, find its hotel and ask for Mick. In the fancy Governor's Suite, there's a baseboard that holds a special treat. Carefully remove it, it should be ajar. But if it isn't, use the crowbar.'"

"Crowbar? She didn't leave us a crowbar," he says.

"Maybe we'll get it from Mick? You think?" I ponder.

"Maybe so. Guess we'll see. I have one in my truck, but the way the clue reads, it sounds like we should have found one from her or something. Otherwise, she would've just said 'use a crowbar.' What do you think?"

"It does sound like that, now that you mention it."

"So where is this old Big Lick?"

"I'm not sure, let me search online." I pull the internet up. "Roanoke, Virginia. That was easy."

"Good job. Now what about the hotel? She didn't give us a name, just 'its hotel.' There can't be just one hotel in Roanoke. What's your take on that?" Clay asks.

"Hmm, I'm not sure. Let me do some more digging." Google is my friend. "There's a hotel simply called The Hotel Roanoke, so that must be it."

"Alright. We'll leave tomorrow morning."

Chapter 41

W E FINISH THE evening just talking on the porch, drinking our coffee, and dreaming about what kind of mountain cabin we want. The sun has gone down, but it's not quite dark yet. We head back inside and decide to take a bath in the luxurious jetted tub for two. It's one of those big, corner garden tubs. Clay runs our water and fills it up. There are candles around the inner ledge by the wall and he lights them as I get undressed. I notice two fluffy robes hanging on the wall next to the shower stall. What a nice touch.

Clay gets in. "Ahh...oh man, this feels great. What are you waiting for, babe?"

"I'm right behind you." I step into the tub and sit across from him. I dunk the back of my head in to get all my hair wet and sit back up.

"You're too far. Come lean on me." He spreads his legs and I move and get in between them, my back against his chest. I start soaping up a washcloth. He takes it from me and finishes lathering it up. He gathers my hair and brings it around my neck to rest on my front and leans me up to wash my back. After he rinses me, he brings me down to his chest again then goes on to wash the front top half of my body. He lingers on my breasts and then forgoes the towel all together. "I'm not fond of the barrier," he says, as he continues massaging my boobs with his bare hands, full of soap.

He splashes water on me to get all the suds off and kisses my neck. "You're so beautiful," he whispers. "I love you, Lynn."

"I know," I whisper back.

He grabs the shampoo and works it through my long, wet hair. I don't know what it is, but there's something so romantic about him washing my hair. He's so gentle, the way he's massaging my scalp with his fingertips, lathering his way down the length of my wavy mane. He leans me down into the tub to rinse it out, and I close my eyes so he doesn't accidentally get shampoo in them. He whispers, "Babe, look at me. Trust me." I do, and I stare up at him. He's so careful not to get the soap in my eyes. It's an incredibly tender moment. We've taken baths together before, but never after having been through something as emotionally draining as we did earlier this afternoon. This is a new feeling. A new experience. We're not talking out loud, but our body language and our eyes are speaking volumes to each other. I can see the love in his eyes. I can feel the love in his touch. I can hear the love in his whispers.

A shield of strength and security covers me. We are naked. Our skin engaged, no barriers between us. But it's not enough. I need more. I want to be closer. Figuratively fastened forever. This must be what they call a spiritual connection. This is a whole new level of love. Ethereal. Transcendental. Existential. I know I've said it before, and I'll say it again, but, God, I am so in love with this man. Unequivocally. Unambiguously. Unconditionally. I don't want to ever leave his side. But sometimes I'm scared that he will leave mine.

After Clay finishes with my hair, he signals me to sit up, and gives me a delicate kiss. Softer than the first time we ever kissed, which was the first moment I knew I was in trouble.

Boy, was I in trouble. I knew my life would never be the same. Sergeant Clay Sinclair put a spell on me less than an hour after I had laid eyes on him.

In the parking lot of that car dealership, when he defined the moment that we exchanged names as 'knowing each other,' he asked me for my phone number and I gave it to him.

"I'll call you," he said.

"Okay." *No you won't.* I got in the rental car I had picked up for work and waved good-bye to him as he watched me drive away. I held his eyes in the rearview mirror until I had to turn.

I had to work late that afternoon, and when I finally got home, I put my stuff down and listened to my answering machine messages. I opened my refrigerator to look for something to eat while they played. One from my mom, one from my sister, and one from Annie. Then came Clay's voice. I froze. He actually called. The same day we met. *This guy does not play games.* My newborn feelings for him escalated at that exact moment. I slammed the fridge door shut and ran over to the machine to rewind it so I could concentrate on his every word. *Hey…Lynn? It's Clay. From earlier. I just wanted to say that it was really great to meet you today. It's about 6:00. I'm sorry I missed you. I'll try again later. Bye.* My heart dropped. I was thrilled that he called but disappointed that I'd missed it. I doubted he would call back again that night. I turned my attention back to the task at hand: finding something to eat. It was almost seven and I was starving. I reheated some pizza and sat down on the couch to eat and watch TV.

At 7:05, my phone rang again. Butterflies. *Is it him? Please let it be him.* I answered the phone.

"Hello?" I asked into the receiver.

"Lynn?" It was him. My heart skipped a few beats.

"Yes. Who is this?" I didn't want to seem too eager.

"Um…it's Clay. From earlier today?" he sounded defeated that I didn't know who he was. Then I remembered, he didn't play games, so I wasn't going to either. I just wasn't used to that.

"I know, I'm sorry. I'm just kidding. I recognized your voice."

"We barely know each other and you're already giving me a hard time? Maybe I should just let you go," he said.

"No, I'm sorry, I just—"

"Ha. Got you back. Now we're even."

"Touché, Clay. Touché."

"So," he said, "what are you doing?"

"Right now?"

"Yeah, right now."

"Sitting on my couch about to eat some leftover pizza."

"Stop. Let me take you out for a real meal."

"What?" *Is he really asking me out? The same day we met?* "But it's Tuesday."

"Soo…what? Tuesdays are only for leftover pizza?"

"What? No," I laughed, "I just…it's just…usually…"

"Usually dates are saved for weekends. Is that what you mean?"

"Yeah."

"That's three days away. I can't wait that long to see you again. And you'll learn, I'm not usual. I play by my own rules."

"So I've noticed."

"Does that mean you're okay with dinner tonight?" he asked again. "You like Italian, right? I mean, you're eating pizza, so I can only assume."

"Um, okay, Clay. I'm going to be straight with you. I am interested in going out to dinner with you, really, I am. Just not tonight. I'm sorry. I had a shitty day. I had to work late and I'm really tired. I would not be very good company."

"Are you telling me you had a completely shitty day?" he asked.

"Well, no, you were the best part of it. I mean that."

"That's what I wanted to hear." His tone of voice let me know he was smiling. "So, Friday, then? Are you good with that?"

"Friday is perfect."

"Good. Seven o'clock?"

"Yeah, I can be ready for seven. And to answer your question, yes, I do like Italian."

"Okay, good. Italian it is."

"Thank you, Clay."

"For what, Lynn?" I loved the way he said my name.

"For not playing games."

"That's not my style. I'll go ahead and let you finish your cold pizza. I'll call you tomorrow."

"Okay." My heart shrunk. I didn't want to stop talking to him so soon after he called.

"Goodnight, Miss Boudreaux."

"Goodnight, Sergeant Sinclair."

I immediately called Annie and told her all about Clay and how I was excited but a bit panicky about my impending date. I hadn't been on a first date in a good while.

"Will you please come over Friday after work and help me pick out something to wear? I don't want to overdress. Or underdress."

"Of course. Where are y'all going?" Annie asked.

"I'm not sure exactly. Somewhere Italian I think."

"He's taking you to Italy? Who is this guy?" she joked.

"Very funny. He asked me if I liked Italian. So, for all I know, we could be going somewhere as casual as a pizza place or as fancy as Gino's."

"Well, don't worry. We'll find you something fabulous to wear. I'll bring over a few pieces too."

"Awesome. Thanks, girl. Now, tell me what's going on with you. How are things with Martin?"

She filled me in on her love life and we chatted for about an hour.

That Friday evening, I was restless, pacing, and clumsy. *What is wrong with me?* My nerves were making me nauseous. I don't know why. I had talked to Clay every night on the phone since the day we met. For hours. I felt like I'd known him forever. He was that easy to talk to. I could be myself, didn't have to try to impress him or prove something to him. I was comfortable. But that night, I was anxious. I hadn't seen him since we met, and even though it had only been three days, it felt like a lifetime. Weird, right?

I kept looking at the clock. *Fifteen more minutes.* I went to the bathroom and checked my makeup again. Relocated some wild hairs and sprayed some more Aqua Net. *Bet you won't move now.* I looked at the clock again. *Five more minutes.*

He knocked on the door. I took a deep breath and answered it. I hoped I looked okay. Annie said I did, and best friends tell the truth, right? We settled on a little black dress of hers that she let me borrow for the night. Couldn't go wrong with that. I can still see it. The dress was sexy, but classy. A sleeveless sheath, with a bit of twinkling metallic inlay, and a slight ruffle at the hem.

"Wow," Clay said after I opened the door. He smiled. My worries vanished.

"I could say the same about you. You clean up nicely, Sergeant Sinclair."

"As do you, Miss Boudreaux. These are for you," he handed me a bouquet of my favorite flowers, lavender roses.

"Oh my gosh, they're gorgeous, thank you. How did you know?"

"Know what?"

"That these are my favorite flowers. Have you been stalking me?" I asked, teasing him.

"They are? Lucky guess."

"I'm sorry. Come in. Please. I'll put these in water and then we can go," I told him.

He did indeed drive us to the elegant Gino's Italian Restaurant. I had never been there before. I looked around and noticed that it was quite a romantic place for a first date. Lights dimmed. A glowing votive on every table. White linen tablecloths. Waiters in tuxedos. But I didn't feel uneasy at all. I was very relaxed with Clay. The waiter seated us and handed us menus and a wine list. As soon as he left, Clay grabbed my hand from across the table. That was the first time we'd touched since we'd met. The fireworks returned. *Could he be the one?*

"Thank you for saying 'yes,'" he said.

"To what?" I asked.

"Tonight. You and me."

"I don't remember saying 'yes' to *that*. What kind of girl do you think I am?"

I'm sure his face turned red. It was hard to see in the low light. But his expression did a one-eighty. Blank stare. Mouth ajar. And he let go of my hand.

"No...not...I meant..." he stammered. *Poor guy.*

"I know. I'm kidding, Clay." I smiled at him and he relaxed. Then he laughed and took my hand back.

"Touché, Lynn. Touché."

"And thank you for asking."

We looked at the menu and he asked me if I wanted a glass a wine. I wasn't really much of a wine drinker at that point in my life. I was more into beer or fruity cocktails, depending on my mood. I asked him to get me what he thought I might like. He ordered a bottle of Cabernet Sauvignon. It was the first time I had ever had Cabernet, and I've never looked back. Of course, I still drink beer, and the occasional mixed drink, but give me a glass of Cab any day.

We had a great first date. The conversation never lulled and we laughed and joked with each other. We took turns asking each other what our favorite music and movies were. Our favorite colors. What we would do if we won the lottery. While we had talked for the last three nights on the phone getting to know each other, there's something about having a conversation in person that is so much better. It's almost tangible.

After dinner, he drove down by the lakes near the LSU campus and we walked around, hand in hand. We talked, we laughed, and we playfully argued over who the best rock star of all-time was.

It was getting late, nearly midnight, and not that I had a curfew or anything, after all, I lived by myself, but I guess he could see that I was getting sleepy, so we went back to his truck and he took me home.

He walked me up to my apartment door.

"Thanks so much for tonight, I had a great time," I told him.

"You're welcome. I hope we can do it again. Soon."

"I'd really like that," I said.

"Okay, I'll talk to you tomorrow," he said, and he kissed me on the cheek.

I blushed. "Goodnight, Clay Sinclair."

"Goodnight, Lynn Boudreaux."

I unlocked the door and went inside. He was so charming. So respectful. He didn't even try to come in, or kiss me. Which I had mixed feelings about, because while I was never one to kiss on the first date, I really wanted him to kiss me. Badly.

About two minutes later, there was a soft knock on my door. I looked through the peep hole to see that it was Clay. I opened the door.

"Hey, you. Did you forget something?" I asked.

"Yeah. This." He took my face in his hands and kissed me. I knew then, that first kiss would be the last first kiss I would have for the rest of my life. It was the softest kiss I'd ever had in all of my existence. That is, until this second, in the tub of a cabin in the woods of North Carolina.

Chapter 42

THE NEXT MORNING, we get up and go back to the main house for breakfast. We sit at the table with the rest of the guests like we are one big family. Breakfast is a feast of sausage, bacon, fried eggs, scrambled eggs, homemade biscuits, grits, ham, hash browns, quiche, and more. My favorite of all the things I eat are the homemade cinnamon buns. Clay has a little taste of just about everything. He reminds me that he's a country man, and country men eat big breakfasts every chance they get. It all looks so delicious, but I don't have room in my stomach for a whole smorgasbord. In addition to the cinnamon bun, I eat some bacon, scrambled eggs, and a biscuit with homemade apple butter.

The owners of the bed and breakfast are so kind and treat us all like kinfolk. We talk with the other lodgers and everyone at the table gives their own account for what brings them to Glade Valley. They are all captivated by our story and curious as to how it will all come together. They encourage me to start a blog so they can keep up with our progress. I tell them about the journal Clay bought me and how I'm writing everything in there, but I think the blog is kind of a good idea too, so I may do it. Clay and I are both surprised at how much they all want to stay informed of our expedition. I get their emails and tell them that I will try and start a blog and contact them when and if I do.

After breakfast, we say our good-byes, hugging each other like we're all old friends. We promise the owners that we will return one day.

Clay and I go back to the post office to cancel Aunt Mitzi's box. The same clerk is there, and we tell her a little about what we are doing. We let her know that Aunt Mitzi and Uncle Sid have passed on, so we need to close the mailbox. She obliges and wishes us well on our travels.

We get back in the truck and Clay puts the address of the Hotel Roanoke into the GPS.

"Look, babe," I say. "It's only a few minutes longer if we take the Blue Ridge Parkway. Let's go that way. I know it's not fall, but I'd still love to drive up that way for as long as we can."

"Sure thing, love." He pushes the button to reroute the course of direction.

"Thanks."

Then he gets his phone out. "Now, how 'bout some Rush?" He's about to press the play button on his screen.

"How 'bout no?"

"What? Why? You love Rush."

"Yes, I do. But it's a new day. My turn again."

"Shit. Alright. Just please don't hit me with disco."

"Okay, deal. I'll surprise you."

"Great," he says, none too excited.

I pull up my *Days of Our Lives* list and "New Moon on Monday" by Duran Duran comes on.

"Okay," he says, "I guess I can live with that. I did go through a painful New Wave phase for a minute in the early eighties."

"New Wave isn't painful. The hairstyles maybe, but the music? No way. Right up there with Disco for me. Anyway, you like it. See? Don't be so quick to reject my stuff."

"I'd never reject your stuff. I'm kind of fond of it. I love all of your stuff," he says as he eyeballs me from head to toe.

"Is that so?" I smile at him.

"Affirmative, ma'am."

"How much?"

"So much, that I would give up watching football if that was the only way to touch your stuff again."

"Whoa. That's some serious love."

"Ask me a serious question, get a serious answer."

"Touché, Sinclair."

We drive for about thirty minutes until we hit the Virginia state line and Clay pulls over so I can get my picture. "Sunday Bloody Sunday" by U2 plays in the background.

"So are you going to start a blog?" Clay asks.

"I don't know. Maybe. I'd have to spend more time on the laptop so it would take time away from us. I'm not sure I want to sacrifice that."

"Well, just think about it, babe. I told you before, I think it's a great idea."

"You saying you don't like spending quality time with me? Talking to me?"

"You can put in a 'comments' section." He laughs and I throw a balled up napkin at him. "Lynn, this whole trip is quality time with you. And of course I love talking to you. Seriously though, I think it would be fun to go back and see things visually after it's all over. I want to be able to relive this trip any time I want with my eyes, not just my memories. I'm having a blast. I know we have pictures, but while things are fresh in your mind, our minds, you can write about it and we can look at it all together later."

"I have my journal though. I don't want to stop using that. I love it."

"You don't have to. You can still use it for notes and then transfer them all to your blog later. I'll help you with the details. We can do it together."

"Okay, I guess I'll look into it. I'll definitely need your help though."

"You got it."

A few miles down the road, I take out keychain number eight again and look at the key itself. I spot something that I didn't see yesterday. I didn't give the key much thought at first, because I know they don't use actual keys in hotels anymore. For the most part, anyway. Just about every hotel has converted to the credit card style keys. I did notice that the key on this keychain wasn't etched, like it won't unlock anything, but I just figured Aunt Mitzi wanted something to put on it instead of it being an empty keychain. So I thought it was just a plain key without the grooves cut into it. But upon closer inspection, I see that it's a small, black, metal sword. At the top end of the hole where it's strung on the keychain is what looks like the end of a tiny crowbar. It has the same type of teeth that a crowbar has, but this one is a much smaller version.

"Babe. I think I just found our crowbar," I say.

"What? Where? How?"

"Look." I show it to him and he inspects it the best he can while driving.

"Holy shit. Sure is. Great eye. I can't believe I didn't catch that yesterday when I was looking at it."

"Well, it was kind of dark on the porch. I didn't see it either."

"Yeah. That's it. Let's blame it on dusk."

"I guess this really is a key of sorts," I say.

We arrive at the Hotel Roanoke around lunch time. I can hardly believe my eyes. It looks almost exactly like Aunt Mitzi's house. Our house. Jeez, will I ever get used to the fact that it's ours now? The hotel is a Tudor style, like *ours*. Except it's enormous.

Clay pulls in for valet parking. "Be careful with her," he tells the attendant as he hands him a twenty dollar bill.

"Yes, sir. She's in good hands," the valet guy says. He gets our bags out of the truck for us and puts them on a bellhop dolly.

We walk through the large carpeted vestibule and see what looks like the façade of the original building before this expansion was added. Worn cobblestone bricks are inlayed from the middle to the floor and faded, red bricks make up the top half. Judging by the look of the older portion, this hotel has been here for a long time. Maybe more than a hundred years.

The lobby itself is gorgeous. It's got an exceptional historical vibe. The huge area is elegant with dark wood walls, decorative tile flooring, antique furniture, chandeliers with little lampshades on each light, and that's just what I can see.

We go up to the check-in desk and I get right to it.

"Hi, is Mick here?" I ask the lady behind the counter, whose nametag says 'Rona.'

"Mick? I don't think he comes in until tomorrow morning. Is there something I can help you with?"

"Can you please tell me if the Governor's Suite is available? We'd like to book it," I tell Rona.

"Sure, let me check." She types into her computer. "You're in luck. It is. How many nights would you like?"

"Just tonight," Clay says. "Is it ready? We'd like to check-in early if possible."

"Um, not quite yet. Shouldn't be more than an hour though, which is still three hours before check-in time. Will that be okay?"

"That will be great, thank you," Clay tells her.

"Would you like to have lunch in The Regency Room restaurant while you wait? I can check your bags for you until your room is ready," she says.

Clay looks at me.

"I could use a drink. I'm hungry, but I don't want to eat yet," I tell him.

"Can you please point us in the direction, ma'am?" he asks Rona as he rolls the luggage cart closer to her.

"It's just through lobby. Can't miss it." She takes our suitcases and gives us a slip of paper with a number on it.

"Thank you," Clay says.

"You're most welcome."

Chapter 43

WE WALK INTO the Regency Room and the hostess seats us at a table. It's a delightful space with white linen tablecloths and various shades of blue throughout. I especially love the cobalt-blue glasses that are set on the table.

"I really just need a drink," I tell Clay. "I'm thinking maybe room service later."

"Sounds good, love. What's your poison this afternoon?"

"Just a glass of wine I think. What about you?"

"I think I'll have the same."

The waitress comes by and takes our order. "I'll be right back with your drinks," she says. She wasn't kidding. Thirty seconds later, our glasses are in front of us. Excellent service.

"To finding answers," Clay says, as he raises his glass.

"To finding answers," I repeat, and we clink our glasses together.

Clay and I enjoy our Cabernet and talk about everything we've done, everywhere we've been, everything we've collected, and everything we've learned so far. We laugh at some of the memories we've made and I make him a promise that I will never scare him again, on purpose, and he apologizes for hiding from me in the first place in that big, scary house in South Carolina.

Two glasses later, Clay realizes that it's time to go check on our room. We pay our tab and get a confirmation that our suite is ready.

We stroll into the room and it's fabulous. Of course, I expected nothing less than that from Aunt Mitzi. And besides, it's a Penthouse. The Governor's Suite. I certainly didn't believe it would be shabby. There's a living area with a fireplace, a full kitchen with a dining table, two bedrooms, two bathrooms, and my favorite part: the rooftop terrace, with spectacular views. We put our stuff down in the master bedroom.

"Wow," I say. "This Penthouse is unbelievable. So grand and cozy."

"I think it's dear."

"Dear?"

"Yeah. 'Dear Penthouse, My wife and I have smoking-hot sex as often—'"

"Is your mind *always* in the gutter?"

"Well, I'm a hot-blooded man, so…yes?"

"Put it on ice."

"That's hard." Clay chuckles.

I sigh and roll my eyes. "I'm going to the bathroom."

"Okay."

As soon as I shut the bathroom door, Clay starts singing "Hot Blooded" by Foreigner, loud enough for me to hear. Typical horndog.

I finish up and walk back out to the bedroom. "Let's get down to business."

"Ah ha. Changed your mind, did you? That 'Dear Penthouse' talk got you all randy, didn't it? I knew it," he said, and starts taking off his shirt.

"No, you goofball. Keep your clothes on. Let's find the baseboard." I laugh as I throw a pillow at him.

"I knew that," he says laughing, as he catches the pillow. "Just thought it might be worth a shot. Besides, Virginia is for lovers, right? It's their state slogan for crying out loud. We shouldn't disappoint them."

"Save it. You check the living room and I'll look around the kitchen and dining area."

We go into our separate spaces and look for a baseboard that is coming apart from the wall. I don't see anything in here. "Any luck?" I yell from the corner near the table.

"Nope. You?"

"No. You check the master and I'll check the spare room. Don't forget the bathroom."

"On it."

I search the second bedroom along the walls and don't see or feel anything off. Same for the bathroom.

"Lynn?"

"Yeah? You found something?"

"I'm not sure, come see what you think."

I rush into the master and Clay is lying on the floor, facing a small wall. He's moved a couple of chairs out of the way along with a small table and floor lamp. The curtains are wide open for the natural light. He looks back at me and smiles as I run in. "What is it?"

"Get down here on the floor with me and feel the baseboard. You can't really see anything just looking down at it."

I walk over and lower myself to his level, flush with the carpet. I see what Clay is talking about. The baseboard is a little crooked, but not by much. I feel with my hands and understand what he means. It's totally off track. "Yeah, that's something. It's painted shut though. How can we do this without damaging anything?"

"We might not be able to. We'll just be really careful, and if we damage anything, we'll let them know they can bill us for the repairs."

"Okay. Here's the crowbar key. I'm gonna let you manage that since you're the handy man. You'll know what you're doing. I'll supervise. Just be careful," I tell him.

He starts to pry the baseboard back a little and the paint starts to chip. Next, he scratches the wall. Yep, we'll be paying for a little patching up. Then, a small section of the baseboard breaks free and pops off, with barely any effort on Clay's part.

"Whoa. That was way more painless than I expected," he says.

"Good job. Okay, what's in there?" I ask.

"I can't see a thing."

"Stick your hand in."

"Negative, Mrs. Sinclair. Not without knowing what lies in wait. Did you bring your little flashlight by chance?"

"Yeah, in my purse." I get up and dig through my bag until I find it and hand it to him. Then I get back down on the floor. He shines the light in the void.

"Crap."

"What? Do you see anything?"

"Yeah, a little white box," he pushes his hand in, "but I can't reach it. My arm is too thick past my wrist. You try."

"Um, negative, Sinclair. Horror movie gauge."

"Well, find me something long and thin, then, scaredy-cat."

"How long?"

"The box is about eight inches back."

I go back into my purse to search for a ball point pen, which I'm not even sure will be long enough, but then I come across my retractable back scratcher. "Will this work?" I ask as I stretch it out to its full capacity.

"Perfect."

I'm back on the floor, holding my breath as he scoots the box out using the back scratcher as an extension of his arm. It scrapes along the concrete of the foundation under the wall.

"Is the box metal?"

"I think so," Clay says. "It's kind of heavy too. Heavy metal," he snickers.

"Ha. That makes sense. Never know, the place might have had a busted pipe over the years and flooded the room, which could've ruined it. Once again, Aunt Mitzi thought ahead."

Clay comes out with the box and it's full of dust. Who knows how long it's been hidden in the walls. He gets up and retrieves a Kleenex from the bathroom to clean it off and hands it to me. It's a small box, about four inches square. I open it up. It's a typewriter letter. An old one, round like a button. Maybe from the 1920s. The letter B.

"What in the world…"

"Well, it is another key," Clay says, turning the disk over in his fingers.

"Huh," I express, feeling a little dense. "Sure is. She's getting trickier. Do you think we're supposed to find an old typewriter in the hotel? Maybe that's what Mick is for."

"I don't know, Lynn. She said to ask Mick first. If we were supposed to find something else using this, and if it was supposed to come from Mick, she probably would have said to ask him after we found it."

"True. Okay. I'm starving, Clay. You?"

"Yeah, famished."

"Let's order some lunch now."

"Good idea, babe. What do you want?"

"Whatever, just order me something. You know what I like."

"Yes. I do." He winks at me and I smile at him.

Chapter 44

I WAKE UP TO Clay next to me on the bed, turning the TV on. I look at the clock. It's 6:30 in the evening. I can't believe I've been sleeping for four hours. I hit Clay with a pillow. "Don't we have a living room you can make that noise in?"

"Yes. But you need to wake up."

"Why?"

"Because if you don't, you'll be awake all night."

"Ugh. Okay. Did you fall asleep?"

"Yeah, 'bout an hour and a half. I've been up since four."

"What have you been doing?"

"Took a shower. Sat out on the terrace for a little bit. Called CeCe to check on her and the house. Everything's good. Sends her love."

"Why didn't you wake me sooner?"

"I tried. You grumbled and told me to leave you alone."

"I did? I don't even remember that. I'm sorry."

"It's okay. You obviously needed it. We both did. Who knew the road could wear you out like that? You feel like getting up and sitting outside? It feels nice."

"Let me wake up. Is that coffee I smell?"

"Put a pot on before I woke you. Your cup is on the bedside table."

"Thanks, babe." I sit up and drink my coffee and then take a quick shower.

The sun falls, and the sky becomes an enchanting shade of indigo. Since we had a late lunch, we decide on a plate of cheese and grapes with a bottle of wine for dinner. We eat on the terrace outside our room. Clay lights some candles and pours us each a glass of Cabernet.

The view of the mountains is spectacular from up here. You can see for miles. I get why they call these the Blue Ridge Mountains. A bluish haze hovers over the peaks in the distance. I don't know if it's the reflection from the color of the sky at dusk, or if it's an illusion. Either way, the jagged silhouettes of the far-off mountain tops are worth witnessing. At least once in your life.

I notice a large glowing star at the top of one of the nearby peaks. I can't tell if it's formed out of neon lights or bulbs though. I wonder what that's about.

"So, what do you think the significance of the typewriter letter 'B' is?" Clay asks.

"Hmm, I don't know. Baywood? Bernice?"

"Bank?" he adds, as he eats a grape and takes a sip of wine.

"Good one."

"Maybe it's nothing."

"It can't be nothing. It has to be something. Otherwise, what's the point?" I ask.

"Well, we still have a lot of miles to go. I'm sure we'll find out."

"Yeah." I finish my glass and pour myself another one.

We talk more about how beautiful it is up here and contemplate our future cabin some more. We laugh and try to come up with as many 'B' words that we can think of, some of them having nothing to do with anything, like 'birthday,' 'brick,' and 'bear.' Then Clay turns it into a dirty game.

"Balls," he says with a laugh.

I snicker and go with it. "Booty."

"Beaver."

"Bondage."

"Big, bouncing, boobies!" he exclaims. I laugh so loud that I bet the parking lot heard me.

"Okay, you need to stop, you're going to get us in trouble."

"Well, let's take this party inside then, shall we? Prove that Virginia really is for lovers. And hey, you forgot one," he says as he picks up our plate.

"What?" I ask

"Blowjob."

I roll my eyes and grab the wine.

I wake up to a bad dream. No, a nightmare. I look at my phone. It's 2:40 in the morning. I dreamed that she…that bitch, Alexa, came back. And Clay chose her over me. My breathing is accelerated. I'm sweating and jittery. My mind starts wandering. Clay is sound asleep. I get up and quietly go back out on the terrace for some fresh air, careful not to wake my husband. I lean on the railings and take a few deep breaths to calm myself down. It smells like rain.

My mind is wobbly. I can't stop thinking about that dream. It brings back more bad memories for me. Not long after we got married, I was cleaning the house one afternoon while Clay was away at a training exercise. I moved the dresser to sweep behind it and there was a crumpled piece of paper that fell to the floor. I picked it up and opened it. It was a letter, from Clay to Alexa. It made me cringe to read it, but I had to, right? I remember it word for word. Every once in a while, it rears its ugly head. Like now.

> *Alexa,*
>
> *You have no idea how much I love you, and wish you would change your mind. I can't stop thinking about you. My bed is empty without you. My heart is empty without you. I'm a wreck. I know you said for me to move on, but nobody on Earth will ever take the place of you. You are my soulmate and I miss you like crazy.*
>
> *Why are you giving up on us because of something that may*

never happen? We can't predict the future. Don't throw the baby out with the bathwater. I could just as easily be taken away by walking out the front door. Anybody could.

Don't you remember all the good times we've had? All the experiences? All the great rolls between the sheets? Nobody else will ever be able to quench my thirst and hunger the way you do.

Why are you doing this to us? I really wish you would think about this. Please, come back to me. I don't want to go on without you. If you don't, I will respect that. But just know, I'll always love you and I'll never love anyone else the way I love you. Please give us another chance.

Love, Clay

I started crying the second I began reading it. I burned it and never told Clay I found it. Obviously he never gave it to her. I consoled myself by imagining that he balled it up and threw it across the room to where it landed, stuck between the wall and the dresser, completely forgotten. Had he known it was back there, surely he would have trashed the letter for real when he got rid of all her stuff. I still wonder what made him throw it away instead of giving it to her. I'm thankful though, because what he wrote was enough to make anybody go back to anyone. But, was what he said true? Will he always love her? Did he just settle for me? Does he still think about her? Will I ever be enough for him? So many questions and fears I have, but I can't ask him, because I'm not sure I want to know the answers. I know he loves me. But, is it the same as he loved her? Is it more? Or less?

Then, my mind travels further away, and I start thinking about how hard it must have been for Aunt Mitzi and Uncle Sid to hide their relationship. I think about their babies. What happened to their babies? Why did they get taken away? That's just not fair. I cry for her and Uncle Sid, which leads to my other deep-rooted fear, and I cry for us.

I hear the door open behind me. I don't turn around. I try and hide my tears, but he knows.

"Babe. What's wrong? What are you doing out here?"

I don't answer. I hear him walking up behind me. He engulfs me in his arms and rests his chin on my shoulder. I almost shrug it off without thinking.

"Love. What is it? What's the matter, Lynn?"

"It's nothing," I can't tell him why I'm really upset. The dreadfulness I felt when I woke up made me feel so betrayed, like he was really leaving me for her. It fed into my deep-seated anxiety. I know it was just a dream, but it felt real. I don't even want him touching me right now. And that letter was most definitely real. I try to dry my eyes. I try to think of something feasible, something that Clay will believe is the reason I'm upset. "Well, it's not nothing. I couldn't sleep and came out here and just started thinking. Just about everything. Everything Aunt Mitzi and Uncle Sid went through, you know? And it makes me so sad for them. I never had a speck of knowledge that any of it ever happened. And their poor babies. What happened? It's just so heartbreaking. And then I started thinking about us, and…"

He turns me around and hugs me hard. "I know," he whispers, "I know. Come on, let's go back inside." I follow him back to bed and he lets me cry myself to sleep in his arms.

I don't know what time I fell back to sleep, but it's daylight now, and I wake up to the rain. I hate traveling in bad weather and Clay hates driving in bad weather. Who doesn't?

He's still sleeping. I hate to wake him up. He stayed up with me and soothed me until I stopped crying. But I know we've got to get up and see what's next on the list. I kiss him on his shoulder and he turns over to face me.

"Hey, love," he says in a gravelly voice.

"Mornin', babe."

"You okay? It's been a while since you broke down like that."

"Yeah. Thank you for taking care of me."

"I'll always take care of you." He rubs my arm and kisses the top of my hand.

"We should get up and get going."

"Yeah."

After I shower, I order room service for breakfast and pack up. By the time Clay gets out of the shower, breakfast is here and we sit down at the table to eat. I get the cipher out and read it to Clay.

"Ready?" He nods as he takes a bite of his omelet. "Okay. 'In Maison Blanche outside the largest room, inside the tall case, you'll find something to exhume.' Well, we're going to the White House."

"Sweet," Clay says. "Always wanted to tour that place. What's a tall case? And do you have any idea what the largest room is?" he asks.

"A tall case is a grandfather clock. I've heard Aunt Mitzi refer to hers as such. I don't know about the largest room. I'm sure that's easy to find out about online." I do a search on my phone. "The East Room," I tell Clay.

"The White House is going to prove tricky for us, Lynn. It's kind of a big deal."

"Maybe we'll get further instructions once we're there. Aunt Mitzi wouldn't throw us to the wolves."

"I hope you're right. So, should we go ahead and check out or see what Mick has to say?" Clay asks.

"I think we should wait. We'll leave our bags here and if there's nothing else, we'll come back and get them, then check out."

I finish my waffle and we head to the lobby to see if Mick is here yet. I see an older, short man, pushing eighty, mostly bald with a fringe of gray hair above his ears. He leans on a cane at the check-in desk. He reminds me a little of Yoda from *Star Wars*. Old Yoda, on Dagobah. "I bet that's him," I tell Clay.

"Seeing as how everyone we've been told to ask for has been at least seventy, I bet you're right."

"Hi," I tell the man. He doesn't have a nametag. "We're looking for Mick."

"That's me," he says with a smile. "Mick McGarrett. Can I help you?"

"Yes, I hope so," I say. "We may be ready to check out. I'm not sure yet. We're staying in the Governor's Suite."

"A lovely room, isn't it?" he asks.

"Yes, sir, it sure is," Clay says.

"Is there something wrong with the room?" he asks.

Clay and I look at each other. Yeah, we ripped up a baseboard and scratched the wall.

"No, sir. It's perfect," I tell him. "But..." I don't know what to say or how to address this.

"Mitzi Santini sent us," Clay finally says. Thank God.

"Mitzi, you say?"

"That's right," I reply.

"Ah. Clay and Lynn, I presume. I've been waiting for you. But, I'm sorry to hear that Mitzi has passed on. She was a lovely lady."

"Yes, she was. I miss her like crazy," I tell him.

"And Sid…what a hoot he was." He gets a little closer to us and lowers his voice. "Is everything okay with the room and *board?*" he asks with a wink.

"Um, actually, well, you see, we uh," I stammer.

"I chipped the paint and scratched the wall," Clay whispers.

"Think nothing of it. It's taken care of. And so is your room. No charge."

"Wow, really?" I ask.

"Yes," Mick says. "Did you find what you were looking for?"

"We did. Is there anything else you can tell us? Give us? Show us?" Clay asks.

"No, son, I'm afraid not. There will be more to come. You'll see."

"Alright then," Clay says.

"Mr. McGarrett, how did you know Aunt Mitzi and Uncle Sid?" I ask.

"Well, when this hotel was first built in the late eighteen-hundreds, it was mostly a stop for people traveling by railroad. The great Salvatore Santini stopped here sometimes on his way up the east coast for business. As you probably know, his son Giovanni followed his father's footsteps and took over the bank. He stayed here as well. Even donated some money for an expansion in the thirties. In fact, it was so substantial, that the owners wanted to pay tribute to Giovanni. Wanted to name a wing after him or something. But he was humble, and didn't want the recognition. So instead, he gave them the idea to turn the new façade into its Tudorean style, modeled after his home. And, like his father and grandfather before him, Sid came to the Hotel Roanoke on his way to New York for business, and Mitzi came with him sometimes. Without them, we wouldn't have been able to reopen in nineteen-ninety-five, after having been closed for six years. That's why your room is on the house. We wouldn't be here if it weren't for Mitzi and Sid. Along with many other private and public donations."

I was speechless. "Oh...just...my God...I had no idea. I never even knew about this place," I tell Mick.

"The Santinis were a modest bunch. It's so great to meet you both, finally. Now I can retire. It's been a rough last few years for me, having to keep this secret, and my health has not been up to par. I was debating passing on the Santini Secret to my protégé, Rona, but no need now. Really, though, it's been a pleasure meeting you both. Lynn, you favor your aunt a lot. Beautiful young lady, you are."

Holy crap, he even spoke like Yoda. "Oh, thank you so much. I've heard that I favor her a couple of times on this trip. And thank you for bearing the burden of this secret for so long. I do hope you feel better soon and are able to enjoy your retirement."

"Thank you, dear. Now is there anything else I can do for you?"

"Well, actually, I was wondering if you had any Christmas ornaments for sale. I took a quick peek in your gift shop, but didn't see any ornaments. I'm trying to collect them from everywhere we go."

"Let me take a look and see if there are any left from last season. Or if you would prefer, I can have Rona send you one when the twenty-seventeen design is completed. Since you're here this year."

"That would be fantastic, thank you. I would love one from this year."

"No problem. I'll make sure Rona doesn't forget you. And if you don't receive one by Thanksgiving, you give her a call."

"Thanks so much, Mick. Here's our address." I write down our address and give it to him. He promises to give it to Rona.

Mick calls a bellhop for us and we go back up to gather our belongings and then back down to check out. I give Mick a hug and Clay shakes his hand while apologizing for the minor damage to the room, then thanks him for taking care of it.

"One more thing," I say to Mick. "What is that star at the top of the mountain in the distance? I could see it from the terrace."

"Ah, yes," he says. "That's the Roanoke Star. It's the world's largest freestanding, illuminated, man-made star. It was constructed in nineteen-forty-nine, and Roanoke has been nicknamed Star City of the South ever since. It was originally supposed to only be lit to kick off the Christmas season, but the residents loved it so much, the Merchants Association decided to keep it lit year-round."

"Oh, wow, what a story. I love it," I tell him.

After a bit more chit-chatting, we get back in the truck and head out on the road.

Chapter 45

CLAY PUTS 1600 Pennsylvania Avenue into the GPS and we see that it's about four hours away. You can guess what he does next.

"Okay, love. Let's jam," he says.

"Make it good," I tell him.

"All my stuff is good." He punches a couple of buttons on his phone and "Immigrant Song" by Led Zeppelin comes on. He starts in with the high-pitched, wailing cry, in unison with Robert Plant. I love watching and listening to Clay sing. He's so animated, and he's got a really good voice. I was pleasantly surprised to learn that, the night before he left for his deployment to Operation Desert Shield, when he sang "Babe" to me.

I take the keychain out and look at it, even though we know where we're going and what we're looking for. It's a simple keychain with an acrylic American flag fob. Well that makes sense. The key is small and tarnished. Brass I think. It's about three inches long with an open bow and a single bit.

"Check it out, babe." I show it to Clay.

"Cool," he says, as he turns the radio down a few notches so we can have a conversation. "I love those old bitted keys. How are we going to get into that clock without being seen? This is going to be a really challenging situation. You realize we'll risk going to jail. There are cameras all over the White House. Secret Service is all over the place."

"That's it." I say. "I don't think we can be sneaky with this one. We could definitely end up in jail. Or at least detained. We need to look for the Secret Service and find the oldest individual. I bet there's a connection to Aunt Mitzi or Uncle Sid."

"Not a bad idea, love. I mean, there *had* to be a connection at some point. Whatever it is that we're looking for had to be hidden, you know? Aunt Mitzi and Uncle Sid, if he was involved in this clue, had to be able to leave it some kind of way. And they got out unscathed. So, you know what they say, 'Where there's a will, there's a way.' Right? We definitely have the will. I think you just thought of our way," he says.

"Okay, so we'll go with that. We'll probably need to stay the night. I'll book us a room." Ozzy Osbourne's voice comes through the speakers as "Crazy Train" starts playing. "You know," I say, in a subject changing tone, "I bet when Mick said that Mr. Santini didn't want any recognition for his donation to the Hotel Roanoke, it was because of Al Capone's gang. It was right around that time. Somebody from Chicago could have discovered the information and found him if they had named a wing after him."

"You're probably right. That makes a lot of sense. Do you remember Aunt Mitzi and Uncle Sid traveling that much? I don't."

"Yeah, they traveled plenty. I never knew where they went every time, but sure. She told me once that their goal was to make it to every state in—oh...Clay...they've been doing this for years."

"What do you mean?"

"She told me. They wanted to visit every state in the nation. That was more than twenty years ago. Twenty years."

"Holy shit. You think they were hiding things and planning this for us all along? For twenty years?"

"It's sort of turning out to look that way. I thought she only started this nine or ten years ago maybe. Why us? Out of everybody. That long ago. Why us?"

"Well, she said it herself. You had a special bond. Right? That has to be it."

"There has to be more to it than that."

"She loved you immensely, Lynn. Maybe it was just that simple."

"I don't know. And she loved you, too, you know?"

"I know. The feeling was mutual. I loved both of them. Uncle Sid was great."

"Yeah, he was," I say. "He was. God, I miss them."

Clay reaches over and grabs my hand. "Modern Love" by David Bowie starts playing.

"Hey."

"What?" I ask as I look up at him. I know my sage is going to say something to make me feel better.

"You still wanna argue that David Bowie wasn't the greatest rock star of all-time?"

I laugh out loud. I was not expecting that. At all. "Oh, babe," I say as I'm still laughing, "that's a twenty-seven-year-old argument you won't win with me. I've said it before and I'll say it again. I love David Bowie. Definitely one of my top-ten favorite artists of all-time. Maybe even top-five. But best rock star ever? I don't know. I'm sticking with my original choice."

"Steven Tyler."

"Yes indeed."

"I still don't understand your fascination with him. Don't get me wrong, I love Aerosmith, but…" He rolls his eyes and shakes his head. I know he wants to lecture me, again, on David Bowie's literary influences and success as a producer with Lou Reed and Iggy Pop outside of his own body of work, but he bites his tongue.

Truth be told, I really do think David Bowie is the greatest rock star of all-time. But on our first date, I was the one who asked Clay that question, and when he answered with 'David Bowie,' I thought it might be fun to initiate some playful banter. So I threw out Steven Tyler as the greatest. He was the first person that came to mind.

That night, as we were walking along the lakes of LSU, Clay stopped. "Wait just a minute. How can you not like David Bowie? That's blasphemous."

"I didn't say I didn't like him. I love David Bowie. I don't know…just the way Steven Tyler dances on stage. He's got such a presence. He's loud. I love that." That is all one hundred percent true.

"But Bowie was a visionary, reinventing himself over and over. There's no way you can argue that Tyler contributed more to the rock world than Bowie. This might be our first and last date, Lynn Boudreaux."

Is he serious? "So this is a deal breaker?" I asked. He smiled, grabbed my hand, and started walking again.

"Well, that all depends."

"On what?"

"Who's your favorite guitar player?"

To this day, I haven't told Clay that David Bowie is my first choice. I like seeing him get worked up about it, trying to prove to me that there's never been anybody better than The Bowie. And probably never will be. We were devastated when we heard about his death last year. Clay gets so passionate when he talks about Ziggy Stardust and everything else that makes up David Bowie's five-decade career. And I whole-heartedly agree with him.

I smile inside, watching Clay as he contemplates holding court in his truck to prosecute me for what he believes is a real obsession with the Aerosmith frontman.

"Steven Tyler. Sheesh. Okay…" he says, obviously restraining himself, "but, who's the best guitarist of all time?"

"Jimmy Page. No question."

"That's my girl." He smiles at me.

I guess he did know what to say to make me feel better.

Chapter 46

"LYNN, WAKE UP," I hear Clay say as I'm being nudged. "I just thought of something."

"What? What's wrong? Are we there yet? What time is it?"

"It's almost eleven. We're going to need tickets to get in. What if you have to reserve them? Like in advance? What the hell are we gonna do?" he asks.

"Shit, I didn't think about that. Lemme check." I look online. "Dammit. You have to get them at least three weeks in advance. Through frickin' Congress. It's literally an act of Congress to get into the White House for a tour. Shit. What now?"

"Okay, don't panic yet. That's what I wanted to know. I may have a connection."

"What? Who?" I ask, as he pulls up a contact on his phone to a chick named Pam. Who the fuck is Pam? He taps the call icon and I hear ringing.

"Hello?" a female voice asks. Pam, I assume.

"Pam?"

"Uh, yeah. That's who you called. Who's this?"

Oh good. She doesn't know.

"Clay. Sinclair."

"Clay? Wow. I didn't think I'd ever hear from you again."

Just what the hell does she mean by that?

"Yeah, well, here I am."

"What's up? You alright?"

"Yeah. Sort of. You still have that connection in DC? I'm in a bit of a pinch."

"Jesus, Clay. That depends. What the hell did you do? Oh, God. Do I want to know?"

"Nothing. I just need a ticket to get in the White House. Two tickets."

"The *White* House?"

"Yeah."

"When?"

"Now."

"Shit, I don't know if I can make it happen that fast. I need at least a couple of days to get you on a list."

"I don't have a couple of days. I have a couple of hours."

"Why are you just now calling me?"

"Long story."

"I'll see what I can do. Who's the other entry for?"

"My wife. Lynn."

"Oh. Alright."

She sounds kinda pissed off all of a sudden.

"So, you think you can get two tickets on short notice?"

"Maybe. Is this a good number for you?"

"Yeah. My cell."

"Okay. Give me a few. I'll call you back."

"Thanks, Pam. I owe you."

"Damn straight. Sit tight."

Click.

"Who the hell was that?" I ask. He sighs. He doesn't want to tell me. "Clay? Who?"

"Pam."

"No shit. Who's Pam?" He exhales a deep breath and rubs the back of his neck.

"We went to high school together."

"So what. Why the hesitation?"

"Well…" he sighs yet again and throws me a few nervous side glances.

"Well, what?"

"She's...Alexa's sister."

"Alexa? *The* Alexa?"

"Yeah." The crack in his voice makes him sound like he's thirteen years old.

"Why the fuck do you have her number?"

"I ran into her at the airport a few years ago. Before I retired, when I was on my way home from training. She was with her husband, who's in the Navy, who has a brother that works for the Pentagon. They were on their way to visit him."

"Why didn't you tell me? And you've had her number in your phone for over three years? What the hell, Clay!" I yell.

"Well, I didn't want to have this fight, for one. And I didn't think it was a big deal. We were all on a layover. The three of us had a beer in the airport bar. Said if I ever needed anything to let them know. She took my phone and put her number in. I forgot about it till just now. All my numbers just keep getting transferred with new phones, you know? I don't check off which ones I want to keep. Besides, look, it came in handy."

"Yeah, we'll see about that. She probably hates me because of what I did to her crazy-ass sister a lifetime ago."

"No, Lynn. She doesn't. She's not like that."

"Well she didn't sound too happy that the other ticket was for me."

"Who cares if she didn't?"

"I care."

"Lynn. It's fine. She's okay. She knows her sister is crazy."

"Right. Sure. You dated for two years. It took you long enough to figure it out. Blood is thicker than water."

"Lynn, come on, babe. I—"

The phone rings through the speakers and cuts him off. He presses the button on his steering wheel.

"Hello?" he asks.

"Done," Pam says.

"Seriously?"

"Seriously."

"Aw, man, Pam, thank you so much."

"You're welcome. Is Lynn with you now?"

He looks over at me. "Yes."

"Can she hear me?"

"Yes," he says.

"May I speak freely, Clay?" she asks.

"Uh, sure," he tells her.

"Hey, Lynn. I don't know if Clay told you who I am or not, but I'm Alexa's sister."

"Yeah. I know," I say, with a healthy level of cattiness.

"Listen, you did the right thing way back then," she says.

Clay looks at me and give me a "See?" look with his eyebrows.

"Uh, thanks." I do feel better. "And thanks for doing this for us. It means a lot. You have no idea," I tell her.

"Yeah," Clay says. "What do I owe you?"

"Tours are free. But you can buy me a drink. I'm in town. Would love to meet you, Lynn."

Clay and I look at each other. He lets go of the steering wheel with all but his pinkies, and flips his palms up. It's his way of asking me if I want to do that. I shrug my shoulders and nod. Why the hell not…

"Uh okay, where? When?"

"I'll text you," she says. "Looking forward to it."

Click.

"Wow," I say.

"See, babe, I told you. She's alright."

"Maybe you dated the wrong sister."

"No, I definitely dated the right one. Because if Alexa and I had not split up, I never would have met you, and that would be tragic."

"Good answer."

Chapter 47

W E GET TO the White House and finally figure out where we're supposed to go. It took a couple more phone calls to Pam to find where the special guest list area was, but we made it inside the house. The house of all houses, in this country anyway. Being here is very surreal, like stepping inside your TV. It reminds me of when I saw the Statue of Liberty for the first time.

Clay and I make it through all the checkpoints and security scans. The tour is self-guided, which is perfect for us. We tour the State Dining Room, Red Room, Green Room, Blue Room, and finally we are nearing the East Room. I can see the clock from here. We wait around for the crowd to pass and I'm starting to get hot flashes. I keep grabbing at my own hands. I see a few security guards, but nobody that looks like Secret Service.

We get up to the clock and we just kind of check it out, like we're interested in how lovely it is. But it's rather plain. There's no window in the door where the pendulum swings and no fancy moon dial at the top of the face. The keyhole is right there. The key is right in my pocket. I could just hurry and open it.

Around the corner comes an elderly gentleman. He doesn't look like a G-Man, or how I always imagined they would look: beefy with a bulge from a shoulder holster under his arm, like Fox Mulder wore on *The*

X-Files. But he's dressed in a suit. And hardly beefy. He must be a hundred years old. He walks right up to us.

"It's a fetching clock, isn't it?" he asks.

"Yes, sir," Clay says.

"Do you have any questions about it?" he asks us.

I try to think of something. "What is it made of?" I ask him.

"Well, it isn't *clay*. Or *linen*."

We both look up, surprised.

He continues, "The *key* is in the details." He looks at us and winks.

Clay and I look at each other and know this is our guy.

"Yes, sir," Clay says.

I get a little closer and whisper to him. "Do you know who we are? Do you know why we're here?"

"I do. And yes. This is no coincidence. I've been watching the monitors like a hawk ever since I heard of Mitzi's passing. I'm so sorry for your loss, dear."

"Thank you, Mister…I'm sorry, I don't know your name."

"It's probably better that way. Just call me Smitty. I'm in charge of all the clocks in the White House," he states.

"Can you get in there for us? We didn't want to get in trouble and get hauled off by the Secret Service," I say, in a hushed tone.

"I need to see your key, dear Lynn," he whispers back. "For validation of your identity."

"Of course." I nonchalantly pass him my key and he gives us a side nod with his head that tells us to give him some space. I assume it's so we don't draw attention from others. We step away and feign interest in some of the paintings. From my peripheral vision, I see Smitty take a large key-ring full of keys from inside his suit jacket. He sticks one of the keys in the face of the clock and winds it up. Why isn't he opening the door? Maybe he's trying to look unobtrusive, keeping a low profile while executing his duties. He's the clock man. Just doing his job. And excavating a secret.

The door of the clock opens. Then, a small snap, like something is being unfastened. I see out of the corner of my eye that he retrieves a dark colored envelope taped to the upper back corner of the clock. He shuts the door and walks past us without saying a word, but skillfully hands Clay the key and envelope.

"Smitty?" I ask.

He turns around, but doesn't say anything. He waves us off. When he gets to the end of the hall, just before he makes the corner, his voice echoes, "You'll get your explanation. In due time. Carry on."

"What just happened?" Clay whispers.

"I don't know, but let's get the hell out of here," I tell him.

We make it back to the truck and Clay checks his phone and sees that he has a text from Pam with details on where to meet her and what time.

We check-in to the hotel and go up to our room to relax. I'm ready to read this letter. Clay tells me that Pam wants to meet us at a bar named The Gibson. He looks it up and says that it's about a fifteen minute drive from the hotel.

He gets another text. "She wants to know where we're staying."

"Why?" I ask. He's texting her back, probably to tell her. I put my head down on the pillow of the bed.

"I don't know," he says.

It's raining again. "Great," I say, "I really don't feel like getting out in this mess. Maybe we should take the metro thingie," I tell him.

"She's sending a car for us," he says.

Damn. Who is this woman? Oh well, at least we don't have to drive and try to find a parking spot. I don't want to like this Pam, but she did do us a huge favor by getting us in the White House. She's even sending a car for us, and she told me I did the right thing regarding her sister. So why am I feeling so off about her?

Clay is texting her back. Again. He gets a reply right away and he smiles, which doesn't help the situation any. I put my emotions to the side, roll over on my back, and open the envelope.

"Lynn, what are you doing? I thought you were going to wait for me," Clay says.

"You seem a little preoccupied with *Pam*. What's going on there?

Something I should know about? Why are you so smiley and flirty? Were you ever with her? Before the other one?"

"What makes you ask that?"

I bolt upright. "Answer the question, Clay!"

He sighs. "Yes."

"Shit. I fucking knew it. How many other skeletons are in your closet?"

He stares at me and squints his eyes. "Why are you doing this?" he asks. "That was forever ago. Some thirty-five years."

I do the math. He was sixteen. Oh, I get it now. We all have our firsts. Clay wasn't mine. But mine is not here, in the same town, right now, wanting to meet us for a drink.

"Oh…nice…how convenient of you to leave out that little morsel of information. Ignorance is bliss, and all that shit, right? Text her back and cancel. This isn't happening."

"What? Don't be ridiculous, we're all adults."

"I'm sorry if I don't feel like having drinks with the girl you lost your virginity to, so you can talk and laugh and reminisce about old times while I sit there like an idiot. No thanks."

"Why are you acting so jealous? You're being irrational."

"And you're a little too eager to see her again. Tell me something, Clay…how is it that you wound up with both sisters? And how does this Pam girl not hate you if you dated her sister for two years after she took your v-card? Huh?"

He comes and sits next to me on the bed. "It's complicated."

"Well, nevermind then. Spare me the details. I don't think I want to know." I lie back down on the bed and turn away from him. I can hear him clicking away on his phone, obviously texting her back, canceling.

"It's done. I'm sorry. I wasn't thinking. But, really, Lynn, I don't get you sometimes."

"What's not to get? You know everything about me." He lies next to me and puts his arm over me. He tries to spoon me, but I keep my legs straight. I'm not in the mood to be cuddled.

"No, Lynn. I don't. Not really. Even you said that, the other day. Remember? I don't want to know though. I just don't understand where the insecurity is coming from, that's all," he says softly. "I thought we were way past this. Lynn, we've been married almost twenty-six years. How many times do I have to tell you and show you, that you're it for me? There's never been another thought of anybody else since the second I met you."

I bend my legs and let him fit into them. Am I being irrational? I don't think so. Nobody can tell me how to feel, not even Clay. Emotions are raw and the one thing we can't control. We can only control how we react to them. Is my reaction justified?

"I'm sorry," I tell him. "Obviously I knew you had a first. I just didn't know who and especially that it was her sister."

"Hey. We never had those conversations, about who and how many we were with before. What happened in the past doesn't matter now. I only know one name from your past. And that's enough. I don't want to know who else. I don't like the thought of anybody else ever having touched you."

"I don't like it either. That's why I don't want to go tonight. I'm sorry if that makes me jealous and irrational and insecure. I don't know why I get like this. I just feel sometimes that I'm not enough for you. You do know what happened to me. I guess maybe I'm just paranoid. And yes, even after all these years."

"Lynn. Seriously. I am not him. I would never do that to you. I hate that you were hurt by him, but more than that, I'm glad. Because it's part of who you are. And I love every part of you...mind, body, and soul. And if Max hadn't cheated on you, our paths would never have crossed. I would have never met you."

That was a fact. Max was my ex, before I met Clay. He and I had worked together. I caught him screwing the big boss, right on her desk in the middle of the day. She thought he'd locked the door. I think he wanted to get caught. Not necessarily by me, but that's what happened. So the bigger boss wrote them both up. Rightfully so. And Max transferred to another agency. Then three months later, the bigger boss told me to take the work vehicle to the shop, where I met Clay. That would have been Max's job.

"Well, that is true. I guess it was fate," I say to him.

"Yeah. It was. And I'm sorry I put you on the spot with Pam this afternoon," he says.

"You didn't. She did. At the time I felt like it was okay, because she did help us get in. And…that was before I knew. Were you ever in love with her?"

"No. We were practically kids."

"Were you her first?"

"No. She used me. She didn't give a shit about me."

"I don't know what's worse."

"It doesn't even matter, because it was so long ago."

"And so, then, how is it that you're on speaking terms with her?"

"Guys don't hold grudges like girls do. Besides, it's not like I've actually been talking to her. I hadn't seen her in *years* before I ran into her at the airport. I didn't even recognize her. She's the one that came up to me. And like I said, she put her number in my phone. I didn't ask for it."

"You didn't delete it."

"I had to catch a plane, to get home to you. And then I forgot about it."

"So, how did you end up with her sister? Years later."

"Alexa is four years younger than I am. I didn't know her from school. I met her out one night at a party. She had just turned eighteen when we got together. When I went to pick Alexa up the first time, Pam answered the door. It was just a coincidence."

"And you kept dating?"

"Yes. Pam was married by then and just happened to be visiting her parents' house when I picked Alexa up for our first date."

"Wait…does Alexa know about you and Pam?"

"No. Not that I'm aware of. I sure never told her."

"Interesting…"

"I told you it was complicated."

"Is her husband in town now too? Or is it just her?"

"I think it's just her."

"Text her back. We're going."

"Lynn. We don't have to, I already cancelled. Told her you weren't feeling well."

"Well I've had a miraculous recovery. Tell her to send the fucking car."

Chapter 48

"OH, REALLY, MRS. Sinclair? You're fully recovered?"

"Yeah. I'm all better. Text her."

"Yes, ma'am." He gets his phone back out and texts her.

Without warning, my body starts tingling. I'm feeling frisky. Clay's right. The past doesn't matter. And forgiveness frees the heart. Not that Clay needs forgiving. I didn't even know him when he was sixteen. But now, he is my man, my husband, my heart. I'll be damned if I'm going to let her get the best of me. Maybe she really has nothing sneaky and condescending on her mind. Maybe she really is an okay person. But I hate the fact that I know she was his first. And I hate that she used him. I need a confidence boost. I look at the clock. It's 5:30. Plenty of time. I'm going to give Clay an afternoon he'll never forget.

"Take off your clothes," I tell him.

"What?"

"Just do it." He obeys without hesitation.

"What about you?"

"Don't worry about me. Remember Birmingham? After dinner in the Presidential Suite?"

"Uh, yeah. One of my favorite nights."

"Remember how I told you there might be more?"

"I do." He gives me a seductive smile.

"Close your eyes." He submits and I run to my suitcase and get out the sleep mask I brought and rummage through my purse for a couple of things. I slip the mask over his head and cover his eyes.

"Babe? What are you doing?"

"Shh. Just keep your eyes covered. No peeking. I'm keeping your hands free, but don't even try to touch me. Pretend your wrists are bound to the bed."

"Whatever you say."

I get undressed and get some ice from the bucket as quietly as I can so he doesn't have any idea what's coming. I take a piece of the frozen water and start at his neck. He winces and sucks in air, like I've hurt him. I know I haven't so I don't react. I drag the ice down and circle the two most sensitive areas on his chest.

"Oh, God. Lynn. What are you doing to me? Jesus, that's hot."

"No, it's cold," I whisper.

"You know what I mean."

I get one of the chocolate peanut butter candies from the bag I took out of my purse and squeeze it, spreading the peanut butter and chocolate on my finger, and I put it in Clay's mouth. He sucks the sweetness off of it, making sexy sounds as he does so. I literally see him getting harder, growing before my eyes.

"Lynn, I swear, I'm going to explode soon."

"No. You're not." He tries to touch me, blindly feeling for me, and I shoo his hand away. "I said your hands were bound, remember?" I circle the ice cube around the tip of him and he cringes again.

"Okay. Yeah, that's gonna put things on hold for a minute," he says with an uneasy laugh.

I take the back scratcher and a ball point pen that I grabbed from my belongings. The pen has a soft marabou feather pouf at the top. I lightly run the feathers up and down Clay's torso while I use stronger pressure on the back scratcher. I bring Clay's senses to a whole new level. He's squirming. I'm loving it.

"What are you doing to me? Oh my God."

"You like that?" I ask.

"Yes. Hell yes."

I repeat the sensation. Delicate with the feathers, but harder with the back scratcher. Then I lean down and trail my tongue up the path of the scrapes until I get to his neck. He breathes in deep. I take his hands and bring them up to my breasts and let his fingers touch my tips.

"Babe. Seriously. Got dammit. You're killing me."

I put his hand to my center and let him do his own exploring so he can feel how much I want him.

"Holy shit," he whispers.

Then I move his hands away.

"Lynn. I mean it. Fuck, babe."

Well, alright then. I take the mask off and we are joined in an instant. Moving like untamed animals. Clay is shouting with each thrust. He's never been this vocal in our lovemaking. Though, I'm not exactly sure that's what you'd call what we're doing right now. It's savage. Fierce. Powerful. Deep. Passionate. Real.

I lie next to my husband and he kisses me.

"You never cease to amaze me, Lynn. God, that was electrifying."

"It kinda was, wasn't it? Another one for the playbook?"

"Fuck yeah."

He kisses me again, then we get up and get dressed. I'm feeling pretty good about myself, and ready to go meet this Pam chick.

A limo pulls up at 7:00 and we get in. The driver takes us to a curb on the side of the street and stops, like this is where we get out. I don't see anything that looks like a bar. But he says this is it. So we go ahead and exit the vehicle.

"Um, Clay, I don't see anything that says 'The Gibson' on it. No marquee, nothing."

"Me either."

"Make sure she told us the right place. Do you think the driver got it wrong?"

Clay texts Pam and she replies that it's just a door. No sign. It's like a speakeasy. Secret.

"Well, there is a plain door right here," Clay says.

"Let's take a look," I say.

He opens it and we walk into an enclosed shadowy alley. There's one dim light bulb dangling above a stool at the end. We head down and wait. For what, we don't know. A few minutes pass and a girl comes down some stairs. She doesn't say anything, but writes something down on a clipboard. She looks up and stares at us. I thought she was waiting for us to give her a password. Then she smiles, her black lipstick a stark contrast to her white teeth. "Follow me," she says, and brings us in. We tell her we're meeting somebody and she lets us look around. The place is so dark, flickering candles on tables our only source of light. The glow within the frosted votives bounces off the walls, barely amplified by the mirror behind the bar. I am really digging this place. I love the speakeasy concept.

Pam, I suppose, sees us and waves us over to a red velvet booth. She is gorgeous. Like pin-up gorgeous. She's got long, straight, jet-black hair and full, red lips. She stands up and gives Clay a hug. I don't like that, but I let it slide. She's tall, with perfect curves and perfect boobs. She's wearing a crimson dress that hugs her perfect figure in all the right places.

"Lynn, it's so nice to meet you," she says and then gives me a hug too. Okay, well, so far, so good. Mostly…

"You, too." Lie. "Thanks again for your help this afternoon. We really appreciate it." Truth.

"No sweat. My brother-in-law has more pull than I thought."

We sit down and a waitress brings us menus. The drink names are rather unique for a bar. I'm contemplating between the Simmer Down and the Purple Rain when Pam orders one called Teen Romance. Okay. Maybe she just likes the drink. I don't know if she's playing games, but I order the Afterglow, even though there were other drinks I'd have rather tried. I don't care what it tastes like. Clay orders one called everything. com. He's clueless.

"So, tell me," she looks at us from across the table, "what brings you both to DC and the White House?"

Clay tells her our story and I fill in some of the parts he skips over. She doesn't look at me once. She's totally focused on him. But, he is doing most of the talking. That could be why.

We finish our first round of drinks and Pam calls the waitress back over.

"This time, I'll have the Remember That Time...?" she tells the waitress.

I shit you not. That's what she ordered. And she looks at Clay when she asks for it. Okay, she's seriously doing this on purpose. I don't know if she has any clue at all that I know about them, but she's making me uncomfortable. Clay too, I can tell. His leg is bouncing up and down. I squeeze his thigh under the table and still it. And then I order my new drink.

"I'd like the Sets My Soul on Fire, please." Pam looks at me and I meet her eyes.

Clay orders next. "I want the Blindfolded and Bound." He looks at me and winks.

My man. Well played, Clay. Well played. He's catching on. This may turn out to be a fun night after all.

"Interesting place," Clay says, as he looks around.

"Yeah, it's really cool," I say.

"Yeah, we found it quite by accident," she says.

"We?" Clay asks.

"Travis and I."

"I thought your husband's name was Jerry."

"Jared. Travis is my brother-in-law."

"Oh," Clay says.

The waitress brings our new cocktails to the table. I take a deep pull from the straw and, oh holy hell...it burns down my throat. I look at the menu again and read the ingredients. There's habanero syrup in it. Of course there is. That must be the 'Fire' part of the drink. They weren't kidding. But I don't care. I'm going to suffer through it. I can't look like a wuss.

"So," Pam says next, "how's the job treating you? Still chasing bad guys?" she asks Clay.

"No. I retired about three years ago."

"Wow. Retired. Lucky. I wish I could get lucky." Jeez, really? "Lynn, what do you do?"

"I just retired too, about a month ago. I was a curator at a museum."

"Well, isn't that nice? Both of you retired. The world is your oyster."

"What about you, Pam?" I ask. "What brings you to DC? Work?"

"Sure, you can call it that." That's all she says.

"Are you still working for the airline?" Clay asks her.

"Yep. Not for very much longer, though. They won't give me the trans-fer I want, so...I don't know what's next. Maybe I'll retire, too. Waitress!" she snips, and shakes her empty glass up in the air.

The waitress responds to her beckon. Alright, let's see what she gets this time.

"Things I Still Remember, please."

Are you fricking kidding me? She is unbelievable. And every time, she looks at Clay. The waitress looks at me for my next drink. "Erotic Seduc-tion," I tell her. I read the description this time. It's a much sweeter drink with apricot liqueur. Hopefully it will quell the firestorm in my mouth.

"My drink of choice this go round," Clay says, "is the Come Harder," with another wink in my direction.

Yes. I love it. I'm really starting to get tipsy. We are slamming these drinks back. I can maybe do one more, and I know exactly which one.

"Soooo, Pammmm," I slightly slur, "where iss ya husban'?"

"My husban'...hmmm. He's workin' in th' Mid'l East. Somewheres. Over there. I can't keep up wit'im."

Good, she's a little drunk too. At least I'm not the only one tripping on my words. I wonder if she's really here for work of if she's got some-thing on the side with her brother-in-law. She seems the type.

"I know, iss hard when they're away," I say as politely as possible.

"Iss no biggie. I'm use'ta it," she says. "Clay? I talked ta my sister ear-lier. Tole'er I was havin' drinks wit' ya t'night. Said ta tell ya hey."

Why is she doing this? Why is she bringing her up? I'm getting really antsy to leave. I don't say anything, and I hope Clay doesn't give her the time of day about his ex.

"Okay," he says. Good.

The waitress brings our next round of drinks.

"Lynnnnn," she turns her attention to me. She touches my arm and leans closer to me from across the table. Her eyes are wide and a little glassy. "Juss so ya know, I can't stan' my sister. I've had a bone ta pick wit'er since I was ummm…" She looks like she's trying to count in her head. "Twenny-two. She don' know 'bout it, so I gotta preten' and play nice, but I never laughed as hard's I did when I heard ya had'er arrested all them years ago. That made m'year. So, thank ya." She raises her glass to me and pounds her drink back.

"Um, you're welcome?" I fake a smile and drink some more.

"Clay," she says, "you 'member th' time we were juniors an' we had that big tess a group'a us went ta study at th' libarry for?"

Clay leans all the way back in the booth and stares at her. The color in his face drains. He shakes his head at her as if to say, "Don't go there." He puts his hand on my leg.

"C'mon, Clay. I know ya r'member that night."

"Pam," he says, a touch of anger in his voice. "Don't."

What the hell is this about?

"Oh, no," I say. "Please do, Pam."

"Welllll…less juss sayyyy…a coupl'a us di'nt get much studyin' done." She winks at Clay and he glares at her. "N'body ever went ta th' dark corner of th' rocks and fossils section. Or should I sayyyy…sex-tion."

Holy fucking shit. He lost his fucking virginity in the fucking library? I shove Clay's hand off my leg and it's my turn to glare. At him.

"Jesus, Pam," Clay says.

"Lynn," she says, "ya don' look sa'prised. Didja know?"

"Some of it." Clay looks down in shame, his jaw clenched. He's mad and embarrassed. As he should be. I know he wants to jump across the table and wring that harlot's neck. I'm not going to react the way Pam wants me to. She wants a fight out of us. And now I'm doing the math. Since she was twenty-two, huh? Yeah, I knew it. That's how old they were when Clay started dating her little sister. Now I know why she can't stand her. It's Clay. She did have a thing for him. And sounds like she still does. Nothing will sober you up quicker than knowing a chick is trying to make a play for your man. I touch Clay's leg and he looks at me. I give him a gentle smile and he relaxes. My eyes tell him that I'm okay. I can't really hold this against him. It was so long ago, and way before we knew each other. The color comes back in his face and he winks at me. But it's definitely time to go. I give Clay another squeeze on his leg to signal.

"What is wrong with you, Pam? You didn't need to go there," he says to her.

"Wha'ss wrong? Juss talkin' 'bout th' good'ole days."

"I'd hardly call them that. Anyway, it's getting late," he says. "We've got another long day of driving ahead of us. We need to go."

"Oh nooooo. But we're havin' such a good tiiiime," Pam says.

"Are we really?" I ask her with a tilt of my head. "We need to get up early."

"C'mon. One more drink. I'll be good. No more mem'ries. I'll call th' limo ta take ya back after we order."

I look at Clay and shrug. I guess we have time for one more since we'll have to wait for the car.

"Okay," he sighs. "One more drink."

"Great. I'll tell th' driver ta be on 'is way then." She texts someone. I really hope it's the driver and she's not pretending in order to keep us here longer. I want to get out of this place. Like now.

Pam summons the waitress over. "For m'final drink of th' night, I want The Man I Forgot I Loved." Is she serious right now? She's looking Clay dead in the face. Thank God he doesn't see her. He's looking at the menu.

"I'm going to have the Bitch Please!" I tell the waitress, as I give Pam a blatant look, to let her know what I ordered was really how I felt. She rolls her eyes.

The waitress looks at Clay. "Bye Felicia! for me."

I laugh out loud. I can't help it. Clay grabs my hand and squeezes it. He joins me in laughter.

"These drink names are so creative," I say, still laughing.

"Yeah," Pam says. She lowers her voice a seductive octave and says, "They are."

Clay jumps back in the booth as soon as she says that.

"Alright, that's it. Let's go, Lynn." He gets up.

"What happened?" I ask.

"Yeah, Clay. Wha'ss wrong?" she asks in a child-like voice.

"Let's just go. Come on, babe. We'll find our own way back to the hotel."

He's serious. Shit. I get up and follow him. I look back in Pam's direction and she's laughing. We get back outside. It's stopped raining.

"What the hell happened, Clay?"

"She fucking stuck her foot between my legs and...nevermind." He pulls up the Uber app on his phone and requests a ride.

"What? What did she do? Did she feel up your balls with her foot?" I start to go back inside and he pulls me back.

"Forget it, it's not worth it. She's not worth it."

"God. I knew she had a thing for you. The drinks she ordered? Could she be any more obvious?"

"Yes. And she was. I'm sorry, Lynn. I swear I had no idea. She never behaved like that when I was with Alexa. We had to act like we didn't know each other."

"And the *library*? Jesus, Clay. That's rich. Real classy."

"Here it comes. I knew you wouldn't just let that one go."

"Can you blame me?"

"No. I know. I'm not proud of it."

"How did you even know what you were doing? In the freaking library. For your first time." I half laugh.

He gives me another half laugh back. "It's not rocket science. I know where it goes. Don't worry, it didn't last long. Are you really mad about that?"

"I'm not happy about it. But I suppose it doesn't matter much." If he only knew some of the places I had sex before we got together. He'd probably be shocked. Or turned on.

The Uber pulls up and we get in.

"Fairmont Hotel," he tells the driver.

"Are you okay?" I ask Clay. "Did she hurt you?" I put my hand on his center and rub him a little.

"Don't do that." He smiles. "And no, she just surprised me. That's all. I'm sorry. We shouldn't have come."

"Hey, it was my idea to go ahead with it. I'm the one who's sorry. God, what a piece of work. She must be really unhappy with her life."

"Yeah. And her poor husband. I bet she's fucking around on him with her brother-in-law."

"That's what I was thinking, too. The library? Really?" I smile at him and he leans over and kisses me.

He takes his phone out.

"Who are you calling?" I ask.

"Nobody. I'm deleting her fucking number."

"I love you."

"I know."

Chapter 49

THE SMELL OF coffee hits my nose and I stir. I stretch and hear Clay in the shower. I get up and go to the bathroom.

"Mornin', love," he says, with a head full of shampoo. "Sleep okay? How's your head?"

"Mornin', babe. Yeah, I slept great. No hangover. Water and aspirin before bed does the trick. I wasn't really drunk though, especially by the time we got back here. Last night was crazy, huh? I'm glad you made us leave, I was beyond uncomfortable," I say as I get ready to brush my teeth.

"Yeah, me too. I was actually ready to go after she ordered her second drink, but I didn't want to be rude, you know? I felt like we owed her for getting us in the White House," he says.

"I know. I think we paid her back plenty," I say.

"Well, we did leave her with the tab."

I laugh. "You almost finished?"

"Yep. Why don't you join me instead?" he smiles.

"Okay. But no fooling around. We need to get going." I take off my clothes and get in the shower with my husband.

"Party pooper. You're taking the fun out of it." He gives me a good-morning kiss.

"So sorry." I turn around for him to wash my back.

"So, what's next?" he asks. "Where to?"

"I don't know. We still haven't opened the envelope from the clock. That's next. Then we'll figure out where we're going."

"Oh yeah. The envelope. I can't believe you haven't opened it yet."

"I know, me either, really. I was just too wound up and aggravated last night. Figured what's a few more hours. Better to open it with a fresh mind after a good night's sleep."

"So," he says, "where's the craziest place you ever had sex?"

"What?"

"Answer the question. You know mine."

"Craziest or riskiest?"

"Whoa. You have one of each? Please…answer both."

Shit. Me and my big mouth. "Clay. We don't—"

"We do. Come on, Lynn. I'm not gonna be mad. This is just for fun."

"Fun?"

"Fun."

I sigh. "Okay. Craziest would have to be the haunted house ride at the fair."

Clay laughs so hard that it makes me jump.

"What's so funny?"

"Nothing." But he's still laughing. "Oh my God. That's excellent. And ballsy. Pun intended. Is that ride even long enough?"

"I was seventeen. So was he. You tell me."

"Touché. How did you even manage that? Those cars are so small."

"I was wearing a skirt."

"Ah. Okay, now what's your riskiest? Don't tell me. The top of the Ferris wheel?"

"No." I pop him with the wet washcloth. He flinches and I laugh. "It's kind of cliché."

"So."

"Under the bridge downtown."

He laughs again and starts singing "Under the Bridge" by the Red Hot Chili Peppers.

"Jesus, woman. Are you crazy? Do you know how many drug deals go on down there?"

"Yeah. Luckily there weren't any there that night. At least not that I saw." I move under the water to rinse my back and wash my hair. Clay soaps up my front. "No funny business, Mr. Sinclair. I know how your mind works."

"You can be such a spoilsport sometimes, Mrs. Sinclair," Clay says, as he playfully bites my boob. "Alright, you're good to go," he declares, as he slaps my butt. I jump at his hand hitting my wet bottom. That stung a little. "Let's get out before I can't control myself."

We exit the shower, dry off, and get dressed. Clay fixes us more coffee and orders room service while I put my makeup on and fix my hair.

I sit at the table and stare at the envelope.

"You gonna open that?"

"Do you think we should try and get in touch with Smitty so we can talk to him about Aunt Mitzi and Uncle Sid? I mean, you know, not on the White House grounds? Maybe meet him for lunch or something? He could've been part of their scheme in hiding the envelope for so long, since he's in charge of all the clocks. He might not have been able to speak freely."

"That's a good thought, but he did say that we would get answers 'in due time.' However long that's supposed to be."

"True." I open the envelope.

"What is it? What does it say?" Clay asks.

"It's a bunch of handwritten numbers. I think it's another cipher," I tell him.

"Is it a pattern? How do the numbers read?"

"It doesn't look like a pattern, other than there are four sets of two numbers, separated by commas. But the numbers themselves look pretty random. I don't see any correlation from one number to the next."

"Sounds tricky. Okay, so what do you think?"

"I'm sure there's a method to her madness, we just need to figure it out," I say.

"Maybe they're dates? Or coordinates?"

"I don't think so. It's too many numbers for dates."

"What about dates and times?"

"Hmm…that could be. The first one would be January fourth, at nine nineteen. Is that date and time significant to you?" I ask him.

"Nothing I can think of," he says.

"Come take a look."

He slides over to my side of the table and we look at it together.

01 04 09 19, 01 01 16 04, 24 04 03 10, 08 04 15 20,
04 28 02 14, 18 06 09 06, 02 15 26 02, 06 04 06 05,
07 19 22 04, 03 16 02 06, 01 04 03 05, 02 36 10 07…

It goes on and on for almost two pages. Number set, after number set, after number set.

"What do you make of it?" I ask him.

"Well, since the numbers are handwritten," he says, "it's obviously not another kind of font we'd have to figure out that would need translating like the first one we found in the box of keys. It's gotta be something else. Something simple, I bet. Like a book. Lots of ciphers are decoded using a certain book."

"Oh my God. Literally. Her Bible." I say. "Duh."

"That has to be it. Where is it? Did you bring it in or is it in the truck?"

I get up and go to my suitcase and get it out. "Haven't let it out of my possession since I got it out of the trunk of that fifty-seven Chevy."

"So," he says, "the numbers probably represent the book, the chapter, the verse, and the word. Another letter from Aunt Mitzi."

"Wow, two letters almost back to back. She must really have known we would want some answers by now."

"What time is check-out? This could take a while. It's pretty long," Clay says.

"Not till one. I think we'll be okay. It's only nine."

"Okay, cool. Let's get down to it."

"Alright, here's the Bible and my notebook. I'll tell you the numbers. You look everything up and write down the words," I tell him. "I can't know what it says until it's done."

I give Clay the numbers and he translates them into words. I see his face frown a couple of times. I was afraid of that.

About halfway through, I don't hear pages turning anymore. I look up and Clay is spaced out. "Hey." I knock on the table and he flinches. "You okay?"

"Yeah."

"Do you want to talk?"

"No."

"You need a break?"

"No. I'm fine. Keep going. What was the last one?" I repeat it and we move on.

A few lines down, Clay's eyes clench shut. He tries to keep tears from spilling out of the sides.

"What is it?" I ask. He opens his eyes. They're red, glassy, and wet at the corners.

"It's just…you'll see. Sorry. Let's finish it."

We get all the way through, which takes close to two hours, and then he hands me the notebook with the letter from Aunt Mitzi.

"Will you please read it to me, Clay? I don't know if I could get through it without falling apart. I have a feeling I know what's coming, and I just need to listen."

"Yeah, babe." His voice is a virtual whisper. He knows what it says, and he knows what it's going to do to me.

> *"My two darling loves,*
>
> *'I hope you are enjoying your time together. As promised, I'll be answering more of your questions, beginning with your second stop.*
>
> *'I know you have wonders about our attempted adoption. Both of them. We tried for years after we got married to conceive. I even got pregnant a couple of times, but miscarried. We finally decided to adopt. It took a while, but we were at long last told about a baby boy, and we immediately put forth motion to bring him home, and we did. Nevertheless, it was not meant to be, for his birth mother changed her mind and took him back. We were devastated. I managed to get pregnant again, but alas, suffered another loss. Then, word came from afar that there was a baby girl available, and again, we jumped at the chance to be a mother*

and father. However, the second birth mother also changed her mind, and we decided we could not go through this again, and we gave up. It was just not meant to be for us. I don't know what was harder, losing them or having them stripped away. We grieved together, we cried together, we mourned together. And then we accepted it together. We moved past it the best way we knew how. We focused on each other. I had other babies in my life that I loved with all my heart, like you, sweet girl. I know you and Clay had your own struggles with fertility. I wish you had come to me, but I know it's a hard issue to bring up, so I never did.

'You may recall the man you met at the bank. We go way back. His family owned the piece of furniture where you found the post note. I hope that helps answer that question.

'You will meet several people along the way that we have old ties to, like the man in the White House. He was a friend of your great Uncle Roman. He's been employed by the White House for nearly seventy years. I hope you and Clay have had fun and will continue to do so. There will be more answers later.

'Love always,

'Your dear, old Aunt Bernice'"

Well, naturally, as expected, I am bawling. But I chuckle at the last line. I guess 'Mitzi' is not in the Bible anywhere.

"Are you okay, Lynn?" Clay is at my side.

"Yes and no," I say through tears, my makeup ruined. "I wish I had talked to her about us now. I didn't know she would understand that well. I didn't know they struggled like we did, though I think it had to be worse for them, actually having gotten pregnant, more than once, only to lose them. Not to mention holding babies that you thought were yours, not once, but twice, only to have them taken from you. That's just horrific and dreadful. They didn't deserve that."

"I know. Come on, let's go sit on the bed."

We get up and get comfortable in the bedroom. "She's right though. The best way to get past that is to concentrate on each other, try not to focus on it," I say.

"Right. That's what we did. That's what we're doing."

Tears overrun my eyes. "I'll just never understand. Everybody always says that God has a plan. Then why are there crack whores in this world, throwing away their babies in dumpsters? Women and teenage girls who don't even try, or want them to begin with...they get pregnant. And then people like Aunt Mitzi and Uncle Sid, and us, that wanted so badly to be parents...and it doesn't happen. How is that God's plan? How did Aunt Mitzi never lose her faith after all of that? Because I've lost some of mine. And I didn't endure near as much. How could she have been so strong and why am I so weak? I know I had to accept it, and I made my peace with it, but there will always be a hole in my heart that's unfulfilled. Empty. How can you mourn the loss of something you never had? How can you not question God? He says in the Bible to be fertile and multiply, but yet he doesn't give that ability to all women? Then why not just give it to the ones that want it? Why not make the ones who throw them away infertile?"

"I don't know, babe. I'll never understand either. It makes me sad, too. Nobody would have made a better mother than you."

"I'm sorry I couldn't make you a father. You don't know how much guilt I feel because of that. And how much fear I have because of it. Even now. You deserve to be a daddy."

"Lynn, don't do this to yourself, it's not your fault. What do you mean by 'fear'? What are you afraid of?"

"That you'll leave me. And find somebody that can give you what I can't." I fall into him and sob uncontrollably.

"Jesus, Lynn. Are you serious, love?" He's holding me tight. "Have you been carrying this for our entire marriage? Why haven't you ever said anything? Why didn't you talk to me?"

I can barely get the words out. "I was scared that if I even mentioned it, you would contemplate it and leave. Trade me in for somebody younger and fertile, so you could go multiply and carry on your name."

"Oh, God, babe. It all makes so much more sense now."

My tearful voice is less than a whisper. "Please don't leave me."

"Lynn. Look at me, love." I look up at him and he wipes under my eyes with his thumbs. "I would never leave you, not because of that, not because of *anything*. That's not who or what I am. Sure, I wanted kids. I know we both did. But it just wasn't in the cards. We were dealt a different hand. I don't know why. And no, it's not fair. But that would never be a reason for me to leave you, babe. Please put that thought out of your mind. You don't need to worry about that, or have any fear of it. You, Lynn, *you,* are my world. Nothing and nobody else. If we had been lucky enough to become parents, sure, our kids would be part of my world too, but it's just you and me. I'm all yours. You are all I need. Just you."

I hug him like I've never hugged him before. Tighter than when he got off the plane from his first deployment. A bit of a weight feels like it's been lifted off of my shoulders. I knew I married an exceptional man.

Clay and I tried for so long to get pregnant. On my twenty-fifth birthday, he asked me to stop taking my birth control pills. He wanted to start a family. I was thrilled. There was nothing I wanted more. I didn't expect to become pregnant right away, but after about six months, I started to get concerned. It just wasn't happening. There were times when I was late and I would get a little excited, but it would always turn out to be just that—a late period. The woes of being irregular. A full year later, after eighteen monthly disappointments, we finally went to the doctor. We did everything we could afford to do. I took fertility drugs, which weren't covered by insurance. Clay was checked and his count was fine. Better than fine. I had my tubes checked for blockages. They were clear.

Over the course of several more appointments in as many months, my doctor discovered that I had a bad case of endometriosis. "But, I don't have any pain," I told her. "Just my regular cramps." She said that it was entirely possible to not have pain with endometriosis and that my irregular cycles combined with the endometriosis was probably what was keeping me from getting pregnant. Oh yeah, and the kicker…she said I probably wasn't even ovulating. But I had a monthly cycle. I know what you're thinking. *How is that possible?* It happens. So it was all me. My fault. I'm the reason Clay is not a daddy.

I had several surgeries over the next ten years to get rid of the endometriosis, hoping that would help, but it didn't. And it always came back, which is why I had surgery for it so many times. We finally gave up. And then I had to listen to everybody. *Put it in God's hands. Quit trying so hard.* Or my personal favorite, *It'll happen when you least expect it.* Bullshit.

Nothing pissed me off inside more than when people would say that to me. I always least expected it. And it never happened. *What about adoption?* Sure, all for it. Do you have ten thousand dollars you'd be willing to give us? *Have you thought about in vitro?* Of course we did. But again, money was the issue.

I know people truly didn't know what to say, and they were just trying to be comforting, but nothing ever eased my sadness. And it's not like it was ever the topic of much conversation, but when it was, there it was.

"I'm sorry, Clay. I'm sorry I never talked to you about my fear. I was just so petrified of losing you."

"I'm not going anywhere. You're stuck with me. Like it or not. Got it?"

"Yeah."

"Hey. You wanna try again? For a baby? We have the money now." He brushes my hair behind my ear and kisses me on my forehead.

"Do you?"

"I want whatever you want."

"That's not an answer. See, this is what I'm terrified of. It's so much easier for a man to become a father later in life than it is for a woman to become a mother."

"Babe, you want my real answer?"

"Yes."

"I think it's a little late for us. Besides, as much as I would have loved for it to happen back then, even as recent as ten years ago, I don't as much now. I love my life with you, the way it is. We can sleep as late as we want. Eat ice cream for supper if we want. Pick up and go whenever and wherever we want. Like now. Have sex whenever and wherever we want. Like now. We couldn't do that if we had kids. And in case you didn't know, I like having sex with you. A lot."

I laugh a little. "Okay, good, I feel the same way." I kiss him.

"So, you feeling a little better about everything?" he asks.

"Yeah. And look at Aunt Mitzi, still counseling me through her Bible from the beyond. Who knew she would get me to finally admit one of my biggest fears to you. I'm so sorry I never said anything, Clay. You deserve better than that from me. I'm really sorry."

"It's okay, babe. I get it now, where your insecurity comes from. I understand. Now, what else is bothering you?"

"Nothing, why?"

"You said you just admitted one of your biggest fears to me. Lynn, you know you can talk to me about anything. What is it? What are your other fears?"

Oh shit. I slipped up with that one. Damn you, subconscious. Crap, what do I say? I can't tell him about the letter. I don't want to. I'm not ready.

"I just worry about you."

"I already know that. What is it that you're not telling me?"

"Nothing. Just that…it's more often than you know. Where do you go when you drift off sometimes?"

"Don't worry about me, Lynn. I'm fine. I'm handling it."

I really do worry about him. But at least he dropped the subject. "Okay. I'm sorry."

"It's okay. Now," he brings me into him, sitting on the bed. I wrap my legs around his waist. "Can we at least pretend we're trying for a baby?" he asks, as he starts unbuttoning my shirt.

Chapter 50

"CLAY, WAKE UP." I shake him and jump out of bed to get redressed.

"What's wrong?" he asks in a groggy voice.

"It's almost twelve-thirty. We have half an hour left to check out."

"Shit. Good thing you woke up."

I'm running around, making sure we have everything packed. I check the bathroom again. Crap, I look frightening. I cried off all my makeup and my hair is a mess. I do the best I can to fix it with what little time we have.

"Come on, Clay," I yell from the bathroom, as I wash my face and forego my beauty regimen for now.

"Do we have time for coffee?" he asks.

"Probably. If we take it to go. Everything is packed, except for our toiletries. Get dressed first."

I get done in the bathroom and go ahead and make a small pot of coffee while Clay finishes putting his clothes back on. I really hate being rushed, so I call the front desk and ask for a late check-out. They give us till 2:00 this afternoon. Okay, good. I can breathe.

"Babe, we have till two. I went ahead and called for a late check-out."

"Thank you. Now I can enjoy my coffee."

"Yeah, I need some too. And now we have time to figure out the next clue."

"Right. Hit me with it."

I dig the list out of my purse.

"Ready?"

"Yep." He fixes our coffee and brings it to the table.

"Okay. 'Find the museum of the Initial railroad, a blushing end is where the secret is stowed.' Any ideas off the top of your head?"

"Let me think…initial railroad…maybe the first railroad?"

"The word 'Initial' is capitalized, if that helps."

"Yeah, probably another clue within a clue, like the rest have been. What does the keychain look like?"

I dig out key number ten. "It's the Monopoly man. From the board game," I say with a laugh. "He's pewter and holding the Boardwalk card." I show it to Clay. The key is long, brass, and bitted, with a peanut shaped hole in the center of the bow.

"Ah ha. 'Initial' railroad, then, would be B and O. Like in the game. Don't you remember playing Monopoly as a kid?"

"Of course. Who didn't?"

"We need to find the B and O Railroad Museum."

"That stands for Baltimore and Ohio, right?"

"Right. And my guess is that since we're right here by Maryland, we're headed to Baltimore," he says. "What's the rest of the clue again?"

"It's, 'a blushing end is where the secret is stowed.' A red caboose."

"Has to be. Good job, love."

We finish our coffee, check-out, and get back on the road.

We drive through a few neighborhoods before we get out of DC. I almost missed my Maryland sign. I never did see a welcome sign for Washington DC, so I suppose a picture of the White House itself will have to do.

I take my phone out and get ready to play some music. I'm in a country mood, so I hit the *Get My Country On* playlist. Since I know this is Clay's least favorite genre of music, I'll find a good party song I know he can tolerate. Yes. "You Never Even Called Me by My Name" by David Allen Coe will be okay with him. That's a fun song. I know at first, he'll roll his eyes, but by the end, he'll be singing along, the way he always does whenever this song plays. And there go his eyes.

"Clay, come on, you love this song."

"Only at a party when I have a beer in my hand and I'm already half drunk," he says.

"Fair enough. But I'm not changing it."

Of course, by the end of the song, he's singing. I knew it.

I take out my journal to write down a few things while "You Look So Good in Love" by George Strait starts playing. I'm not writing to transfer anything to any online blog for later, which I still haven't looked into, but just to reflect on the last couple of days. I learned a lot about myself. About Clay. Things I thought might drive a wedge between us, when in fact, they brought us closer together. I didn't think that was possible. I'll still worry though, and that may never go away, no matter how confident I am on the outside. The fear of him leaving me is deep. I hope it goes away though. I absolutely want it to.

"What'cha doin', babe?" Clay asks.

"Just writing about us."

"What about us?"

"Mostly about how the last couple of days went and how crazy they were. And how beneficial they were."

"Beneficial how?"

"Cathartic. For me."

"I can see that. For me too."

"How so?"

"I finally saw why you felt the way you did."

"You mean feel the way I do."

"Lynn, c'mon, I thought I put your worries to rest."

"I can't just turn them off within a few hours."

"Are you saying you don't believe me?"

"No, of course I believe you and everything you said, but it's just hard to flip the switch in my head that easily."

"Alright, now you're losing me. I thought the subject was closed."

"It's psychological. For me. It's my inner demon that I have to fight. I know you're not going anywhere, Clay."

"Do you?"

"I have faith that you won't."

"Lynn. You don't need faith for that. Faith is for something you can't see. I'm right here. You need to know it. Believe it."

"I do." I will. I'll get there.

"Okay then." He grabs my hand and doesn't let go until we get to Baltimore.

Why is this so hard? He's telling the truth, I know it. Why can't I trust that he won't leave me? Even after all this time. I know why. It's the other demon. I don't want to say her name, not even in my head. Why am I so intimidated by a freaking ghost from his past? Why do I continue to let her existence bother me so when Clay has never given me a reason to doubt his love for me? It's that damn letter. The one that's weighed on my mind for twenty-seven years.

Chapter 51

W E PARK IN the lot at the B&O Railroad Museum. It's a roundhouse building with a circular glass structure of windows and rotunda at the top. Outside in the rail yard I see locomotives, old passenger cars, boxcars, freight cars, vintage sleepers, flatcars, and of course a couple of cabooses. Some train cars sit right on the edge of the parking lot. We park right next to one of the old engines.

Inside, we're struck by the grandeur of the museum. American flags hang all around from the center of the building under the glass windows. Antique engines and passenger cars are exhibited throughout the place.

I see one caboose. The entrances are blocked with chains, as they should be, but I'm not sure how we're going to get around them.

"Clay, there are people everywhere," I whisper. "We'll never get into that caboose. Should we try the ones outside first? Or do you think we should look for someone and tell them our story and that we have a key?"

"Let's try outside first. Chances are, we'll be able to get in without being noticed. I know we can just ask, but I kind of like the sneaking around."

"My thoughts exactly. Let's just hope whatever we're looking for is in one outside."

We head back outside and find the caboose marked number 2222.

"Okay," he says, "you keep watch. I'll try to get in."

"Good, I was going to suggest that anyway. You with your stealth-like abilities. Plus, you're sprier than I am and will be able to jump the chains blocking the entrance. Good luck, babe." I give him the key and snap a few pictures of the caboose.

"Thanks."

He gets up to the door of the caboose and I hear him mutter a plethora of curse words.

"Shit, Clay, what is it?" I yell in a whisper.

He looks back at me. "It's got a frickin' padlock on it now. It needs a modern key. Not this antique crap." He jumps down off of the landing and comes back to my side near the caboose.

"Well, maybe that's not it. There's another one over there, and it looks older than this one."

"Okay, lemme go try that one. Stay on watch."

Clay runs up to the other caboose. He shakes his head. Same thing.

"Dammit. What do we do now?" I ask as he's back in my ear shot.

"We're gonna have to ask somebody to let us in."

"Crap, I was afraid of that. That always makes me so nervous. You know, it's always better to ask for forgiveness than permission."

"Well we can't break in, Lynn. And I can't walk through walls."

"I know, it just sucks."

Just then, a man in a conductor's uniform comes walking around the corner. "You interested in the caboose?" he asks us.

"Uh, yes, sir, actually," Clay says.

"Well, come on in. I was just about to open it up for visitors."

"So, it's okay for us to look around inside?" I ask.

"Sure. There's commentary and everything. Just press the button," he says.

"Oh, thank you." I say.

"What are the odds?" Clay whispers to me.

Since we're the first ones on board, we have the whole thing to ourselves. Hopefully we find something before other people start filing in.

The caboose is so clean. I'm sure this is not a historically accurate representation of how an active caboose actually looked, which no doubt would've been covered in soot and smoke from the engines, because I bet the all-male crews on board never minded a little grit and grime.

There's an old cast iron cook-stove similar to a pot-belly style, a lantern hanging on the wall, and a small stainless-steel sink that reminds me of something you might see in a prison. Small metal rungs are attached to a section of wall under the upper seats, like a ladder. Below the elevated seats are tall, skinny cabinets that resemble lockers, only without locks. Just door handles.

"Clay, you check these locker cabinet thingies, I'll check the stove."

"What are we looking for?"

"I dunno, but I bet we'll know it when we see it," I tell him.

I lift the cast iron cook-lids off the stove and poke around in there with my flashlight. I don't see anything except rust. I try to turn the draft controls at the bottom, but they won't budge. Next I open the stove door itself. More rust. I can hear Clay digging all around in the corners of the cabinets under the seats.

"Any luck with the lockers?"

"Nothing clear. Hand me your flashlight." I give it to him and he looks up, down, and all around with the beam of light inside each locker. "No, I don't see anything."

"Feel with your hands. Maybe there's a dip. A pocket. Or something." He inspects them again, sliding his palms all over the interior, plucking them to listen for sound variations, but still nothing.

Then he checks the bench seat and I investigate a storage box in the corner. Nothing and nothing.

"What are we missing?" I ask. "Are there any hidden panels in the walls? Or the floor?"

"I don't think so, but I'll look again."

Then it hits me. The lantern.

"Clay. The lamp."

"Oh yeah. Good thinking. There's gotta be something in there."

"Can you remove it and take it apart? Carefully?"

"Please," he says with heavy sarcasm.

"Sorry, sometimes I forget that you're skilled in so many areas."

"Oh, why Mrs. Sinclair, are you trying to make me blush again? You want me to turn the color of this caboose?" he asks, teasing me, as he takes the light down off the wall.

"Well, that depends."

"On what?"

He takes off the globe from the base of the burner.

"On how soon we can get to the next hotel. God forbid I give you blue balls again."

"Touché, babe."

He unscrews the burner from the base and looks inside. I'm waiting with bated breath. This is our last shot at finding something. He looks back at me and grins.

Chapter 52

"THE LETTER 'C,'" he says.

"As in another typewriter letter?"

"Yeah. See?"

He takes it out and hands it to me. I examine it while he puts the lantern back together. Just as he's about to hang it back on the wall, the employee back comes inside.

"Son, what are you doing?" Oh crap.

"I uh...we just...there was...okay, here's the thing."

Clay tells the man our story and I show him the typewriter key.

"Well, alright," the conductor-man says, "so long as you take it with you. I'm so tired of that rattle. Didn't know what the hell was in there. Never dawned on me to take the damn thing apart."

And just like that, he's gone. Clay and I have a nice laugh over it and I get back to checking out the key a little closer. "It's the same style as the 'B' we have. Like, from the same typewriter," I observe.

"Yeah. Okay, let's get out of here and figure out where we're headed next."

"Wait, I want to go back in and browse the gift shop. See if they have any ornaments."

"Alright. Let's go check it out."

We go back in and find the gift shop. I'm thrilled to see that they do have Christmas ornaments. I haven't been able to find very many at the places we've been. Most of them will have to be made with the pictures I take. We didn't even check to see if they had any at the White House because we were ready to high-tail it out of there. I'll order one online. I'm sure they exist.

Sadly, I don't see any caboose ornaments, but there's a glass ball ornament with the B&O Monopoly board game square on one side and the B&O capitol dome logo on the other. I have to get it, since it coincides with the keychain we have for this stop. I also buy a coffee mug with a picture of the museum and its history.

"Okay, ready to go?" I ask Clay.

"Yeah."

He takes the bag from me and holds my hand as we walk to the truck. I get in and get the cipher out.

"Alright. 'In the capital of the second smallest state, find the museum with Nipper. Try them all till you find the right one to activate, hopefully you leave a little chipper.' I have no idea about anything other than the first part. It looks like we're going to Dover, Delaware," I say.

"Nipper?"

"Yeah. It's capitalized. Maybe a person or nickname of something?"

"Maybe. What's the keychain look like?"

I look in the box. "It's a record. Like an old LP."

"Hmm," he wonders. "Maybe it's a music studio museum. Do a search for Dover, Delaware and Nipper. I don't know who or what Nipper is."

I look online and search. "Well, well, well… it's the Johnson Victrola Museum. Nipper was the RCA dog that was looking into the Victrola on their logo."

"Ah…very cool."

I give Clay the address and he keys it into the GPS.

"About two hours. We're gonna need to spend the night. I'll find us a hotel," I tell him.

"Wow, babe. Do you realize that so far, Maryland is the only state where we haven't spent the night?"

"Not true. We didn't stay in South Carolina."

"Oh yeah. Well then, do you want to keep going or do you want to find a place here? We can head to Delaware in the morning."

"You know what? Let's stay here. Make a night of it. I'll check the Baltimore hotels."

"Sounds good to me. I bet there's some good nightlife in Baltimore, too. Maybe we can find another brewery or something," Clay says.

"Or something."

"You didn't like the brewery in Athens?"

"No, I loved it. Just thinking maybe we can find something different. But if not, I'm all for another brewery."

I look up the local hotels and book a suite at one with a view of the harbor. Clay is navigating through his phone. Probably looking up the nightlife. He takes out his credit card and buys something. I see a barcode on his screen. Concert tickets? That would be cool.

"What'cha buying?"

"Don't worry about it." Ooh, I love surprises.

I punch the address to the hotel in the GPS. "Sweet, only seven minutes," I say. "Full steam ahead."

"You trying to make a joke, babe?" He puts his card back in his wallet and throws it in the console.

"Yeah. Not funny?"

"Sorry. You need more *training*."

I laugh at his pun. "Well, maybe you can help me get back on *track*."

"There you go. That one wasn't lame."

"Call my jokes lame again, Mr. Sinclair, and you won't get any of this caboose tonight."

"Another good one. And touché, Mrs. Sinclair."

Clay and I get all checked in to the hotel and unload our stuff in our room. We've got a great view of the harbor. There are several luxurious yachts moored in the boat slips and some sailboats anchored out on the water. I can't wait to see what the panoramic scene looks like at night, with all the lights reflecting in the marina.

"So, babe. What did you find for us to do tonight?" I ask.

"Something fun."

"Give me a hint."

"No."

"Why?"

"Because it's more entertaining for me if I keep you in the dark." He gives me a wicked smile.

"A concert? I saw you buying tickets to something."

"Not a concert."

"Is it a romantic dinner cruise in the harbor?"

"No. But that sounds nice. But, no. Sorry."

"Pub crawl?"

"Stop trying to guess."

"It's a pub crawl."

"It's not a pub crawl."

"Ghost tour?"

"Stop it. I'm not telling you."

"Ugh…alright, fine. I like surprises anyway."

"I know you do. So, let it be one. I'll tell you this though. It's something we've never done together before. And you need to get ready now. Wear something casual and comfortable. We need to leave ASAP."

"Oh, that sounds interesting. So, like a t-shirt and shorts?"

"Yeah, perfect."

I get dressed and we head down. Clay hails a cab. The driver asks where we're headed and Clay hands him a piece of paper that I can only assume is the address of where we're going, so as to keep it a secret from me. I have no idea what we're doing, but I'm a bit giddy. I love when Clay surprises me.

We are literally in the car for only about ten minutes when we pull up to Camden Yards.

"A baseball game? Really?" I ask with high-pitched enthusiasm. No pun intended.

"Yep. The Orioles versus the Washington Nationals."

"Oh, Clay, this is so cool. I've never been to a major league game."

"I know. I've been to a few before, when I was a kid. My dad took me to some Astros games. But, you and I have never been to one together. And I've never seen the Orioles, so this is all new for me, too."

"Thank you, Clay. I love this surprise."

"Good, I'm glad. Come on, we have to hurry. The game's about to start."

We rush to our seats, which are pretty good considering Clay just bought them about an hour ago. We're on the first level right by third base. The game should start in about twenty minutes.

"These are great seats. How did you manage this on such short notice?" I ask Clay.

"It's not exactly packed, so these were easy to get. You hungry?"

"Yeah, now that you mention it."

"Okay, I'll go grab us a couple of hot dogs and beers. I don't see any vendors in the stands around here."

"Hopefully the line isn't too long, I don't want you to miss anything."

"Me either. I'll be right back."

He gives me a kiss as he leaves his seat. Clay truly is an amazing man. An amazing husband. An amazing lover. Just all around amazing. I actually hate that word, 'amazing.' It's so overused that its essence has diminished. But, there really is no better word to describe my husband.

So here I am again, alone with my thoughts in the stands of Camden Yards. Though I guess I'm not really alone, per se, since there are at least a few thousand people around me. But, without Clay by my side, I do feel like I'm by myself sometimes. Therefore, my mind wanders. I think about how wonderful our life is and how fortunate we are to be on this quest together. All of the memories we're making, thanks to Aunt Mitzi and Uncle Sid. I can finally check 'go to a professional baseball game' off my bucket list.

Clay knows me so well, inside and out. His arranging this game for us makes me love him more and doubt him less. But, I just can't shake that subconscious feeling of uncertainty I have regarding her. You know who I'm talking about. With Pam still so fresh on my mind from last night, it reminds me of the other one. I can't help but think that Pam's sister might be on Clay's mind, too. Does he still think about her? Does he ever dream about her? Does he ever wonder what his life would be like if she wouldn't have left him that last time? He'd be a daddy if he'd married her instead of me. I wonder if he thinks about that.

That thought leads me to recall the time I came back from one of my doctor's appointments. The appointment where I learned that I didn't ovulate and probably wouldn't be able to conceive. I was twenty-seven. Clay was supposed to come with me to the doctor, but he got called into an emergency meeting at the police station. I cried all the way home from that appointment and walked in the door with puffy, red eyes. Clay was home when I got there.

"What are you doing home?" I asked him.

"I left the meeting early. I'm sorry I couldn't go with you to the doctor. But, I wanted to be here when you got home. What's wrong, babe? What did they say?"

I started crying again and sat on the couch next to him. He put his arm around me and pulled me close.

"I can't," I said through tears. "It's impossible."

"What's impossible? The doctor told you that?"

"Not exactly, but she might as well have. I don't ovulate. I'm sorry, Clay. I'm sorry."

"Why are you apologizing? You didn't do anything wrong. Are you okay? Physically?"

"I guess. I mean, it's not life threatening, just heartbreaking."

"I'm so sorry I wasn't there with you, Lynn. Fucking work."

"It's okay. I probably needed to let all these tears out by myself anyway. I asked the doctor if this was the end of the road and she said we could always try to adopt, or medically, the next step would be to make an appointment with a specialist for in vitro."

"What's that?"

"It's where they take my egg and your sperm and put them in a petri dish and then after it's ready, they implant it into me and hope it takes."

"A test-tube baby?"

"Yeah, that's the term most people are familiar with. The doctor said the procedure is gaining momentum."

"How much does it cost?"

"It's insanely expensive, so yeah, this is probably the end for us. But she said no doctor in their right mind will ever tell a patient that it's impossible to become pregnant because miracles happen every day. So we just have to hope and pray for a miracle. I'm sorry that my body is broken and there's basically a snowball's chance in hell that we'll become parents." I laid my head in his chest and cried some more.

"Hey. Lynn. Look at me, love."

I looked up into his crystal-blue eyes and he wiped my tears away. "What?"

"You are not broken. Your body works just fine for me. And you know, I love our life. It's perfect the way it is. I married you because I love you. Not because I wanted kids. If you get pregnant, that would just be a bonus."

"That's the sweetest thing ever," I told him, and of course, I started crying again.

Chapter 53

"WHAT DID I miss?" Clay asks as he comes back with our hotdogs and beers.

"Um, nothing. Looks like you're just in time. They're getting ready for the first pitch." I wouldn't know if he'd missed anything anyway, since I was lost in my thoughts.

The Orioles come on in the bottom of the first inning and score a homerun right off the bat. Literally.

"Holy shit." Clay says.

We jump up and down and cheer like we've been lifelong fans of the Baltimore Orioles. It's thrilling.

"Oh my God, that was fun," I say as we sit back down. "Good thing we finished our food and drinks."

"Yeah. Otherwise beer and mustard would be all over us right now," he says with a laugh.

The Orioles score two more homers in the first inning, which keeps us on our toes. Clay catches the third homerun ball. There's a kid a few rows in front of us that's about twelve years old who almost caught it with his glove, but it bounced right out and landed in Clay's hands like magic. Without even giving it a thought, Clay looks at me and says, "I'll be right back." He goes down and gives the kid the baseball. The boy is ecstatic, with wide eyes and a huge smile. Clay gives him a high-five. It looks like the dad is trying to pay Clay for the ball. Clay won't take it. I know he won't. He shakes the dad's hand and claps the boy on the shoulder. When he gets back to his seat, he tells me that the boy said he will remember this day forever and that he'd been trying to catch one for three years.

We're having the best time. We laugh and cheer, eat stadium food, drink stadium beer, and have great conversations with some true Orioles fans sitting next to us. After tonight, Clay and I are in that number. Our Orioles win the game with a score of six to four. We'll be fans of this baseball team from here on out.

We get back to the hotel and we are both tired, but keyed up. It's getting pretty late and I just want to crash, but Clay has other plans.

"Come on, babe, let's go down to the hotel lounge and celebrate the win with a drink."

"Clay, I'm kinda tired. We've had a long day. Besides, the lounge closes soon."

"C'mon, Lynn, one drink. Then we can come back up and relax. You promised me some caboose anyway." He winks at me.

"I did, didn't I? Okay, one drink. But that's it."

We go down to the lounge and I get us a table while Clay orders for us. He comes back with a Michelob Ultra for me and a Loose Cannon IPA on draft for himself. He raises his glass and I do the same with my bottle.

"To the Orioles and a renewed appreciation for baseball," he toasts.

"Cheers," I say, as we clink our drinks together.

"So," Clay says, "we have ourselves a letter 'C' now along with our 'B.' What do you think that could stand for?"

"I don't know. 'C' could be for 'Chauvin,' since that's our family name. 'B' could still be for 'Bernice.'"

"Or, 'BC' for 'Before Christ,'" he says.

"The letters do look like they came from a typewriter before Christ."

Clay nearly spits his beer out. "Good one, babe. But wouldn't they be Hebrew letters if that were the case?" He smiles.

"No, they're from a Latin typewriter, like Caesar used."

"You're just full of the jokes tonight," he laughs.

"Thanks, I'm here all week." I play a little air rim-shot and give my best 'badum bum chhhh' sound effect with it.

Clay wiggles his fingers in front of him on a pretend keyboard. "Veni, vidi, vici." He pulls an imaginary sheet of typing paper from the invisible platen and laughs again.

"You're so silly," I tell him. "It might still be too early to speculate though. With the letters, I mean. There could be more coming, since we have two now. God only knows how many we'll end up with in the end."

"True," Clay replies. "So, tomorrow, the Victrola Museum. What do you think is there?"

"No telling. Although, my guess would be a lot of old record players."

"You're seriously on fire tonight, woman." He laughs and takes another sip of his beer.

I smile. "I have my moments. Maybe she donated one of her Victrolas. She and Uncle Sid had several over the years that I know of, and there's only two left in the house."

"Huh. Interesting. I only recall seeing the one in the den. Where's the other?"

"It's in the third bedroom on the right, upstairs. In the corner by the bed."

He closes his eyes. "Oh yeah. Okay I see it now."

We talk about the game some more and how much fun we had.

"You were so sweet to give that kid the ball," I tell him.

"Well, it was his. He would have had it if it wouldn't have bounced out of his glove. Besides, I'm not a complete asshole."

"No, not entirely." I wink at him. I take the last sip of my beer and shake the bottle from side to side to show Clay I'm finished and to signal that I'm ready to go. "Lounge closes in five minutes." He gulps the last few swallows of his beer down and we head upstairs.

Back in our room, I walk over to the window to look out into the harbor. It's even more beautiful at night. The dramatic glow of the lights dancing on the water is mesmerizing. I can hear the faint sounds of metal cables clanging against aluminum masts like nautical wind chimes. Clay comes up behind me and wraps his arms around my waist as he rests his chin on my shoulder.

"Dazzling, isn't it?" I ask him.

"Yeah. Very captivating. This is a great view. Great room." Then he slowly whispers into my ear, "Great bed."

"Oh really? You've tested it already, Mr. Sinclair?" I ask with a smile as a tingle blazes up my spine.

I turn around to face him. He doesn't answer me, not even playfully. His eyes are kindled from a place beyond words. He's ignited. He grabs the back of my head with one hand while his other one is still around my waist, pulling me closer. He charges into me, kissing me hard. I kiss him back, fueled by passion. He tastes like beer and smells like cologne mixed with the outdoors and a hint of sweat. He smells like a man. My man. His pheromones are flammable, making me burn for him. He lifts me up by my butt and I wrap my legs around him while kicking off my sandals. Clay carries me over to the bed and throws me down. Whoa. This is different. "Undress. Hurry," he tells me, as he shreds himself of his clothes. We're naked in seconds. He lies next to me on the bed and touches me. He feels how ready I am for him.

"Oh, God, babe," he whispers, "You're so wet. I love feeling you like this. It's so fucking hot."

"It's what you do to me," I whisper back. "I love how you make me feel."

He kisses me again as he continues stoking me between my legs and stirs the inferno already within. I reach down for him and he's as ready as I am.

In a hushed voice, I ask, "Clay, what are you waiting for? I need you."

"I know," he mutters back, "but I'm putting you at bay for a bit. I'm in control tonight."

"No fair," I say to him with a slight laugh. But I know, it's payback time for Birmingham. And yesterday in DC. Intensity meter blown.

He takes his hardness and rubs the tip up and down my slick center, teasing me, tantalizing me, tormenting me. He's feeding my fire. Fanning my flames. Furthering my flare. God, I just want him inside me. How long is he going to torture me? I'm a ticking time bomb, waiting to be detonated. Just when I think I'm going to combust, he finally lights my fuse.

Each strike initiates a shower of sparks. Each spark singes me with sizzling intensity, until we are engulfed in wildfire. Excitement is gauged by the dispatch of signals between our eyes. Body heat rising. Pressure building. Flashpoint rushing. Until finally, we are rescued by the explosion, followed by the collapse, and we simmer into smoldering embers.

Chapter 54

CLAY WAKES ME up with a kiss on my forehead. "I've got your coffee ready. There wasn't much creamer. I hope it's okay."

I stretch and sit up to take the mug from his hands. "Thanks," I say, still half asleep. I take a sip. "It's fine. What time is it?"

"Eight fifteen."

"How long have you been up?"

"Since about seven. I went to the gym, showered, and then brewed the coffee."

I take a few more sips from my mug, then get up to go to the bathroom. I grab a quick shower and brush my teeth.

"Clay?" I semi yell from the bathroom.

"Yeah, babe?" he answers back.

"Can you check and see what time the Victrola museum opens please?"

"Sure thing, love."

As I'm in the middle of blow-drying my hair, Clay enters the bathroom with a sour look on his face. "What? What's wrong? Don't tell me they're shut down."

"No. Just closed. They reopen tomorrow."

"Shit. So now what?" I ask.

"Let's stay here again tonight. I can take you on that romantic harbor dinner cruise."

"Aww, babe, I would love that."

"Consider it booked."

After I do my hair and makeup, I get dressed and join my husband at the table with a fresh cup of coffee. He's reading the paper with a smile on his face.

"Good news?"

"Check it out. We're famous." He slides it my way and there's a picture of us with him catching the ball from the game last night.

"Oh wow. Cool. That's getting laminated and going on the scrapbook tree. Maybe even at the top, since we're stars and all."

He snickers. "I agree. Definitely a night to remember," he says. "Down to the last seconds of it." He winks at me.

"Yup, I must say, that was also quite memorable, Mr. Sinclair."

"Oh, really now? What was your favorite part, Mrs. Sinclair?"

"It was all good. But I think just the way you started it, going from zero to a hundred in milliseconds. You set me on fire."

"Mission accomplished." He leans over and gives me a kiss. "I love you, babe."

"I know."

Chapter 55

CLAY STARTS THE truck. "Whose turn is it? I've lost track."
"Yours."
"Good." He hits the shuffle button on his playlist. "Uprising" by Muse starts playing. "Hell yeah. I haven't heard this song in a while."

"It is quite the jam," I say. "In fact, it's on my *Badass Songs* playlist. Turn it up."

When we arrive in at the Johnson Victrola Museum in Dover, there are no other cars in the parking lot.

"Are you sure they're open?" I ask Clay.

"Their webpage says they are. And look, the lights are on. It's still a little early though, we might be their first visitors of the day."

"True."

"You'd think people would be lined up to look at old record players on a Wednesday morning," he smiles.

"Goofball. Okay, let's check it out." I get the clue out again to refresh our memory. "Basically, we have to try and unlock all the Victrolas until we find the right one."

"Yikes, that could take a while. At least there's not that many people here."

"Yeah," I say, "but that means the employees will be watching us that much closer. Probably."

"And if we run into that, we can always tell our story. They might lead us right to it."

"Maybe so. We'll just see what happens. But yeah, I like sneaking around, seeing how far we can get without having to explain ourselves." I fold the cipher back up and put it back in my purse, but keep the keychain out.

Clay opens the door and Victrolas are everywhere. All shapes, sizes, and colors. Some are simple, tabletop versions with small horns. Others are more ornate with large horns and detailed cabinets. There's a section in the middle of the museum where several of the loveliest Victrola horns are hanging from the ceiling. My favorite one is painted a light-blue, inside and out, with groups of pink rosebuds on stems with leaves encircling the opening.

We are soon greeted by a curator who starts telling us some of the history and I'm half paying attention, fascinated and distracted at the same time. After her spiel about felt plungers and RPMs, she lets us explore the museum at our leisure. I breathe a small sigh of relief.

I notice a collection of Nipper memorabilia in a corner. There are tons of various pieces with the little dog looking into the Victrola. The famous painting is called *His Master's Voice*. There's a stained glass rendition, salt and pepper shakers, stuffed animals, and ceramic Nippers of all sizes.

"You want to make this interesting?" Clay asks me.

"What do you mean? It's already interesting."

"No, I mean, do you want to make a bet on which one will open?"

"Oh. Sure. I bet it's one of the fancier ones."

"Well, of course, right? Too easy. Which fancy one though?" He looks around. "I bet it's—"

"Wait. What are we wagering? What do we win?"

"Satisfaction of being right."

"No. You said interesting. That's boring."

"Alright, Mrs. Sinclair. What do you propose?"

"If I win...I drive for the next week."

"Negative. Next option."

"We get a pool."

"A pool? At home?"

"Yeah. Build us a whole backyard oasis."

"Done and done. You don't even need to bet me for that, Lynn. If you wanted a pool, you could have just said so. You know I won't say no to you for anything."

"Except to drive the truck."

"Yeah. Except for that," he smiles. "Come on, let's just look for the Victrola."

We try to open a few of the more elaborate Victrolas, but the key doesn't work on any of them. It either won't fit or fails to turn. So we try some of the basic ones. They don't unlock either. Then, I notice something that seems out of place. There is a gigantic ceramic Nipper, about five feet tall, right next to one of the swankiest Victrolas I've ever seen. The machine is vaguely familiar.

"Maybe this was part of the clue," I tell Clay. "Since she mentioned Nipper and that we'd have to try all the Victrolas till we found the right one. Maybe it's been this one all along. This Nipper is not even in the collection in the corner. It's too big."

"Yeah, good job. And right next to this far from ordinary Victrola. That's gotta be the one," he says. "Go ahead. Unlock it."

The gold-leafed Victrola stands at about four feet tall. The doors are painted with a couple of angelic women playing lyres. They're dancing in colorful dresses. On the side of it, there's a man, clothed in a blue suit. Maybe he's searching for the origin of the music that the ladies are playing on the other side of the cabinet. It reminds me of Keats' poem, "Ode on a Grecian Urn." The Victrola's gilded surface and elaborate artistic design are signs of affluence. This was for a rich man's parlor. Moving closer, the placard that accompanies the lavish old-timey record player comes into view.

```
On loan to the Johnson Victrola Museum from
the personal collection of Mr. and Mrs. Sal-
vatore "Sid" Santini of Baywood, Louisiana.
To remain until further notice from Lynn
and/or Clay Sinclair.
```

Yep. I knew I'd seen this Victrola before. And apparently, Uncle Sid's name was really Salvatore. Named after his grandfather. Something else I didn't know.

"Holy crap, Clay. This is ours if and when we want it."

"What? Are you serious?"

I show him the small notecard placed near the bottom of the Victrola. "I would love to take it now, but I know the truck doesn't have room for it."

"Or the security," Clay says. "Plus, the Victrola doesn't have Bluetooth."

"Ha, ha, ha. Somehow I doubt any of the records that would play on this would be in your list of favorites."

"Touché. Let's see about having it shipped to the house after we get home. Not that I don't trust CeCe in handling it, but I don't want her to hurt herself, trying to find a place for it."

"Good idea," I reply. "Okay here goes nothing." I put the key into the golden cabinet and turn. *Click.* The two smaller top doors open to reveal the shelves originally used to store the records. But instead, I find an envelope. To neither of our surprises, inside is a note from Aunt Mitzi:

> *Dear Loves,*
>
> *My gift to you this leg of your tour is this Victrola itself. I have fond memories of this exquisite piece. It was a wedding present from Sid's father to his mother and was handed down to us with the house.*
>
> *When we started this little adventure for you, we thought this would be a great find for both of you. We found out about this museum and made the trip up here to let them use it on display until you discovered it.*
>
> *We've already paid to have it moved for you, so whenever you're ready, just say the word. It's been arranged that the movers will even take it inside and set it up where you want it.*
>
> *I hope you both enjoy having it back in the house. May you find as much pleasure in it as we have found over the years. We loved swaying to the sweet melodies coming from it. We would waltz to "Three O'clock in the Morning" by John McCormack, one of our favorite songs. You'll find that record still in the house.*
>
> *As always, Love, Aunt Mitzi and Uncle Sid*

"Well, that answers one of our questions. At least we can have it delivered to the house now and Cecilia won't have to worry about it," I tell Clay. "I can't believe it though. I forgot all about this Victrola. I remember asking Aunt Mitzi what happened to all their Victrolas, and all she told me was that they sold them, except for the two left in the house. I wonder where the rest of them are. Maybe they really did sell the others, or gave them to Uncle Sid's side of the family. I bet Enzo has one."

"Probably so," Clay says. "Okay, well are you alright with finding the tour guide and asking them to ship it to the house now? It'll be there when we get back."

"Yeah, that sounds perfect. Should we put it in the room upstairs with the other one?"

"That's not how stereo works, babe." He smiles. "How about we put it in one of the other bedrooms, so we can spread them out?"

"Even better," I agree. "I really want that huge Nipper, but I'm sure he's not for sale."

"Yeah, I doubt it. Would be a neat addition to the house though, wouldn't it? Maybe we can find our own little Nipper at some point."

"That would be super cool."

We find the manager of the museum and tell her who we are and give her our story. She's delighted to meet us and promises us that she will set up the transfer of the Victrola as soon as possible and assures us that it will arrive safely.

It starts to rain and we run back to the truck. Clay looks at me and says, "Well, babe, that was an easy one. Where to now?"

I get the list out. "Ready? 'In the Garden State's Colonial Park, the stone cottage is where you'll want to check in the dark. Stay on your toes, make sure you're out before the gates close.' Oh my. That sounds a bit ominous."

"Yeah, most parks close before dark," Clay says. "How are we going to manage that? You have the key?"

"Yep."

"Show me."

"No. That's Missouri. We're going to New Jersey. The Garden State."

"Touché. Again." He smiles at my little joke.

The key is a regular looking house key, and the keychain is a stack of five small stones. They are almost completely flat. I show it to Clay.

"I like it," he says. "Very Zen."

"It is."

"I bet those would skip for miles across water."

"Well, don't think you're ever going to get the chance to prove it, Mr. Sinclair. But, you're right. They'd be perfect for skipping, if they weren't stacked on top of each other and held together by a wire."

"Lynn, seriously, though. How are we going to manage getting into that place at night? Should we tell them who we are or chance it?"

"Let's chance it. Makes for a better story, right?"

"Oh, you finally found your sense of adventure. Good for you, babe."

"Yeah, we'll see. I'm sure it will be pretty unnerving."

"It'll be fine."

"Wonder why though. At night I mean."

"Must be good reason. Maybe it's a greater risk to go during the day, where people could actually see us going in, knowing we don't belong."

"Maybe so."

"Don't worry about it yet. It's just a property right? Like the house in South Carolina?"

"That was different."

"How? If anything, that was worse, because it was private property. At least this is public property."

"Yeah, with authorities that could possibly arrest us for trespassing."

"You're freaking out. Let's just get there first. Now, who's up for some more kick-ass music?"

"Hit it," I tell Clay. "Renegades" by X Ambassadors starts.

After about an hour, we finally cross the Delaware River and make it into New Jersey. No welcome sign though. Bummer.

Clay's phone buzzes and he hands it to me to check his text messages. **Nice catch.**

That's all it says. It's from an unknown number. I read it to Clay.

"What? Who's it from?" he asks.

"I don't know. It's from an unknown number."

"Shit. It's gotta be Pam. She must have seen the paper."

"You want me to respond?"

"Yeah. 'New phone. Who dis?'" he says and we both start cracking up.

I decide not to respond at all. After about ten minutes, she sends another text, which I relay to my husband.

I know you read that, Clay. If you're still in town, why don't you ditch that wife and call me. We can make up for lost time. I've fantasized about you for thirty-five years.

"Now what?" I ask, as my blood begins to boil.

"Just ignore it."

"That's really hard."

"That's what she said."

"Who, Pam? I'm gonna kick her ass. Turn around."

"No, babe, I was trying to be funny."

"Not the time."

Sorry. Really though, just ignore it. Better yet, block her number."

"Good idea."

While I'm trying to figure out the settings on Clay's phone, another text comes through. I read it to Clay through clenched teeth.

You know you want it. I saw the way you looked at me the other night. Come and get it. Followed by a picture of her in bed with nothing but a sheet on and showing heavy cleavage. I don't tell him that part.

"Just how exactly were you looking at her?"

"She's delusional, Lynn."

"Is she? She's gorgeous, Clay. You're gonna sit there and tell me you didn't look her up and down a couple of times? Because I did."

"Maybe I did. I don't remember. I'm only human."

"Wrong answer."

"Lynn, come on. I don't want anything to do with her. She's obviously unhinged. And desperate."

I'm still trying to figure out his freaking settings.

Buzz. It sure is wet.

"What's it say?"

"This bitch has balls."

"That's what it says?"

"No." I tell him what it really says.

"Maybe she's just talking about the weather. It is raining."

"Are you actually defending her?"

"No. Just playing devil's advocate."

"How considerate of you. Ass."

Buzz. This time, it's just a picture, with her boobs completely out. I don't tell him. But he sees it. Damn, she has a nice rack. I see Clay trying to sneak another peek.

"Are you serious right now? Keep your eyes on the road, Clay!" The texts just keep coming, all before I can figure out how to block her damn number. And all of which I read to Clay with hesitation, irritation, and indignation.

Buzz. Tell me you haven't thought about me. I bet you can't.

Buzz. Know why? Because you never forget your first.

Buzz. I've hated Alexa since the day you started dating her. She's an idiot for letting you go.

Buzz. Biggest mistake of her life. She knows it too. Says you're the one that got away.

Buzz. Stop ignoring me, Clay. You won't like the outcome.

"Jesus, she's pathetic. You haven't figured out the settings yet?"

"I'm working on it. Damn this new technology." I'm clicking buttons in his sub settings and menus. His phone is so different from mine.

Buzz. Lynn doesn't know, does she?

"Doesn't know what?" I ask.

"I don't know what she's talking about. What else could there possibly be? I'm pretty sure you know everything."

"Pretty sure? Is there anything more you want to tell me?"

"No."

"So, there is something else. You just don't want me to know about it."

"That's not what I meant. There is nothing else."

Buzz. Too bad Alexa lost your baby.

What. The. Fuck. I can't even read it out loud. Pressure builds in my chest. It's like I forgot how to breathe. My hands start shaking and I silently start crying.

"Babe, what is it? What did she say?"

"Like you don't fucking know, you liar!" I scream through tears.

I throw his phone at him.

"Got dammit, Lynn, I'm driving. What the hell!" He swerves and pulls off the highway at the next exit. He parks in a grassy area off the side of the road down a secluded street and kills the motor. "What is wrong with you?"

"See for yourself. As if you don't already know. You asshole. How could you lie to me about that?"

"What are you talking about?" He picks up his phone and reads it. He looks like he's seen a ghost. "Babe, I—"

"Don't fucking 'babe' me right now."

"Lynn. I didn't know. I swear. I didn't know. I would never keep that from you. Not after everything we've been through."

"I don't believe you."

"What?" His voice cracks.

"I don't fucking believe you, Clay! That's what!"

Buzz. He looks at his phone and shakes his head. He blinks his eyes hard and a tear falls down his cheek. He gives me his phone.

Oops. Did I just let the cat out of the bag? That's something even you didn't know. Life's a bitch, ain't it?

My God. Shit. "Oh, Clay," I whisper.

"Don't. Just. Don't."

"I'm sorry, Clay. I—"

"I said don't fucking do this right now, Lynn!"

He gets out of the truck and slams the door.

Chapter 56

HE'S FUMING. SEETHING. Livid. He walks back and forth, runs his hands through his hair, and takes a few deep breaths. At the bed of the truck, he pulls the tailgate down and flips the bedcover open. I watch as he sits in the back, brings his knees up, and lays his head down, his chest heaving. All I want to do is get out and hug him, but he needs space.

I pick up his phone. No more texts. Pressing a few more buttons, her number is finally blocked. That fucking bitch. How dare she. If he didn't know, then it had to be after they broke up the last time. After he wrote her out of his life and made her do the same. Why wouldn't she tell him she was pregnant though? That's just cruel.

Clay seems to have calmed down. A little. The rise and fall of his chest has decreased to a slower surge. God, I'm the worst wife. How could I not believe him? I was so wrong for that. I can't imagine what's going through his head right now. All I can do is sit here and look at him. I won't move or speak until he gives me permission.

It's been fifteen minutes. I bite my lip and fidget with the buttons on my shirt. He finally looks up and sees me watching him. He motions with his head for me to get out of the truck. Shutting the door with just a click, my feet tread lightly to the back of the truck. I climb in, sitting across from him. My mouth stays closed.

"I need answers," he says.

"I know."

His eyes are bloodshot.

"Lynn. I—"

"I'm sor—"

"Let me finish. I don't know what I'm more hurt by. The fact that Alexa hid this from me or the fact that you didn't believe me. I've never lied to you. For you to think that...that fucking cut. And as for the baby, I don't know what to think. I don't know how she could keep me in the dark about something that important. I don't know why Pam felt the need to share it after all these years. That was a real bitch move on her part."

He stretches out and scoots to the end of the truck, hanging his legs over the edge of the tailgate. I get as close as I can to him and do the same. My arm wraps around his waist and he gets up. So I get up. I take a step towards him and he takes a step back. I meet his eyes, reach for his hands, and slowly pull him into me. He doesn't resist. He hugs me tight and buries his head in my shoulder and cries. We stay that way for a few minutes. Neither one of us says a word.

He eases his grip on me, lets go, wipes his eyes, and takes a few more deep breaths. He walks to the passenger side of the truck. I start to follow him.

"No. You're driving. I can't." He gets in and shuts the door.

Whoa. I'm driving? I look on my phone for the nearest hotel. There's one just on the other side of the Turnpike. Perfect. I get in the truck and head in that direction.

"Where are you going?" Clay asks.

"I'm not driving the rest of the way in silence. And we're not doing the park like this. We're sorting this out right now. All of it."

I pull into the hotel parking lot and get out. Clay stays put, staring out the window at cars with unknown drivers rushing by on the highway. I go in and get us a room. Clay comes into the lobby with our suitcases just as the clerk hands me the keys.

We head up to the room and I open the door. Clay drops the bags at the entrance. In a daze, he goes straight for the bed and lolls down on top of the covers without even taking off his shoes, as if he's relied strictly on muscle memory. He faces the window, away from me. I get in behind him and wrap my small self against his muscular frame the best I can. He's still upset and I don't blame him.

"Clay. I was awful to you. I'm so sorry. You don't deserve that, especially from me. You're right to be angry with me."

"Angry's not what I am, Lynn."

"Hurt. I'm sorry I hurt you. I never want to do that again."

"You crushed me, Lynn," he whispers. "I felt like I couldn't breathe." I hear him sniff. I can't see it, but I know his eyes are tearing up again.

"I know." I prop myself up so I can see his face.

"If I tell you something, I mean it. I've never felt so vanquished. So dismissed. By you of all people." Gravity lets a tear fall from his eyes.

"I know." I kiss him on his shoulder. "I'm sorry," I whisper.

He turns over in my direction. "Babe. Don't do that again. I don't know if I can take it."

"I won't."

I run my fingers through his hair and give him a peck on the lips.

He sits up and gets his phone out. He scrolls up and down, looking for the texts I guess.

"I finally figured out how to block her number," I tell him. He punches in a few things and then hits the call button on speaker.

"Well, well, well…" Pam says when she answers.

"Give me Alexa's number."

"Now why would I do *that*?" She asks in the cattiest voice I've ever heard.

"Because, you fucking bitch, I need answers. She has some explaining to do."

"What's to explain?" She sounds a little drunk, too.

"Fuck you, Pam."

"Ooh, is that how you talk to somebody who has what you want? 'Cause I've got something you want. Don't I, Clay? Don't you want what I've got?"

"I swear to God, if—"

"Relax, Clay. Here."

Clay writes the number on the hotel stationary. He hangs up and re-blocks Pam's. He takes a deep breath and dials his ex. It rings four times before she answers.

"Hello?"

"Alexa."

"Yeah? Who is this?"

"It's Clay. Sinclair."

Silence.

"Hello?" he asks. "Are you there?"

"Uh. Yeah. Sorry, I just…wow. Clay. Been a long time." She sounds genuinely surprised to hear from him. "What's—"

"Look, I need to know why you never told me about the baby."

"What? What are you talking about?"

"Don't play dumb. I ran into Pam. She filled me in on your little secret."

"That bitch. She swore. You were never supposed to know."

"Are you fucking kidding me? Why the hell not?"

"I…it…we…"

"Answer the fucking question, Alexa!"

She sighs. "I didn't know I was pregnant. It was after we had broken up the final time. I went to the emergency room with severe pain and bleeding, and found out I was having a miscarriage. I'm sorry, Clay, but it was over before it started. I would have told you if I'd known. I figured since there was no baby, no us, there was no need to burden you with that."

"It didn't cross your mind once that it might have been my right to know?"

"It crossed my mind several times. I didn't know what good it would do. You told me to leave you alone. Forget about you. So I did. I tried. For months after. And by the time I got enough courage to tell you, it was too late. I went to tell you. But you'd moved on. You weren't even in the country."

Oh my God. The first night she came to his house while he was deployed. That had to be when.

"What choice did I have at that point? Besides, your new girlfriend had me arrested and I had to promise not to go back there or she would reinstate the charges, which was so ridiculous by the way. I just wanted to talk to you."

No you didn't, bitch. You wanted him back.

"You picked a real winner, Clay. I hope you're happy."

Fuck you, bitch. He is.

"I am. And Lynn did the right thing. Don't blame her."

"She threatened me."

"She *warned* you. And you egged my house! What did you expect?" He shakes his head and sighs. "Forget it. That's all in the past. Thank you for answering the question."

"Whatever. Look, I'm sorry, Clay. I'm sorry Pam did that to you."

"That part's not your fault."

"You and I were great together, Clay. I'm sorry I threw it away."

"Don't be. I'm not."

Click.

He throws his phone on the floor and lies back down. He stares at the ceiling, his face an expressionless mask.

"What are you feeling?" I ask him.

"Part relief. Part sadness. Part fury. Towards Pam."

"Explain the rest."

"Well, I'm slightly relieved that she didn't intentionally keep an actual pregnancy from me."

"Do you believe her?"

"Yeah, I do. After all this, there's no reason for her to lie."

"I know why you're sad. I'm sad about it too. I'm sorry, Clay. Truly. I am."

He sniffles and starts tearing up again. "It's just not fair," he says shakily. "I didn't want to be with her anymore, but I would have been there for that baby."

"I know you would have. I know. Come here." He lays his head on my chest and I wrap my arms around him. We both cry for the loss of his angel baby. He out loud, and I silently.

Chapter 57

CLAY FALLS ASLEEP in my arms and I sit there holding him, rubbing my hands through his hair, trying to get him to unwind. He falls asleep, and eventually, sleep finds me as well.

I'm awakened by the need to pee. I don't want to disturb Clay though, he's sleeping so soundly and looks so calm. My arms and legs slowly untangle from Clay's. He squeezes me, telling me to remain. I do. Even though that didn't help matters with my bladder. I run my fingers through his hair some more and hear him fall back into a slumber. But I really have to go now. My motions are cat-like. Stealthy. Sneaky. Slinky.

"No. Don't leave me. Stay," he whispers, as he embraces me with a firm grip.

"Babe, I have to go to the bathroom. I'll be right back, I promise." He lessens his grasp and lets me up so I can go.

After the bathroom, I sit back in bed and scoot as close as I can to him. He rests his head back on my chest and drapes his arm over me. I rub his back and soothe him back to sleep.

My thoughts meander. I wonder how different our life would have been if their baby had survived. He or she would be at least twenty-six today. Clay would have been the best daddy. But would I have been the best step-mom? Would I have accepted it? Would I have resented it? Would it have driven Clay and me apart? Would we have even gotten married? Alexa would have definitely been in the picture, at least for eighteen years. Could I have handled that? I don't know. I begin crying again. For Clay. For me. For us.

I'm trying to be quiet and still, but I guess I'm stirring more than I thought, because Clay wakes up and stretches. I dry my eyes before he sees I've been crying. I can't let this be about me right now. I need to be strong for him. This is his time for heartbreak. His turn to lean on me. His moment to break down. I need to allow him. I owe it to him. Pull yourself together, Lynn.

He blinks and looks up at me. "What's wrong?" he asks.

"Nothing. I'm fine. What about you? You okay?"

"Emotionally drained. But, I'll be alright."

"Can I get you anything? You thirsty? Hungry?"

"A little thirsty, but don't get up yet. Stay with me."

"Sure thing, love."

"Hey, that's my line," he says as he smiles at me.

"I know." I smile back at him.

"Thank you."

"For what?"

"For this. For letting me have this meltdown. For being there. Here. I'm sorry. I'm not used to feeling so helpless. I'm supposed to be the strong one."

"Clay. This does not make you weak. It makes you human. You have nothing to be sorry for. You do know that, right? You did absolutely nothing wrong. You just learned something terrible. You got some of the worst news anybody can hear and you reacted. You're entitled. And on top of how I treated you, which was so wrong of me. I'm the one who has something to be sorry for. Not you. *I'm* sorry."

"Lynn, that's over. I know you're sorry. If the roles were reversed, who knows? I might have responded the same way. Let's just forget about it and move on."

"Okay."

"Okay then."

He starts to get up. I hold him down.

"Where are you going?"

"To get some water."

"No. I'll get it for you."

I go over to the sink and fix him a glass of ice water. He drinks it straight without stopping.

"I guess I was thirstier than I thought."

"Refill?"

"No, I'm okay now. Come lay back down with me. I want to keep hugging onto you."

I take off my shorts and my bra to be more comfortable and climb back into the bed. Clay gets down to his boxers and joins me under the covers. We face each other and he wraps himself around me.

"No funny business," I tell him. "I just want to be here for you."

"You are here for me. Why 'no funny business' though?" He chuckles.

"Clay, I'm serious. I know you're hurting. I'm not going to take advantage of that. And I don't want you to use sex to forget about it."

"I'll never forget about it. But I'm not letting it get in the way of my life with you. I need to be as close as possible to you right now. I want you, Lynn. Right now."

I can tell. How is it that men can be ready to go within seconds? He kisses me and I give in. We spend the rest of the afternoon in bed, using only body language to communicate.

Chapter 58

THE NEXT MORNING, we get up and continue on our way up the Turnpike to Colonial Park Gardens in Franklin Township, New Jersey. Not long after, I finally see a welcome sign and get excited.

"It's my turn for the radio," I tell him, "but you want it?"

"Okay. Why though?"

"I just want you to be happy."

"I am happy." He looks at me and I know my face is giving away some fear. "What is it?" he asks. I'm afraid to say. "Come on, Lynn. Talk to me."

"I'm just a little scared that what we found out yesterday might change you."

"What? I'm still the same person, Lynn. Nothing has changed."

"Hasn't it though?"

"No. Not really. So there's a tidbit of information from my past that came to haunt me. And it may very well haunt me at times in the future, but it doesn't change who I am."

"A tidbit? How can you be so flippant? You were almost a father."

"That's not exactly what I meant. I'm not trying to play it down. I just mean that, yeah, it's sad. But it happened so long ago and I didn't even know about it. Let's say she had it and hid it from me, told everybody it wasn't mine but it really was. *That* would change me. But that's not what happened. I'm still me, babe. And I dealt with it yesterday. It's out of my system. I can't dwell on it, and you shouldn't either." He looks at me reassuringly. "Okay, Lynn?"

"Okay."

"But..." he pauses.

"But what?" I ask, as I run my hand through my hair, afraid of what he'll say.

"I will take you up on your offer."

"My offer?"

He smiles and hits his playlist. "Epic" by Faith No More starts.

A big smile flashes back at him. And I drop the subject. I let it go. If he's moving on, I will too.

"So," I say, after we've driven a few miles, "it seems we'll be spending the rest of the day and into the night at the park. We may need to pack our picnic backpack. They might not have a restaurant on site."

"Oh, that's true. I hadn't thought about that. Guess we should hit a grocery store or drive thru or something on the way," Clay replies.

I look online. "There's a big supermarket up ahead in a few miles. We can pick up some stuff there from the deli."

"Cool deal. Check the flashlight. Make sure the batteries are good."

My hands rummage through the glovebox, find the flashlight, and turn it on. "Pretty bright. But I guess it wouldn't be a bad idea for us to pick up some more anyway."

After stocking up at the store, we make it to the park just before noon.

"Alright, we need a game plan," Clay says.

"Should we have packed our camo?"

He laughs. "No. It's a good thing we thought about wearing dark clothes though. I'm thinking we can just make a day of the park, like actually check it out, have our picnic and all that."

"Yeah? Sounds good. Then what? The park closes at nine. That doesn't give us very long after the sun goes down. How are we going to hide from the groundskeepers?"

"I was thinking we could just evade all the groundskeepers. Keep a low profile all day, you know? Try not to ask questions."

"I guess."

"This place seems to stretch on for miles. See if you can pull up a map or something and find this stone cottage."

I look online and find a map of the grounds, but no mention of a stone cottage. However, I do find some other information about picnicking.

"Well, it looks like their main picnic areas have to be reserved in advance and are for groups of people. But there are a few picnic tables by a different parking lot, back out across the street, in the other section of the park. Should we head there first and eat?"

"Yeah. Let's do that," he says.

Clay starts the truck back up and drives us over to the other lot about half a mile away. We get out and set up our little picnic at one of the tables. I'm happy to finally make use of my retirement present. Our little spread consists of rotisserie chicken, green beans, macaroni and cheese, and fruit salad for dessert. And instead of wine, we have bottled water.

"This sure is some mighty fine vittles you got here, Mrs. Sinclair."

"All your favorites."

"So, what else is there to do around here?" he asks.

I check online again. "Aww, man, we're two days early for the mini golf and the paddle boats. They don't open up for the season until Saturday. That would have been fun. I want to check out the rose garden though, for sure."

We finish eating and then head back to our previous parking spot. We get out and walk towards the Rudolf W. van der Goot Rose Garden. Everything is in bloom and the breeze brings out the perfumes of the flowers. There's a huge fountain in the middle of the garden, surrounded by a stone walkway that branches out in several directions. On either side of each path, rows of different rose bushes sway in the gentle wind. There must be hundreds of varieties and colors. We walk around and I spot Aunt Mitzi's favorites, the Candy Swirl roses. I stop, take a whiff of them, and I have a moment.

"I miss her so much," I tell Clay.

"I know. Me too." He gives me a hug and kisses me on my forehead. "You okay?"

"Yeah," I say with a sniffle.

"C'mon. Let's walk over there and sit down for a minute." Clay points towards the pathway that leads to a gazebo.

We sit down on a bench and I lean into Clay as he puts his arm around me. "Is it weird that I can feel her presence here?" I ask.

"No, not at all. We know she was here, and she's with you all the time. In your heart."

"I know, but I mean, I can like…sense her."

"Still not weird."

My eyes close and we sit in peaceful silence for a few minutes. The only thing I hear is water trickling in the fountain and birds singing. Tranquility.

"Clay?"

"Yeah, babe?"

"How are we going to find this cottage? This place is almost seven hundred acres. If we're going to keep a low profile, how do we not ask somebody? We're gonna have to."

"No, I don't think we'll need to." He elbows me. "Check it out."

I lift my head up. About a hundred yards away, I see what appears to be the stone cottage. Straight in front of us. It's partially hidden by some tall bushes, so all I can see is the roof and the chimney. But it's definitely a stone chimney.

"Holy shit. Is that it? How lucky is that?" I ask rhetorically.

"I thought it might be nearby, when you saw her favorite roses. Part of the reason why I wanted to come sit over here. Come on, let's go see what we can find out. At least see if that's it for sure, and if the key looks like it will work," he says.

We get up and walk the way to the cottage. The closer we get, it's evident that it is in fact a stone cottage, and I fall in love with it. It's so charming. The small house is made up of various shades of light tan stacked stones all around. Four sets of double casement windows are set across the front. One is ajar, the breeze provoking it to flap back and forth on its hinges in small successions, squeaking like an old swing with rusted chains. A stone path leads to the front arched doorway. Ivy has taken over the entire east side of the house, except for where the windows are. And of course it's surrounded by some of the most beautiful flowers and shrubbery. The door does have a modern lock so the key on the keychain will hopefully open it up. Windows close to the rooftop indicate that the cottage has a second floor, but I don't see how the ceiling could be very tall for the upper level.

"Okay," Clay says, "I think the key will work."

"Clay, this cottage is very well taken care of. What if someone actually lives here?"

"Then at dark, if we see lights on, we knock on the door. So. Now we wait."

"No. Now we find something else to do to pass the time. There's an arboretum, a sensory garden, and even a bocce ball court. All within walking distance. What do you want to do?"

"Bocce ball? We haven't played that since before Uncle Sid died. That sounds fun."

"I know. I used to love playing during the holidays at their house. We should fix the court back up in the backyard. Still plenty enough room for our future pool, too," I muse.

"I love that idea," Clay replies. "What exactly is a sensory garden?"

"It's actually called the 'Fragrance and Sensory Garden.' It's designed for people to be able to touch, see, and smell the flora. All kinds of aromatic flowers and herbs are planted, and there's also some textured grass and shrubs. I think it would be a great place for those with special needs, you know? Especially for the visually impaired."

"Wow. That sounds pretty cool. Okay, after I whip your ass at bocce, we'll check it out."

"You? Whip my ass? At bocce? You forget I was practically raised in the backyard with that bocce ball court, Sinclair. You sure you wanna go there?"

"I like a challenge."

"You're on. Prepare to be embarrassed."

We stroll over to the bocce ball court and play a round, which of course I win.

"Best two out of three?" Clay asks.

"If you insist."

Clay wins the second bout. That's okay. I let him. But now, the unthinkable unfolds before my eyes. He is about to win the third round too, and not because I'm allowing it. However, on my last play, my red ball spocks his green ball out of the way and kisses the jack ball. I jump up and down with excitement, throwing my hands in the air. "Yes!" I shout, as I triumph in our final game.

"Alright, Mrs. Sinclair. You win." He addresses a make-believe crowd. "Ladies and gentlemen, the winner of the gold medal in Bocce Ball Olympics of Colonial Park Gardens is…Mrs.…Lynn…Sinclair-air-air-air…" He places a pretend gold medal around my neck. "Well done, ma'am." He bows to me.

"Thank you, sir." I blow kisses and wave to the imaginary cheering spectators.

"I can't believe I'm married to an Olympic champion. We should celebrate." In a surprise move, he sweeps me off my feet into his arms. I let out a playful scream and grab onto his neck as he swings me around a few times, the two of us laughing. My stomach drops like I'm on a rollercoaster.

"Oh my God, Clay, put me down. I'm gonna lose my lunch." I bury my head in the crook of his neck.

"Oh no, we can't let that happen. Okay, on your feet." He sets me down, gives me a kiss, and slaps my butt.

"That was fun. I haven't felt like that since I was a little kid." Holy crap. I'm dizzy, staggering around like I've had ten drinks. The sky is below me and the grass is above. I almost fall, but Clay saves me and my arms wrap around him to catch my balance.

"You alright, babe?" he asks with a little laugh.

"Yeah, just a little woozy. How are you not wobbly?"

"Do you know how much I've had to train over the years to not react in such a way?"

"No," I laugh.

"I'm as cool as a cucumber."

"Of course you are. Okay, now let's go check out the sensory garden, shall we?"

"We shall."

We wander towards the sensory garden and I can instantly smell a mélange of lavender, peppermint, basil, rosemary, magnolia, lemon balm, and more. Rows of lovely Fountain Grass with its fuzzy, buff-colored plumes shoot towards the sky from the ground. Patches of pointy, bright-blue, rounded mounds of ornamental grass occupy another section of the garden. I've never seen that type of grass before. It reminds me of those retro fiber optic lamps from the seventies. Or like a garden full of blue porcupines. I get closer to the sign and see that it's called Spiky Blue Fescue.

"Whoa," Clay remarks. "Real live bluegrass."

"Yeah, I really like that. I want to get some of that for our house."

"You got it," he says. "I hope it grows in Baywood."

"Well," I say, "we've managed to kill several hours now. It's almost six thirty." I check online to see what time sunset is. It's at 8:04, with the last light at 8:34. "About an hour and a half till the sun goes down. It'll be dark by eight thirty. Which gives us less than half an hour to get to the cottage, find whatever it is we're after, and get out."

"Okay. Let's go chill out around the cottage by that gazebo where we were earlier and wait for dark to fall."

"Okie dokie." We walk back over to the gazebo and sit down.

"Alright, we need a hotel room." Clay says, as he starts to look online. He punches in a few buttons on his phone. "We're all set."

"Now we wait."

"The cottage is dark, thank goodness. Now's our chance," I say.

"Yeah, let's run for it."

"Run for it? No way, I don't want to bring any unwanted attention to us. Let's just walk fast."

As we make our way out of the gazebo, it starts to drizzle. Great. Just what we need. The petrichor that results is pleasant though. I love that smell, when the rain first hits the ground.

"Shit," I yell in a whisper. "This sucks."

"Not really," Clay whispers back. "This weather is just what we need. No groundskeepers will be out."

"Good point. Let's hurry though."

We hustle our way to the stone cottage and Clay unlocks the door, inching it open without a sound.

"Any idea what the hell are we looking for?" he asks.

"No, but I'm assuming since there's only one key, we'll know it when we see it, as per usual."

"I suppose so," he says.

We hurry inside and shut the door behind us. It's pitch dark, and if it weren't for the rain, you could probably hear a pin drop. Looking around with the flashlight, it becomes obvious that the cottage is used mostly for storage and partially as a makeshift greenhouse. There are plants all along the windowsills and some are sitting on tables throughout the bottom floor. A child's drawings and colored pictures frame the air conditioning intake vent.

Outside, it starts raining harder.

"I think I see why we were told to come at night, since this is clearly not open to the public," I say.

"You're probably right."

"I don't see anything that stands out as to the significance of this place or why we're here. Do you?"

"No."

Just then we hear a thud upstairs.

"What the hell was that?" I ask, a slight tone of terror in my voice.

"I don't know. Let's go see."

"What? Are you crazy?"

"Come on, Lynn. Nobody else is here."

"How do you know?"

"They would have come down by now."

"Maybe they're sleeping."

"Not likely. The park's not even closed yet."

Thump. Thump. Thump.

"Oh my God, Clay. I'm scared." I'm hanging on to his shirt for dear life. He's going up to the second floor. Why are we following the noise? We are in yet another scene of our sporadic horror movie. A cricket chirps and I nearly shit myself.

Thump. Thud. Scrape.

Oh hell no. "Clay, stop." I whisper loudly. We are halfway up the stairs.

"What, Lynn?" he whispers back. "It's probably nothing. Just a tree limb on the roof or something."

"Dammit, I'm freaking out." Visions from urban legends and slasher flicks of madmen in slickers with hooks for hands are in my head.

"I've got you, Lynn, I'm right here. It's okay."

A loud clap of thunder tears through the night followed by the unmistakable hair-raising resonance of a music box's melodic tinkling. Seriously, could this situation get any more cliché?

"Holy shit, now I'm creeped out," Clay says.

"Oh no you don't, Sinclair. You're not flipping on me now. Move along, cowboy."

We rush the rest of the way and make it into what looks like a small bedroom. The ceiling is sloped, as are a couple of the walls, accounting for the small space. There's an iron daybed with a little bedside table next to it. A closet, half open. And a desk, of which the jewelry box rests on top near the window, sitting next to a creepy doll with unsettled eyes.

"This must be the groundskeeper's quarters," Clay says.

"Perfect. We've stumbled into the very place we were trying to avoid. I feel bad, Clay. This is somebody's personal living space. It looks like a little girl lives here too. We've never done this before."

"Yeah. We should hurry then."

"We should hurry regardless."

Thump!

We both gasp. Clay shines the light to where the noise came from, towards the closet. A wire hanger with something draped through it is sagging on the knob between the door and the jamb. Apparently, when the air conditioning kicked on, it swayed the door and made the hangar bump against the frame. Okay, that explains that. Another clap of thunder rattles the windows by the desk, knocking the doll over and the music box starts again. Whew. No ghosts here.

"Lynn, dear?"

I was wrong. That was Aunt Mitzi.

Chapter 59

"D ID YOU HEAR that?" I ask Clay.

"Yeah, the thunder is what made the music box chime."

"No. I heard Aunt Mitzi's voice."

"What? No. I didn't hear that. Are you sure? What did she say?"

"Yes, I'm sure. She said, 'Lynn, dear?' like she was asking for me. Am I going crazy?"

"No, babe. You're not crazy. You said you could sense her. Maybe she really is here."

"Aunt Mitzi? If you're in this room…help us. Show us why we're here."

More lightning flashes. It highlights something I hadn't noticed before. In the corner of the bedroom, there are a few framed pictures.

"Clay, move the flashlight over to that corner. I saw something."

As the beam of light shines on the wall, I see it. There's an 8x10 photo of Aunt Mitzi. An old picture, like from the sixties.

"That's it," Clay says.

We walk over to the picture for a closer look. It was originally a black-and-white photo, but it's been hand-tinted with color. Beautiful Aunt Mitzi, holding a bouquet of her favorite roses.

"She looks kind of sad, don't you think? She's barely smiling," I say.

"Maybe she was tired."

"Look. There's a caption." I take Clay's hand with the flashlight and move it to where I can read it.

```
Mitzi Santini, 1966 Rose Garden Jamboree
Champion, with her prize-winning Candy Swirl
roses. We are honored to have her special
breed of roses in our gardens.
```

"*Her* Candy Swirl roses?" I ask. "*Her* special breed? Oh wow, Clay, did she create them?"

"Seems like it. You didn't know about this?"

"No. Never. Why would she keep this a secret? This is wonderful. It should have been celebrated. In the family, I mean. No wonder these were her favorite. She made them. I knew she loved roses, but, no, I never knew she was into breeding them. She just keeps getting more and more intriguing."

"Should we take the frame?" Clay asks.

"I would love to, but no, I don't think we should. Remember, she said to use our own judgment with the things we find. So, as much as I'd love to have this, I feel like it would literally be stealing."

"But breaking and entering is okay with you?"

"We didn't break in. We have a key. Anyway, this photo belongs here. It should stay. Come on. We'll just take the knowledge."

"And a picture," he says. "I mean, a snapshot."

"Yes." I get my phone out and capture it the best I can.

Clay takes the frame off of the wall.

"What are you doing?"

"There might be an envelope behind it."

"Oh wow, good thinking. Hurry, though. It's ten minutes to nine."

Clay lifts a few of the clips holding the photo in the frame and slides the cardboard-backing out.

"Huh. Well, look at that." he says.

"Unbelievable." I grab the envelope. "The rain has stopped. Let's get out of here."

We make a run for it and get back to the truck without being spotted. I think. I hope. Maybe the groundskeeper had the night off. Or maybe he or she was preoccupied in another part of the park. Whatever the case, we make it out of the park at 8:58 and are safely back on the road to our hotel for the night. Someone shuts the gate as soon as we pull out of the parking lot.

"That was close, babe," Clay says.

"Yeah, I was extremely freaked out though. I swear, I know I heard Aunt Mitzi's voice. She was there, Clay. I felt her."

"Oh, I believe you. After all the crazy shit we experienced in there, I know she pointed us in the right direction."

"I'm just glad to be out of there. I was so scared we were going to get caught."

"Me too. But we didn't."

"Hallelujah. What on earth possessed you to look for an envelope behind the frame?"

"Um, I don't think it was anything on earth. I think it was Aunt Mitzi. In some cosmic corner of my mind, I heard the word 'envelope,' like a whisper from my subconscious."

"See? She was there."

"I would be inclined to believe you, love. So, are you going to open it?"

"Oh. Duh. Of course." I take it out of my pocket and run my finger under the sealed flap. "Oh look, Clay."

"I'm driving, babe. And it's dark. Just tell me what it is."

"It's a four by six copy of the picture with her roses, with the caption on the back. And there's a letter from her."

"That's great, babe. Now you'll have an actual picture instead of the crappy one you took on your phone. What's the letter say?"

I turn on the flashlight on my phone and read it.

"*Dearest loves,*

I do hope this finds you. I know I didn't give a clue about it, but I figured by now, you would have become accustomed to expecting an envelope from me.

I hope you enjoyed finding out about my roses. Only a few people in the family knew that I bred them. Now you know why they were my favorites, though there's a bittersweet reason for it. It's actually a sad story, which is why it wasn't well-known and reveled upon in the family.

'It happened completely by accident. You see, Uncle Sid always acknowledged me as a mother on Mother's Day, and vice-versa on Father's Day, given that we had lost a few babies in our years of trying for a family. It was a personal thing we did, just between us.

'One year, Sid gave me a red rose bush. The next, a white rose bush. I was actually pregnant on Mother's Day that year, but shortly after, I miscarried. After the doctor released me back to regular household duties, I went into the garden and clipped all the roses off the bushes and planted them in one big flower pot. I cried the entire time, my tears mixing in the soil. I didn't have the heart to tell Sid I didn't want the roses anymore. Every time I looked at them, they reminded me of our losses. But I couldn't bear to just strip them of their beauty by throwing them away, so I only planted the stems with the blossoms. I thought for sure they would die. But they stayed in that pot, thriving.

'I would cut every bud from the original bushes before they would bloom. Sid saw me, but never questioned. I figured he thought it was a coping mechanism. He was right. I know he didn't mean for them to give me heartbreak, but that's what happened. He never gave me another rose bush.

'A couple of years went by, and the next thing I knew, there were my Candy Swirl roses, growing amongst the reds and whites in the flower pot. They had mutated spontaneously, which is very rare. They were a freak of nature. It was a miracle they ever came to be. I like to think my tears in the soil may have had something to do with it, but who knows.

'As a bit of therapy, Sid suggested I enter them into the rose world as a new breed, so I did, never expecting anything to come of it. To my surprise, it was a big deal and they were a real crowd pleaser to the American Rose Society. I was sent many requests to speak at garden shows, rose symposiums, and horticultural conventions over the years, but of course, given the background of

how my roses emerged, I could never do it. Though I was happy that so many people loved my roses. It did help with healing my heart. It was as if our angels were giving joy to the world.

'I received a mailing one year about the Colonial Park Rose Jamboree and I decided to enter. We made a trip out of it and fell in love with the gardens and grounds. Winning the competition was the icing on the cake.

'As time went on, my roses gave me such delight, but I was still never able to speak publicly about their conception, for lack of a better word, because it was difficult to get the words out without falling apart.

'So now you have the story. Don't let it bring you down. It has a happy ending. I will forever love my Candy Swirl roses, and I'm thankful for the happiness they brought others.

'Love, Aunt Mitzi'"

"Wow," Clay says. "That's something."

"Yeah. What a story. I'm glad we found this envelope, otherwise we may have never known. I can't believe it though. I'm finding out so much about her. It makes me miss her that much more. I wish I could just talk to her again, have an actual conversation. I just want to give her a big hug."

"You will. One day."

"I suppose so. I'll be so glad to see her."

"Well, let's hope it's not anytime soon."

"Right," I chuckle.

We check into the hotel and settle in.

"I'm gonna look for the next key." I dig in the box of keys to look for the number thirteen keychain.

"What do we have?" he asks.

"It's a rhinestone dollar sign. With a small silver key. Looks like another filing cabinet key."

"Hmm…a dollar sign keychain with a filing cabinet key. It can't be a safety deposit box then. Maybe just a bank with another cabinet in store? Surely there's another bank in our future."

"I'm willing to bet there will be more than one. We still have thirty eight states after the next one. I can't believe we're only on number thirteen. It feels like we've been on this trip for months already, but tomorrow will only be two weeks since we left."

"Probably just seems that way because we've constantly been on the go, haven't slowed down much."

"True."

I get the cipher out. "Alright, here's the next clue. 'In the country's largest city, money's history is displayed. In a case where safety can help, there are products to trade.' That is rather cryptic. I don't get it. So what do you think?"

"All I know for sure is we're headed to New York City. The rest, I'm too tired to think about right now."

"Yeah, that's all I get out of it too. And I agree. Let's sleep on it."

Chapter 60

THE NEXT MORNING, we put our sleuthing caps on.

"She says 'money's history is displayed,'" Clay ponders, "like the history of money. History. A bank museum maybe? See what you can find on that."

I look on the internet for bank museums in New York City. "The first thing that pops up is the Museum of American Finance. There's also the Museum and Gold Vault Tour at the Federal Reserve Bank of New York. Sounds like we may have a couple of contenders."

"Hmm...anything else?"

I look further down the list of results from my search. "Yep. Here's a listing for the Capital of Capital Museum. Jeez, this may prove harder than we thought. We may be there a while."

"What's so wrong with spending a couple of days in the bright lights and big city?" he asks.

"Nothing, actually. I love New York. Maybe we can stroll through Central Park and do a couple of other touristy things too. We haven't been there in forever."

"That sounds good. Yeah, we haven't been since before September eleventh. I'd like to see the memorial. Pay my respects."

"Me too. Okay, let's look at the clue again so we can try to narrow down where we should go. Or do you think we should just start with the Museum of American Finance, since that's what popped up first?"

"Yeah, we can lead with that. It seems everything that has been at the top of all your searches is where we need to be."

"Alright. Now to book a room." I book us a suite at Le Parker Meridien. "You ready to go? We're not that far from the city. Maybe about an hour or so, I would guess."

"Sure. Let's hit the pavement."

Once in the truck, I give Clay the address to the hotel and yep, it's only an hour away. It'll probably take us longer to get there though, seeing as how it's New York City. Traffic hell.

The lobby of the hotel is beautiful. All cream colored marble with a huge skylight in the middle. We check in and drop our stuff off in the room.

We decide to eat lunch at the Burger Joint restaurant inside the hotel.

"Okay, Clay. Let's get this clue figured out. 'In a case where safety can help, there are products to trade.' I'm so lost on that. What are your thoughts, puzzle king?"

"Well, let's talk it out. Somewhere that safety can help might be like a hospital, a fire station, or taking shelter from a storm. And products to trade may be the tools used in that scenario. Like bandages, oxygen, food…stuff like that."

"And what the crap does any of that have to do with history of money and finance, smarty pants?"

"Slow down, babe, jeez…we're just brainstorming here. It might not be that at all."

"Sorry, I'm just anxious. Okay, let's try another angle. Products to trade could be like a barter system. That was done before paper money, right? That's history. Different things traded for different levels of value. Something I have in place A that you can't get in place B. Importing and exporting."

"Whoa, I think you may be on to something there. Keep talking," Clay encourages.

"Ports. Lots of things came in and out of the harbor here for trade."

"Things. Goods. Items. Products. Merchandise," he says.

"Yes. All of that. I'm confused as to where the safety part comes in though, like if we're talking about importing and exporting, maybe 'safety' is just a play on words for an actual safe. Like a money safe? Where things were put for safe-keeping."

"You could be right on the money, babe," he says with a smile.

"Ha."

"Maybe," Clay says, "we're looking for a safe or a vault, with something from the past that was popular in exchanging between the states, or countries for that matter. But you said you think the key looks like another filing cabinet key, right?"

"That's what it resembles, but I can't be sure. But I hardly think this small of a key would open a vault. Plus, don't big safes and vaults use combination locks?"

"Yeah, you're right."

"Well, whatever it is, I can't wait to find out."

"Me either," he says.

Clay takes a bite of his burger and I can see the wheels spinning in his head. He's not done contemplating this clue.

"What is it?" I ask.

He puts his finger up until he swallows his bite. "What if it's something at Wall Street?"

"Explain," I say, shoving a few fries into my mouth.

"Well, that's where the New York Stock Exchange is. Money, money, money. The 'trading floor' is there, where people trade their stocks, right? And, Wall Street is named for the wall that protected the residents of the New Amsterdam settlement, keeping them all 'safe' from harm. Make sense?"

"Total sense. You're so freaking smart. But…"

"What?"

"That doesn't seem like Aunt Mitzi's style."

"Her style?"

"I mean, most of the places she's sent us to have been museums."

"So? You don't think she'd have an ace up her sleeve? Maybe Uncle Sid helped with this one. He was the big money man. I'm sure he spent some time on Wall Street."

"I don't doubt that. The Museum of American Finance is on Wall Street anyway. Guess I left that part out. So, how 'bout this...if none of the museums pan out, we'll go to the Stock Exchange."

"Alright. I guess. I just really think that's it. It makes the most sense."

"We'll see."

We finish eating and take a cab to the Finance Museum. The building is on the site of New York's first bank, the Bank of New York, which was founded by Alexander Hamilton. Talk about historic. Crazy, right? This actual bank building was opened in 1929 though. Still pretty historical.

"Where do you want to start?" Clay asks.

"I guess it doesn't really matter. Let's just look around."

We walk through a few exhibits. Rows and rows of monies from centuries and decades gone by are presented behind plexiglass in the circulation exhibition. There's a portion on bank robbers, the Alexander Hamilton room, an area about bonds, information about the stock exchange, and so much more to see. Then, on the back wall of the museum, I see it.

"Clay?" I turn around and he's gone. I find him over by the information and technology spot, which showcases old ticker machines and typewriters. "Babe. This way." I point to my left. He looks. He sees. He smiles. There, is the section I believe we're looking for.

"Commodities. Wow, how did we miss that? It seems so obvious now," he says.

"I know. Do you think this could be it then? Instead of the Stock Exchange?"

"I guess we'll soon find out."

We start at the end, since that's where Clay was standing, even though it's a little unnatural to start backwards. "Corn. Cotton. Butter. Cheese. Coffee. Cocoa. Livestock. What does this have to do with safety?" I ask.

"Alright, stop."

"Should I collaborate and listen?"

He laughs. "Precisely. Let's look at the clue again. Read the key words."

I take it out of my purse. "Money. History. Displayed. Case. Safety. Help. Products. Trade."

"Okay," says Clay, "well I see why she says 'displayed' and 'case.' Here we are. At a display case. The key might fit this display case. It could be something in here. Right here. Now…let me think. Safety. Help. Safety can help."

While he's pondering out loud, my eyes wander to the other end of the display. I see it. What we're here for. I turn Clay around. There, at the beginning of all the commodities, is oil and gas. With a big-ass yellow gas can, boldly labeled SAFETY CAN. He smiles wide.

"It's not 'safety can help,'" I say, "It's just 'safety can.' I guess she didn't want to give it straight to us."

"No, she wants to make us work for it. Well played, Aunt Mitzi, well played. So, I guess this is the place."

"I guess so. Now the fun part. Open it without anybody seeing. Fat chance."

"Let's just go for it," he says. "We have a freaking key."

"Naturally, the can is in the most difficult place to reach. It's all the way at the end. This is not going to be discreet."

Clay unlocks the case and I get at the end and swing the door back as little as possible. The can is big though. It's about a foot in diameter and about eight inches tall. This is going to be cumbersome. I grab the bulky gas can and I hear something rattle inside. Just as I'm about to open the cap and see what's in there, the inevitable happens.

"Yeh, we gotta tehn-sitty-two in Cahmmodahties," a gray-haired security guard, with a very thick New York accent, says into his radio. That's police code for Breaking and Entering in Progress. Super.

Chapter 61

"HOLE IT RIGHT dare. Put the can down. And yous," he points at Clay, "step away from the display," he orders. The guard projects such authority that Clay puts his hands up and does as he's told.

"Uh," Clay stammers, "we're Clay and Lynn Sinclair."

"I didden acks faw ya names," he barks.

I know that was Clay's way of trying to get us out of this. Maybe they've heard about us.

"Sir," I implore, "we have a key. Please call your manager."

I know we're in trouble, at least for the moment, but I just want to turn over that gas can. It's right there. As the security guard is preoccupied on his phone now, I flip open the lid and try to look inside. Clay gives me wide eyes, telling me to stop.

"Yeh," the guard says. I can't hear the other end of the conversation. He's got ear buds on. "You shaw? ... Neggadiv ... Yeh, but ... Yeh, Sinclair ... Ahrite ahreddy ... Yeh, I got it ... Tehn-faw." He looks over at us. "Yous free teh go. Aftah yous find whateva it is yous lookin' faw. Sahry. I'm new."

We smile at him and I know Clay is as relieved as I am. "That's okay," Clay tells him. "Thank you."

"Yes, thank you officer. I'm sorry, we should have identified ourselves when we first got here this morning," I tell him.

"Fuhgeddaboudit," he says as he walks away.

"Okay, let's see what's in this bad boy. Here, hold your hands out," I say as I dump the gas can over.

Clay opens his hands and out falls some rust. And another typewriter key.

"I knew it," I say with a smile.

"And now we have an 'S.'"

"So. 'B,' 'C,' and 'S.' That has to be for 'Bernice Chauvin Santini.' When are we going to find out what to do with these?"

"I don't know," Clay replies.

Clay puts the gas can back in the display case exactly like we found it.

"Where to now, love?" he asks.

"Let's go to Central Park."

"Sounds good."

We take a cab to the park and walk for hours. We start at Strawberry Fields, and "Strawberry Fields Forever" happens to be my favorite Beatles song, so you know I have to take a picture by the sign. There's a John Lennon Memorial adjacent to Strawberry Fields. It's a big, circular mosaic with the word 'Imagine' in the middle. People come here every day and leave flowers, as a way of paying tribute to the slain Beatle.

We walk over to the serene Bethesda Terrace and Fountain. This area of the park is one of the most famous, as many scenes from movies and TV shows have been filmed here. I love the statue at the top of the fountain—an angel that stands over four small cherubs. The cherubs represent health, purity, peace, and temperance. It's called *Angel of the Waters*. I take a picture for my journal.

Next, we head to my favorite part of the entire park—The Mall. It's not what it sounds like. It has nothing to do with shopping. The Mall is a corridor of sorts, flanked by rows of beautiful American elm trees that shade the path. It must be at least ten degrees cooler here. Clay and I take a rest on one of the benches.

"Babe, this has been a great day," I tell Clay. "I love this park. I wish we had something like this back home."

"Me too. Maybe we can make our own little Central Park in the backyard. Lord knows there's enough land back there."

"Oh, Clay, I love that idea. Let's do it. Boy, we have our work cut out for us when we get back, huh? Our renovations, a backyard oasis with a pool, revitalize the bocce ball court, and our mini Central Park. I can't wait."

"We'll call it the Santini Sinclair Sanctuary. What do you think?"

"Perfect. Absolutely perfect. But, are you sure? That's really a lot of work, Clay. You know I will help you, but—"

He interrupts me by pulling me in for a kiss. "I'll do anything for you, Lynn. If you want a park, I'll build you a park."

"I love you. Thank you, Clay. You're the best."

"I know," he says with a smile.

We get up from our respite and go check out the Balto dog statue. I love that movie. The story is inspirational, and the title character is voiced by my favorite celebrity, Kevin Bacon.

We round our afternoon off with a fun ride on the Central Park Carousel and a delicious lunch at Tavern on the Green.

After eating, we saunter back to the hotel, stopping at Umpire Rock along the way for a few photo ops. There are flecks of quartz and mica throughout the huge boulder-spread, along with other minerals, which make it sparkle and glitter in the sunlight. It's very impressive and seems sort of magical.

Upon returning to our hotel room, we both kick off our shoes and crash on the bed, facing each other.

"It's been a long day," Clay says,

"That it has. But it's been wonderful," I say as I feel my eyes getting heavy.

"Come here," he replies. I turn over and affix myself to his body. He hugs me closer and we float into dreamland.

My eyes open as I lie fully clothed on the hotel bed. I don't know what time it is, but it's gotten dark. We must have really been tired. Clay is motionless, his breathing calm, his arm still draped over me. I take his hand and link mine to it. He stirs and kisses me on the cheek.

"Sorry, babe, I didn't mean to wake you," I tell him.

"It's okay. What time is it? How long have we been sleeping?"

"No idea. I didn't want to move to check."

He rolls over and grabs his phone. "It's eight thirty."

"Oh my gosh, are you serious? I'm guessing we really needed that nap."

"Yeah. And I feel like I could go right back to sleep. I know we're in one of the most exciting cities in the world, and we haven't been here in forever, but would it be okay with you if we just stay in tonight? This trip is really catching up to me."

"Of course," I tell him, "I was thinking the same thing. We can chill here and figure out the next clue."

"Okay. Get the key and cipher ready." He gives me a kiss and starts to get up out of bed.

I hold him down. "Where are you going?"

"Bathroom."

"Oh," I give him a smile and let him go.

While Clay is occupied, I find the cipher. He soon joins me at the table.

"Ready?" I ask him.

"Hit me."

"Alright. 'On Fayerweather Island, in a house of light, once again, you should go at night. Upon your entrance, make your way towards the skies. Look behind the mason with a dragon that flies.' Whoa. Again in the dark? I'm guessing 'house of light' is a lighthouse. That's easy enough."

"A house of light could be a greenhouse."

"It could."

"Or a church."

"That too. But, she says we need to climb to the top and find, what? A brick, I guess?"

"Yeah, with a dragonfly on it. So that probably rules out greenhouse. But still might be a church. In the bell tower." Clay gets up and does an impression of the Hunchback of Notre Dame, yelling, "Sanctuary! Sanctuary!"

"Okay, Quasimodo, calm down," I say laughing at the way he has distorted his face.

He laughs and sits back down. "Alright, Esmeralda, any idea where this 'Fairweather Island' is?"

"Fayerweather. F-A-Y-E-R. And no. Lemme check." I pull up the internet on my phone and search. "It's off the coast of Connecticut. And it does have a lighthouse, so that answers that. It doesn't look very easy to get to. Once we get to the island, we'll have to go on foot part of the way. The road only goes so far. Looks like we have to cross a breakwater to get to the lighthouse."

I show Clay the aerial view of the terrain. There's a footpath of large, mostly-flat rocks that have been built up as a bridge to get to the lighthouse from the parking lot at the end of the street. It looks rather uneven in areas.

"Jeez," Clay says. "We'll have to be careful. By the looks of it, it'll probably take us an hour to walk from the lot to the lighthouse. That stretch looks like it's at least a mile long, and with the jagged ground, it'll be tough. For you."

"What are you saying, Sinclair?"

He smiles. "Nothing. I'm just messing with you, love. You can handle it. So how far are we from the island?"

"About two and a half hours. Then the walk to the lighthouse itself."

"And the nearest city?" he asks.

"Bridgeport."

"We'll need a room there for tomorrow night."

"Yeah."

"So, maybe since we know we don't need to be there until tomorrow night, we can do Ground Zero tomorrow afternoon and whatever else we feel like. I'm sure we'll have time."

"That sounds good," I tell Clay.

"You have anything else in particular in mind?"

"Not really. We can play it by ear. See where the day takes us. I like having no plans sometimes. Like today. Even though I knew I wanted to go to Central Park, nothing beyond that was planned and we had the best time."

"Yeah, we did."

Chapter 62

I WAKE UP AND look at the clock on the nightstand. It's 7:43 in the morning. I need to go to the bathroom, but I don't want to get out of this bed. It's so comfortable. Clay is still sleeping. At least I think he is. His back is facing me, so I can't really tell. It sounds like he is though. I scoot up behind him and put my arm over his side. He doesn't move. Definitely sleeping. About ten seconds later, I find out that I was wrong. He takes my hand and moves it down for me to feel him. Oh no. I can't do this now. I need to pee.

"I can't," I whisper. "I gotta go. Gimme a minute. I'll be right back."

He kisses my hand and lets me go. I head to the bathroom and before I finish, Clay struts in. Naked in all his glory. And he's ready.

"What are you doing?" I ask as I laugh. "I told you I'd just be a minute."

A coy smile crosses his face. He heads for the huge shower without saying a word. His eyes, unusually dark, are holding mine, and saying plenty. A lavish waterfall spills from the gigantic shower head. Clay cocks his head to the left, telling me to join him. Okay then. Can't argue with that. Far be it from me to debate the nature of this sexy beast before my eyes. I kick off my bottoms and take off my top. He gives me an 'after you' gesture with his hand for me to go in first. I walk into the shower and he slaps my bottom.

We stand under the extravagant rainfall and soak ourselves. He opens his mouth, fills it with water, swishes it around, and spits it out. His version of a quick brush of the teeth, I presume. I copy him. Moving towards the back of the shower, my hand brushes against his leg. He grabs my hand and makes me feel him. I smile. As I'm washing my hair, Clay lathers up a washcloth. He washes the top half of my body, taking his time with my breasts. He trades places with me so I can rinse my hair out. Clay continues with the towel, washing down the front of my legs and up the back of them. As I lean my head backwards to get all the rest of the soap out of my hair, I'm surprised, but not really, as he takes one of my breasts into his mouth while groping the other one. Then he takes the cloth and rubs it between my legs while kissing my neck. He playfully bites my shoulder. I kiss him and press our bodies together. Taking the washcloth, I scrub his back. He slips a finger into me, then strokes it up and down my center. I can feel how slick I am. He's as hard as cast iron against me and I look into his beautiful blue eyes. His suggestive eyes. He puts his hands under my butt. That's my cue. I drop the washcloth and grab him around his neck. He hoists me up and I wrap my legs around his waist. He gets us into position and we become one. Oh man, he feels so good. It's been a long time since we've done it in the shower. Too long. He turns and leans against the wall for leverage and I move up and down, in slow motion, enjoying every inch of him. I speed up, and ride him, until we are spent.

We finish our shower, laughing and carrying on like newlyweds. We dry off, brush our teeth for real, get dressed, and head down to the front desk to ask for a late check-out.

We move on to Norma's for breakfast. We are seated at a table in the middle and handed menus.

"You know," I say to Clay, "I read that this restaurant got voted the number one breakfast place in all of New York City."

"Looking at the list of options here, I don't doubt it. Lucky for us it's in our hotel."

A pretty blonde waitress comes to our table and introduces herself as Johnelle. She takes our order and says she'll be right back with our coffee.

There's a small gathering of people sitting next to us, late sixties to early seventies in age. They are having some kind of party. Another older couple joins them and the sweet little lady gets so excited upon seeing the rest of the group. "Happy annavoysawee," she exclaims in that wonderful New York accent, as she hugs the celebrated couple. "The big foive-oh!" She reminds me a little of Aunt Mitzi, spunky and full of life.

"That's so sweet," I tell Clay upon witnessing their merriment.

"Yep. That'll be us one day."

Johnelle comes back with our coffee in a French press and sets it on the table with two mugs and a bit of lagniappe. "This is a sample of our daily smoothie," she says as she gives us each a shot glass full of said daily smoothie. "Berry-mango. Made fresh. Enjoy! Your breakfast will be out shortly."

"Thank you," we say in unison.

"My pleasure," Johnelle replies.

After breakfast, we make our way to the 9/11 Memorial and Museum. It's all so overwhelming and sad. All of these innocent people that lost their lives on that dreadful day. All of the memories of where I was when I found out what happened come flooding back. All of the emotion and fear come back.

I was at work filing some papers, listening to the radio. "Everything You Want" by Vertical Horizon was interrupted with breaking news. An airplane had just hit the World Trade Center. We ran into our conference room and turned on the TV, just in time to see the second plane hit. Gasps echoed throughout the room.

Our director immediately labeled it as an act of terrorism. Deep down, we all knew. But he's the one who said it out loud. He made it real. The hair lifted up on my arms and neck. I was shaking. I started crying. I heard whispers around the room. People were talking about me. People I didn't even know that well.

"Her husband's in the military," one said.

"He'll be called to go to war," another declared.

"Poor Lynn," stated somebody else.

And before I knew it, I saw stars. And then blackness.

Everyone was hovering over me when I opened my eyes. The room had filled with more employees during my blackout. My face was being patted with a cool rag.

"Is she okay?" someone asked.

"Lynn, can you hear me?" my director was asking, snapping his fingers. "Yes. What happened?"

"You fainted," he said. "You were out for two minutes."

He sat me up and gave me water. I regained composure, as best as I could anyway.

Other people were crying too. Some of the men in the room had stone-cold, ashen faces. I wasn't the only one with a spouse in the military. Several people had sons and daughters in various branches as well.

I knew Clay was going to be called for another deployment. I was terrified, but I couldn't let him know. I had to be strong for him. I didn't want him to go, but it was his job. I signed up for that fear when I married him. I worried about him when he was in Operation Desert Storm, but that time was different. What happened on September 11, 2001 was a blatant act of terrorism on our country and Clay had to defend America. There's a big difference between being worried about the love of your life and being scared to death you'll never see them again. I thank God every day that he came home to me. Healthy. Safe. Whole.

Clay brings me back to reality. "You okay, babe?" he asks.

"Yeah, just counting my blessings," I say as I wipe a tear away.

"Hey," he says as he takes my face in his hands, "I count mine too. Every day. Some of my brothers weren't as lucky. But I'm so thankful I was able to come home to you, in one piece. So grateful."

He hugs me tight and I don't want him to let go. I feel like we're saying good-bye all over again. These painful feelings were buried for so long, but now here they are. The anxiety, the trepidation, and the anger. I start crying, thinking about all the 'what ifs' I thought about back then. I try to pull myself together.

"I'm sorry," I say. "All the feelings just came back."

"It's okay, love. It's natural to feel this way about all of this. It was an awful time for our country and it still is. We're still fighting over there because of this. It's okay for you to feel this way."

"I'm just so glad you're out. I don't know what I would have done if—"

"Shh...shh...it's alright, love, I'm right here. I made it back. And I'm not going anywhere without you again."

We walk without speaking, reflected in the bronze panels above the cascading fountain at the footprint of where the North Tower once stood. The only sounds are the falling waters and the echoes of our footsteps. Clay breaks the silence. "Are you ready to go? Find something a little less tragic to do the rest of the day?"

"Yeah. I don't think my heart can take any more sorrow right now. I'm glad we did this though. It's good to remember."

"Never forget," he says.

"Never forget," I whisper.

Chapter 63

WE SPEND THE rest of the day being tourists, visiting the Empire State Building and South Street Seaport. After another long afternoon of sightseeing, we make our way back to the hotel and get ready to take another nap.

"Set your alarm, please Clay? So we don't oversleep before we need to get up and get our stuff together to check-out."

"Sure thing, love. What time? Six?"

"Yeah, that should be good. That gives us a couple of hours to sleep before we need to get on the road and it'll be pretty dark by the time we get to the island."

He sets his alarm on his phone while I shut the sun out with the curtains.

Clay and I are back on the road by 6:30.

"What does the keychain look like, Lynn? We figured the clue right off that we forgot about the key."

I dig around in the box for the number fourteen keychain. "Well, it's a lighthouse lantern. Imagine that. And it's a little flashlight too. Cute. The key is just a regular key, like a house key." I dangle the keychain in the air to show Clay.

"Cool. So…tunes?" He asks.

"Sure. It's your turn again."

"It is? I can't keep up." He presses a button on his phone and "Cum On Feel the Noize" by Quiet Riot fills the cab of the truck.

We get to the parking lot for the lighthouse a little after 8:30. Clay and I make sure to bring our flashlights.

"Clay, are you sure we should be doing this? It just seems dangerous. Check out the rocks. They look rickety."

"Are you serious?"

"Yes and no. Mostly yes."

"Lynn. We did not come all this way to turn back now. Aunt Mitzi wouldn't send us here if it was dangerous. Those rocks have been there a hundred years. I'm sure they're sturdy enough. Besides, we need the piece of the puzzle, right?"

"Okay. Yeah, I know. Alright. Let's just be careful. Hold my hand the whole way."

"Sure thing, love. Come on. It'll be okay. Look how cool the lighthouse is, all lit up."

"It looks miles away. We'll be here all night."

"We got nothin' but time."

He packs the flashlights in a backpack while I get each of us a bottle of water out of the cooler.

We walk over the rocky terrain for the better part of an hour and finally make it to a section with smoother ground. The lighthouse still seems forever away. At least we have a clear shot to it. No major obstructions appear to be in our path.

The beacon from the lighthouse along with the moon, which is almost full, are helping to light our way.

"Why do you think she wanted us to come here at night?" Clay asks.

"I don't know. Maybe the same reason as the stone cottage? Because if people were there during the day and we just waltzed into the lighthouse, we'd be followed, and the lighthouse isn't open to the public."

"Makes sense."

"And…I know Aunt Mitzi. She loved lighthouses. They're so much prettier at night, with the light shining. She'd want us to see that. You don't get the same effect in the daylight."

"True. Plus, it's a little more adventurous. Like, what if it's haunted?"

"Please don't even mention that."

"Too late." Clay starts making ghost sounds to try and spook me.

"Dude. Seriously. Quit."

"Maybe it's a friendly ghost, like Casper."

"That wouldn't be so bad I guess." We both laugh.

As we get a little closer, the smell of burning wood invades my nose.

"Something's off," I tell Clay.

"What do you mean?"

I notice an orange glow dancing from the area behind the lighthouse, out of our view. Shit.

"Clay, stop," I whisper.

"What's wrong?" he asks out loud.

"Shh. Somebody's there."

"What?" he whispers back.

I point. He sees what I see. Somebody has lit a fire.

"See?"

"Shit. Maybe it's nothing. Maybe just a homeless man. I don't hear anything so it's not like a bunch of people sitting around drinking and causing mayhem. Maybe it's a couple of teenagers having sex. It is Saturday night. Let's keep going."

"We should have brought the gun." He gives me a look. Even in the dark, I know that look. He brought it. Thank God. You just never know.

"Lynn, I'm not going to let anything happen to you." He takes his pistol out of the backpack and keeps it at the ready.

"I know. Okay, I feel a little better now."

The further we get, the more apprehensive I become. I hear rustling.

"*Who's there?*" an angry voice asks from behind the lighthouse.

"We don't want any trouble, sir," Clay says.

"Get out of here!" he screams.

"We don't mean any harm," Clay assures him. "We need to get something that was left for us and we'll be on our way."

"Left where?" he yells.

"Inside the lighthouse," Clay tells him.

We walk closer still. The man comes out from behind the lighthouse.

"It's locked." The man's voice eases somewhat.

"We have a key," Clay says.

We're nearly fifty feet from him now. He doesn't look homeless. Pretty clean-cut.

"You do?" he asks.

"Yes," says Clay. "I promise, we'll be in and out and not a bother."

As we approach him, I can tell that the man is in his late sixties and dressed fairly well, in jeans and an old Grateful Dead t-shirt. He hasn't shaved in days. White hair sticks out from a Red Sox baseball cap. His eyes are red, like he's been crying. Or maybe smoking pot.

"I'm sorry, didn't mean to scare you if I did," he says, and his demeanor has totally changed. "I come out here on the anniversary of my wife's death and have a bit of a pity party. This is where I asked her to marry me. We were married almost forty years when she died five years ago. Nobody has ever come when I'm here. I was a little startled. Forgive me for shouting. Name's Dixon." He holds out his hand.

So he was crying. Poor guy.

"Clay," he says as he shakes Dixon's hand. "Sorry for your loss."

"Lynn," I say, but I keep my grip on Clay.

"So, how is it that you have a key to this old lighthouse?"

We give him the abbreviated version of our story and he's curious to see what's inside the antiquated house of light.

"We'll just be a few minutes, hopefully," Clay tells him.

The lighthouse, which denotes the entrance to Black Rock Harbor at the island, is octagonal in shape and made of stone. It includes three stacked sets of windows on one side, with the door directly across from the group of windows. The tower is painted white with a wrought iron fence around the lantern room. The vent and lightning rod top it off.

I read a bit of history on the lighthouse before we got here and found out that it was deactivated in 1932, when two automated lights were constructed offshore. Solar panels keep the illumination of the lighthouse alive, but it's not intended for navigational aid.

"Say," Dixon says, "you kids mind if I join you? I could help you search for whatever it is you're looking for. I've just never seen the inside. It would mean a lot to me."

Clay and I look at each other. We don't know this guy. Do we trust him enough to help us? What if he finds the brick before we do without telling us and takes what's behind it? We could lose a piece of the puzzle. Clay is a better judge of character than I am, so I let him answer Dixon. If he trusts him, then I will too.

"Sure, we could use an extra set of eyes. We're looking for a brick with a dragonfly on it."

"Thanks, you guys."

Clay unlocks the door and opens it. It's musty as hell. Dank. Sultry. I smell mold. The three of us climb the circular iron staircase up to the landing just below the lantern. Our flashlight beams shine all over the natural bricks inside, looking for one imprinted with a dragonfly.

"Anything, babe?" I ask Clay.

"Nothing yet. You? Dixon?"

"Sorry, no," Dixon replies.

"Me either. Are you sure we're looking for a dragonfly? She said 'look for a dragon that flies.' I mean, it could literally be a dragon."

"Maybe so. But regardless, I haven't seen either one of those. Wait. Lynn, check this out."

Clay moves his beam of light to a stone at about the six-foot mark. I see a very faint stencil of a wing.

"Well, I'll be damned," Dixon says. "You really are on a scavenger hunt."

"More like a treasure quest," I say. "Clay, that must be it. The edge of the mortar around it is cracked too, so see if you can shimmy it out. I won't be able to reach it."

My husband, being six-foot-two, has no trouble. He does his best to loosen the stone, but it barely budges. He opens his backpack and takes out a screwdriver. He works it between the brick and mortar and finally gets it to come out. Clay peers inside the void.

"What's in there? Gold? Gemstones?" Dixon asks.

"It's nothing," Clay says with a sigh.

"Nothing? Shit. What now?" I ask.

"Maybe this wasn't it," Clay says.

Then, as he goes to replace it back in the wall, something falls from a hollow in the stone.

"Holy shit," Clay says.

"Oh, thank God."

We look at each other and grin.

"What in the hell?" Dixon asks.

Clay bends down and picks up our prize.

"So, what do we have?" I ask.

"Another typewriter key. 'L.'" He shines his flashlight at the stone, examining it. "Well…they carved a space in the rock itself to hold the key."

Dixon walks over to us. "Can I see?"

"Sure," Clay hands it to him.

"A typewriter key, huh?"

"Yes. This is our fourth one to find," Clay answers.

"What's it mean?"

"We're not sure yet," I say. "Maybe this one stands for 'lighthouse.'"

"I don't know," Clay replies. "We'll figure it out."

"This is a good find for us."

I take some pictures inside the lighthouse. Dixon takes one of Clay and me together, then I set the timer on my phone and put it on the windowsill to get a snapshot of the three of us.

While Dixon is admiring the view from the window, Clay puts his gun back in the backpack.

We walk back down the spiral stairs and as Clay locks the lighthouse back up, I take some photos of the outside of the structure. It really is beautiful. Especially with the moon in the background.

"That oughta do it for us," Clay says.

"Yeah. We'll be back on our way now, Dixon. I'm sorry to hear about your wife. I hope you find some peace tonight."

"I'll be okay," Dixon says. "Thanks for your concern. And thank you so much for letting me come up there with you. Norma would have loved the view from up there. You guys be careful heading back. These rocks can be tricky."

"Yes, sir," Clay says. "Thanks. And thank you for your help up there. Have a good evening, Dixon." They shake hands.

"You too, Clay. Lynn."

"Bye, Dixon. It was nice meeting you," I say.

It only takes us about an hour to get back to the truck. It was a little easier going the opposite direction since we kind of knew what to expect. We make it to our hotel in about fifteen minutes. It's almost midnight by the time we check in.

"Straight to bed?" Clay asks.

"Yes. I'm too tired to even look at the next clue or try to figure out what the 'L' is for. Let's sleep on it and start with a fresh mind in the morning."

"Okay, love."

We climb into bed and Clay scratches my back until I fall asleep, which takes mere minutes.

Chapter 64

"LYNN," I HEAR Clay's voice as I'm being shaken with gentleness. "Wake up. Breakfast. Coffee."

I'm not ready to get up yet. My muscles are aching. Must be from the night's trek across uneven rock. My stomach is growling. How is he so lively? And that's not how he usually wakes me up. Where's my morning kiss on the cheek? I give him a grunt and keep my eyes closed.

"Come on, love. It's time to get up. What are you waiting for? Your breakfast is going to get cold." I hear him walking back over to me and he leans down to press his lips to the side of my face. There it is. "Lynn," he says softly. He gives me another peck on my cheek. "It's ten o'clock."

My eyes pop open. I sit up and rub them. "Ten? Why did you let me sleep so late? How long have you been up?"

"You were sleeping so hard. Snoring, even. And I hate waking you up. Except in the middle of the night." He winks at me and I smile. "I got up about seven, I guess. I went to the gym and worked out. Came back and showered and I've been reading the newspaper. I know you don't like sleeping late though, so I went ahead and woke you. Plus—" he gestured towards the steaming plates on the table.

"Thank you. Yeah, I'm not a fan of the day passing me by. I'm so sore though. My muscles, head to toe. You're not?"

"No, I'm fine. You're probably hurting from walking all of that jagged path to the lighthouse last night." He strides back over to the table and starts gathering my breakfast together on a tray.

"Well, it turns out you were right when you said I couldn't handle it, even though you were joking. I guess I'm not in as good of shape as I thought."

"There is nothing wrong with your shape, Mrs. Sinclair."

"Ha. Thanks, babe. You know what I mean. Maybe I should hit these hotel gyms more often."

"Maybe you should. Not that you need to, I just love watching you run those treadmills. Sexy as hell." He smiles at me and brings me my breakfast in bed. "Since it'll probably pain you to get up…here." He sets the tray over my legs and puts my coffee on the nightstand. "Poor love. I'll find you some aspirin or something."

"Thank you. I need something stronger than aspirin though." I begin eating my breakfast and take a sip of my coffee. "Did you eat already?"

"Yeah. Sorry. After my shower. Since we skipped dinner last night, I was starving when I woke up. Especially after I got back from the gym."

"Okay, then you can read the clue while I eat. It's in my purse."

"Oh wow, really?"

"Well, I'm hungry. And can you bring me some Aleve please?"

"Sure thing, love." He digs around in my purse for the medicine and the clue sheet, then comes and sits next to me on the bed and gives me the pills.

"Thanks. So what's it say?"

"Let's see. 'In the nation's smallest state, more answers await. The same kind of place as clue number two, the oldest one in the opposite of Easterly is where you need to pursue.' Okay, a bank in Rhode Island is all I get from that without searching online. 'Easterly' is capitalized. You have any ideas?"

"No, that's all I understand too. But the opposite of Easterly would be Westerly. Right? Find the key," I tell him as I take a bite of toast.

"Yes ma'am," he says, and he gets up to look for the keychain. He rummages through the box and finds number fifteen. "It's a picture of a piggy bank. And another safety deposit box key along with a tiny, little mortise key. So," he says walking back to the bed, "probably more papers.

Not sure what this small key could be for. A locket maybe? Do lockets have keys?"

"I don't know. Maybe if it's kind of a big locket. Let me see the key?" He shows me. "That looks like it might be an old diary key. She said we'd get answers. Maybe they'll come from that."

"Maybe so. As for your other observation, yes, Westerly would be the opposite of Easterly. If it's that simple." He picks up his phone and starts searching online. "Got it."

"What did you find?"

"Washington Trust Bank in Westerly, Rhode Island. Founded in 1800."

"Wow. Okay, good."

"Says here it was the first bank to use George Washington's likeness on currency, sixty-nine years before the federal one-dollar bill was issued."

"Holy cow. Now that's some trivia for ya."

"Now, what about the 'L' from last night? What do you think about that?"

"Not sure. She kind of threw me off with that one. Although, her middle name was Lorraine, so that's probably it."

"Could be. You finished?"

"Yes, thank you so much for bringing me breakfast in bed." He takes my tray back to the table and I finish off my coffee.

"You're welcome. You want to rest some more or what?"

"I need to shower. How far is the bank?"

"Oh I forgot to look." He checks. "A little over an hour. Shit."

"What?"

"I just realized it's Sunday. Banks are closed."

"Ugh. Okay. Nothing we can do about that then. So I think I'm going to go soak in a hot tub instead of shower."

"Take your time. Can I get you anything else?"

"No, I'm fine, thanks though."

Tiptoeing to the bathroom, my legs tell me they'd prefer to stay in bed.

Chapter 65

MONDAY MORNING, WE get to the bank and find someone to help us with the safety deposit box. Upon opening it,
we do in fact discover an old diary. And a large, brown envelope. The diary is old and worn. It's got a dark-brown leather cover, with
scratches that were no doubt caused by much love and use by Aunt Mitzi
over the years. The words 'A Line A Day' are impressed in the cover, and
there is indeed a lock, to which this small key belongs.

I open the diary. The pages are yellowed. As I flip through it, a small
gust of air enters my nose with that old-book smell. The same one you're
hit with when you enter a library.

"You open the envelope," I tell Clay. "I'll wait to read the diary."

"Okay, are you sure?"

"Yeah."

He opens it up and starts nodding. "I was hoping this is what it was
going to be."

"What is it?"

"It's the original title for the Brougham. Glad to finally have it in my
possession. Now, we just need to find the dang thing. Do you want to go
somewhere private and read the diary?"

"I think I'll be okay reading it on the road. We can figure out the next
clue and head that way while I read through the diary."

"Alright then, our work here is done. Let's head back to the truck and figure out our next destination."

Back in the truck, I get the cipher out. "Okay. 'In the town where the first shots of the American Revolutionary War were fired, there's something for you that I have acquired. In a melodious locale, there's something to strum. The place rhymes with 'auditorium,' and they're waiting for you to come.' Whoa. Okay…I never did that well with history, but if my memory serves correctly, the American Revolutionary War started with the Battles of Lexington and Concord, right? In Massachusetts?"

"Right," Clay says. "So we're headed to one of those cities probably. The keychain?"

I dig it out. "It's a statue of a soldier or somebody, standing on a big rock." I show it to Clay.

"Ah," he says. "I know that statue. I've been there. Some of my travels are finally paying off. Remember, I spent some of my training at Fort Devens up there. That's the Minuteman Statue. We're going to Lexington."

"Alright, cool. And a melodious locale that rhymes with auditorium? A concert hall, maybe?" I ask.

"Well, she says she's acquired something and they're waiting for us. So it must be some sort of store or retail space. A music shop? Something to strum is more than likely a guitar, right? That would make the most sense."

"Could be any stringed instrument. Guitar, banjo, lute. Hell, even a harp or a violin. Some people strum those. But it's probably not that."

"That's true, I suppose. And I doubt it's a harp. She'd have known we couldn't take that with us. I hope it's a guitar though. Look up music shops in Lexington."

I search and find it. "Got it. First one in the list is The Music Emporium. Which kinda rhymes with auditorium, so that has to be it. Inspecting this small key, I guess we're looking for a musical instrument case. And, quite possibly, you're about to score yourself an actual guitar, babe. Do you even know how to play?"

"Not very well. I started trying to learn in high school, but then I got sidetracked with the Guard, college, and trying to figure out what I wanted to do with the rest of my life. Never picked it back up. I doubt it's like riding a bicycle. I may have to reteach myself. But, the thought of having an actual guitar to play…that would be awesome. I really hope that's it."

I look at Clay in his Candlebox t-shirt and picture him practicing how to play "Far Behind." He's frustrated at first, which is cute in my eyes, but he's so aggravated. He gets the hang of it though, and I didn't think my husband could get any sexier. Mmmm…now I really hope it's a guitar too.

"What are you thinking about?" Clay catches me in my daydream.

"Just imagining you playing a guitar. It's very, uh…shall I say…arousing? You'll rock it."

"Oh yeah? Well…alrighty then. If it's not a guitar, I'm freaking buying one. I never thought of it as an aphrodisiac." He gives me one of his wily, half-smiles. I wink back at him.

He starts the truck and we're on our way to Lexington. I open the diary and see that it starts shortly after Aunt Mitzi and Uncle Sid got married. I do another quick thumb-through and notice that the last entry was on July 8, 2013. It's a letter to us.

"Clay. The pages at the end are addressed to us. Here's to hoping for some more answers."

"Nice. Read it to me. Are you sure you don't want me to pull over somewhere?"

"No, I'll be okay. I've shed so many tears already that I don't think I have any more left in me."

"Okay then, go ahead. I'm all ears."

I take a deep breath, hoping that I'm really able to spare myself some tears this go-round, and begin to read.

> "*My sweet darlings,*
>
> *'Here come some more answers your way. I will start with a few rather simple things.*
>
> *'First, Clay, I will tell you that you'll find the car you're looking for somewhere in the Midwest.*
>
> *'Second, you may be wondering how I became known as Mitzi, when my given name is Bernice, even though it's not abnormal that half the population of the south isn't called by their*

given names. Your cousins T-Boy, Bootsie, Foo-Foo, Jethro, Tater, and Dinky are proof of that! Anyway, I digress…So, when I was just about three years old, the winter was long and cold. I received a pair of handmade mittens for Christmas. I loved them so much, I never wanted to take them off. Mama called them my 'mitties' and apparently, I tried to repeat her, and came out with 'mitzies.' So, the name stuck. Sorry it's not more glamorous than that.

'Now, Mississippi Coltrane. Remember him? He's not from Mississippi and wasn't even born there. In the early sixties, after he got the job with the Bank of Baywood under Mr. Santini, Sid and I took him under our wing, since he wasn't from here and had no family or anybody else that he knew in town, and we became great friends. He and Flo even had a bit of a romance. In 1965, Colt, as he was known, got an offer to be the bank manager at the First National Bank in Clarksdale. It was a great opportunity for him, and he jumped at the chance. He asked Flo to go with him, but her life was in Louisiana, and she couldn't leave, not even for him. So they went their separate ways. When Sid and I decided to do all of this for you, I knew we could use him as a connection, and I gave him the nickname Mississippi Coltrane so I could use 'Miss Cole' as a clue. His real name is Colton Murphy.

'Next, here's a bit of info I'm sure you didn't know. A few years after I married Uncle Sid, there was another young man that had eyes for me. He would send me flowers, much to the dismay of Sid. They came from a secret admirer, and at first, I thought it was Sid playing games. But he swore it wasn't him, and I could tell by his reaction, he was telling the truth. Not long after the weekly flower deliveries to the bank started, I realized who it was. This other man was few years younger than me, and supposedly had been smitten with me for most of his life. I used to look after him when I was a teenager. As a boy, he had told me that he loved me, but I just thought it was puppy love on his part. Mere fondness more than anything else. Of course I would tell him I loved him too, because I did, as a caretaker does a child. I never thought in a million years that it would become something more than that *for him. There was nothing he could do to take me away from Sid, no matter how sweet, albeit inappropriate, his gestures were. Especially since we were already married for several years when he started pursuing me. And besides, I would always see him as a little boy, nothing more. His name was Lorenzo. You know him better as Father Angelo. A bit of a shock, right? Sid threatened him, in a roundabout way, that if he made any more advances towards me, he would be 'dealt with accordingly.' Had I known Sid would say that to him, I would have handled the situation myself. Next thing I knew, Lorenzo joined the seminary. He told me after, when I ran into him in the store one day, he didn't want anybody else, and since he couldn't have me, he decided to devote his life to God. He did make a wonderful priest, and over time, Sid was able to finally acknowledge him at church without ire.*

'Now…the quilt and the old house in South Carolina. That home belonged to the family of Sid's sister-in-law, Valentina, Enzo's mother. The quilt is a family tree quilt that my sisters and I, your grandmother included, quilted in the late sixties. We quilted one for each of the remaining Chauvin siblings to be handed down from generation to generation. The one your Grams had was lost in the tragic fire that took her life. If only that quilt had been the only thing taken from us. I've missed her so much over the years.

'And now, I'll tell you about something you've probably been scratching your heads over. The typewriter keys you've found… there are only four, so you don't need to look for any more. The letters stand for your names: Clay and Lynn Boudreaux Sinclair. As for what to do with them, you'll know it when you see it. You're six states away from the reveal.

'Lastly, you'll remember the Tallahassee Automobile Museum. Perhaps you met the owner, Mr. Moe Castinella. Maybe you even met his wife, Eden. She is the baby girl that we adopted and then had to give back. We thought it was an eerie coincidence that her name was Eden, as we had named her Eve. Several years before Uncle Sid died, we decided to hire a private investigator to try and find both of the babies we tried to adopt. We vowed not to

interfere in their lives and we wouldn't ever tell them of our failed attempts, but we wanted to know how they were doing. We were thrilled to learn that our PI had tracked down our baby girl. She's a beautiful woman and it did our hearts good to know she had been well taken care of and had a good life. Upon learning that her husband owned an auto museum, we elected to donate the '57 Chevy, so that we'd have some kind of connection to her, even though she'd never know. The PI we hired never did find our baby boy, which we had named Douglas. It seems like it would be the opposite, doesn't it? After all, our boy was adopted in state, while our girl was not. I do hope our boy has had a good life and didn't wind up in trouble or something worse.

'Well, I hope this has answered more of your questions, maybe some you didn't even have to begin with. Please enjoy reading my diary. You will even find more pieces of information that you didn't know. I love you both, dear hearts. I hope you are having a wonderful trip.

'Love, Aunt Mitzi

"Whoa," I say. "That's some heavy stuff right there."

"No joke," Clay replies.

"I can't believe Eden was their girl. That is so weird, to know that she was right there with us. I strangely feel a bond with her now, but of course I'll never say anything. She would have been my cousin. Oh my God Clay, that means…the hitchhiker would have been my cousin too. Shit. I can't wrap my brain around that."

"Well…not really. Had she actually been adopted by Aunt Mitzi and Uncle Sid, chances are she would have never met and married Moe. Therefore, her children would be different."

"True. Still though, kinda creepy, right?"

"Yeah. Hey, I didn't know your grandmother died in a fire."

"She didn't. Not directly. She was able to get out in time, but not soon enough. She was taken to the hospital and died of smoke inhalation."

"Oh, crap, that's awful. I'm sorry, Lynn. What caused the fire?"

"Old, faulty wiring. It was in the middle of the night."

"Where was your grandfather?"

"Working offshore. Mom said it was my Grams that always dreaded a call about an accident on the oil rig. Never thought it would be the other way around. I don't remember much, I was only four, but I remember the family being really sad. And I remember the funeral. Grampa didn't live much longer after she died. A couple of years. I think he literally died of a broken heart. The older I got, the more I missed that I didn't have grandparents on my mom's side. But Aunt Mitzi and Uncle Sid were there for me and CeCe."

"I'm glad you had them. And that they had you."

"Yeah, me too. Ever since my dad's parents moved to Indiana in the late seventies, I've hardly gotten to see them. Once every few Christmases they would come down, but now they're too old to travel that far."

"Maybe we can stop and see them on our way through, when we get to that state."

"Oh, that would be great, Clay, thank you. So, speaking of…the Midwest, huh? I bet you can't wait till we get to that part of the country. I wonder what state it's in."

"I don't know. But yeah, can't wait."

"Man, how 'bout that story about Father Angelo? I told you he had a thing for her. I knew it. I just didn't realize it was that deep. And to join the priesthood because he couldn't have her? That's some serious heartbreak. How bold of him to send her flowers though, even after she was married. He's at least eighty-five, I'd say. Maybe a little older? Aunt Mitzi was ninety-three, so anywhere from five to eight years age difference. That's so bizarre though, right? He was probably scared of Uncle Sid, bless his heart."

"Well, he was in the wrong though, Lynn. You don't put a bid out for the farmer's livestock when it's clearly not for auction."

I laugh at his choice of words. "Did you just make that up? I've never heard that before."

"You know what I mean. You don't go sending flowers to another man's wife."

"I knew what you meant, I just never heard you say that before."

"Yeah, I made it up. Good one, huh? Anyway, that's playing with fire.

He broke one of the commandments. And then joined the priesthood? You don't see the irony in that?"

"Wow. That's true."

"Sending flowers to her was ballsy though, I'll give him that, but you mess with the bull, you get the horns. I know you've heard that one."

I laugh. "Yeah, I see your point."

"Well, here we are. The Music Emporium. Let's go see what this key is for," Clay says. He looks up to the sky and whispers, "Please let it be a guitar. Please let it be a guitar." I smile as I think the same thing.

We enter the store and a small bell hits the glass door on our way inside. A guy behind the counter looks up and smiles. "Hey guys, how can I help you?" he asks. He's a little older than us, with shoulder length blond hair. He's wearing a Tom Petty t-shirt and has a few tattoos up and down his arms.

"Hey, man," Clay says in a casual tone, like he's known him for years. "We have a strange situation."

"Sounds interesting. What'cha got?"

"We have a key to a musical instrument case, but we don't know what the case looks like or what kind of instrument it's for. Except that it has strings." Clay hands him the key.

"Please tell me you're Clay and Lynn."

"We're Clay and Lynn," I tell him.

"Finally," his face lights up. "O'Neil Martin. Damn glad to meet'cha," he shakes Clay's hand and comes from behind the counter to give me a hug.

"Uh, nice to meet you too," I say. Good thing I'm a hugger.

"Sorry, I just can't believe you're actually here. I know exactly which case it is. It's been waiting for its rightful owner. I'll be right back," O'Neil says to us.

"Don't get your hopes up Clay, it might not be a guitar." I point to all of the instruments hanging on the wall of the store. In addition to guitars, banjos, lutes, and violins, there are ukuleles, mandolins, and lyres hanging from the walls. And some instruments I've never seen before. But I do see a harp in the corner.

"I know. Whatever it is though, I'll be thankful to have it."

O'Neil comes back with a case in the shape of a guitar. "Here you go. This thing hasn't seen the light of day in over four years."

"Four years?" I ask as Clay unlocks the case.

"That's right," O'Neil says.

Clay opens the case and seems rather pleased. No, that's an understatement. I haven't seen him this excited since the Brougham. "Holy shit, babe. Look at this."

"It's beautiful." It's so shiny. Aside from the white pickguard, the colors are yellow in the innermost ring, orange in the center, and black on the outer edge.

"It's a nineteen-sixty-one Fender Stratocaster, three-tone sunburst," O'Neil tells us. "The little old couple paid almost ten thousand dollars for it, but it's worth more than that now. Then they left it with me. They only took the key. They made me promise to hang on to it and said that you would be around some time or another to pick it up. I've had it in my office ever since."

"Somehow, I'm not surprised by any of that," I tell him. "There's barely a scratch on it. You can tell it was definitely well taken care of all these years." I turn to Clay. "You definitely have to learn how to play now."

"I will," he says. "I promise."

"May I?" O'Neil asks, gesturing to the guitar.

"Oh, please. Be my guest," Clay tells him. "I need to hear what it's supposed to sound like, so I know it's not broken when I try." Clay hands O'Neil the guitar.

"Metallica fan?" O'Neil asks.

"Who isn't?" Clay smiles.

O'Neil plugs the guitar into a small amplifier on the counter and starts playing "Enter Sandman." I have a small list of 'heavy' songs that I like. This is one of them. We are really digging the performance. Clay is banging his head like he's twenty-five again, the way he did when we saw Metallica in concert back in '92 in New Orleans. The Stratocaster sounds great and O'Neil is an exceptional player.

I happen to look down into the case during our impromptu show, and I notice a small, satin drawstring bag that had been resting under the neck of the guitar. I pick it up and open it.

Chapter 66

INSIDE IS A silver charm bracelet, with charms that represent every-where we've been so far. My eyes fill. I guess it was inevitable. Clay notices me wiping my eyes. I tried to be nonchalant, but oh well. O'Neil brings his recital to an end.

"I'm sorry, I didn't mean to stop you from playing, which sounded awesome by the way."

"That's okay. Thank you. And thank you, Clay, for letting me play this beauty. Wish it was mine. I'll give you two a moment," O'Neil says. He walks back to his office.

"What is it, babe? What's wrong?"

I show Clay the bracelet. "Look at this. It was hiding under the guitar. The charms are in order of our stops. Except the first one is a key, which I guess just symbolizes all of the keys." We look the charms together. The head of the key is heart shaped with 'LOVE' spelled out as the bit. The charms continue with our travels. There's a postcard, a rhinestone dollar sign, a small piece cut out from an actual map with Birmingham in the center, a Bible, a greyhound, a quilt, an envelope, the Roanoke star, a grandfather clock, a caboose…and then I see one that really makes me smile. "Oh, look. There's a little Nipper looking into a Victrola. Oh my gosh, I love this so much."

"This is really special, babe. I know you'll always treasure it."

"For sure."

There are also charms of a cottage, the letters NY encrusted with rhinestones and a red dangling apple, a diary, and the last one on here is an electric guitar. Imagine that.

"I'm putting this on right now. She knew I would love this. Thank you, Aunt Mitzi."

"I guess we both scored on this stop."

"Yeah. We did."

O'Neil comes back out of his office. "You guys okay?"

"Yeah," I tell him. "This was hiding inside the case under the guitar. It made me cry happy tears. I'm so sorry I did that in the middle of your playing."

"That's really nice. I'm just glad it wasn't my playing that upset you," he smiles. "Is there anything else I can help you with today? How 'bout an amp to go with that fine Strat?"

"Oh. I hadn't thought about that," Clay says. He waltzes over and starts looking at some of the amplifiers on display.

"Clay, I don't think we'll have room for an amp in the truck."

"I'm just looking at these small ones. There's room."

"Small ones?" O'Neil asks. "Please, don't insult the Strat. It's not meant to be played on a small amp. It almost killed me to plug it into the one at the counter. Here, let me show you, if I may?"

"Sure," Clay says.

If my insides had eyes, they'd be rolling. We seriously do not have room in the truck for a huge amp. We barely have room for the guitar. I give a polite smile to O'Neil as he picks the guitar up and plugs it into a large amp and reprises the song from earlier. The difference in the sound is mind-blowing. Even I'm impressed.

Clay looks at me with question marks in his eyes. I mouth the words, "Okay. You can get it," since he can't hear me speak over the badass guitar playing through the amp. He walks over to me and kisses me in the middle of the store. O'Neil stops playing mid-chorus.

"Should I leave again?" he asks with a smile.

"Not at all. Just thanking m'lady. We'll take the amp."

"Yeah, it sounds great. You were right," I tell O'Neil. "But, is there any way you can have it shipped to our house in Louisiana?"

"You got it," he says to me. "Clay, you'll really get your money's worth out of this amp. It's the same kind Aerosmith would practice with on their tour bus. I used to roadie for them."

"Are you shitting me?" I ask.

"Nope. Great bunch of guys. I had to quit though. One wrong turn of my foot, I slipped and fell off the equipment trailer, brought a speaker down with me. Bulk of it landed on my shoulder and nearly crushed it to pieces. Ended my gig."

"Man. That sucks. I freaking love Steven Tyler," I tell him.

"Yeah," Clay says. "She thinks he's the greatest rock star that ever lived."

"Seriously? Of all-time? Hey, I love the guy, but…over Bowie?"

Clay and I start cracking up. "That's exactly what I keep trying to tell her," he says. "No offense to Steven Tyler."

"Hey, I get it. Don't have to convince me. Sounds like you have a bit of work to do with Lynn here though," he laughs. "But seriously, Steven's a great guy. I owe him my life."

"I bet you've got some stories," Clay says.

"You have no idea. I could write a book."

"Maybe you should," I tell him.

"Maybe I will," he winks at me.

"Well, O'Neil, it's been fun visiting with you and picking this baby up," Clay says as he locks the guitar case. "But we need to get back on the road. Thanks for everything. Especially for taking care of this and shipping the amp. I hope I can do them both justice."

"Hey, you will. Just practice as much as you can. If you lived 'round here, I'd give you free lessons. So great to meet you both. You guys be careful on the roads." He shakes Clay's hand again and gives me another hug. The bell dings on the door again as we walk out.

"That was one of my favorite stops," Clay says.

"I guess it was. I got myself a rock star now. Is there such thing as a quadruple threat?" I smile at him as we get back into the truck.

"I'm far from rock star status, babe. I'm like, a kindergartener on Grandparents' Day."

I laugh out loud, remembering the performance my kindergarten class sang for Grandparents' Day at school. Everybody was so off key. Half of us kids forgot the words to the songs the teachers tried so hard to get us to learn, the students playing tambourines were out of sync, and the projection of our voices was low and flat.

"You'll get there. I know you will."

"So, where to now?" Clay asks.

"Let's see." I get the cipher out of the console. "The clue says 'Find the Hale House in the Granite State. You'll find one of three highboys, and inside a drawer, there's something to excavate.' See if you can find out where that is while I look for the key."

"Okay," he says as he searches on his phone, "but what's a 'highboy?'"

"A tall chest of drawers on legs."

"Oh yeah, I've seen those. Okay, so we're looking for a dresser full of dirt."

"What?"

"She said there's something we'll have to excavate. Did you remember to pack the shovels?"

"Goofball." I push him in his shoulder and he laughs.

He looks at his phone again. "Okay, there's a listing for a William Hale House and another listing for a Hale House at the Woodman Museum. They're both in Dover, New Hampshire. Another Dover. That's cool. Which one do you want to go with?"

"The second one."

"You sure? Why?"

"The word 'museum' stands out."

"Okay. Oh, shit."

"What?"

"They don't open till Wednesday."

"Ugh...seriously? That's two days away."

"Yeah, that kind of sucks. You wanna try the other Hale House? They're open. And it was at the top of the search online."

"Yeah, but if it's not that, then we'll be stuck in a tiny town for two days."

"Alright. Hey, we're not too far from Boston. You want to make a little side trip there then? Our anniversary is tomorrow."

"Aww, you remembered."

"Have I ever forgotten?"

"No. And yes, Boston sounds fun. I've never been there."

"I know. You'll love it. We can be there in about a half hour." He starts the truck.

"Sweet." I clap my hands and bounce up and down in the seat like a little kid. "Can we go to the Cheers bar? That was always one of my favorite TV shows."

"Of course we can." Clay is amused at how animated I am. "How are you feeling? I mean with your muscle aches?"

"Better, but still a bit sore. That long, hot soak in the tub did me some good though."

"Okay, good. We can check-in and then go do something touristy if you want. Or do you just wanna do Cheers today?"

"I'm thinking Cheers."

"Sweet. So am I."

The next morning, I'm stirred by Clay enclosing me into his firm body. He is my cocoon and I'm about to awaken after an eight hour incubation.

"Lynn," he whispers.

I maintain my state of semi-consciousness, not ready to morph just yet. But I grab his hand and link our fingers, so he knows I'm not ignoring him. He lightly pushes himself against my backside and I'm aware of his need.

He's closer to my ear as he whispers again, "Happy anniversary, love."

I smile to myself. "Happy anniversary, babe," I whisper back.

As I try to roll over and face him, he steels himself, maintaining possession of my body. Okay, he wants me to stay put. He reduces pressure over me, but I don't move. He gives me a soft peck on the cheek and then removes my panties. He kisses the outer edge of my ear, knowing that if

I wasn't ready before, I will be now. He parts my legs slightly and strokes me. I let out a breathy moan. He turns my head in his direction and kisses me with urgency. That kiss, combined with the sensation at my center, makes me almost lose it right then. He positions me just right—flawlessly, seamlessly, effortlessly—and enters me from behind, taking ownership of me with bravura. Insistent. Intense. Intimate. He kisses my neck as he moves gently inside me, taking his time, savoring these moments. Clay continues taking advantage of my front being free to explore and circles his finger in the perfect place while driving into me a bit faster, a little harder, and a lot deeper, effectively hitting my G-spot. I'm on the brink of losing control, but I want to wait until Clay is ready. Finally, after several more minutes, he signals me and I know he's there. We both surrender, simultaneously, and our bodies engage in a series of reflexes. Winded, we lay there together, giving each other soft kisses between our heavy breaths.

"God, Lynn..." Clay huffs, "Do you know how much I love you?"

"I have a pretty good idea. Right back at you. And I really like that position."

"Me too. I love being able to feel you inside and out at the same time."

"Mmm...that is a good feeling. I love you, Clay. Happy twenty-six."

"Happy twenty-six."

"What should we do today?" I ask him.

"Oh, it's already been planned. I have a surprise for you."

"What? How did you find time to plan a surprise?"

"I have my ways, Mrs. Sinclair."

"You're unbelievable, Mr. Sinclair. I don't have anything for you though. I knew we'd be on this trip and—"

"Shh," he cuts me off. "Don't worry about it. It's okay."

"No. It's not. Wherever we go today, I'm going to find you something."

"Lynn. That's not necessary. Just spending time with you is all I want. All I need."

"I'll make it up to you, Clay. I want to."

"Well, alright then, if it makes you feel better. You did just let me buy an amp. That can count."

"That's true. But not what it was intended for. That's a bonus."

"I'm not going to fight you over getting me a present." He smiles at me as he sweeps my hair behind my ear. "I promise you though, you can't top what I have planned."

"Oh, really? Well, then…let's get to it, shall we?" I smack him on his sexy ass for a change and jump out of bed to get dressed. He laughs and follows my lead.

Clay continues the morning by taking me to eat our first meal of the day in an area just outside of Boston called Allston. The restaurant's name is, get this…The Breakfast Club. I love it, because he knows that *The Breakfast Club* is my all-time favorite movie. The eatery is reminiscent of an old diner, one that looks like a train car, except instead of the usual '50s style décor, there's '80s memorabilia all over the place. I spy lunch boxes from '80s movies and cartoons all along the top shelf, running the entire perimeter of the restaurant. There's a statue of the Stay Puft Marshmallow Man from *Ghostbusters*, various movie posters and black-and-white stills, framed albums of '80s bands and soundtracks, and so much more. It's practically a museum. Clay might be right. I doubt I'll be able to top what he has planned for me today, and this is just the beginning.

I look over the menu and see the heading named Library Specials. So, without a doubt, I'm going to choose the meal named after my favorite character from the movie: The Criminal. Clay gets The Basket Case, as it comes with a ton of food. The meals we order don't really match what the characters ate in the movie, especially since Bender, who was labeled 'The Criminal,' didn't eat anything for lunch in *The Breakfast Club*. But then again, we're here for breakfast. Not lunch. We leave with full bellies.

After breakfast, we drive back into the city and take a stroll through the Boston Public Garden and the nearby Boston Common. These two parks are so lovely and romantic with their features of ponds, fountains, many varieties of flowers and trees, bridges, and more. Or maybe it's just the state of mind I'm in.

At the pond in the Public Garden, there is a fleet of long pontoon boats that you can ride, with giant fiberglass swans perched at the end, pedaled by a tour guide. The pedal boats have about six rows of benches, which are occupied by lots of tourists, and we want to be alone today, so we opt out. Although it looks like it would be fun, it just isn't ideal for lovebirds wanting to spend the day together.

We continue walking around and I spot a sign for the Edgar Allan Poe statue. Ever since I read "The Tell-Tale Heart" in junior high, I've been a bit fascinated with Poe. This life-sized likeness of him is the color of the Statue of Liberty, though it's bronze-based instead of copper. Here, Poe is rushing down Boylston Street, his coat blowing in the wind. His right hand grips a suitcase, halfway open, suspended in time, from which a raven flies out and stacks of manuscripts fall. A heart, which represents the aforementioned short story, sits upon the pile of papers. Ironically, though Poe was born here, he hated Boston. He's probably rolling over in his grave because of this bustling immortalization that stands in the city for which he had such disdain.

As I'm taking pictures of the statue, Clay spots a store called Leather World and wants to go inside. He says he needs a new duffle bag. I follow him in and he checks out the bags. I notice a section of leather wallets. I know Clay's current wallet is old and peeling at the edges, so I discreetly pick up one that I know he'll like for his anniversary present. He's engrossed in looking for just the right duffle bag and doesn't even see me checking out at the register. Good. "It's for my husband," I whisper to the clerk, and point in Clay's direction with my head. "It's our anniversary."

"Happy anniversary," he whispers back. "Great choice. Would you like it giftwrapped?" he softly asks.

"No thank you. Your logo gift bag will be just fine." It's small enough to put in my purse. Clay is oblivious as to what's going on at the cash register.

I walk over to where Clay is and he finally decides on a beautiful duffle bag, dark-chocolate in color, with pockets galore and that fresh leather smell. It also has wheels and a telescopic handle so we don't have to carry it. Perfect for our current lifestyle on the road.

Around 3:00, Clay takes me for a late lunch at Top of the Hub, an upscale restaurant fifty-two floors above the Back Bay. It has an awe-inspiring 360 degree view of Boston and a romantic ambiance of white linen tablecloths, candles, flowers, and piped-in smooth jazz.

Our waiter comes to take our order. "Good afternoon. My name is Keith and I'll be taking care of you today. Can I start you off with a glass of wine? Or one of our unique signature cocktails? An appetizer, perhaps?" he asks.

"No appetizer for me, thanks," I tell him, "but, I will try your Pear Drop Martini."

"And for you, sir?" Keith asks Clay.

"I'll have the lobster bisque and an extra dirty martini, please."

"Yes, sir. I'll put your order in and be right back with your drinks."

Keith scoots off and Clay turns his attention back to me.

"So, how's your day going, Mrs. Sinclair?"

"Perfect, Mr. Sinclair. I still don't know how you managed all of this on a whim. We didn't even know we were coming to Boston."

Clay smiles. Not just any smile, but one of his sly smiles.

"What?" I ask. "What did you do, Sinclair?"

"I may or may not have pre-planned this side trip for our anniversary."

"What? Are you serious? You sneaky little devil. How did you do it?"

"You nap a lot."

I smile at him and shake my head. "So, the place in New Hampshire is really open right now?"

"No, actually. It really is closed until tomorrow. That was pure coincidence. But, I was going to suggest we come here first anyway. I knew you'd say yes."

"You are something else, babe. I still have nothing for you." I think about his gift inside my purse.

"Don't worry. There's plenty of time left in the day for you to redeem yourself," he says with a little laugh.

"Clay, come on, I feel bad enough. You went through all this trouble just for me. For us."

"It wasn't any trouble, love. And I'm kidding, you know that."

Keith brings our drinks and Clay's lobster bisque, then takes our orders for our entrées.

"You were right though, I don't think I can top this." His wallet is nice, but it won't match what he's done for me today.

"I know." He smiles again. "And it's not over yet."

"You mean there's more?"

"Of course there's more. It's not even close to sunset."

"I don't deserve you."

"Don't be ridiculous, Lynn. It's not like it's a job to love you. I wanted to do this. I wanted to make this a special anniversary."

"All of our anniversaries are special, babe."

"But none of them have ever been in Boston."

"Well, that's true. This one is just extra special then."

Keith brings our entrées and we tell him we'd each like a glass of Cabernet.

"So, what do you think could be in that highboy?" Clay asks.

"Hard to say. The only time we've gotten close to being right is when we think we might get a letter with some answers. And the guitar was a pretty good guess. What do you think?"

"I don't know. Maybe more answers?"

"Nah, I doubt it. She just gave us some. At this point, I don't even have that many unanswered questions. So that's what we'll probably get... more questions," I snicker.

The food is delectable, the drinks are great, and I've just finished off the best Boston Cream Pie for dessert I've ever eaten. I mean, it had to be, right?

Before Keith brings the check, Clay orders a bottle of the Cabernet we are drinking to go. To go?

"What are you up to, Clay? Are you crazy? That's a *four hundred dollar* bottle of wine."

"I just thought it would be nice to have a bottle back in our room later. Are you okay with that?"

"Yeah, but, I'm sure we could get a bottle from room service. Then you wouldn't have to carry it around. Or spend that much money."

Four hundred bucks for a 2012 bottle of Morlet Passionnement Napa Valley Cabernet Sauvignon. It probably sells for half this price online. What is he thinking?

"I doubt we could get this wine in room service. And nothing's too good for you, love. Besides, it's just money."

"I keep forgetting we're better off financially now. You really know how to spoil me, Clay. I promise, I will try and make it up to you before the night is over. I just can't imagine what else you have up your sleeve."

"You won't have to wait long. We're going there now."

354 | Rosie Politz

We get back in the truck and head to another park area of Boston known as the Esplanade. Clay parallel parks and we walk across The Arthur Fiedler Footbridge at the corner of Beacon and Arlington Streets. To our right is a huge grassy area that has a big stage with an impressive semi-circular Art Deco cover.

"That's Hatch Shell," he explains. "The Boston Pops play there on the Fourth of July and they have other outdoor concerts, movie showings, and stuff like that out here."

"Cool. But, we're obviously not here for a concert, since the field is practically empty. So, what are we doing here, babe?"

He takes my hand. "Close your eyes."

"What?"

"Close your eyes, Lynn. And keep 'em closed until I tell you to open them."

"Okay."

"Promise."

"Okay, okay. I promise."

We walk for what seems like eternity in my blackness, although it's literally only about a minute. Clay stops and puts his hands on my shoulders.

"I'm going to sit you down on this bench. I'll be back in a second."

"Where are you going?"

"I'll be right back. Keep your eyes closed, Lynn Sinclair. I mean it."

"Okay, Clay Sinclair." I give him a playful salute. He takes my face in his hands and gives me a peck on the lips.

"Eyes closed," he whispers as he sits me down.

He doesn't walk far because I can hear his voice, but I can't tell what he's saying. A couple of minutes later he comes back and takes my hand.

I get up. "Can I open them now?"

"No. Just another minute."

He guides me about twenty feet or so and tells me to open them. I'm in total wonderment at what I see. There's a Venetian Gondola, complete with gondolier in full regalia. There's also a gentleman seated with a guitar.

"Oh my God, babe. This is gorgeous."

"Good surprise?"

"Great surprise."

"Come on. They opened exclusively for us."

"What do you mean?"

"Their season doesn't start for a couple of weeks. But I told them our story and they agreed to do one early. They don't even usually do them during the week when they are open."

"Oh, Clay, this is just too much. I just…" I start tearing up.

"No, don't cry, babe. This is a happy time. C'mon, let's get in the boat."

I nod and follow him while wiping my eyes, and we carefully get into the gondola. Our gondolier, Leo, and the musician, Ken, greet us and tell us happy anniversary.

We settle into seats that are much more comfortable than I first thought they would be. There's a dozen roses waiting for me, too. Ken begins to play softly as we take off.

"I just can't believe you did all of this, Clay."

"Why?"

"It's like something out of a fairytale."

"So, does that mean I'm your Prince Charming?"

"Charming doesn't even begin to describe what you are," I smile. "I love you. So much."

"I know. I hope you saved room for some more dessert."

"Oh, I don't know about all that. I'm stuffed. What else could you have possibly done?"

Clay points to a basket full of cheese, crackers, fresh strawberries, and chocolates. There are also two wine glasses.

"So, this is what the wine was for?"

"Yes, ma'am. The basket came with the tour, but we shouldn't let all those chocolates and strawberries go to waste, right?"

"No, no, no. That would be a travesty," I say with a chuckle. "I'm sure I can squeeze a few down. This day just keeps getting better."

"The sun should be setting soon. We'll have the best seat on the Charles River." He retrieves a corkscrew from his pants pocket, opens the bottle, and pours us each a glass of wine.

I lean into Clay and give him a big kiss, not caring about the eyes on us. We glide down the river talking about our day and key moments of our trip as a whole, we laugh about old *Cheers* episodes, drink our wine, eat strawberries and chocolates...and then out of nowhere, Leo starts serenading us in Italian, singing along with the music coming from Ken's guitar. I shake my head at Clay. It's all so absolutely perfect.

The sun has almost set, and Clay was right. Stunning. On the other side of the river, the Boston skyline is lit up in all its glory, and again, it makes for a fantastic view from our perspective.

"How long do we have?" I ask Clay.

"The tour is an hour, so about another thirty minutes or so."

"I don't want this day to end."

"There's still a lot of time left on the clock, love. We don't have to go to sleep tonight." He winks at me and I smile at him.

I hear something knock the side of the gondola. "What was that? Did we hit something?"

"I don't know," Clay says.

I look at the gondolier and he points in the water. I scan over the side where I heard the noise and there's a bottle floating right next to the boat. I look back up at Leo.

"Go ahead," he says, "Pick it up. It's okay. It's safe."

"Okay, cool. Here, hold my glass, Clay." My hand reaches down into the water. I turn my attention back to Clay as I bring it up. "This must be part of their shtick. Very neat. But, I'm sure you already knew that, right?" I smile at him as I ask. When I turn my head back to the bottle, I see there's a piece of paper rolled up inside.

"What is it?" Clay asks.

"It's a real live message in a bottle. Probably a lover's fortune. It will say something like, 'May your love be forever magical' or 'Love is like a river, forever flowing.' Whatever it says though, I'm sure we'll be able to relate to it."

I open the bottle and shake the scroll out, untie it, and begin to read it.

"'*Dear Lynn...*' wait, this is for me?" I ask Clay. My mind tries to make sense of this.

"Yes," he replies with a smile.

"How did you...nevermind..." My eyes begin to water again.

"Are you going to finish reading it?"

"Yeah. I'm sorry, I'm just so overwhelmed with everything. I don't know if I can read it out loud though, without full-on crying."

"It's okay then, read it to yourself. I know what it says." He gives me one of his adorable smiles and puts his arm around me.

I return to the parchment and continue reading to myself.

> *Dear Lynn,*
>
> *These past few weeks have been some of the best of my life. Our life. I will be forever grateful that Aunt Mitzi and Uncle Sid chose us to send on this cross-country expedition. This quality time with you has been priceless, and I will cherish the memories we're making for the rest of our days.*
>
> *You have made me the happiest man alive since I met you, and I love you more with each passing moment. You're my best friend, my lover, my rock, my soulmate. My life would be imperfect without you as my wife.*
>
> *Happy 26th Anniversary, babe. I love you.*
>
> *Love, Clay*

Of course I'm sniffling and trying not to let the tears fall, but a couple have escaped from my eyes. "Clay, that's just beautiful. Thank you. I feel the same way, you know. I love you. So much. This has literally been the perfect day. I want it to go on forever." I smile and give him a kiss. "Happy anniversary, you incredible man." I roll the letter back up and stick it in my purse.

"You're welcome. And I thought you might say that, about this being the perfect day, because I know you so well. I found a song to commemorate today. I want you to listen to it." He turns around to Ken. "Would you mind holding off, just for a minute? I want to play her this song."

"Sure," Ken says. "No problem."

Clay takes his phone out and scrolls for the song he's talking about. He tells me that the song is called "Perfect Day" by an artist named Holley Maher. I listen to the song, and it is perfect. Perfect lyrics with a perfect melody. I honestly don't know how I ended up so freaking lucky to have this man as my husband.

Guilt washes over me as I remember my feelings of doubting him. My head hangs down. I'm ashamed of myself. How could I ever be uncertain of his love for me? I hate being this insecure. I hate that a smidgen of my reservations remain. My eyes well up, but this time they're not happy tears. They're angry tears. I'm furious with myself. But I play it off as Ken begins playing his guitar again.

"Babe, that's one of the most romantic songs I've ever heard, and it does fit with everything I'm feeling right now." That's mostly true. "I swear, I don't know what I did to deserve you."

"You didn't do anything but be yourself. And that's who I fell in love with."

He kisses me again and wipes my tears away. We have another glass of wine and just as we finish it up, we're back at the dock.

We make it back to the hotel and before we get out of the truck, I pull the small gift bag out of my purse. "Happy anniversary, babe. I hope you like it."

"What's this? How did—when did—oh, I see…Leather World, huh? When we were eating, you said you didn't have anything for me yet. Hmm…now who's the sneaky one?" He opens the small gift bag and pulls out his new wallet. "Oh, Lynn, this is perfect. Thank you so much, love. I needed a new wallet."

"I know. You really like it though? It pales in comparison to the day you gave me."

"I love it. And you know I like the bi-fold better than the tri. So yes, it's spot-on. Exactly what I would have picked out for myself. Thank you."

"Good, I'm glad you like it. And you're welcome." He gives me kiss, then we get out and go up to our room.

Clay lets me enter first. Just when I think the day is over, I walk into the room and there's a path of rose petals on the floor, leading to the bathroom.

I gasp at my husband. "Clay," I whisper. "This is unreal. Oh my God."

"You like?" he asks.

"I love," I tell him.

We follow the path to the bathroom. The huge tub is filled with a steamy bubble bath, more rose petals, and candles all around.

Clay kisses me in the candle light and we undress each other, then we climb into the tub and relax in the bubbles. I lean my back against his chest and he wraps his arms around me and kisses my shoulder.

"So," he says, "perfect ending to a perfect day?"

"Clay, this goes beyond perfect. Seriously, movies aren't even made of what you did for me today. For us. This has been the most romantic day of all days ever on the planet."

"Wow, really? I just thought I was doing something nice and thoughtful."

"That's why you're the best. You don't even know how awesome you are."

"Oh, that's where you're wrong, babe. I know I'm awesome. I just wanted to make sure you did."

"Humility and modesty. Two traits I had no idea were in you," I mock him and we both laugh.

"I'm serious though, Lynn. There are no lengths I won't go to, to show you how much I love you. I can't possibly, practically in your own words, do anything else to prove it to you. Whatever is in your head, you need to exorcise it. I'm not going anywhere."

"I know that." I do. I believe it. I know it. For crying out loud, I finally know it. And I am about to exorcise this demon. "I just have one question."

"Shoot."

"Did you mean everything you said? Am I really your soulmate?"

"That's two questions. But yes, I did, and yes, of course you are. Where is that coming from?"

Here goes nothing. "A letter I found once. That you wrote to her."

"What letter? When? To who? Found where?"

"A letter begging her to come back to you. You said *she* was your soulmate and you would never love anybody again the way you loved her. Nobody would ever quench your thirst and hunger the way she could. Nobody would ever take her place. It was balled up behind your dresser. I found it not long after we got married when I was cleaning while you were at training."

"Fuck." He lets out a long sigh. "God, Lynn. It's no wonder you've felt the way you have. I'm so sorry you had to find that. You know that was way before I met you, right? I thought I had gotten rid of everything. I forgot all about that fucking letter. I thought I threw it away. I guess I missed the garbage. Got dammit, this is all my fault. I should have made sure it went in the trash. You've carried that on your shoulders all this time, too, haven't you? This...in addition to being worried I'd leave because you couldn't get pregnant."

"Yes," I say with a lump in my throat. "That letter has nagged at me from time to time. But this is not your fault, Clay. It's mine. I've let the doubt plague me for so long, wondering if you settled for me. If I really made you happy. If you loved me like you loved her."

"Settled for you? Are you kidding me? If anything, I feel like it's the other way around. I'm the one who's lucky...how you put up with my long hours working and the weekends when I'd have to leave for training all those years. And of course you make me happy. More than happy. And no, I don't love you like I loved her. My love for you is so much deeper. So much more profound. Concentrated. Richer. Unfathomable. I could go on and on about the way I love you."

I take his hands and kiss them. "I had a bad dream while we were in Roanoke that she came back and you chose her over me. That's why I got up and went outside, when you found me on the terrace. That's what I was crying about. Mostly."

"Jesus. Okay. What else?"

"That's it."

"That's it? Really?"

"Really. Clay, I promise you, my doubts and fears are gone. Quashed. It may have taken forever for me to see clearly, but—"

"Why couldn't you just believe me though? Why did it take all this today for you to finally have confidence that I love you like I do?"

"It wasn't really just today. I've always known, Clay. I have. I just had this psychological affliction from that letter, and I was too insecure to ever bring it up. Besides...the other day, when you had to call her, about...you know...and she said she was sorry she threw what she had with you away.

You snubbed her and hung up on her like she was nothing. That was solid for me. 'Don't be. I'm not.' I told you, I don't deserve you."

"And again, I'm telling you, don't be ridiculous. Are you sure there's nothing else from my past that's weighing you down? Get it all out right now."

"I swear. That was it. God, it feels so good to be free of that. I'm sorry, Clay."

"Hey, it's okay, love. I'm just glad it's all out there. I guess we just unlocked something else, huh? And you had the key the whole time."

"My God, you're right. I guess we did."

"I had no idea you ever saw that letter. You have to know that I was in a bad place when I wrote it. I was desperate and I didn't know what to do. I guess it was more like therapy for me to try to get over her than anything else. I threw it away and never thought about her again."

"Thank God you never sent it to her. She would be in this tub with you right now instead of me."

"I didn't send it to her because I didn't mean it. I didn't want her back. She nearly destroyed me. I didn't deserve that. And then I met you. You were what I needed. You taught me what real love was. What real love is. You're here in this tub with me because of who you are and because you are the only real love of my life. I love you, Lynn. All of you. Inside and out."

I look up at him and he kisses me on my forehead. I turn over and lay facing him. Some of the water splashes out of the tub and a bunch of bubbles fly up, which land on Clay's head. We laugh and I rub them into his wet hair.

"Let's get out," I whisper.

He drains the tub and we barely dry off before we are in bed, making the best love of all the love ever on the planet.

Chapter 67

THE NEXT MORNING, we make our way to Hale House in Dover, New Hampshire.

"Tunes?" Clay asks. "Who's turn?"

"Okay, sure. It's mine," I say as I smile at him.

I search for a playlist that I haven't listened to yet. I come across the one titled *Color Me Happy* and I hit the play button. "Orange Crush" by R.E.M. begins.

"Oh, that's a good one," Clay says of the song playing through the truck.

"Yeah, one of my favorites."

"So, have you heard from Cecilia lately?"

"Not in the last few days. I'll text her and check on things."

After I send CeCe a text to get an update on the house and everything, my phone buzzes with a message from Annie. **Hey girl, sorry to interrupt you on your trip, but just wanted to tell you... you were right about Stone. I mean, as far as you might have guessed.** She adds a couple of winking emojis.

My boisterous laugh startles Clay.

"Jesus. What's so funny?" Clay asks.

"Nothing."

"That was not a 'nothing' laugh."

"Girl stuff."

I text Annie back. **Are you kidding? That's great to hear. And you are not interrupting anything, especially with something like that. So things are going ok I take it?**

"Is everything alright with the house?"

"I don't know yet, still waiting to hear back from CeCe. That last text was from Annie."

"Oh. What's up with her? Anything wrong?"

"No. Quite the opposite."

"Ah. She and Stone finally did it, huh?"

I laugh again. "Yup."

"So, what's so funny about that, then? I think that's pretty cool."

"Um, well...how do I say this? I may have told her that if he was anything like you in the bedroom, she would be a happy camper."

He smiles. Of course he smiles. "Did you, now?" he asks, with a trace of gratification in his voice.

"I did. In so many words."

"So, I'm guessing she was pleased, then?"

"It would seem so."

A reply from Annie comes back. **Things are going great. It's only been a month or so since we started talking and hanging out, but I really like him. A lot. It's so weird being with him like this after having known him as just a friend for so long. We're taking things kind of slow though.**

I answer. **I can understand that. He still has a bit of a wall up thanks to Crazy Daisy. But so happy for you. Keep me posted.** I send her a winking kissy face emoji with my text.

She responds with **Thanks. Will do.** And a heart emoji.

I get a response from CeCe as "Pink" by Aerosmith starts playing. "Cecilia says everything's great. The Victrola arrived and they put it upstairs in the bedroom where we wanted it. She sent a picture. It looks great in the corner, brings out the curtains. See?" I show him and he agrees.

"So, what does this keychain and key look like? Did you find it?"

"Yeah. It's just a round piece of granite with a small, old-fashioned skeleton key. I mean mortise key. Or whatever you call it." I show it to

Clay. With its speckled flecks of beige, gray, and brown, the granite on the keychain almost matches what we had in the kitchen at our old house.

"That reminds me of our old countertops," he says.

"Funny, I was just thinking the same thing. I wonder if she did that on purpose. Regardless, it's nice to have a little reminder from our previous kitchen. I did love our other house, but I'm so happy to be in Aunt Mitzi's. Our place now."

"Yeah, I was pretty proud of our Craftsman. But, like you, I do love where we'll be spending the rest of our lives. All the extra space inside and room outside."

"So much love has come and gone throughout that house over the years. And I love that we live in the place we got married. Makes it that much more special." Clay takes my hand and kisses it near my wedding rings.

We drive up to the John Parker Hale House and park on the street in the front. It's a Federal style, three-story, red brick building, with seemingly more windows than bricks. We learn that the house is one of four buildings on the campus that makes up the Woodman Institute Museum, including a genuine colonial garrison.

The tour is self-guided. To our surprise, there are no velvet ropes or stanchions of any sort, which makes me happy. Docents are on standby and spread throughout different sections of the house in case visitors have questions.

We meander through Hale House and Clay grabs my hand as we move from exhibit to exhibit, looking for the highboy. We are surprised to discover that Lucy, the daughter of the house's namesake, was secretly engaged to John Wilkes Booth during the time that he killed Abraham Lincoln. Her picture was even found in Wilkes' pocket upon his own death, twelve days after he assassinated the President.

The first floor showcases many artifacts from the history of Dover, New Hampshire, including antique tools, pewter, china, glassware, and so much more. Clay finds interest in a vintage police officer uniform and antique firefighting equipment and supplies. He's fascinated by how primitive it all is, especially the head gear that firemen had to wear. Some of the helmets and masks remind me of characters from *Star Wars*. I take a few pictures.

Upstairs, we enter a room and finally see one of the highboys. The room is full of antique furniture. A beautiful Victorian couch, upholstered in off-white silk brocade, and an Edwardian mahogany corner chair with lyre-shaped supports, catch my eye. Clay and I walk over to the highboy and tug on the drawers. They all open, so this is not our piece.

Moving into the room across the hall, we find another highboy. The showcase of antiques continue into this room. There's a really cool conversation chair inlaid with bone and mother of pearl in a floral pattern. Those kinds of chairs have always been on my list of wants.

"I don't think this is it either," Clay says. "The keyholes are fake."

"Yeah, I see that. Well, the next one should be it, then. Whenever we find it."

We go through a couple of other rooms and there's no sign of a highboy. In the next place we enter though, I see it.

Up against the wall between two of the windows, there it stands. The prettiest of all three. It's a Queen Anne-style with cabriole legs, an intricately carved fan in the bottom middle drawer, scalloped apron, and a broken pediment arch complete with flame finials.

"Okay, this has to be it," Clay says.

"I sure hope so, and I hope whichever drawer is locked, that whatever is supposed to be inside is still there."

Clay tries opening the drawers while I get the key out of my pocket, and four of the five open.

"That's your cue," he says.

I unlock the remaining secured drawer. Inside I find an old red View-Master, like the one I had when I was a child. There are also a bunch of reels in a case to go with it. I hurry and take it out, so as not to be seen.

"A View-Master? This was one of my favorite toys when I was a little girl."

"Mine too. What's on it?" Clay asks.

"I'm not sure. Here, hold this." I give him the case of reels and then I put the viewer up to my eyes and look up towards the light. "Oh, Clay. They are pictures of Aunt Mitzi and Uncle Sid's wedding. She must have had them converted to these three-D reels just for this. I've never seen them before."

"You've never seen her wedding pictures?"

"No. I mean, yes, I've seen her wedding pictures before, but not in three-D. I've never seen these reels before."

"Let me see."

"Hold on a minute." I flip through them again. The springy feel of the lever and the click-clack sound of each advance to the next frame brings me right back to my childhood. I give it to Clay when I finish my second round and he flips through the pictures.

"Cool, right?" I ask.

"Yes. Very. Okay, let's go find one of the docents. We can tell them who we are. Somebody working here probably knows why the drawer was locked."

"Yeah, we'll let them know it's empty now," I smile.

After talking to one of the employees, she calls several more over to meet us. They've all heard about us and a few had met Aunt Mitzi and Uncle Sid. I showed them what we found in the highboy and they were thrilled for us.

We get back in the truck and I open the case that has the rest of the reels in it. There must be at least a hundred more sets of reels. They are dated and neatly labeled in Aunt Mitzi's handwriting. I pull one from the middle that's marked 1965. The old familiar smell of glue and plastic from the reels invade my nose.

"Oh my God, Clay. These are of Aunt Mitzi and Uncle Sid at what looks like The Empire Building."

"What?"

"Yeah." I flip to the next frame. "Now they're outside with the building in the background. That's definitely The Empire Building." Next one. I gasp. "It's the car."

"Which car? *The* car? Lemme see."

I hand it to Clay and he peers into the eyepieces. "Holy shit. Oh, just look at that baby. I can't wait to get my hands on her. I can't believe these pictures are in color. Now I know what shades to use. Thank you for this, Aunt Mitzi. I'm going to fix her up good as new. I'll treat her right and make you proud."

"Well, now I see the significance of it. That must be why she gave you the Brougham there."

"Yeah, must be," Clay agrees. "I could sit here and look at this all day, memorizing the specs…man. I can picture myself repairing her in the garage."

"You can still do that, but later. We need to figure out where to go next. In the meantime, I'll be taking a gander at all these reels."

"Aww, babe, that's not fair. I want to look at them with you. I can't do that while I'm driving."

"Okay, you're right. I'll read more from her diary instead then. But first, yeah, we need to see where to go next."

"What's it say?" Clay asks as I unfold the paper.

"Um, let's see. 'In the city where the author of *The Shining* resides—"

"Yes!"

His excitement, for whatever reason, made me jump and my heart skip a beat. "Jesus, Clay, you scared the crap out of me!" I slap him with the sheets of paper in my hand. "What's the deal?"

"Sorry. I'll tell you in a minute, keep reading," he says, with a smile so wide I can nearly see all of his teeth.

"I'm starting over so I can try and process the full clue. Zip your lips. 'In the city where the author of *The Shining* resides, there's a warehouse to find where something hides. At 10 Parker Street, the place is Big Red's. Find an old box for voting, and watch out for the Feds.' What in the fresh hell? The frickin' Feds?"

"Who cares about the Feds? What I want to know is, do you know who wrote *The Shining*?"

"I know it's one of your favorite movies. Oh, yeah…that's why you're giddy. Stephen King."

"You're damn right it's Stephen King! This is gonna be great."

"Okay, so where does he live? Obviously somewhere in Maine."

"Bangor. And as far as the rest of the clue goes, it sounds like we're looking for a ballot box, inside a warehouse named Big Red's."

"Yeah, but um, can we back up to the 'Feds' part? Why would we need to watch out for the FBI? Maybe it's a place known for stakeouts," I say.

"Aunt Mitzi wouldn't send us any place dangerous. You know that."

"So, then, what other kinds of Feds are there? Federal what? Federal Express? Maybe it's a Fed-Ex distribution center warehouse. But then, where does Big Red's come in?"

"Maybe it's just a federally run warehouse," he says.

"Named Big Red's?"

"I don't know, love. Maybe Big Red's is another clue inside itself. Let me think. Big. Red."

"Big Red soda. Maybe it's their warehouse."

"You're messing up my mojo, Lynn," he laughs, "but good call. I love that stuff. But it's a southern thing, based in Texas. I doubt you can even get it up here. Now, time to zip *your* lips, ma'am."

"Sorry, babe. Proceed with your puzzle-solving strategy."

"Okay. Big. Red. Probably not Big Red soda. Big Red gum? Hmm… cinnamon. Red Hots. Hot Tamales. Hot Damn. Goldschläger. Fireball. Hey, maybe Big Red's means it's a firehouse. For big, red fire trucks. Or maybe they build fire trucks at this warehouse."

"Oh, good thinking, babe. I love how you can do that, just ponder out loud and come to a possible conclusion. But, wait, firemen aren't federal employees."

"No, not usually. Maybe she just needed something to rhyme."

I laugh. "Maybe she did. Well, either way, we have an exact location. Let's go north, shall we?"

"We shall."

Chapter 68

I'VE GOT ABOUT three hours to read some more of Aunt Mitzi's diary. I open it to a random page, dated September 3, 1945.

"You want to hear some diary entries?" I ask Clay.

"I'd love to. Read away."

"'*Yesterday marked the end of the war. I'm so relieved. We have been on pins and needles for so long, wondering if we're next. I'm grateful that Sid was never drafted.*' Wow. That's a pretty heavy entry."

"That's all it says?" Clay asks.

"For that day in that year. This is a five-year diary. Each page has the day printed at the top, starting with January first, but there are only a few lines meant for writing the day's events. She had to write the year in. The number nineteen is pre-printed and she wrote the two-digit year after it. Four lines per day per year. Five years per page. It's not like today's journals, with all blank pages where you can write till your heart's content."

"I see. Read me something else."

I flip through to another random page. "July 8, 1950. '*It's a beautiful day today. Rita and Louis are coming over for a cookout. She is bringing her three-bean salad and I'm cooking my famous strawberry pie for dessert.*' Oh good, not everything is going to be so serious."

"Tell me more about this famous strawberry pie. Do you have her recipe? I don't believe I've ever had it."

"I don't either, now that I think about it. I don't ever remember Aunt Mitzi making strawberry pie. Apple, definitely. Blueberry, sometimes. But never strawberry. Strange."

"Hmm…interesting. I loved her blueberry pie. That was my favorite. Especially with Uncle Sid's homemade vanilla ice cream," Clay says.

"Agreed."

I flip a few more times and read some more accounts of her days. Most of them are pretty routine, everyday musings. Then I find one that strikes a chord. I sigh.

"What is it, babe?" Clay asks.

"April 12, 1949. '*Went to hospital with pain. Doc admitted. We lost another one today. I was about three months with child. Why does this keep happening to us?*' I hate that for them. Ugh. I can't read any more right now."

"I'm sorry, love. Why don't you put some music on. Take your mind off of things for a minute. Maybe take a nap."

"Okay."

I get my playlist out and since I'm not feeling very enthusiastic at the moment, I opt for the one titled *Slow Jams*. Ed Sheeran's "Fall" commences.

I reach up to scratch my nose and the bracelet on my arm calls my attention. I examine all the charms again. I look out the window for a while and watch as we pass the world by. My mind drifts. I just can't believe that Aunt Mitzi and Uncle Sid did all of this for us. It continues to astound me.

"You alright, Lynn?"

"Yeah, why?"

"You just seem a little distant, that's all. Are you sure you're okay? What's on your mind? You know you can talk to me, love. About anything."

"I know. I'm just amazed at everything. All that we've done on this trip. All that we've learned. All that we've experienced and acquired. All that we have to look forward to. I'm just really exhausted. I feel like I could sleep for days."

"I hear ya, babe. We'll be there soon, then we can rest some more."

"Okay, yeah."

"I Can Dream About You" by Dan Hartman begins to play.

"You know," Clay says, "this song got me through some rough moments when I was deployed. Both times."

"What? Really? You never told me that."

"I know. Whenever I had some down time, which wasn't that often, I would get really sad, missing you. And I would listen to this song. It made me feel closer to you, even though we were thousands of miles apart."

"Aww, Claaay," I say, dragging his name out. "I can't believe I never knew that. That's so sweet. I did the same thing, though. I had a whole mix tape of songs that reminded me of you and us. Well, the second time, it was a CD, but anyway, I would listen to it over and over while you were gone, when I was by myself. I would play it every night while I was lying in bed, thinking about you, and sometimes I'd cry myself to sleep."

"Now, see? I didn't know that. I guess we're even." He snickers a little and I smile at him.

"Shadow was good company for me while you were gone the first time. He was my connection to you. I felt like sometimes, when I talked to him, I was talking to you. I'm so glad we don't have to worry about you being deployed anymore."

"Me, too." He looks at me and gives me one of his lovable grins. "Shadow was a great dog. I miss him. We should get another dog when we get back."

"Yeah, we should. I've been thinking about that myself, in the back of my mind. Playing with Fred before we left reminded me of how much I love having a dog. It's like you read my thoughts. How did I wind up with such an impeccable man?"

"I appreciate that, babe, but hey, I'm not without my faults. You know that. It's not easy being me sometimes."

"Clay, you haven't had an episode in a while. Are you okay? Or are you hiding them from me again?"

"What? No, Lynn. I'm fine. But yeah, I know, it's been a while. Sometimes I feel like it's the calm before the storm. You know they can hit me at any second. I've been walking on eggshells around myself, just waiting for something to go down. Athens was a close one."

"I know. You're still taking your meds, right?"

"Yes, Lynn. I'm taking my meds. Haven't skipped a dose."

"Good. I'm here for you, Clay. If it happens, we'll work through it just like we always have."

"I know. I know. Thank you." He grabs my hand and kisses the back of it.

Clay wakes me up when we get to Bangor and I stretch. "How long have I been out?"

"About an hour and a half."

"I'm sorry, you should have woken me sooner."

"It's okay, I know you said you were exhausted. We're almost there."

We're driving down Main Street and I notice a fire station to my right just as Clay starts to slow down.

"That must be it. But the address is wrong. Wouldn't it be Main Street?" I ask.

"Yeah," Clay says. But it's on the corner of Main and Parker here, so we'll just go check it out and see what we find. You know we'll have to explain everything first."

"That's okay. I kind of figured that."

We pull into the parking lot of the fire station and go inside. A firefighter who looks to be in his thirties with dark hair and a goatee walks up to us.

"Can I help you?" he asks.

"Yes," Clay says, "I hope so. We are Clay and Lynn Sinclair. We're here for the ballot box."

The fireman crinkles his brow and rubs his goatee. "I'm sorry. Ballot box?"

Clay and I explain everything to him and he still doesn't seem to understand.

"Let me see if the sergeant knows anything." He starts walking down the hall. "Hey, Sarge? Can you come see for a minute?"

"What is it, Doyle?" I can hear the sergeant ask from another area. Doyle, apparently, is relaying our story to him. The sergeant gets up and I gather that they are both making their way back to us.

"I'm sorry, I don't have a clue as to what this is all about," he says to us.

"Oh. The clue. That might help," I say.

I read it aloud to them and they look at each other with hard faces.

"What's wrong?" Clay asks. "What happened?"

"Follow me," says the sergeant. "You're at the wrong address."

"I thought we might be," I say.

We follow him back outside and he points across the street.

"I'm sorry," he says, "but your Big Red's warehouse has been demolished. A couple years ago. Nothing left but dirt and slab."

Oh shit. This isn't good.

To be continued...

About the Author

ROSIE POLITZ IS a down-home Cajun girl who loves to travel and hates to cook. She has a Bachelor of Arts degree in Anthropology from LSU and works in the tourism industry. She's a seasoned photographer, a 1980s pop culture trivia fanatic, and an avid list maker. Some of her favorite pastimes include playing board games, planning parties, and singing karaoke. She collects flamingos, wind chimes, and commemorative glasses from her travels. Rosie is married to her husband, Tommy, and they reside in the Deep South, where Tommy does most of the cooking. While she's written poetry throughout her life, *Key Moments* is her first novel.

Rosie is busy working on further installments of her Key Series. In the meantime, please visit rosiepolitz.com for up-to-date information and join her mailing list for exclusive material. She would love for you to follow her on facebook.com/rosiepolitzauthor, Twitter @rosiepolitz, and Instagram username rosiepolitz.

www.ingramcontent.com/pod-product-compliance
Lightning Source LLC
Chambersburg PA
CBHW030652120726
47905CB00001B/176